Amy Andrews is a multi-award-winning *USA TODAY* bestselling Australian author who has written over fifty contemporary romances in both the traditional and digital markets. She loves good books, fab food, great wine and frequent travel—preferably all four together. To keep up with her latest releases, news, competitions and giveaways, sign up for her newsletter at amyandrews.com.au.

Lifelong romance addict **JC Harroway** took a break from her career as a junior doctor to raise a family and found her calling as a Mills & Boon author instead. She now lives in New Zealand and finds that writing feeds her very real obsession with happy endings and the endorphin rush they create. You can follow her at jcharroway.com, and on Facebook, X and Instagram.

Also by Amy Andrews

Tempted by Mr Off-Limits
Nurse's Outback Temptation
Harper and the Single Dad

Royally Tempted collection

Forbidden Fling with the Princess

Also by JC Harroway

Mistletoe Baby Mix-Up
The Paramedic Roommate Pact

Jet Set Docs collection

One Night to Sydney Wedding

Royally Tempted collection

One Night to Royal Baby

Discover more at millsandboon.co.uk.

FORBIDDEN NURSE NEXT DOOR

AMY ANDREWS

DOCTOR BOSS WITH BENEFITS

JC HARROWAY

MILLS & BOON

All rights reserved including the right of reproduction in whole or in part in any form. This edition is published by arrangement with Harlequin Enterprises ULC.

This is a work of fiction. Names, characters, places, locations and incidents are purely fictional and bear no relationship to any real life individuals, living or dead, or to any actual places, business establishments, locations, events or incidents. Any resemblance is entirely coincidental.

Without limiting the exclusive rights of any author, contributor or the publisher of this publication, any unauthorised use of this publication to train generative artificial intelligence (AI) technologies is expressly prohibited. HarperCollins also exercise their rights under Article 4(3) of the Digital Single Market Directive 2019/790 and expressly reserve this publication from the text and data mining exception.

® and TM are trademarks owned and used by the trademark owner and/or its licensee. Trademarks marked with ® are registered with the United Kingdom Patent Office and/or the Office for Harmonisation in the Internal Market and in other countries.

First published in Great Britain 2026
by Mills & Boon, an imprint of HarperCollins*Publishers* Ltd,
1 London Bridge Street, London, SE1 9GF

www.harpercollins.co.uk

HarperCollins*Publishers* Macken House, 39/40 Mayor Street Upper, Dublin 1, D01 C9W8, Ireland

Forbidden Nurse Next Door © 2026 Amy Andrews

Doctor Boss with Benefits © 2026 JC Harroway

ISBN: 978-0-263-41988-7

Printed and Bound in the UK using 100% Renewable Electricity
at CPI Group (UK) Ltd, Croydon, CR0 4YY

FORBIDDEN NURSE NEXT DOOR

AMY ANDREWS

MILLS & BOON

This book is dedicated to Sheila Hodgson, editor extraordinaire, who loved the romance genre and most especially authors. You were a constant in the shifting sands of publishing, the north star, and you are so terribly missed.

Vale, Sheila, and thank you for all the HEAs.

CHAPTER ONE

CARO EASTWOOD HAD been a nurse for a decade so there wasn't much in this life that could throw her off her game. She'd seen it all—adrenaline-inducing emergencies, heart-breaking emotion and enough bodily fluids to last a lifetime—and no matter what a shift threw at her, she just took it in her stride and got on with whatever needed to be done.

Certainly being rudely woken in the early hours of the morning and ordered to evacuate her accommodation due to some kind of calamitous structural problem with the building had been slightly challenging, but she'd got on with that, too.

What she couldn't countenance, as she moved carefully through the dark surrounds of her—supposedly unoccupied—temporary digs in search of a light switch—which was not conveniently located next to the front door—was the sudden appearance of a large figure.

A large, man-shaped figure.

She froze, her pulse an alarmed thrum, as he strode into the open-plan kitchen off to her right and yanked open the fridge. The door obstructed her view of the front of him, including his face, but light flooding his body revealed a *lot* of skin. The only thing between him and naked was a towel anchored low on narrow hips.

Who the hell was *he*? And what the hell was he doing in

Warwick's house casually rummaging around the fridge? Unless Warwick, who was in Istanbul at a symposium and not due back for two more days, knew all about this person being in his house?

Which made more sense. Because who broke into a house to strip out of their clothes and raid the fridge?

But perhaps the bigger question was, what the hell was she going to do about it if he *had* broken in? He seemed sizeable from here so she doubted she could take him, even if attempting to do so was something of which she was capable. She could use her *nurse voice*, which usually got her through most situations. She just wasn't sure this was one of them.

Maybe she could slowly back out? He hadn't seen her, so it was a plausible option. She could find a hotel, which had been plan A until Hudson—her brother and owner of the evacuated apartment—had insisted she crash at Warwick's.

Hud and Warwick were best friends, so he knew where the spare key was kept.

Of course, Warwick was also *her* brother-in-law—*ex*-brother-in-law—so they were hardly strangers. Not that their paths had often crossed since she'd divorced his twin brother.

As she stood stock-still in a swelter of indecision, fate—in the form of a furry beast—took the wheel. The cat meowed loudly into the preternatural quiet and scared the absolute bejesus out of her, causing her to yelp and take a step back, stumbling in the process and going down.

She only just caught a glimpse of the guy as his head started to emerge from the fridge before her feet lost contact with the ground. Unsurprisingly, flailing her arms and grasping at the air didn't help and she landed on her back, smacking her head on the hard, unforgiving floorboards.

Air expelled from her lungs in one involuntary '*Ooof*' as a starburst of pain exploded at the point of contact followed by an instantaneous hot prick of tears, which she squeezed back as she shut her eyes and waited for the immediate pain to dissipate.

Clenching and unclenching her fists, Caro sucked air in and out of her nose as she performed a quick head-to-toe inventory, mentally poking and prodding every inch of her body to make sure it was only her head that was hurt. Before it was done the cat took her continuing reclined posture as an invitation, climbing on top to sit down on her belly.

Just to add insult to injury.

Weirdly though, all she could think was, *Warwick has a cat?* Or did it belong to this robber person? Was that his MO? Break in, get naked, have a snack, bring the cat? Was the cat some kind of…accomplice?

Or maybe she was concussed?

Just as the pain was starting to ease—which felt like minutes but was probably only seconds—and Caro's eyelids were fluttering open, light flooded the previously darkened house, stabbing her eyeballs, which she scrunched shut.

'What the blazes?' a voice thundered from up above somewhere before turning astonished. '*Caroline?*'

Caro's eyes flew open. Only one person apart from her mother ever called her by her full name—and only if she was annoyed or emphasising some point. Wincing at the retina frying light, Caro squinted until a head loomed over her blocking it.

Yep…that was the person. *Warwick Devlin.* Hudson's bestie and her brother-in-law.

Her *ex*-BIL.

Who was almost naked as he towered over her, his forehead furrowed. Dark wavy hair fell forward and it was damp, she belatedly realised, as if perhaps he had just come from the shower and wasn't naked robbing himself. His jaw was also dark with whiskers—more than an eight o'clock shadow, less than a three-day growth.

'It's Caro,' she muttered irritably because even all these years later she remembered the prickle of those whiskers against her skin. And because, even though it was probably just the head knock, she still liked the way he said Caroline too damn much.

Hold on, Caroline. That was what he'd whispered to her over and over—urgently and earnestly—that night all those years ago, never again calling her Caro.

'What the hell are you doing here?'

Caro opened her mouth to explain but where in the hell did she even start and why was *he* here anyway, when he was supposed to be in Turkey? Also, there was something different about him that she couldn't pinpoint and it was really bugging her too. 'Me? What the hell are you doing here?'

'I *live* here.'

Right. Yes, of course. But he was supposed to be away. That was what Hud had said, right? She winced as she tried to remember through the smarting of her head and the low buzzing noise filling her ears and reverberating through her torso.

Wait, no. Not buzzing. *Purring.* She glanced down to find the slender caramel Siamese with freaky blue eyes still sitting on top of her like she was its own personal mat. The cat was looking between them as if was listening intently like some high priestess adjudicating an argument.

'You have a cat?' Which somehow, with her head starting to throb, seemed a much more pressing question to ask someone who'd always been a dog guy.

'Yes.'

'Since when do you like cats?' Maybe that was what was different about him—he was a cat person now?

He grunted. 'It adopted me.'

Like that explained everything. Caro winced as she felt gingerly for the lump that must surely be there.

'Are you okay? Did you bang your head?'

'Of course I banged my head,' she said testily, because she should be worried about her Glasgow coma score but instead she was distracted by how tall he was all the way up there and how nicely delineated his calves were and whether or not he had anything else on under that towel. 'I banged everything.'

'Here.' He offered his hand. 'Let me help you up.'

Caro would have liked to have refused but, lying on the floor like a cracked egg, her thoughts just as scrambled, she figured some assistance wouldn't go astray. Plus, there was a cat sitting on her.

'Thanks,' she murmured, reaching for his hand.

'Move, Heidi-ho,' he said in a tone as gentle as the nudge from his bare foot. The cat gave a huffy *miaow*, slinking off Caro's belly, her head held high.

He pulled then as Caro tried to coordinate bone and muscles in a body as disjointed as a discarded marionette, somehow managing to stand upright, even if she did sway a little as his hand slipped from hers.

'Whoa,' he said, reaching for her again, his arm slipping around her waist, her hand splaying in the small of his back just above the towel.

It was gallant and gentlemanly but it felt like neither of those things as their bodies met. A hot, wild zing pulsed at their point of contact and instead of feeling perfunctory it felt...*taboo*. Caro fought the urge to lean into him, shuttering her eyes against the tug, but that only attuned her to the warmth and vitality of his flesh and the scent of freshly showered man that eddied around her like a flurry of warm snow.

It would be so easy to linger, to lean in and nuzzle the ridge of his collarbone that was in her direct line of vision. And it was *so* tempting but...

What the hell? This was *Warwick*. Maybe she really did have a concussion.

'Thanks, I'm good,' she said, straightening and pushing back a little, her hand dropping from his body as his arm slid from her waist.

'Do you have a cut or a lump?'

He didn't ask if he could palpate her skull, he just did, automatically slipping into doctor mode as his fingers found their way to the back of her head and sifted through the shoulder-length fluff of her strawberry-blonde hair, methodically examining.

'Quit playing doctor,' she grouched. 'You're a paediatrician.'

Undeterred by her grouchiness, he continued to probe. 'Which makes head bumps my bread and butter.'

She winced again as he found the lump. '*Ow*,' she complained.

'Yeesh.' He grimaced as he palpated it. 'Nasty.' He removed his hand from her hair, leaving a trail of goose bumps prickling across her scalp in its wake. Holding up two fingers, he asked, 'How many fingers?'

Caro shot him a *seriously?* look but answered. 'Two.'

'What day is it today.'

Sighing with exaggerated patience, she said, 'Sunday. Just.'

'And what about the year?'

'The year of our Lord 2025.' She folded her arms. 'And my brother's name is Hudson and you are Warwick, his best friend. *Your* brother is Brad. He is your twin and my ex-husband.'

Caro wasn't sure why she'd gone *there*. Maybe because she'd come close to sniffing him just now and she needed to remind *herself* exactly who he was. Even if Warwick and Brad were non-identical twins and, as such, *nothing* alike.

'My mother's name is Joy, my dad's—'

'Yeah, yeah.' He held up both of his hands in surrender. 'I get it. You're neurologically intact.'

If he'd been anyone else, Caro might have laughed at the medical speak but it was so typically Warwick. He'd always been such a nerd boy. *Aha*…that was what was different.

'You're not wearing glasses.'

She'd known him for twelve years—she'd been eighteen the day they'd first met at Hud's twentieth birthday party—and hadn't ever seen him without his glasses. Admittedly she hadn't actually seen him for almost three years—since a paediatric endocrinology conference where they'd spoken about a dozen words to each other because he'd apparently been too busy and important for chatter—but he had been wearing glasses then. The rimless kind that made him look nerdy-hot.

According to the woman who had sat beside Caro during Warwick's paper on the latest research findings on diabetic ketoacidosis in children, anyway.

'Oh…no.' He started to lift his hand as if he was going to adjust his frames before also realising he wasn't wearing them. 'I've switched to contacts.'

Caro opened her mouth to tell him they suited him but shut it again. The man was clearly well put together. He didn't need any more compliments.

'So...' He shoved a hand through his hair, bare biceps and several muscles in his chest bunching to aid the movement, which made her hyperaware of their state of dress. Or *un*dress where he was concerned. 'Is there a reason why you're breaking into my house at almost three in the morning?'

Caro blinked. Surely they weren't going to have a conversation with her covered neck to toe in baggy clothes—a shapeless jumper over a turtleneck skivvy, saggy track pants and well-worn Uggs—and him nothing but a towel? She might not be concussed but acres of Warwick's flesh was causing her IQ to drop several points.

'Do you think you could—' she flapped her hands in his general direction '—put some clothes on before we chat?'

It was his turn to blink as he looked absently down his body. 'Oh, right.' He nodded. 'Be right back.'

He strode away, past the kitchen and into a room she couldn't see from her vantage point, leaving Caro to ponder the events of the last ten minutes as she gingerly prodded the egg on the back of her head. It had been a truly bizarre night.

She hadn't thought things could get any more surreal than emergency vehicle lights strobing up and down the street and across the façade of the apartment block like some scene out of an American cop show, but she'd been wrong. She'd been given half an hour to vacate, performed her very best slipping-on-a-banana-peel act and found out that her ex-BIL was a cat person now.

And he lived in a house. Like a *proper* house.

Eager to get out of the frosty Canberra night, Caro hadn't paid much attention to it as she'd walked up, but, looking around now, she realised it was a proper grown-up house. From the polished floorboards to the art hanging on the wall, from the cushions on the couches to the potted plants dotted around this big open central room, from the fireplace to the fancy red appliances sitting on the kitchen countertop to the *cat*—none of it fitted the 'swinging bachelor' vibe she'd expected.

It was a settling-down house. A long-term house. A *family* house.

'Sorry about that.'

Warwick strode back into view fully dressed now in boxers and a T-shirt that looked old and soft and very, *very* touchable. He looked fit and vital and perfectly at home, like he was comfortable here in this house that should have a swag of kids running around in it and the delightful aroma of baking bread coming from the oven.

'Do you want a cup of tea or something? Coffee? Hot chocolate? Something stronger. I'm having a whiskey.'

He moved as he spoke, crossing in front of her as he headed towards a long retro-style sideboard sitting against the far wall, passing a couple of caramel-leather couches placed in a U-shape around a fireplace. Warwick reached his destination as Caro said, 'Um, sure, thanks. Whiskey.'

God knew, it had been one of those nights.

He selected a bottle from the half-dozen that sat on top of the sideboard and cracked the lid. The heavy thunk of tumblers being turned over was followed by the splash of liquid into glass then the metallic noise of a lid being screwed back on the bottle.

Picking up both drinks, Warwick returned to her side and handed her one. She took the proffered glass, which was some kind of fancy cut crystal, appreciating the weight in her hand. There were no cheers or tapping of their tumblers together as Warwick swallowed half of his in one hit. Caro went at a more sedate pace, taking a small sip.

It'd been a long time since she'd shot neat whiskey. Something *he'd* taught her how to do, she remembered absently. Back when they'd all lived in the share house.

'So,' he repeated. 'You're here because?'

'Hud didn't message you tonight about his apartment?'

'Nope.'

'He was supposed to message you.'

Hudson, a paramedic, lived in an apartment south of the city overlooking Lake Tuggeranong. He'd taken six months off work and was finally doing that trip around Australia he'd been planning since high school. Caro, at a crossroads in her life, had volunteered to house-sit while he was away, scoring a job in the paediatric ward of the Canberra City Hospital, which she started on Monday.

'Maybe because he thought I was still at the symposium he'd wait till morning. What about his apartment?'

'Apparently there's an issue with two of the lower-ground apartments developing massive cracks in their walls and chunks of their ceiling falling down. Some kind of emergency officials were called in to investigate and they found some foundation subsidence and recommended the entire place be evacuated. I woke at one thirty to a knock at the door telling me I had half an hour to grab some things and get out.'

She'd been there for only two days. *Welcome to Canberra.*

'Holy shit.' Warwick paused, his glass halfway to his mouth. 'Is everyone okay?'

'Apparently yes. They're evacuating out of an abundance of caution et cetera et cetera. They're going to let us know something more definitive tomorrow but for now—'

His brisk nod interrupted her. 'You had to get out.'

He said it so grimly Caro was left with the distinct impression he didn't want her here. Damn Hudson—she should have gone with plan A.

'I...rang Hud to let him know and ask him if he had anything important he wanted me to take out with me in case the whole damn building decided to collapse overnight, and he asked me where I was going and I said I was going to ring some hotels, and then he said that I should come here because you weren't home for a couple of days and he'd let you know.'

'Of course.'

His tone was dismissive, like an automaton. It sure as hell didn't fill her with the milk of human kindness. Caro had assumed that at some point, particularly when Hud came back, she'd see Warwick again. Maybe even semi-regularly. She'd even been looking forward to it, old memories of laughing and kidding around filling her with the kind of hazy nostalgia that made a person feel warm all over.

But Warwick Devlin was not giving off nostalgic vibes just now.

'It's just for tonight,' she clarified. Today was Sunday, her first shift was Monday which meant she had a day to come up with an alternative. 'I'll find something else in the morning.' There was probably a serviced apartment she could get somewhere.

'I said it's fine, Caroline.'

No. He had *not* said that. And even if that was what his dismissive *of course* was meant to imply, he resoundingly did *not* sound fine. But Caro wasn't going to call him on it. Not at almost three in the damn morning.

'Why *are* you home?' she asked, changing the subject.

He shrugged. 'My paper had been presented and I'd heard there might be some industrial action at Sydney airport, which I didn't want to get tangled up in and have to bump any of my appointments later this week, so I decided to come home early. I landed in Sydney a few hours ago and drove straight home.'

Caro winced. That was a three-hour drive on top of a very long flight. 'You must be wrecked.'

Maybe that was it? He was jet-lagged. Maybe that was why he was being so…unwelcoming. Not that she'd expected a hug and an effusive greeting, landing on him like this out of the blue and after several years of no contact, but a smile might have been nice. A quick hug for old times' sake?

'Yup.' He grimaced. 'All I thought about on the drive was shower, food and bed.'

'And I threw a spanner in the works.' She pulled a face. 'Sorry.'

'It's—'

'Fine?' She quirked an eyebrow as she interrupted, which finally earned a smile.

'Look, I'm sorry.' He rubbed his jaw. 'I'm tired and you surprised me and—'

'It's fine,' she repeated teasingly as she interrupted again.

Caro wasn't sure why she was teasing, why she was hoping to coax that small smile into something bigger. Something that went all the way to his eyes. It worked, though, and a tightness in her abdomen, which she'd not consciously noticed, loosened.

He sighed. 'Do you have anything to bring in from the car?'

'I just brought a carry-on bag and it can wait till the morning.' She was wrecked too and, between the tropical climes of the indoor heating and the seductive tug of the whiskey, she was sleepy.

'How about I show you to your room and then we can have a more lucid conversation some time tomorrow?'

Sounded like a plan to her.

Caro quickly knocked back the rest of her whiskey, almost choking as it burned *so good* all the way down. 'No need,' she murmured huskily, her vocal cords still recovering from the hit of alcohol. 'Just point me in the direction.'

His gaze drifted to her mouth and locked there for several beats, which didn't feel very brother-in-law-like, and she licked her lips nervously. Had she dribbled some whiskey? But then the moment passed and his eyes snapped back to hers.

'Two rooms that way.' He pointed past her to her left. 'Take your pick.'

'Thanks,' she said as she passed her empty glass to him, which he accepted automatically. 'Goodnight, Warwick.'

'Goodnight, Caroline.'

She turned on her heel and walked in the general direction of that finger, her legs stupidly weak. Whiskey legs. That had to be it. Not the way he'd called her Caroline. Or the fact that she could feel the laser beam of his gaze, fanning her from nape to heel.

Which didn't feel very brother-in-law-like, either.

CHAPTER TWO

Warwick watched Caroline go until she'd disappeared from sight, wishing that gut clench he'd always felt around her wasn't *still* there. His eyes were gritty and felt like they'd been removed from his sockets, rolled in gravel and stuffed back inside his head, yet he didn't miss a single detail, despite all those shapeless layers, of her lush curves. Curves he'd committed to memory years ago.

Dreamed about far, far, *far* too often.

How was it possible to still be crushing on this woman—his brother's ex-wife—all these years later? Surely his ridiculous infatuation should have passed by now?

He was thirty-bloody-two. A successful paediatrician with his own private practice, which focused mostly on endocrine disorders, particularly type one diabetes. He was involved in a critical and potentially game-changing pancreatic research study. He was a sought-after speaker on the medical lecture circuit.

Hell, he was a sought-after *date*. Not that he actually went on many.

And yet Caroline Eastwood—who'd been married to his twin brother—was still his Achilles heel. And now she was in his house...

He'd known she was moving to Canberra and had assumed he'd see her from time to time but had figured that would be planned and he could mentally prepare himself for the impact. He hadn't expected it to be tonight. When he was too damn tired to sort through his complexity of feelings where she was concerned.

A loud miaow dragged him out of his fevered thoughts and Warwick glanced down to find Heidi winding herself around his legs. She'd wandered into his house—starving and scruffy—the day after Warwick had moved in and written a note on his fridge.

Get a dog.

He'd turned her away but she'd kept showing up and, when it had become apparent from his enquiries she didn't belong to anyone, despite a pock-marked tag proclaiming her to be Heidi, he'd taken her in. That had been two years ago. There was no dog and she was still here.

She treated him with haughty disdain about ninety per cent of the time, but there was something kinda nice about having her draped around his head earphone-style overnight and being woken to the deep, content rumble of her purrs.

He scooped her up as his phone buzzed in his pocket and he pulled it out, tapping on the notification on his screen. A text.

Hey dude.

Warwick almost laughed at the typical Hudson greeting. No one since high school had called him dude aside from Hud.

How's Turkey? Hope you're getting laid and having some fun and not being boring super nerd all the time.

Hud thought Warwick took life far too seriously. Which was bullshit. But then Warwick thought Hudson took life far too lightly, so he guessed that made them even.

There's been some issue with my apartment and Caro's had to get out in the middle of the night. I figured as you were OS it'd be okay for her to crash at yours tonight. We'll know more tomorrow re the apartment sitch but she might need to stay a bit longer if the building is uninhabitable for a few days. I'm assuming that's ok. You'll hardly know she's there.

Warwick blinked at the screen. *Hardly know she's there?* He laughed. There was *zero* chance of that. He was jet-lagged as hell yet, from the moment he'd realised the identity of the woman splayed on his floor, he knew he was doomed to lie awake all night and think of nothing else *but* Caroline.

Glancing at Heidi, Warwick shook his head. 'I'm screwed.' Her long slow blinks seemed to concur and he sighed. 'Come on, then, let's at least pretend we're going to get some sleep.'

Switching out the lights on his way, Warwick headed to his en suite, where he brushed his teeth and popped his contacts out before tumbling straight into bed, resigned to a night of staring at the ceiling counting sheep. And yet, despite the consternation knotting his insides, his eyelids drooped almost immediately.

Maybe it was the jet lag or maybe it was knowing that the woman who was never far from his mind was now not far from him *at all* and, as calamitous as that was to his equilibrium, it was also somehow soothing…

Warwick woke an indeterminate number of hours later from a sleep so deep and dreamless—thank you, God—he didn't even know where he was for a moment. Perhaps because his feline headphones were nowhere to be seen. Or heard. Or maybe because he'd expected to hear the amplified call to prayer echoing down the Bosphorus that had woken him every morning the past five days.

But there was only silence. Because he was home now. Right, *yes*. Home. This was definitely his bed.

Twisting his head, he levered himself up onto his elbows to look at the luminous dial of his bedside clock. It was three. In the afternoon. So he'd been asleep for…twelve solid hours. And it was… Sunday. Collapsing back against the sheets, he shut his eyes again, knowing his first official appointment wasn't until Wednesday and that he could probably sleep until then if Heidi let him.

And then the events of last night all came flooding back and Warwick's eyes pinged open. Something wrong with Hud's apartment. *Caroline*. Caroline in his house. Caroline, his sister-in-law. His *ex*-SIL. Tripping over, banging her head, needing a place to stay.

Just for tonight.

Throwing back whiskey like she was nineteen again. Licking her lips as if she hadn't imbibed for a long time.

He shut his eyes on a silent groan. Not only had he stared at her mouth as she'd licked her lips, but he'd been far from welcoming. Not rude exactly, but he'd hardly rolled out the red carpet. Sure, he'd been tired and her being in his house had thrown him for a loop, but it was hardly her fault the foundations of Hud's apartment were dodgy.

She'd been a friend in need. And they *were* still friends, he supposed, even if he'd kept a distance—both mentally and *actually*—as much as possible since she and Brad had split.

Still, he'd rather she *was* here, with no threat of a building falling on her head, because, as hard as it was to be physically close to her, if anything happened to her...? A world without Caroline in it somewhere, even if it was far away from him, would be infinitely worse.

Warwick strained to hear any signs of life outside but could hear nothing. Maybe she'd already gone? Found a place to go and vamoosed. Left him a note. Or a text. Tiptoed out of his house and his life. For someone who wanted her here about as much as he wanted to drill a hole in his head, that thought was extra depressing.

Warwick groped for his glasses on his bedside table and jammed them on his face as he checked for messages on his phone. None. Swinging his legs out of bed, he quickly dressed in jeans and a T-shirt and strode out of his room, bed unmade. If she'd left it was because of him and he had to fix it because, of course, she could stay here.

Should stay.

Complicated personal family dynamics aside, Caroline was his best friend's little sister. She could stay as long as she needed. God knew, the house was big enough. And he was a big enough boy to put aside his stupid, *juvenile* crush and be the perfect host.

'Caroline?' he called, looking around for her, slightly panicked now when he couldn't see her or even any evidence she'd *been* here.

Good one, *dufus*.

He checked his phone again—nothing. Quickly, he scrolled to Hudson's number—he'd know where she was, right? His finger hovered over the green call button. No, he couldn't call Hud. He was thousands of kilometres away—he didn't need a call as to his sister's whereabouts from the guy he'd charged with looking out for her during this whole evacuation thing.

Scrolling on, he found Caroline's number. He had it because, for some reason, Hud thought he should. Not that he'd ever called it—*ever*. But he'd never been able to bring himself to delete it, either. Hell, it probably wasn't even hers any more. It was all he had though, so it was a good place to start.

Tapping the green call button, he put the phone on speaker, the ring echoing around the room. And that was when he heard it, an answering ring from somewhere. *Outside?* His pulse leapt as he glanced at the large sliding doors that flanked either side of the central fireplace and, without giving it any thought, he headed in their direction.

By the time he reached them Caroline was coming at them from the outside, phone in one hand, coffee mug in the other. Tapping the end-call button, Warwick slid the door open, welcoming the crisp embrace of afternoon air cooling his fevered imaginings.

He hadn't driven her—Hud's sister—away.

'You're awake,' she said with a smile. 'You really were wrecked.'

Warwick didn't know what he'd expected after last night but she was her normal friendly, breezy self and the sick bilious slick that had jettisoned into his stomach at the thought of her being gone instantly soothed.

'You're back to your glasses.'

'Yeah.' Warwick suppressed the urge to touch the sleek black frames. 'My eyes are a little irritated this morning. I don't think the air con in planes agrees with my contacts.'

'They do look a little bloodshot,' she observed. 'I hope you don't mind me making myself at home.' She waggled the mug at him. 'But it's such a glorious day and I found a nice sunny patch to laze.'

She chatted like he hadn't been grumpy and irritable last

night. And stared at her mouth as she'd thrown down her whiskey. Which soothed the tension in his body.

'And those trees.' She pointed at the three Japanese maple trees, the leaves of which were all currently turning glorious shades of red. 'How could a person who grew up in a place where leaves are always green resist them?'

Warwick had to admit that autumn in the nation's capital was a magnificent time of year, despite the cold. And having his own mini version of it in his backyard was what had appealed about the house. 'They were all red when I bought the house.'

A house far too big for him.

She nodded as she stared at the trees. 'I get that.'

Warwick blinked. Just like that, Caroline had accepted the purchase everyone else had questioned. Why would a single guy want to own a massive four-bedroom house in the burbs that screamed two kids and a dog? Even if it was an amazing house in one of Canberra's poshest suburbs and a stone's throw from Lake Burley Griffin.

But the trees had reminded him of his sister—Gina—whose favourite colour had been red. Reminded him of long-ago days playing in their backyard with her and Brad when their home had been happy and full of laughter. Before she'd died and cast a long dark shadow in all their lives.

Gina would have loved those trees. And the fact Caroline approved warmed him right through to his core.

'Getting a little chilly now that the sun is off the yard though.'

She brushed past him as she came inside smelling like sunshine and coffee. Unlike last night there was nothing baggy about what she was wearing today. Fitted jeans that showed off how her waist cinched in and her hips flared out and a snug khaki skivvy that cupped breasts he'd spent over a decade trying not to think about.

She'd scraped her hair up into a ponytail at the back of her head but most of it, he noted as he absently watched her walk to the kitchen, appeared to have fallen out, wisping against her nape. Warwick remembered how often she'd lamented her fine, can't-do-a-thing-with-it hair.

He also remembered how he'd stroked it that night as he'd whispered urgently for her to hold on, *hold on, Caroline*, as the ambulance siren had squealed overhead.

'I have some good news and bad news,' she said as she placed her mug on the drainer beside the sink that sat at the far end of the central island. 'What do you want first?'

She was teeth-achingly chipper, considering how disastrously this supposed new chapter in her life had started. Which only made Warwick feel worse because he knew deep in his bones that she was compensating for his lack of enthusiasm.

Realising she was looking over her shoulder waiting for him to answer, Warwick slid the door shut to ward off the increasing chill and said, 'Good news.' As a doctor, he'd learned that a spoonful of sugar really did help the medicine go down.

'I can get a serviced apartment from tomorrow at Tuggeranong. Hopefully with sounder foundations.'

She gave a half-laugh at her joke as Warwick's heart sank. It didn't feel particularly good. Which was actually *bad*. Less than twenty-four hours under his roof and barely any words spoken between them and he already craved more of her company.

'And the bad news?'

'Hud's apartment is screwed.'

Okay, that did sound bad. Shoving his hands in his front

pockets, he ambled to the kitchen, halting at the opposite end of the central island, leaning his hip into the counter. 'Define screwed.'

'Well, not his apartment per se, but the building itself. An official from the council engineering department called this morning to say they needed to do further assessment, which would probably take a week and if it's an issue with the foundations, which she highly suspected it would be, then it would need to be fixed, which, worst-case scenario, could mean it's uninhabitable for a couple months. Might be less. Could be more.'

'Well crap.' Hud had bought the new-build apartment a year before Warwick had bought this house and been stoked with the lake views and how easy it was to jump on the highway and get to the ski fields without having to go through the city.

Caroline smiled. 'That's exactly what Hud said.'

'So, people can't even go back and get their stuff?'

'They'll know more after the assessment apparently. She said in all likelihood owners will be allowed back in to grab what they want out of their apartments before they commence work on the foundations.'

'Is Hud coming back?'

She shook her head. 'I managed to dissuade him. For the moment, anyway. There's nothing he can do here other than pace and rant about the lack of information and how slowly everything is moving.'

Warwick grinned. 'Sounds like Hud.'

'Right?' She returned his grin and it felt like old times, shaking their heads over her brother's famous impatience. 'I told him I'd keep him UTD and to chill.'

'And that worked?'

'That and some female voice in the background saying

she was taking a shower and needed someone to scrub her back.'

Warwick blinked at the unexpected turn the conversation had taken and the deadpan way Caroline had delivered the information about her brother getting naked in a shower with some random woman. Now sex was between them the atmosphere suddenly felt loaded but then her lips quirked into a smile and, to his surprise, Warwick laughed.

So did she.

He'd always tried to avoid any sexual connotations in conversations with Caroline but, for God's sake, they were both grown adults who'd known each other for a long time. Surely, they could have a laugh about her brother—who they both knew and loved—getting lucky on the road somewhere?

Surely, he could stop being so bloody guarded around her all the time.

Because it felt good, the sound of her laughter wrapping around Warwick in a cloud of nostalgia. Like an old cloak, one that he'd just found at the back of his closet having forgotten about years ago.

Until their laughter naturally petered out, of course, and they were just looking at each other across the kitchen like two people who'd forgotten what to say to each other.

Caroline recovered first. 'You must be starving. I noticed there's bacon and eggs in the fridge—can I whip you up some?'

Warwick was about to shake his head but then his stomach growled and he realised he was hungry. When had he last eaten? His 2:00 a.m. fridge raid that had been interrupted by the arrival of Caroline. And that slug of whiskey—if that counted.

Probably not.

'Um, sure,' he said, more for something to say than any proclivity for a fry-up.

Not that she'd waited for his answer, crossing from the sink to the fridge and yanking it open. She liked to feed people. He remembered that. It was her love language. Not that this was *that*, of course, but it was her default setting. Even when she'd come home from the hospital and was supposed to be resting, she'd cooked batch after batch of brownies.

She and Brad had argued about it. He'd wanted her to rest and Caroline had insisted she was *fine* as she'd cooked almost maniacally in the kitchen. Brad had looked at him helplessly when Warwick had called in to check on her and he'd given his brother a let-her-do-what-she-needs-to-do shrug. Because he hadn't known what the hell was best either, but had figured she probably did.

So he and Brad and Hud had eaten brownies for breakfast, lunch and dinner for days.

'I can't believe you go away for a week,' she said as she grabbed ingredients, 'and your fridge is fuller than mine after I've done a shop.'

'Cheray picked up a click and collect for me when she dropped Heidi home earlier this evening.'

Arms laden, Caroline shut the fridge door with a foot-hip manoeuvre, quirking an eyebrow at him. '*Cheray*, huh?'

If he wasn't very much mistaken that emphasis wasn't as light and flirty as her eyebrow might suggest. 'She's my EA.'

'You get your *secretary* to run errands for you?' Her voice as she unloaded her armful onto the counter-top of the central island left him in no doubt that she considered this an egregious act of overstepping boundaries.

'No, I get my *friend* Cheray, who also just happens to be my terrifying, efficient *EA*, to mind my cat and pick up some groceries for me. From time to time. Her five-year-old son is obsessed with animals.'

'Sounds like she's a keeper.'

Warwick couldn't tell if she was being genuine or facetious. 'She is.' Cheray had come to him as a temp for a month not long after her partner had died leaving her with no life insurance, a huge mortgage and a one-year-old.

She'd been so damn good, he'd offered her a permanent job.

After opening several cupboards, Caroline located a frying pan and placed it on the gleaming surface of his fancy induction stove top. Next she grabbed a sharp knife from the block then reached for the nearby wooden chopping board. Her movements were efficient and flowing. It was like watching someone familiar with cooking perform a culinary ballet.

'I have a hotel reservation that's available from four today,' she said casually as she sliced open the bacon packaging. 'So I'll just make you this and be out of your hair.'

Warwick blinked at the announcement, which at least drew his gaze to her face and not the interesting shift of her breasts beneath her skivvy as she set about cutting the fat away.

Out of your hair. Fuck's sake—that was the last thing he wanted.

Hudson had asked Warwick to put a roof over his sister's head. Sure, he had no idea about Warwick's hopeless bloody crush, but what did that matter when he had a house with plenty of spare rooms? He'd for sure feel guilty rattling around in here knowing Caroline was forking out money to stay somewhere else.

Proximity would be a definite issue for him, but he was thirty-two years old, he could just suck that the hell up. After all, this place was clearly big enough for both of them to stay out of each other's way and, what with her shifts and all the extra hours he spent working on the research data, the probability they'd see much of each other was low.

'Please don't go.'

Her hand faltered mid slice. It was only for the briefest of moments but he clocked it before she continued the action. 'It's fine.' She shook her head, her gaze trained firmly on the job at hand. 'It's all sorted.'

'No. It's not.' Warwick pushed off the counter and rounded it, coming to a halt about a foot from her position, leaning his hip into the benchtop again. 'I'm sorry I wasn't very welcoming last night.'

'It's fine,' she repeated.

He remembered how he'd used that word last night when it had decidedly not been fine and now she was doing the same thing. Except they'd smiled a little over it then, something that didn't seem likely now.

'No. It's not.' He placed a stilling hand on hers to stop her cutting, which was suddenly getting on his last nerve. He wanted to say what he should have said last night and he wanted her to know he meant it.

She did stop but now his hand was on top of hers and he was conscious of the fact he was touching her—*Caroline*.

Snatching his hand back, he took a steadying breath. 'It was rude of me. There is no need for you to move to an apartment when this place is huge and is a much closer commute to your work.'

She shook her head. 'I've already imposed enough.'

Imposed. God, had he been that much of an arsehole? 'You haven't. Friends don't impose, you know that. And it's just a week.'

Glancing up at him then, her eyes met his. They were

brown too but where his were dark and monochrome, hers were lighter with flecks of amber. 'Or maybe two months.'

'*Maybe*,' Warwick emphasised.

'I…don't want you to feel obligated.'

Warwick hated that his standoffishness last night had made her think he was doing this out of obligation. Sure, she was Hud's sister and Brad's ex, but he'd offer anyone he knew in this situation a bed, why should Caroline get any different treatment?

'*Pfft*. There's no such thing with family.'

She held his gaze. 'But we're not family any more, are we?'

There was a whole lot of history in that sentence Warwick didn't even want to think about, because the truth was they might not officially be family any more, but the two of them had been through an experience that transcended family.

And he knew she knew it too.

He shrugged. 'Once a Devlin, always a Devlin. And even if you weren't—' *My brother's ex.* 'You're my best friend's little sister, that definitely makes you family.' And doubly off-limits. 'Not to mention how pissed your brother will be at me if I let you go live in a *serviced apartment* when I have three spare bedrooms.'

She smiled. 'Luckily he's a long way away.'

'Like that'll stop him.'

Hudson had been so pissed at Brad for cheating on Caroline, which had ultimately led to the end of the marriage, Brad had blocked his number for a couple of years and to this day things between the two former friends was lukewarm. Warwick and Hud had always been closer than Hud and Brad, but Warwick was under no illusions that Hudson's loyalty was to his sister first.

'Come on, Caroline.' He smiled and it was harder than

it should have been because as much as he wanted her to stay, he knew it would be a challenge. 'Please. Do it for the trees if for nothing else.'

It must have worked because a smile tugged at the corners of her mouth. 'The trees are pretty amazing.'

'And they're only going to get better before they lose all their leaves.'

She nodded slowly. 'It *would* be more convenient to work than living out at Tuggeranong.'

Warwick grinned. 'Much.' About ten minutes as opposed to twenty-five to thirty.

'I'd have to insist on paying you some rent.'

An immediate vehement rejection formed on Warwick's lips, but he tempered it because she had that determined gleam in her eye he knew only too well. She'd looked exactly the same when she'd announced she was going to run a marathon in her first year of uni. She'd done it but mostly because so many people—Hud and Brad, *not* him—had predicted she'd chicken out.

'If I was temporarily dislocated and needing a place to stay for a few weeks, would you charge me rent?'

She shot him a dirty look but didn't answer because they both knew she wouldn't. 'I can't just land myself on you like this.'

'Could I not just land myself on you?' Now *there* was a thought.

'Hmm.' She narrowed her eyes as if she was scheming up another way to pay her way. 'How about I do all the cooking and cleaning?'

Warwick frowned. 'I don't need a housemaid.'

'I have to earn my keep somehow.'

Warwick was not proud where his brain went—it seemed to be leaping on any comment that could be misconstrued in a sexual way and going wild. Like exactly what Caroline could do to earn her keep. Bloody hell, he'd spent the last twelve years of his life suppressing these kinds of thoughts, he *would not* give them free rein now he and Caroline were going to be roomies.

Christ, if *Hud* could see inside his head there'd be trouble. He didn't have to ask the man to know that one Devlin brother screwing with his sister was one too many for Hud.

'Do you still cook that lemon meringue pie?'

She smiled. 'I sure do.'

'Fine, then, keep me supplied in that and we'll call it even.'

'That's it?'

'That's it.'

She regarded him for long moments and Warwick kept his gaze steely and unwavering until finally she huffed out a breath. 'Okay, *fine*. But let's review the situation at the end of the week, okay? See how it goes. You might be down on your knees begging for me to leave by then.'

Warwick almost groaned out loud as she planted *that* thoroughly wicked thought in his head. For God's sake— was she trying to kill him?

'I could leave my shoes everywhere. Have the TV volume up too loud. Turn on every light in the house and not turn them off again.'

As long as she didn't leave her underwear draped around his furniture, Warwick was pretty sure he could cope with some general slovenliness. 'No worries,' he agreed, just to get her off topic. 'We'll review after a week.'

She stuck her hand out then, clearly wanting to seal the deal with a shake. Warwick didn't think it was wise to touch her again quite so soon after the last time but if that was what she needed...

He slid his hand in hers for the most perfunctory shake but she held on a little longer, her gaze earnest. 'Thank you,' she murmured. 'I really appreciate this.'

She let go then, but not before Warwick felt as if she'd been holding his heart. 'No worries.'

'Now.' She opened the carton. 'You like your eggs easy, right?'

It didn't surprise Warwick that she remembered such a detail but that wasn't where his libidinous brain went. 'Yes.' He cleared his throat. 'Thanks.'

Easy. Just like him.

CHAPTER THREE

CARO WAS A little nervous walking into the ward the next morning at eight despite her extensive experience in paediatrics. She'd worked in a large Brisbane children's hospital in both A & E and ICU as well as several other general paed wards in smaller regional hospitals. When tragedy had struck her life and she hadn't been able to face nursing kids for a couple of years she'd worked a stint in the operating theatres of a private hospital.

So, it wasn't the work itself stirring the butterflies in her belly—it was the unknowns. The other nurses. The person in charge. The rosters. The fair division of labour. The dynamic between the doctors, the nurses and the allied health people. The level of support from the hospital hierarchy if the shit ever hit the fan—would they have your back?

Put short, it was the *vibe*. Something less tangible but that could make or break a job.

As directed in her welcome email, Caro made her way to the nurses' station situated about halfway down the wide hallway that led from the front swinging door all the way to the bank of windows at the far end. The familiar sights and sounds of morning life on a ward kept her company.

Breakfast trays being collected, nurses dashing in and out of bays, babies crying, older children playing, teenagers chatting and laughing, cleaners mopping, the low murmur of ceiling-mounted televisions above each bed, parents soothing fractious toddlers, a giggling little escapee with a plaster on one leg running down the hallway, a nurse in hot pursuit.

The video clip and soundtrack to life on a paediatric ward. And Caro loved it.

A blonde woman about her age wearing the same uniform Caro was wearing—pink scrubs, the hospital logo on the pocket of the shirt—was leaning her elbows on the high top of the station next to several bed charts that were open to the medications page. A utility bag was strapped around her waist, the front bulging with what Caro assumed to be tools of the trade. Scissors, forceps, tape, a pen, some spare gloves and a slim torch for pupil checks.

She was talking to a middle-aged woman dressed in civis sitting inside the U-shaped station at the desk, which was lower than the high top. A stack of charts was at her elbow, a corded phone held to her ear with her shoulder, leaving her hands free to tap on a keyboard.

'Hey, I'm Caro Eastwood,' she greeted. 'The new RN starting today.'

'Oh, hey, welcome.' The blonde woman's smile was quick and genuine as she held out her hand and they shook. 'I'm Haley.'

She tapped her name badge, which was round and sported a cartoon version of her face in the middle complete with blonde hair pulled up in a high ponytail. Beneath, in pink letters scrawled in a childlike font, was her name.

'This is Trudy.' She pointed to the woman sitting at the desk. 'Sometimes Trudes or Trude-a-loo or even Trude-a-licious. She's our admin officer and none of us would know where anything was if it weren't for her.'

'Just you,' Trudy's dry comeback was quick but affectionate.

Caro laughed. 'Nice to meet you.'

'I think the boss wants to see you, yes?'

'Yes. I have a meeting with her in five minutes. Can you point me to her office?'

Haley nodded. 'Let me show you the staffroom first, where you can stash your bag.'

Five minutes later, her bag stowed in a locker and the butterflies in her stomach now fully settled after such a warm reception, Caro knocked on the nurse unit manager's door. A muffled command to enter had her twisting the handle and opening the door.

'Hi, Caroline.' The black woman behind the desk looked about forty and had a full set of amazing locs, tied back loosely with a red, black and yellow scarf.

She was wearing the NUM uniform of a navy skirt with a geometrically patterned blouse, the hospital logo on the pocket. Removing bright-orange-rimmed glasses that had been perched on the end of her nose, she stood and offered her hand. 'Glenda Stephenson.'

Caro crossed to the desk, noticing that Glenda was sporting a similar name badge to Haley's, her caricature complete with matching hair and orange glasses. She made a mental note to source one for herself as she shook her new boss's hand and said, 'Caro, please.'

Now more than ever the long form of her name only felt right coming from a very different set of lips. It had been a lot of years since she'd heard it so consistently but these past twenty-four hours had certainly made up for that. Imbued with all their history, Warwick said it in a way that struck like the vibrations of a tuning fork—resonating deep in her gut.

Caroline was *their* name.

'Sit, please.' Glenda gestured to the chair opposite.

They indulged in some basic small talk for five minutes, where Caro gave a brief retelling of her musical accommodations before they got into the nitty-gritty of the ward and its routines and Glenda's expectations. The older woman was a no-nonsense straight talker, which Caro appreciated, but there was a twinkle in her eye hinting at a sense of humour.

Then she turned the spotlight on Caro. This was the first time they were meeting as Glenda had been away when Caro was interviewed via Zoom and she went back through some of Caro's employment history.

'It's good to have such a highly skilled nurse on our team.'

Caro smiled at the compliment. 'Thank you.'

'Seems like you're a bit of a…' one eyebrow quirked as shrewd eyes looked at her over orange frames '…rolling stone?'

Caro thought it was more observation than criticism, but it was true she had moved around a bit these past seven years.

'This is your first time out of Queensland though?' Glenda continued. 'Big move considering how different the Canberra weather is from the tropics. Why here?'

Moving from one of the warmest states in the country, where winter days were generally temperate and quite lovely, to minus-degree nights, frosts and iced windscreens would definitely take some getting used to. But more and more this past year, Caro had found herself craving roots again.

After losing the baby everybody had wanted to coddle her and that was what she'd needed at the time—her parents hovering, ready to slay dragons. But after a couple of years she'd known she had to make a change or for ever become this tragic figure of pity.

So, she'd taken her life back.

She'd moved away, moved around, worked in different hospitals, lived with different people in share houses, as she'd done in her uni days. She'd made friends and had fun and nobody knew or cared about the baby or her ill-fated marriage.

And she'd needed that too.

But Hud going away for six months had coincided with her recently turning thirty and his entreaties over multiple years for her to move to Canberra had finally resonated.

'My brother lives here.' So did Warwick. But how could she possibly have known she and her ex-BIL would end up being roomies?

'You're close?'

Caro smiled and nodded. 'We are.' The answer seemed to please Glenda, who beamed approvingly, and Caro felt like she'd passed some kind of test.

They moved on to discuss the four paediatricians that consulted and Caro almost laughed out loud as Glenda whispered conspiratorially, 'I know we're not supposed to have favourites but Dr Devlin is the nicest of the lot. He does a diabetic clinic at the hospital every Wednesday afternoon and all our newly diagnosed type ones are automatically admitted under him. The kids love him. So—' she winked '—do their mothers.'

Caro did laugh then. Warwick was certainly easy on the eye. Especially in nothing but a towel. She'd been too blinded by Brad's gargantuan personality and dazzling good looks back in the day to really register the attractiveness of his quieter, more serious, bespectacled brother. At least though, for twins, they had been easy to tell apart.

'He is charming,' she agreed, because it felt weird not to acknowledge she knew him now they were specifically talking about Warwick.

'Oh, you've met him?'

'Yep. He's actually my brother's best friend. And... I was married to *his* brother for half a second a bunch of years ago now.' She didn't think her boss needed to know they were also currently cohabiting seeing as how it was only temporary.

Glenda blinked. '*Really?*'

Pressing her lips together, Caro nodded. 'Uh-huh.'

'Okay. Well. That's...' the sparkle Caro had glimpsed earlier twinkled from Glenda's eyes '...convoluted?'

'A little, yes. But we're also friends, so it's all good.'

They *were* friends. It was just, as Glenda said, convoluted. It was hard to think of her history with Warwick without thinking about how he—not Brad—had been there the night she'd lost the baby. How it had been him, *not* her husband, who had held her shaking, cold, bloodied hand in the ambulance as she'd floated in a woozy haze of grief and despair.

Friends seemed such an insipid descriptor for what they'd been through together.

Thankfully, Glenda's phone rang, bringing the discussion to an end. Seeing Warwick again had stirred enough memories, she didn't want to have to think about them at work too. And she had a two-day mandatory new-staff orientation to attend.

'That's my sign,' Caro said with a smile. 'Orientation starts soon.'

Glenda reached for the phone. 'I'll see you on Wednesday.'

Caro left the office as Glenda picked up the receiver. She waved at Trudy as she passed by the nurses' station and laughed at the same little escapee toddler from earlier who shot her a cheeky grin.

There were definite good vibes here and she couldn't wait to start.

* * *

Caro was surprisingly tired when she arrived home—no, *not* home—at four thirty. It wasn't like she'd done anything all day but sat on her butt and listened to a bunch of different people talk about a bunch of different hospital policy and procedures with about two dozen other new staff from varying hospital departments.

None of it was physically demanding but it was a brain drain and she was feeling it as she let herself in to find the house empty. She called out to Warwick but there was no answer and she wondered where he was as disappointment washed through her system. She'd actually been looking forward to seeing his face.

Which was completely ridiculous. What in the hell was wrong with her? Why on earth was she so damn keen to see her ex-BIL's face?

Thankfully Heidi—such a strange name for a cat—distracted her by winding around Caro's legs in greeting. 'Poor baby. Did your person go out and leave you all alone?' She crouched to pet the sleek, soft fur that ran from head to tail. The cat miaowed indignantly, leaving Caro in little doubt that she didn't need anyone but *herself* in this house.

'I bought you a treat.'

Heidi clearly knew exactly what those words meant as she slipped out of Caro's reach, padding regally to the kitchen. Caro had been to the local grocery store on her way home to pick up the ingredients for the pie she'd promised Warwick and had spotted some tinned sardines on her way out.

She emptied a tin onto a saucer and the cat, apparently approving of the offering, ate the fish with relish as Caro unpacked the paper bag containing two more tins of sardines, several fat yellow lemons, eggs, a couple of packets of plain sweet biscuits and condensed milk. Also two bottles of red wine.

Because it was red wine weather, for sure.

The air had a real nip to it and the night was drawing in and she wondered again where Warwick might be before she stopped herself, refusing to give that thought any latitude. Pouring herself a glass, she set about making her famous no-fuss, quick-and-easy lemon meringue pie, instead.

It had been a while since she'd made it but, thanks to the three lemon trees that had grown in the backyard of her childhood home, making it was pure muscle memory as she cut and squeezed the lemons.

As a kid, Caro, had wanted to be a chef and had nearly gone down that route, toying with going to culinary school in Paris. But then her mother had got meningitis when Caro was fifteen and there'd been a lot of hospital visits during that time that had left an impression. By the time her mum came home, Caro had changed career track.

She wondered as she blitzed the biscuits for the pie base how differently her life might have turned out if her mother hadn't fallen ill and she'd gone to Paris. She'd have probably never met Brad, or met him much later, anyway. She might not have had her head turned so quickly. Might not have given into the giddy rush of it all. Might not have got pregnant and married at twenty-one.

And divorced at twenty-two.

But she *hadn't* gone to Paris. She'd studied nursing in Brisbane and cooked for enjoyment instead of perfection. As well as stress relief and exam anxiety. All her friends had benefited from cakes and pies and biscuits as they'd swotted for exams together or received a special delivery if they'd had a tough prac shift or when they'd witnessed their first death or been through the adrenaline-fuelled experience of their first session of CPR.

Food had gone from a career option to an expression of love and, although she didn't cook as often as she used to any more, the motion and routine, the aromas of herbs and spices and whatever was cooking in the oven, were deeply satisfying.

Just like this pie. The glossy, citrusy filling had oozed luxuriously into the shell and even having to improvise a piping bag for the meringue topping had made her happy. As happy as the multiple, perfectly formed, teardrop dollops of meringue that stared back at her as she slid the pie into the oven.

Taking a quick shower while the pie cooked, Caro dressed in track pants and a long-sleeved T-shirt the colour of the lemons she'd just used, before following her nose to the kitchen twenty minutes later and pulling the pie out of the oven. Fluffy white peaks of meringue now toasted delicately brown greeted her, along with the mouth-watering aroma of citrus and pastry as she set it on the centre island to cool.

Her disappointment that Warwick still wasn't home was starting to morph into a tiny dart of worry, which was ludicrous but still didn't stop her checking her phone in case he'd texted while she was in the shower.

Nothing.

She told herself not to worry. He could be out doing any number of things. Like shopping. Or working out at the gym. Or visiting friends.

Hell, he could be out on a damn date.

The thought came out of nowhere and sank like a lead balloon. Maybe she could text him? Nothing weird or demanding. She wasn't his mother or his girlfriend. Just a *hey, shall I keep you some dinner?* Or, *where do you keep your xyz's?* Something that might produce a response and give her proof of life without being nosy or pushy.

An acknowledgement that he wasn't dead in a ditch somewhere.

Her gaze fell on the pie again and she smiled. Perfect! Snapping a quick pic of it—okay, maybe she styled it a little with a filter—she attached it to a text.

Not bad, even if I do say so myself.

That was fine right? No questions, no pressure, just... food porn. But, who didn't like that? Tapping send, Caro set it free before she could second-guess herself any more. They were friends. Friends texted each other, right?

That done, she put Warwick and his whereabouts firmly from her mind. The pie would take about twenty minutes to cool and she was starting it whether he was home or not.

In the meantime, she had a glass of wine to enjoy.

Warwick had worked up a real sweat on his run. He didn't ordinarily go for any longer than thirty minutes but the jet lag was kicking his arse so he'd pushed himself to go further. When he hit the sack tonight he wanted to be deep down in *bones and muscles* tired. So tired jet lag didn't stand a chance at waking him at 3:00 a.m.

So tired he wouldn't lie awake in his bed wondering about Caroline in her bed. Did she sleep arms and legs akimbo? Or not? Did she snore? Or not? Did she talk in her sleep? Or not? Did she wear pyjamas?

Or not...?

He needed to be too tired to think about that kind of shit. Because he had a lot of nights ahead of him and that didn't bode well if he was awake half the night thinking about things he shouldn't be thinking about. But once her text had arrived there was no way he was slogging it out here any longer when he could be indoors enjoying the culinary mastery that was Caroline Eastwood's lemon meringue pie.

Sure, he enjoyed the exercise and found it a really good antidote to work-related stress. And the city teemed with cycle paths and walking tracks like this one around the lake, where the reflections of trees glowed like lit matches as the sinking sun set red and gold leaves ablaze.

But it was no match for Caroline's pie.

Letting himself into the house ten minutes later, he toed off his shoes, sweeping the main living area, expecting to see her in the kitchen or curled up on the couch, but both were disappointingly empty. He glanced in the direction of her bedroom. Maybe she was taking a shower? But, *nope*. Do *not* think about her in the shower, douchebag.

Pie, Warwick. Go eat some pie.

On cue, his stomach rumbled and he turned in the direction of the kitchen, striding purposefully, the white fluff of the top revealing itself in more intricate detail the closer he drew. It was a work of art, he realised as he rounded the central island, his taste buds eagerly anticipating as his mouth salivated. He could smell the citrus and the sweetness of toasted meringue, which she'd piped all fancy-like as if she'd bought it from a patisserie, not home-cooked it.

Almost too pretty to eat. *Almost*.

Opening the cutlery drawer, he grabbed a knife and fork before opening another drawer and retrieving a plate. As he sliced into it, he noticed the bottle of red to one side of the counter and then he heard the door slide open and looked up to find Caroline swathed in the soft cashmere throw from the couch, empty wine glass in hand, heading in his direction, Heidi the cat at her heels.

'Didn't take you too long,' she teased.

She looked warm and soft and relaxed, her cheeks pink from the fresh air and maybe the wine, and he imagined for a moment how wonderful it might be if they were together and she were welcoming him home. He'd spent a lot of time thinking about her over the years in hot, passionate terms but now she was here, under his roof, he was wondering how great it would be to be free to open his arms and have her walk straight in.

How wonderful it would feel to have her slide her hands around his waist, link them around his back and press her cheek to his chest. How nice it might be to drop a kiss on top of her head then rest his chin there and just stand for long moments, revelling in seeing each other again after a day apart.

Like a couple.

'I didn't know you were a runner,' she murmured, interrupting his flight of fancy as she drew to a halt on the other side of the island, her eyes roaming over his chest.

Warwick had started his run in his hoodie but had removed it about ten minutes in and tied it around his waist, leaving him in a loose tank top, which was now damp with sweat. Something Caroline could hardly miss as her gaze lingered on his biceps and the beads of sweat in the hollow at the base of his throat.

If he wasn't very much mistaken, her nostrils might even have flared a little.

'Well... I wouldn't exactly call me a runner,' Warwick demurred as a flush of heat, not related to exercise, travelled south. 'I don't do marathons or anything. But the paths here are incredible and so accessible and it gives me a period of time where I'm not focused on anything other than my body.'

Which, at the moment, included her.

'To be honest,' he admitted with a smile, 'I'm not much of a fan of the actual hard work of it, but the scenery round the lake is beautiful and distracting.'

Just like her.

'And I know at the end of it,' he continued, ignoring that *not* helpful thought, 'those endorphins will kick in and I'll feel really bloody good. For at least…ten minutes.'

She laughed. 'I get that. Don't forget *I* ran a marathon back in the day.'

'I remember.' That was his problem. He hadn't forgotten a thing about her in their entire history of acquaintance. Not a damn thing.

'Only because everyone was sure I couldn't do it.'

'Not me.'

Her smiled faltered a little before she said, 'No. Not you.' Their gazes meshed for a beat and time seemed to stop before her smile resumed its full wattage. 'Anyway, after forty-two kilometres, I reckon those endorphins lasted, oh…at least *eleven* minutes.'

It was Warwick's turn to laugh. 'That bad, huh?'

'Brutal.' Her expression left him in no doubt the the experience was seared on her brain. 'I much prefer the endorphins you can get from eating something really good. Like pie.'

Warwick liked the way she thought. And if Caroline wasn't his ex-SIL or Hud's sister and they were just a man and a woman, he'd have easily added, *or from truly amazing sex*.

But he was *not* going to say that.

'I agree.' Warwick nodded because her pie *was* good. Opening the drawer again, he grabbed another fork and plate, passing them over. 'I assume you're having a piece too?'

'Yup. But you know the best way to eat it? In the privacy of your home, of course?'

Where Warwick's brain went then was not for any kind of public consumption. *Jesus Christ, man—do not think about smearing it all over her body and licking it off.* The rate his libido was going he'd have to head out for another run. 'Nope.'

She picked up her fork. 'Straight from the dish.'

'Oh, really?'

Warwick quirked an eyebrow, loving that she'd revealed this about herself. Lusting after her all these years was one thing, but being shown behind the curtain of her life to something she did when no one was watching was another. There was the fantasy of her, which he'd idealised over the years, and the reality of her, which was surprising and different and so much more fascinating.

Placing his plate on top of hers, he brandished his fork as he pushed the pie dish to the middle of the island, halfway between them.

'I like the way you think.'

She grinned as her spoon spliced through the fluffy waves of meringue. 'Cheers,' she said, lifting her loaded spoonful to him.

'Cheers,' he returned, lifting his, and they smiled at each other as they tapped.

It felt a little debauched as he brought it to his mouth, eating it like this. Like how two grown adults might eat it in bed together after a long session between the sheets, and his brain was back at smearing it over her body again.

But then he shovelled his into his mouth and that was forgotten as his eyes fluttered shut and his other hand slid to his stomach. He didn't know if it was her skill or the ingredients or because it had been a very long time since he'd tasted her speciality, but flavour exploded in his mouth, the meringue melting on his tongue as the sweet crunch of the base provided the perfect balance to the tartness of the citrus.

He hummed in satisfaction, savouring both the taste and the wave of nostalgia as he opened his eyes to find her gaze intent on his face—on his mouth. Which, frankly, was almost as satisfying as the pie even if she did immediately look away again.

'You are seriously wasted on nursing,' he murmured as his tongue ran along his teeth, hunting down every last morsel before he reloaded. 'You should open a pie shop.'

She laughed, her hand covering her mouth as she chewed and swallowed. 'Maybe I will.' Dropping her hand, she went in for another spoonful. 'One day.'

Warwick stilled as his brows drew together. 'Do not joke about that.'

Lifting the spoon to her lips, Caroline lifted a shoulder. 'Never say never.'

He was about to chastise her for teasing him but then she slid that spoon into her mouth and he went a little dizzy and lost his place in the conversation. 'You know,' he said as he dragged his eyes off her, ploughing his spoon into the dish again as he changed conversational track, 'I remember the first time I ever tasted your lemon meringue pie.'

She blinked as the spoon slid from her mouth. 'You do not.'

Oh, but he did. 'I do.'

Warwick grinned around his mouthful. She'd been nineteen and she and Brad had already been together for six months. She'd moved into the share house near uni with Hud, him and Brad, taking the fourth bedroom, but had moved into Brad's room within a month.

Not that her parents had known.

'I'd called into your parents' house to pick something up for Hud and you were home for the weekend helping your mother cook for some party they were having.'

'Oh, yes. I remember that, too.'

He wondered if she remembered it in as vivid detail as he did. She'd had some kind of bandana thing in her hair and been in frayed cut-off jeans and an ABBA T-shirt and she'd scratched her arm on the lemon tree.

'I thought the custard wasn't quite tart enough. Mum disagreed.'

Warwick nodded as he heaped his spoon again. 'And I cast the deciding vote.' He'd tasted a lot of Caroline's cooking—although he'd called her Caro at the time—so he'd been eager to settle the dispute.

'In my favour, if I recall correctly.'

'Of course.' He shoved the spoon in his mouth and quickly swallowed. 'I knew which side my bread was buttered on.' He'd scored two mini lemon meringue tarts to take with him as a consequence *and* she'd started making them at home, too.

She laughed as she loaded her spoon again and took another mouthful. 'Brad was never a fan.'

'That's because Brad's an idiot.'

Warwick loved his brother, but they were very different people. They might have shared a womb—Brad was two minutes older—but they weren't identical in *any* way. Sure, everybody *loved* Brad because he had a big dazzling personality, but he'd always been a bit of a butterfly, flitting from one shiny thing to the next.

The fact he'd stayed with Caroline for a few years—*married* her even—had surprised everybody. His becoming a cosmetic surgeon and moving to LA had not.

Caroline laughed again. 'He's not an idiot.'

Quirking an eyebrow, he said, 'He let you go, didn't he?'

He kept his voice light but still, it sliced through the convivial atmosphere with all the finesse of a rusty machete.

Warwick winced as Caroline's laughter petered out. Why in the hell had he said *that*? They'd been having fun and he'd gone and put a downer on it all by reminding her of a really shitty time in her life.

She shrugged. 'We were both young.'

Warwick all but ground his teeth. *The man* cheated on her two months after she half bled to death from miscarrying his baby and she still made excuses for him. But it was a topic they'd never discussed and it was hardly the time for it now, either. So instead of telling her what crap that statement was and how she'd deserved better, Warwick just grunted and hacked a bit more pie off with his spoon. Possibly more aggressively than was warranted.

Caroline followed suit with much less vigour and they ate the next mouthful in silence while he silently castigated himself. Well done, *dickhead*. Remind her of her brief marriage. And the baby she lost.

Swallowing the mouthful that suddenly tasted like paper, Warwick placed his spoon in the dish. 'Think I might hit the shower.'

'Good idea.' She swallowed, a slight smile hovering on her mouth. 'You stink.'

Her warm flippancy surprised a laugh out of him as their eyes met and Warwick took a breath. With two words she'd reminded him of a time when they'd often bantered and neutralised his faux pas, for which he was immensely grateful.

'I can't promise there'll be any pie left when you get out.'

Warwick grinned. '*C'est la vie.*' Because he knew one thing for sure where Caroline was concerned—where there was one pie, there were more.

CHAPTER FOUR

By the time Wednesday morning rocked around Caro was well and truly ready to get to work. It had been almost seven weeks since she'd worked a shift between finishing her last job and organising her move and she missed it.

She was happy to see Haley on shift with her when she turned up in the handover room ten minutes before seven. 'Hey,' she greeted. 'You ready for this? It's a madhouse out there at the moment.'

Caro nodded. 'Bring on the chaos.'

There were four other RNs on the shift. Dionne, a few years older than Caro and in charge of the shift, introduced everyone. Paul and Julie, both in their forties, had worked on the ward for over five years each and there was Georgie, a new grad who'd been on the ward for two months.

The twenty-eight-bed ward was currently bursting after yesterday afternoon's ENT theatre list but a dozen now tonsil-less kids would be discharged after they'd eaten breakfast, which should significantly lighten the load. Other than that there was the usual mishmash of cases. Anything and everything from respiratory illnesses to broken bones. From mystery rashes to several cases of D&Vs. From burns to appendicitis to a baby with a febrile convulsion.

'Can I get you to take the observation bay closest to the nurses' station, please?' Dionne asked after she'd allocated everyone else their patients. 'We'll have a new patient transferring from Critical Care around ten this morning. Didi Marsh, three years old, newly diagnosed type one admitted in severe diabetic keto acidosis five days ago.'

'Oh. Poor little thing. That really sucks.' Having worked in a PICU setting for eighteen months, Caro knew how precariously ill newly diagnosed diabetic kiddos could get. DKA was a medical emergency for a reason. 'What was her pH?'

'An impressive 6.7.'

Caro blinked. '*Yeesh.* She's lucky.'

'Yup.'

In any *acute* situation that kind of pH would be fatal for most people. But because type one diabetics generally got there at a slower pace, with their bodies constantly compensating on a chemical level to return the body's acid/base balance to within the very tight range of normal, they could get severely acidotic with their systems still chugging along.

Limping, actually. Struggling? Yes. Symptomatic? Definitely. But often, to all outward appearances, managing. Especially little kids who couldn't yet talk to explain their symptoms or tell their parents how poorly they were feeling.

'The pH is back to normal now,' Dionne continued. 'As are the blood-sugar levels and other blood work. She's off her insulin infusion and on injections but she's obviously still weak and recovering so she needs close monitoring for a few days. The family live in a small rural town about five hundred kilometres west so they'll probably be here for a couple of weeks before they feel able to transition home.'

Caro nodded. Didi and her family were going to need a lot of support. Having a child diagnosed with type one diabetes was stressful and scary for families. When that child was particularly young it was even more fraught. Parents were anxious about how they were going to cope and it was her job, in conjunction with a host of other allied health professionals, to look after *them*, too.

Paediatric nursing was never just about the patient.

It was, after all, Didi's parents who were going to have to manage their daughter's condition when they got home. Their rural location would be an extra challenge but it was the hospital's job to make sure they went home with proper services in place.

'I've let Dr Devlin's office know about the admission so I imagine he'll be around at some time later to see Didi.'

Caro suppressed a smile. First day on the job proper, first patient practically and she and Warwick were already being thrown together. She hadn't seen him for years prior to moving and now, not only was she living—rooming—with him, but they were already involved with the same patient.

Just as well she wasn't someone who believed in signs…

'That won't be a hardship,' Dionne said with a wink.

Caro just laughed, not wanting to explain again her relationship with Warwick when she wasn't sure what it was half the time herself. Especially now. When they'd been living separate lives she'd known who he was—Hud's friend, Brad's brother. Now they were practically in each other's pockets and she'd cooked for him and she caught herself looking at him sometimes and thinking things she shouldn't be thinking, she wasn't so sure.

He let you go, didn't he?

Warwick's words *and* his tone from Monday night had left her in no doubt what he'd thought about his brother leaving her, which had felt surprisingly…flattering. But then she'd felt bad because, sure, Brad had screwed up, but she'd been an idiot, too.

They'd been too young. And she'd been too dazzled.

There was a couple of years after the baby when she'd resented him for that but once she'd come out the other side of her grief, Caro had been able to own *her* part in their relationship breakdown. Had been honest about how the relationship probably would have ended earlier, had she not accidentally fallen pregnant.

'Also in that bay,' Dionne said, 'is the nine-month-old baby with the febrile convulsion from two days ago who is still throwing temps. One of the post-op tonsils who had a bit of a bleed and had to go back to Theatre. And the ten-weeker with RSV.' She walked out of the door of the handover room and Caro followed. 'Think you can handle all that?'

Caro smiled. 'I reckon I can.' Although she knew that if any of the four kids had an acute deterioration, the other patients would be neglected until the crisis was resolved.

They wandered into the four-bed bay. Unlike the others that were six beds, this one sat directly opposite the nurses' station and was reserved for patients needing closer observation. Dionne did a quick tour of the bay, showing Caro the layout before someone called her name.

Smiling apologetically, she said, 'If you need to know where anything is, just holler,' before departing.

Austin, the febrile-seizure baby, chose that moment to wake, sitting up and looking through the high bars of the cot as he started to cry.

'His mother's just nipped out to take a shower,' said the mother of the tonsillar bleed whose child occupied the next bed.

'Thanks,' Caro said.

As she made her way to the cot, the little boy pulled himself up on the bars of the high safety rails and stuck both his arms through. One arm was boarded up, IV tubing sprouting from beneath the bandages leading all the way to a pump attached to a pole beside the bed. He looked forlorn and miserable.

'It's okay, little one,' Caro crooned as she reached the cot and released the clasp to lower the bars.

A grizzling Austin fell straight into her outstretched arms and Caro lifted him out, cuddling him to her chest. She couldn't walk with him, given his attachment to the drip, so she just rocked from side to side making nonsensical hushing noises as his little chest shuddered in and out. Propping her chin on a head covered with a fine wispy layer of hair, she noted that he felt warm. The handover nurse had reported him as afebrile at six, so Caro made a mental note to take his temp when his mum got back.

But, right now, she was exactly where she should be.

Her heart expanded as Austin snuggled closer. Her mother had worried after the miscarriage about Caro working in paediatrics. She'd fretted that it'd be too hard—emotionally. Which was, of course, right. There were definitely times of high emotion in her job. And yes, moments like this with a snuggly babe, she *did* think about her baby boy that never was.

He'd have been nine later this year.

But it didn't make her sad. Not any more anyway. If anything it made her feel closer to him and she liked that.

Austin's mother returned a few minutes later apologising profusely but Caro assured her all was fine as she handed the baby over and took his temp. He was febrile again and she administered some Panadol before getting on with her list of chores.

She was double-checking some IV antibiotics with Haley mid-morning, when her new patient arrived in the ward, looking small and forlorn in the bed as the orderlies pushed it into place.

Caro greeted Didi with a big smile. 'Good morning, lovely.'

The little girl had a halo of frizzy, knotty, bed-head curls and looked pale except for the dark smudges under her eyes that emphasised the hollows beneath her cheekbones. She was looking at everyone too warily to return the smile, her lips dry beneath a smear of gloss, both arms secured to padded boards and wrapped in bandages to protect precious intravenous lines.

Caro turned to her mother, who looked utterly wrecked. 'Hey, I'm Caro. I'm going to be looking after you guys today.'

'I'm Leesa,' she said with a wan smile. She blinked back a sheen of moisture but Caro definitely clocked it before it disappeared.

Giving Leesa a gentle shoulder squeeze, Caro said, 'I'm just going to the nurses' station to get handover then I'll be back, okay?'

Handover was a little convoluted as the critical care nurse went methodically through the lead-up to admission followed by the last five days of history but Caro was back at the bedside in fifteen minutes. Didi was sleeping, curled up clutching a teddy bear, so Caro turned her attention to Leesa. 'How are you doing?'

'I'm fine.' Leesa nodded vigorously. 'Obviously not what we expected and there's a lot to learn and figure out but we've got this. We're going to be all right.'

Caro's heart sank even as she smiled and nodded back. Leesa was projecting confidence and positivity, which was awesome, but her hand trembled a little against the bar of the bed rail and Caro suspected she was close to losing it. 'You will be. I know it's hard to see from where you're sitting, but Didi's already made tremendous progress. They wouldn't have discharged her from Critical Care if they didn't think she was ready.'

Leesa gave a tight smile. 'Yeah.'

'It's a lot, I know,' Caro said gently, 'and you must be a little overwhelmed but—'

She shook her head. 'I've been googling everything. We're going to be fine.'

Caro's gaze flicked to the trembling hand and she wondered who exactly Leesa was trying to convince—Caro or herself. 'Have you had anything to eat yet today?'

'My husband has taken Harrison, our five-year-old, for a nap and he's grabbing something to eat and a shower. We're just over the road at the hospital accommodation. I'll go when he gets back. Didi's been very clingy.'

'Of course.' Caro gave her a warm smile. 'How about I get you some toast and a cup of tea or coffee in the meantime?'

Leesa was looking at her blankly like she wasn't really comprehending what Caro was saying, so she just smiled and said, 'I'm guessing white coffee no sugar? And does honey toast sound okay?'

'Thanks,' Leesa murmured.

Caro nodded and was there and back again within five minutes. 'Here you are.' She placed the mug and plate on the adjustable bed table and positioned it so Leesa could easily reach the impromptu breakfast. 'The coffee's not exactly gourmet but it's hot and I didn't even burn the toast for once,' she joked.

That scored her another wan smile but Caro was encouraged as Leesa picked up the mug. 'Dr Devlin should be along to chat with you some time in the next few hours,' she said, then left Leesa to eat her breakfast—or brunch, as the case might be—in peace.

* * *

Of course, as was always the way, he turned up at the worst possible time, just after Caro had performed a finger prick to test Didi's blood sugar. Didi had kicked and screamed and cried through the entire thing, making a process that normally took about five seconds a several-minute ordeal involving a lot of cajoling and pleading from Leesa, who was on the verge of tears herself as she consoled her sobbing daughter.

'Sounds like we're about to get a one-star review over here, Sister Eastwood.'

A low teasing drawl from behind enveloped Caro in a casual familiarity, but also, and quite confusingly, a flood of goose bumps swept over her body at the same time, beading her nipples against the lacy fabric of her bra. Looking over her shoulder, she found Warwick smiling at her as he approached, surrounded by an entourage of junior doctors.

Her pulse did a funny little giddy-up at the sight, which was *extra* confusing. Warwick was family, not…whatever *this* was.

It had to be because it was the first time seeing him in his *Dr Devlin* persona. His professional guise. Which was quite something. Dressed in dark trousers and a checked shirt that was open at the throat, he had a stethoscope slung casually around his neck, looking every inch the consultant paediatric specialist.

He oozed *boss* vibes. Very…dominant and in charge, his unmistakeable authority just a little bit arrogant and yet far more…stimulating than she'd expected.

Flummoxed by her reaction, Caro gave a half-laugh just as the BSL reader beeped: 8.2—not too bad considering the stage of Didi's recovery from DKA. Automatically she held it up to Warwick, which gave her something to do other than panic about her very physical reaction to her *ex-husband's brother.*

He nodded, clearly happy with the result, which was when Caro spotted the name tag pinned to his pocket half obscured by his stethoscope. Like Haley's and Glenda's, it was round, featuring a caricature that sported the exaggerated square jaw of a cartoon superhero, a scruffy face and big, black-rimmed glasses. The name beneath was simply *Warwick* and there was just something so unassuming about it, Caro's legs went a little wobbly.

He turned his attention to Leesa. 'Hi.' He smiled at her as he crouched down beside the chair where Leesa was sitting, a sobbing Didi on her lap. 'I'm Warwick Devlin. You must be Leesa?'

A harried Leesa nodded. 'I'm so sorry about this,' she murmured quietly as she gently rocked her daughter. 'She really freaks out with the finger prick. I think she's still traumatised from the night we first came in and it took so many goes to get a drip in her.'

He nodded. 'Sounds like you might still be a little traumatised too?'

Leesa shuddered. 'It was pretty awful.'

Caro could only imagine. Paediatric IV access could be tricky at the best of times—add to that the level of dehydration Didi would have been suffering and the difficulty increased.

'I just…honestly don't know how we're going to keep doing this,' Leesa whispered, more to herself than to Warwick.

Leesa's faux confidence from earlier had quickly dissolved, the despair in her voice palpable, and Caro's heart went out to her. With Didi hyper-anxious about the finger pricks, which without a CGM—continuous glucose monitor—would be several times per day, life probably seemed quite bleak at the moment.

Might Didi get used to it? Possibly. Or maybe her anxiety would get worse, making every day a battlefield.

Warwick gave Leesa a confident smile. 'You won't have to. We're going to get you hooked up with a continuous glucose monitor as soon as possible. No more finger pricks and you'll be able to keep a close eye on her levels through an app on your phone.'

For the first time since she'd arrived on the ward, possibly, Caro suspected, the first time since this whole ordeal had begun, Leesa brightened. 'Really? The diabetes educator wasn't sure how quickly we could get her on a CGM.'

'I reckon we can get it done asap,' Warwick said with another smile. 'I'll liaise with her after this and we can hopefully have one to go in a few days.'

The flood of relief on Leesa's face practically lit the entire room. 'That would be wonderful.'

'She might not be a fan at first. It's strange having a patch on you all the time, but I think when the finger pricks go away she'll settle to it.'

Leesa nodded. 'I think that will help enormously.'

Warwick turned his attention to Didi, who was now utterly exhausted from her crying jag, her face wet, her breathing coming in discordant hiccoughs. 'Hey there, Didi, I'm Warwick.'

He smiled and waved as Didi regarded him and the people clustered in a group behind him with suspicion. After the little girl had spent five days in Critical Care being poked and prodded by people who looked a lot like him, Caro could hardly blame her.

'Oh my God,' he said suddenly, his eyes bugging. 'Did you know you have something stuck in your ear?'

Didi's expression grew even more suspicious and she snuggled closer to her mother as Warwick reached for her ear then gasped as he pulled back his hand to reveal a big, shiny silver coin in his fingers. 'You have money in your ear!'

Didi's shuddery breathing halted as she stared at the coin in wonder. She looked at her mother then back at the coin, then at Warwick.

'Wait…' Warwick reached for Didi's ear again. She didn't shy away this time. 'You have another one!' He produced another coin and she actually smiled a little. 'Did you swallow a money box? Shall I check and see if there's one in your other ear?'

Didi thought for a moment before she nodded slowly and turned her head, allowing Warwick access to the ear that had been pressed into her mother's chest. Smiling, Warwick repeated the process but this time came back empty-handed. 'No, sorry.' He shook his head. 'Nothing there. But—wait.' He peered closer, inspecting Didi's face. She didn't shrink back. 'I think you have some in your nose.'

Another coin was produced from Didi's nose. 'Did you know she could do that, Mum?' Warwick asked, addressing Leesa.

Leesa laughed. Actually laughed. 'I didn't. No.'

'I think she might be…' Warwick leaned in a little and whispered, 'Magic.'

'I think you might be right,' Leesa agreed, playing along, the most relaxed Caro had seen her the last couple of hours. Didi had also settled right down, watching the little crowd around her with interest, not apprehension. 'We'll definitely be taking her to the grocery shopping from now on.'

The gathered entourage, who had been smiling indulgently at the display, laughed. Warwick offered Didi one of the coins. 'You want to keep it in case Mummy needs it for the mortgage?' More laughter, which obviously went over Didi's head, but she reached for the coin, taking it in fingers encumbered with IV bandaging and tucking it close.

'If you don't mind, we're just going to have a little chat about Didi while we're standing here.'

Leesa shook her head. 'It's fine. After five days upstairs, I'm used to it now.'

Caro smiled at the comment. Critical care nursing and medical handovers were often done at the bedside, which could be both informative and difficult for loved ones. Although, given the way Leesa *and* Didi were looking at Warwick—like he hung the moon and the stars—Caro suspected he could have asked anything of them.

Within a minute of appearing, Warwick had managed to soothe Leesa's shot nerves and calm a fractious Didi. He'd been real and human, he'd got down to Didi's level, he'd been positive and funny and set, not only his patient, but her mother at ease.

Caro couldn't help compare him to Brad, who'd never have introduced himself by his first name or worn a goofy badge. He'd always said he'd worked too damn hard for the title to not use it, and even though they'd split a few years before he finished his medical training she'd seen enough of his YouTube channel—yes, all the trendy cosmetic surgeons had them—to know that his patients never called him *Brad*.

And the *magic*? Lordy... If erect nipples had bewildered her, they were nothing compared to the explosion in her left ovary.

'Nilaa.' Warwick pushed out of his crouch as he addressed the woman in the five-person huddle who was carrying Didi's medical chart. She seemed like she was about twenty-five so probably an intern but, as she was wearing a headscarf, it was difficult to tell for sure. 'You want to run us through the details of Didi's case?'

That was another thing Warwick did. He didn't say *the patient* or rather *my* patient, as Brad did in those videos. Like a lot of doctors, actually. He used people's names.

Nilaa nodded. 'Didi Marsh, three-year-old newly diagnosed type one diabetes admitted five days ago in severe DKA.'

The intern was thorough—she'd obviously done her homework, going through all the clinical presentations and treatments. Then, in a truly egalitarian way, Warwick turned to another intern, who also looked about twenty-five, and quizzed him on the disease itself. The guy seemed nervous but Warwick was encouraging, gently prodding and directing as they talked, drawing the others into a discussion so it was less adversarial.

More conversation than examination.

Damn it, *Dr* Warwick was ticking all her boxes. And if he'd been any other male doctor who had created this much ruction in all her interesting places, Caro might have flirted a little, tested the waters, maybe even suggesting a drink after work if he'd shown interest.

But he wasn't any other male doctor, was he? He was *Warwick*.

'Awesome.' Warwick nodded. 'Well done, everyone. But remember, the most important thing you can do when taking on a new case is to go over the history again with the person at the centre of it all. Given Didi is three, that's going to be her mum or dad. Don't solely rely on the notes or what's already in the chart. Something might have got lost in translation or missed or not noted down.'

He glanced at Leesa, smiling apologetically. 'I'm sorry, I know you've probably been asked to go through this several times already, but would you mind telling us in your own words what happened before Didi was admitted to hospital?'

And because he'd already thoroughly won her over, Leesa didn't hesitate consenting. 'Of course.' She smiled as she absently rubbed her chin across the top of her daughter's head while Didi happily played with the coin. 'Where do you want me to start?'

That statement in itself spoke volumes. Didi and her family had been through a lot and Caro made a mental note to talk to the social worker about getting some kind of counselling/debriefing support for Leesa and her husband.

'Maybe where, looking back, you can pinpoint something that you thought was unusual or odd at the time but makes sense now? If that makes sense,' he said with a self-deprecating laugh.

'Yes,' Leesa said, also with a laugh. 'About a month before, she started weeing right through her night nappies.'

'And that was unusual?'

'Yes. She's not toilet trained yet and she was probably only dry about half the time at night usually, but I was having to change her sheets every few nights or so. We'd had that heatwave though and I'd been forcing both the kids to drink extra, so I didn't really think much of it.'

Haltingly, Leesa laid out the events as Warwick listened carefully, interjecting with questions when he needed extra information or sought clarification.

'My husband was overseas for work and I was staying with my dad and my stepmother in Canberra the morning we called the ambulance. Didi had been irritable from the moment she woke up and had a tantrum when I wouldn't let her have a chocolate bar for breakfast.'

'Were tantrums unusual?'

'They had been, but she'd been having a lot more lately

and I just thought it was those terrible twos that we'd missed and were now the terrible threes. But then, when she was on the kitchen floor flailing around, her shirt had ridden up and I really noticed her ribs. Like…she's never been a chubby child but I've never noticed her ribs before.'

Leesa's brow furrowed and Caro could tell she was reliving those moments, again.

'When she finally calmed down her breathing was really funny and the hairs on the back of my neck sat up and I just knew something wasn't right. I called the health hotline and the nurse asked me if that was Didi she could hear breathing and when I said yes she called an ambulance immediately. And…it was all a bit of a blur from then, really.'

Warwick nodded and asked several more questions before asking Leesa if she had any she'd like to ask. Unsurprisingly, she did, many of them digging into the chemistry and pathogenesis of diabetes, and Warwick stood there patiently answering every one, like he had all the time in the world and not probably a dozen other patients to see.

And not in his usual nerdy medical jargon way—Caro didn't hear glycogenesis or islet cell autoantibodies once—but in simple layman's terms that Leesa seemed to easily grasp. When the questions were exhausted, he laid out the plan for Didi's hospital stay, assuring Leesa they wouldn't send them home until she was confident she had a handle on everything.

'We're going to be in hospital for ever,' Leesa said with a laugh that sounded flat and hollow. 'I'm never going to get a handle on all this.'

Warwick once again crouched down beside the chair and locked eyes with Leesa. 'I know this feels insurmountable right now and that you don't think you'll ever cope and I'm really sorry that this has happened to Didi and your family.'

His voice was low and soothing. It wasn't performative for the sake of his juniors or the ears of the three other mothers in the room. It was just him and Leesa.

'But you *will* get a grip on this, I promise. Everybody at this stage thinks they're going to screw up and they'll never get it and are terrified of the unknown, but that's why we're here. To help. And you and Didi's dad and Didi herself...' He smiled at the little girl. 'You'll all be experts at this before you know it.' He leaned in a little and whispered, 'More expert than me.'

And there went her right ovary. *Yowsers*. Caro mentally fanned herself because *Dr* Devlin was seriously *hot*.

'I'm going to hold you to that,' Leesa said, her voice wobbly.

'Fair. But I'll be holding myself to it too.' Warwick grinned as he stood. 'I'll swing by in a couple of days and see how you're getting on. Meantime...' He fished in his shirt pocket, pulled out a card and handed it over. 'That's my office number. Get my EA, Cheray, to page me if you want to see me before that.'

He departed then with his gaggle of baby doctors and Caro and Leesa watched them go before Leesa turned her gaze to the business card, staring at it blankly for a beat or two.

'Wow.' She glanced up at Caro. 'He's good, isn't he?'

Caro smiled. 'He is.'

'I mean, not that the others haven't been,' Leesa hastened to assure. 'He's just...extra. Like, he really *really* knows and cares.'

'Yeah.' Caro nodded. 'He has juvenile diabetes in his family so he's particularly passionate about it.'

'Oh.' Leesa's gaze shifted to where Warwick had halted, his elbows resting on the high shelf of the nurses' station, his team hanging on his every word.

Caro wanted to tell Leesa about Warwick and Brad's little sister—Gina—who had been diagnosed with type one at the age of eight, so she understood why he was *extra*. Except Gina's diagnosis had been made on autopsy and Leesa didn't need to hear that.

Warwick chose that moment to glance over his shoulder as if he knew exactly what she was thinking. Their gazes met as a small smile touched his mouth.

'Excuse me, Leesa,' she said. 'I just need to check a couple of things with Warwick.'

She didn't hear Leesa's reply, she just headed in his direction, skirting around the nurses' station, their eyes meeting as she approached him from the other side of the desk.

'Why don't you guys go on ahead and get set up for the clinic?' Warwick said, not taking his eyes off her. 'I'll catch you up shortly.'

Glenda had told her in their chat about the public paediatric outpatients clinic every Wednesday afternoon.

'So…' She folded her arms. 'Magic, huh?'

He grinned. 'Works every time.'

Yeah. Didi had been agog. 'Now I'm going to have to learn magic.'

'Oh, I don't know.' He folded his arms so they were now mirroring each other. 'I think someone who made the last piece of lemon meringue pie disappear from the fridge this morning has some pretty strong magic going on already.'

'I'm sorry.' Caro grinned, not remotely sorry. 'Did you have dibs on it?'

Ignoring the question, presumably because neither of them had called *dibs*, he narrowed his eyes. 'Pie for breakfast? Really?'

Caro lifted her chin. 'Yes. Really.'

'That's pretty decadent, don't you think, Caroline?'

The word *Caroline* should be illegal sliding off his tongue, especially when he was dressed as this version of himself. Dr Devlin was pretty damned decadent himself. 'Yes,' she said with a nod. 'Turns out that when you become an adult, you can eat pie for breakfast and nobody polices it. *Or* even cares.'

He chuckled as his gaze drifted to her mouth before returning to her face. 'Being an adult is *so* much fun.'

Caro was pretty sure they weren't talking about pie now, or magic. In fact she had to remind herself that they were at work as she tried really hard not to think about the other adult things a person could do. With another adult person. About which nobody would care.

Although, in their case, there'd be people who would, *very definitely*, care.

Brad for one. Hud for another, who was still low-key pissed at Brad all these years later despite her insisting *she'd* forgiven him. And both sets of parents would probably have…concerns.

Then, of course, there was Warwick. He'd care most of all if he knew she was suddenly thinking about him in a different way, right? Even if he did seem to be enjoying this… vibe between them. Which was, frankly, a little confusing.

'Anyway.' She shook her head. This was not why she'd approached. 'I just wanted to say thank you for putting Leesa at ease like that. She was pretty close to losing it when she got here a few hours ago and you really helped her believe she can do this. I know she appreciates it and so do I.'

Caro knew that sometimes parents needed to hear praise and encouragement from the *person at the top* before they could be convinced they were doing well. And she got that. It was just not that common to find a doctor who fulfilled their part of this unspoken bargain very well—who was good with both kids and parents.

Unlike Warwick, who was clearly excellent.

'Of course.' He shrugged like it was nothing. 'I should be able to bring the CGM with me on Friday. Don't tell her that just in case there's some kind of unforeseen delay from the supplier.'

It was Caro's turn to say, 'Of course.'

'Fancy takeaway tonight? There's a local place that does amazing wood-fired pizza.'

'Sure.'

'I can bring them home with me. Won't be until after six—clinic always runs late.'

Home. It sounded blissfully domestic but it would be dangerous, coupled with these strange thoughts, to start thinking of Warwick's house as home. 'Okay.'

He grinned. 'See you then.'

Caro just nodded this time as he departed, her eyes tracking his progress to the door as she, once again, found herself thinking thoughts that were *very* unsuitable for work.

CHAPTER FIVE

Warwick pushed open the heavy swing doors to the ward on Friday, as promised, CGM in hand. It sounded like feeding time at the zoo as he was greeted with what must surely be every kid on the ward voicing their displeasure at being here. He smiled to himself, glad that he got to come and go and not have to endure this cacophony with no escape.

Glenda came out of the first bay as he passed, a crying baby with a snotty nose and a fine rash that seemed to cover his entire body on one hip, a bundle of bed linen squashed against the other. It was worse than he thought if the NUM was lending a hand. 'Afternoon, Sister Stephenson, the usual chaos, I see.'

She eyed him crankily. 'Why are you so damn chipper?'

He grinned. 'What's not to be chipper about? It's a beautiful day and tomorrow is the weekend.'

Glenda harrumphed. 'What's a weekend again?'

Warwick laughed. They both knew she didn't work weekends either but her point was well made. Tomorrow was going to be just another day for her nurses and the children and their parents.

'Is that for Didi?' she asked, tipping her chin at the box in his hand.

'Yep.'

'Thank goodness. Finger-prick time is a major test of endurance for everyone involved. It'll be a godsend for Didi and her poor mum, who's at her wits' end.'

'Yep.' Leesa's fragile composure had been evident on Wednesday. Having a continuous glucose monitor would alleviate the need for multiple daily finger-prick tests and therefore a lot of Didi's anxiety.

The last thing a young diabetic like Didi needed was a needle phobia considering her insulin, for the moment and potentially other times throughout her life, was being administered via injection. Soon they could put her on a pump that both continuously monitored blood-sugar levels and automatically titrated and delivered the insulin dose accordingly. But…one step at a time.

'Helen called to say she's been delayed.'

Warwick nodded. He'd got the message from the hospital diabetes nurse, who would normally do all the teaching around how to apply the sensor and care for it and how to sync the app and use it, but Warwick had done it plenty of times too and could at least get Didi started while they waited for Helen to join them.

He could have pushed the appointment time and waited to arrive with Helen, but Leesa had been told yesterday they'd be coming and he knew she'd be watching the clock. He didn't want to add to her stress by not being punctual when he was able.

'Caro's down there though,' Glenda added as she dumped the linen in the hamper and switched the grizzling baby to her newly freed hip.

Warwick smiled broader and Glenda arched an eyebrow. Which he ignored. 'Great.' *So* great. 'Thanks.'

He had asked her this morning if she was going to be looking after Didi today. She hadn't been able to be certain, of course, but the fact she was made him smile. Visiting patients on the ward had always been one of the favourite parts of his job—despite it sometimes feeling like stepping into a scene from an apocalyptic movie—but knowing that Caroline might be here in future made him look forward to those times even more.

It sure put a spring in his step now as he covered the distance to Didi's bed thinking about their last couple of nights. They'd settled into a routine of eating and watching TV together and it was starting to feel like old times again, back when they'd all lived together. When things had been easy between them. Even when he'd been nursing the most enormous crush, their friendship had always felt easy.

Caroline was the first person he saw when he entered the bay. She was hanging a new bag of fluid on a child who looked about eight with swollen lips and eyes so puffed up, they were mere slits in his head. The poor kid must have suffered some kind of anaphylactic reaction. Their gazes met and her eyes rounded briefly, like maybe she'd been thinking about him and now suddenly here he was.

'Dr Devlin,' she greeted politely, recovering quickly, a slight smile playing across her mouth now.

'Sister Eastwood.' He returned her smile with one of his own and their gazes held a little. He noticed she was wearing a cartoon name tag today, her caricature sprouting feathery hair from her head and two hearts in her eyes.

'I hope you brought your magic tricks. Didi is not a happy camper at the moment.'

Warwick looked across at Leesa, who was standing, Didi clinging to her like a baby koala, arms clamped tight around her mother's shoulder. The little girl was almost as puffy-eyed as the allergic kid. 'What happened?'

'Blood collector came.'

'Ah.' He nodded. 'Say no more.'

Drawing blood from kids was always fraught but for someone like Didi, already traumatised from her experiences with needles, even more so.

'Well, hopefully this—' he brandished a couple of boxes containing CGM kits '—will help alleviate some of her finger-prick anxiety.'

'Good.' Caroline fitted the IV tubing into the pump and shut the door as she dialled up the delivered amount. 'Helen's running late.'

'I know. I'll start though. I think both Didi and Leesa could do with a pick-me-up.'

'Sure.' She nodded. 'Go on over. I won't be long.'

Warwick approached Didi and Leesa with a big smile. Leesa's return smile was lacklustre, Didi didn't even bother, which almost made Warwick laugh. That was what he liked about kids—there was no bullshit with them. If they liked you, you knew it, if they didn't you knew it too.

It was good to see her looking much better than she had two days ago though, even if she wasn't particularly happy at the moment. There was some colour in her cheeks and more alertness in her gaze. Having read her electronic chart before he'd attended today, he was pleased to see she was also continuing to improve clinically.

But that didn't mean she wasn't totally over being in hospital.

'Hang on a moment.' Warwick fished around in his trouser pocket for what he wanted. 'What do we have here?'

Leaning forward, he plucked a square of gauzy red fabric from behind Didi's ear. She blinked, eyeing the fabric with interest but still not willing to let go of her funk. 'I see.' Warwick nodded gravely, hands surreptitiously back in his pocket again, scrunching the other fabric square into his palm. 'You'd rather a purple one, right?'

Leaning in one more time, he pulled the purple fabric from behind Didi's other ear and handed them both to her. 'Did you know she could do that?' Warwick asked Leesa, his eyes round and incredulous.

Leesa perked up, suppressing a smile. 'More magic?' she asked, her voice breathy and amazed. She glanced at her daughter. 'Incredible.'

'I think you need to consider putting her into a special magic school. There's no telling how magic she'll become with a little training.'

Laughing, Leesa nodded. 'We'll definitely look into the enrolment process.'

'Well, I have the best magic trick of all,' Warwick said, addressing Didi. 'I can make it so you don't need to have any more finger pricks. Would you like that?'

Didi, her head snuggled into the crook of Leesa's neck, her two scraps of fabric clutched in her hand, eyed him for a long moment before giving a barely perceptible nod. 'That would be amazing, wouldn't it, sweetie?' Leesa enthused.

Another small nod.

'Well, ta-da!' Warwick produced the boxes from behind his back with a flourish. 'This is for you. Shall I show you and Mummy how to use it?'

A third nod.

Warwick smiled. 'Okay, then.' He turned his attention to Leesa. 'Is your husband wanting to be here for this?'

'It's fine.' Leesa shook her head. 'He'll be a while. He's taken Harrison out for a few hours because he's going a bit stir-crazy. I'll catch him up.'

'Sure.' Warwick nodded. 'Do you mind if I put one on you first, so Didi can see how it all works and that it doesn't hurt?'

'Yep,' she agreed eagerly. 'Sounds like a plan.'

He smiled. 'Excellent.' Caroline joined them as he said to Didi, 'Would you like to help me put one on Mummy first?'

A curious expression flitted over the little girl's face before she nodded again, shy but clearly interested in the request.

'Okay, then. Leesa, how about we sit on the side of the bed and, Caroline—' he glanced at her as they sat down '—why don't you grab that chair and sit, too?'

Caroline brought the hard, plastic bedside chair closer to the bed, sitting down so close her knees were practically touching Leesa's, for which Warwick was grateful. He didn't have to explain she was going to need to stick close if they had any chance of separating Didi from her mother—Caroline was experienced enough to anticipate it without his explicit instruction.

'Right...now. Didi, you won't be able to see what's going on there so why don't you sit on Caroline's lap?'

Leesa passed Didi over but the little girl started to cry and buck, reaching for her mother. Warwick couldn't blame her. She'd been through the wringer, surrounded by strangers who hadn't given her a moment's peace. It was no wonder her suspicion levels were sky-high.

'Here,' Caroline said, cutting through the noise to hand Didi the packaged sensor that had demo written across the top. 'Can you hold this for Dr Devlin? This is the most important job of all. Only very special magic little girls are allowed to help like this.'

Warwick mouthed thank you over Didi's head, his admiration for Caroline's skills as *a nurse* kicking up another notch as the child's fussing cut out and she stared at the flat disc-shaped device that fitted into the palm of her hand. The little girl inspected the sensor as Caroline positioned her so her little legs were pressed firmly against her mother's.

Knowing they had a small window before Didi lost interest

and started to fuss again, Warwick glanced at Leesa. 'When Helen comes we'll go through everything in more detail, including syncing to the phone and the ins and outs of the app, but for now I think we should just get on with doing it.'

Leesa nodded. 'Yes. Absolutely.'

'We'll place Didi's sensor here, at the back of the upper arm.' Warwick demonstrated on Leesa, who rolled her sleeve up a little as Didi watched. 'There's usually enough fat there and it's not often banged or knocked. A lot of people place it on their abdomen but, for kids Didi's age, especially initially, out of sight, out of mind.'

'And it's waterproof, right?'

'Yep.' Warwick nodded. 'You can take a shower or a bath or go swimming with it,' he said as he smiled at Didi. 'You like to swim?'

'Yes,' she said, her voice faint.

'I bet you're fast too, right?'

Didi shook her head. 'But I can touch the bottom.'

Warwick bugged his eyes. 'Magic *and* aqua kid as well? Is there nothing you can't do?' That earned him a slight smile as he returned his attention to Leesa. 'So, you need to wash your hands first, obviously.' He had a bottle of hospital-strength antibacterial foam and squirted his hands with it generously before he opened the box that contained the preloaded applicator and an overpatch to help secure the sensor.

'Next you've got to clean the area with an alcohol wipe.'

Quickly tearing the top off the packet, Warwick cleaned a patch of skin on the flesh underside of Leesa's arm just below the hem of the T-shirt sleeve. 'Let that dry for ten seconds.' He glanced at Didi. 'Can you count to ten yet or are you too busy working on your magic to worry about numbers?'

'You can count to twenty, can't you?' Leesa said.

'Shall we count to ten?' Caroline said, lightly propping her chin on top of Didi's head as she held both of her palms out flat. 'Ready?' She started counting, putting a finger down as she went. 'One...two...three.'

Didi joined in and Warwick smiled at her before lifting his gaze to look at Caroline, who was concentrating on her fingers as they counted out loud together. His throat tightened a little—she looked good with a kid on her lap and he wondered how often she thought about the baby she'd lost when she was surrounded by other people's babies every day.

Was it hard for her?

Her baby would have been nine soon. Maybe there'd have been more to follow. Maybe Caroline would have had a whole swag of babies. To his brother.

For some reason, sitting opposite her like this, watching her with Didi, that thought was an even bigger irritation than usual and Warwick had to mentally slam the door shut on that thought. Because that hadn't happened. With Brad or anyone else. No other partners or pregnancies as far as he knew. And he was pretty sure Hud would have mentioned it had there been any such news.

Not that Warwick had ever asked after her specifically, but best mates talked.

'Okey dokey, that should do it,' Warwick murmured, getting his mind back on the job. 'Now, if Mummy can turn slightly on the side, I'll show you how the sensor goes in—what do you reckon?'

Didi nodded and Leesa shuffled herself slightly so she was sitting half sideways.

'This is the applicator.'

Warwick picked it up and showed them both. It was made from a hard plastic and was similar in size and shape to the top part of the safety guard that was used with a kitchen mandoline, fitting into the palm of a hand.

'You press it against the skin here that's been disinfected.' He pushed the device firmly into Leesa's arm. 'Then you push this button on the side—' Warwick tapped the button '—and it releases and implants the sensor in one movement.'

'There's a bit of a loud click when that happens,' Caroline said, her voice light and easy-going, but looking directly at Leesa as she conveyed the warning.

Once again, Warwick was glad it was Caroline sitting here because she was right to give Leesa a heads-up. If she was surprised by the sound and startled that could impact Didi, who was watching the proceedings very carefully. The slightest flinch from her mother could influence Didi's own experience with the device.

'But it doesn't hurt,' Caroline assured them.

'That's right,' Warwick said, backing up Caroline's assurance with his own. 'You ready to hear it?'

Another nod but a little more uncertain now as Warwick pushed the button, which did indeed click loudly. Didi blinked at the noise and looked even more uncertain but he pulled the device away to reveal the sensor now sticking to Leesa's arm. 'Wow! Is that it?' Leesa was all round-eyed in faux amazement as she looked at her daughter. 'How quick and easy was that?'

'So easy,' Warwick agreed.

'And it didn't hurt at all, did it?' Caroline asked.

'Not one bit,' Leesa enthused. 'And the best part is no more finger pricks—that's right, isn't it?'

'That's right,' Warwick concurred as he ran a fingertip round the tape that circled the device and secured it to the skin.

'Woohoo!' Leesa whooped, pumping her spare arm in the air.

'Woohoo,' Caroline responded, lifting both Didi's arms and flapping them around, which elicited a giggle.

Warwick grinned. 'I'm just securing it now with this extra plaster.' He removed it from its wrapper, peeled off the sticky backing and fitted it snugly over the top. 'There.' He glanced at Didi. 'How about that? Takes hardly any time at all and no more finger pricks.'

He needed to keep reiterating the fact because while it was easy as an adult to understand that placing the sensor was quick, easy and painless, it wasn't so easy for a three-year-old kid who, after a week in hospital, already had a keen mistrust of all things medical.

'This is so awesome,' Leesa said, looking at her daughter. 'Your turn now?'

Warwick could hear the slight brittleness in her tone and could tell she was trying so hard to be positive and encouraging in front of Didi despite her own anxiety from traumatic memories of the last week and lack of sleep.

'That's a great idea,' Caroline enthused. 'We won't have to do any more finger pricks then. Can I get a woohoo?'

She lifted Didi's hands in the air again as there was no giggle this time. Didi's bottom lip wobbled a little as she turned solemn eyes on Warwick and said, 'Mummy do.'

'Of course.' He nodded vigorously as he stood, patting the spot he'd just vacated. 'You sit next to Mummy and we'll be here just in case she needs a hand the first time.'

There was a lot riding on this first application of the sensor. It had to be smooth and no stress. Reapplying a new one regularly would be a way of life for Didi and her family so the last thing any of them wanted was this process also becoming a battlefield. Didi would have diabetes for life—

unless the research he and so many others were involved in actually found a cure—and this sensor was a vital step in monitoring and managing her condition.

Caroline lifted Didi onto the bed next to her mother and stayed close as Warwick passed the antiseptic foam to Leesa. 'Which arm would you like?' Caroline asked. 'This one?' She lifted the girl's arm and gave it a little shake before dropping it and picking up the other and repeating the process. 'Or this one?'

Warwick was aware Caroline was trying to keep a wavering Didi busy while her mum got herself ready, and was deeply appreciative. He'd never seen her in action as *Nurse Caroline* before but seeing this whole new dimension to her character gave him an even deeper understanding of her as a person.

She might be excellent at baking, but *this* was clearly what she was meant to be doing.

'Hang on a moment,' Warwick said, flickering his narrowed eyes comically as he passed the second box to Leesa. 'My magic fingers will know.'

He squeezed each upper arm as he shut his eyes and pursed his lips like he was getting magical vibes telling him which one was suitable. But, in reality, with Didi being right-handed, it would be better to start with the sensor in her left arm so she wasn't conscious of it every time she used her hands.

It wouldn't take long to lose the awareness of it, but Didi *was* only three.

Opening his eyes, he declared the winner, raising her left hand in the air as Caroline had done and giving it a shake. 'This one, definitely.'

'Okay.' Leesa nodded. 'Leftie it is.'

Caroline attempted to distract Didi as Warwick talked

Leesa through the application, which worked reasonably until the click sounded and frightened her. She started to cry but Caroline was quick to cut it off at the pass. 'That's it now,' she exclaimed, clapping her hands in glee. 'It's all done.'

Didi paused mid-sob and blinked, looking at her mother for confirmation. 'All done,' Leesa confirmed, kissing her daughter's forehead and clutching her close for a moment, tears in her eyes.

'You're doing well,' Warwick murmured, smiling gently.

Leesa nodded, her eyes glassy. 'Thanks,' she said, her voice low and husky. 'It's just… I wish she didn't have to go through any of this.'

'Yeah. This isn't fair and it really sucks and I'm sorry,' he apologised again, 'it's happened to your family.'

He thought about Gina then, about how his poor mother had ever coped with her sudden death and the events surrounding it because of this goddamn disease. How they'd been camping at a bush site for two weeks that hot summer. Warwick remembered she'd been thirsty but then, they'd all been thirsty due to the warmer temperatures. She'd been lacklustre too, just wanting to read in the shade, not play cricket with the other kids at the campsite, but she'd always loved to read more than anything else.

Then a few nights in she'd complained of a headache and gone to bed early. At some stage during the night, she'd left the tent she'd shared with him and Brad. Warwick had stirred and seen her go out but figured she was going to the toilet and gone back to sleep. They'd woken to find her missing. She was found the next day, in a coma she never came out of, her cerebral oedema too advanced.

The autopsy had revealed DKA and it had been concluded that when she'd woken that night, she'd been disorientated and confused and had wandered away from the campsite.

He remembered how empty the house had seemed for the longest time. Reminders of her everywhere—her budgie, her pictures, her fridge art, her handmade Christmas tree decorations that first Christmas without her—but the rooms utterly devoid of the boisterous sound of her laughter.

Warwick was sorry it had happened to his mother—his family—too.

'I don't like it, Mummy,' Didi whispered as she reached for the sensor. 'Take it off.'

Leesa reacted quickly, grabbing Didi's hand. 'No,' she said firmly, shaking her head as she used her other hand to smooth back her daughter's hair. 'It's very important that you don't touch, okay, baby? *Very* important.' She forced another smile and Warwick could see she was trying really hard to be calm but firm, which was exactly what Didi needed from her right now. 'If it comes off we have to go back to the finger pricks again and you don't want that, do you?'

'No.' Didi shook her head, forlornly, her eyes two puddles of blue. 'I won't touch it, I promise, Mummy.'

Leesa nodded through more tears as she once again clutched her daughter to her. Thankfully Helen arrived and gave them something else to focus on. 'I apologise for being late, Leesa,' she said, slightly puffed, as if she'd hustled a great distance to get here as soon as she could.

The diabetes educator might be close to retirement age but had been doing the job for over thirty years at different hospitals and what she didn't know about diabetes care could be written on the back of a postage stamp. She always joked she wouldn't leave her post until they'd found a cure, but Warwick wasn't entirely sure she was joking.

'It's fine, Helen,' Leesa assured. 'Warwick made a start.'

Helen made a show of examining Didi's sensor, giving

her a sticker that said *I've been brave today*, while praising her courage.

'I was just about to get into the app,' Warwick said.

'Excellent.' Helen nodded. 'It's such an amazing tool, isn't it?'

A lot of people Helen's age struggled with technology, but not her—she'd proudly embraced all the new tech that came along, getting across it as quickly as possible so she could teach her clients.

'Here,' Caroline said as she stood. 'Take my chair.'

'Oh no.' She dismissed the offer with a wave of her hand. 'I'm fine to stand.'

But then, as if on cue, the IV pump on the kid with the allergic reaction beeped and Caroline smiled. 'You might as well,' she said. 'I'm going anyway.'

Warwick watched Caroline depart, crossing the room quickly to switch off the alarm so it wouldn't wake the child or the two other sleeping babies in the bay. Dealing deftly with the issue, she added some extra fluid in the chamber before reaching for the chart on the end of the bed and flipping it open. Unzipping the pack that was strapped around her waist, she pulled out a pen and made a notation before closing it again, glancing in his direction for a moment.

Their gazes met and, for a moment, it felt like they were the only two people in the ward as his heart did a funny little double-tap in his chest. Hell, he'd *missed* her. But, more than that, he'd seen her in a different light today and that intrigued him. He wanted to get to know *that* Caroline, not just linger on the past.

Breaking eye contact, she turned away, chart in hand, and departed, and he tuned in again to hear Helen saying to Didi, 'Here, I brought you this.'

She handed over a clear plastic sleeve containing a colouring book and a small packet of colour pencils. Helen herself had worked on the book with the juvenile diabetes foundation to develop something that could be given to all hospitalised kids that were facing a new diagnosis of type one diabetes. The title—*Not All Heroes Wear Capes*—was emblazoned across the front and featured a cartoon picture of a child, wearing a cape, arms folded, chest puffed out, a CGM sensor on prominent display.

'Look at that sensor,' Leesa said, tapping the cover. 'Same place as you.'

Didi, hugging the book to her, seemed to like it very much. 'Thank you,' she whispered.

'No worries, sweetheart,' Helen said. And then, looking at Leesa, she said, 'Let's sync the sensor and I'll talk you through the app.'

When Warwick left the bay twenty minutes later, he found Caroline behind the nurses' station desk putting down the phone. She smiled at him as he approached and came to a halt opposite her on the other side. 'How'd it go in there?'

'Good.' Warwick nodded. 'Leesa might be internally freaking out a lot of the time but she's eager to learn and gets a hang of things quickly.'

She nodded but seemed distracted before she tapped the phone and said, 'That was the council engineering people.'

'Oh, right.' It was Friday. He'd forgotten they were supposed to call with an update at the end of the week. 'What's the go?'

'The damage isn't as bad as they'd first suspected. The repair is scheduled to take approximately three weeks.'

'Oh, that's good news,' he said, feigning a brightness he didn't feel.

And it *was* good news. But was it *so* wrong of him, to have hoped that the fix would take several months? He'd lived alone in his house near the lake with those trees he loved so much for two years and been perfectly happy. But now Caroline had moved in, *less than a week ago*, cooking in his kitchen, eating on his couch, watching his TV, hanging her clothes on his line, lazing on his sun loungers, and it had started to feel like a *home*.

'Hud will be relieved.'

She nodded. 'They said I can go in this weekend and grab anything I might need. I'll ask Hud if he wants anything brought out, otherwise I can make do with what I have.'

'I can give you a hand if he needs anything,' Warwick offered.

'Thanks.'

'You got any other plans this weekend? You start night shift on Sunday, yeah?' She'd mentioned during their pizza sesh that she'd been put on five nights.

Famously not a fan of night duty, she wrinkled her nose. 'Yep.'

Warwick chuckled at the shudder in her voice as he reeled off some places she might like to visit. 'There's plenty of big shopping centres around if you want to check them out. Lots of amazing walks around the lake. The big telescope out at Tidbinbilla is also really interesting. Or if you fancy heading to the coast, Bateman's Bay is only a couple of hours' drive away.'

'At the risk of sounding like a giant nerd, I've been wanting to see the National Portrait Gallery.'

Warwick blinked. 'Really?'

She laughed. 'Yes, really. There's so many places I want to see here. The National Gallery, the High Court—bonus if there's a decision pending—the Royal Mint, Questacon, the War Memorial, Parliament House, the National Arboretum.'

'The *Arboretum*?' Not generally on a lot of people's things-to-see-in-Canberra list.

'Sure. Why not?' She shrugged. 'Obviously not all this weekend but it's my first time ever in the nation's capital. I want to see all the buildings and monuments.'

'I'd forgotten how nerdy you could be.'

So many people had mistaken her as being extroverted because of her association with Brad. But Warwick knew she'd always been a bit more like him. Part of the chorus rather than the star of the show. The one who cheered and supported, who showed their love through small acts of kindness. The one who hung back in the kitchen cooking for the party while everyone else enjoyed the *actual* party.

'If you want to go full nerd and the business of government is your jam, you should check out the parliamentary schedule online and sit in the public gallery during a debate.'

Her lips twitched. 'Something tells me you've done that more than once.'

The merriment dancing in her eyes jagged in his chest. 'It's interesting.'

'You don't have to convince me.' She grinned. 'I'm a total *dork*—' she said it breathily while batting her eyes in a completely exaggerated manner '—for the business of government.'

It wasn't supposed to be flirty or a turn-on, he knew that. It was supposed to be teasing, but just knowing she was into the kind of stuff he was into was strangely arousing.

'There *is* an exhibition currently running at the portrait gallery I keep meaning to get along to. So, if you…don't mind the company…?'

She smiled. 'I'd love the company.'

CHAPTER SIX

THANKFULLY HUD HADN'T wanted anything from his apartment, which meant Caro and Warwick were pulling up at the gallery at just after eleven.

'Wow,' Caro said as they approached the entrance court, which was flanked either side by two enormous cantilevered concrete blades.

She'd seen a picture of it online but it was much more striking up close. One of the newer buildings within the parliamentary triangle, it shared the precinct with the High Court, which sat further along towards the lake.

'Impressive, huh?' Warwick murmured.

He came to a halt beside her, which was when Caro realised she'd actually stopped in her tracks. 'I'll say.'

They wandered in, the warmth of the gallery snuggling around them like a hug as they checked their coats at the cloakroom. It was a stark contrast to the day outside, which, though bright and sunny, had not yet struggled out of single figures.

Inside was even more spectacular. Large, natural-light-filled galleries boasted interesting, thought-provoking portraits. Everyone from famous indigenous Australians to rock stars to bush rangers to royalty. Combined with glimpses of the lake festooned in a riot of colour thanks to the autumn leaves, it was a veritable feast for Caro's eyes.

Then there was him, the perfect gallery companion.

Warwick didn't try to act like he knew every single thing about every single piece of art as Brad would have done, talking a little too loud to demonstrate his intellectual superiority to everyone else in the gallery. Instead he conferred with the prospectus he'd bought when they'd entered—something Brad would never have done—and quietly read from it whenever she stopped in front of a painting that had caught her eye.

He didn't grow easily bored and fidget and check his watch or make jokes about the slightly more modern takes on portraiture they passed as Hud—who was more an outdoors kinda guy—would have. He seemed happy to stand and look at whatever had interested her and converse about it just as she was happy to stand and stare and converse about what had interested him.

It didn't hurt that he was easy on the eye either, which apparently every single woman who spotted him had also noticed. Not that she could blame them. His jeans were snug in all the right places, cupping his ass and quads, and his Superman T-shirt, which sat nicely over the contours of his chest, was giving ultimate superhero vibes. Add to that his black-rimmed glasses he was wearing instead of his contacts and he was the full Clark Kent.

The fact they regarded *her* with admiration and even a little bit of envy also put a bit of a spring in her step. Which was ridiculous, of course—they weren't together like *that*—but the spring refused to be quelled.

Not even the sexy blonde who smiled at him—as if Caro wasn't standing right there—and said, 'Nice shirt,' dented her buzz. Maybe because Warwick barely spared her a passing glance before returning to the passage he was reading on the background to the Albert Namatjira portrait they were standing in front of.

But still, her very presence made Caro pleased that she'd taken some effort with her own appearance this morning. It wasn't the tight black leather pants, white halter top and spiky heels the blonde was wearing, but she knew she looked good in the burgundy cord A-line skirt that skimmed her curves, the khaki turtleneck skivvy that hugged her breasts and her tan, knee-high boots.

Even her hair, for once, sat nicely instead of fluttering around her head in a flyaway mess. Okay, it wasn't a waterfall of blonde *wow*, but it framed her face and drew attention to the autumn shades of her eyeshadow and the flecks of amber in her eyes.

It took them a couple of hours to slowly work their way around all the exhibitions and it was fun and relaxing and went way too quickly. When they got to the end Caro was sad that it was over.

'Fancy lunch at the café?' he asked. 'It's really good.'

Caro loved that Warwick knew what the café was like because it meant he really was a regular, which she admired. And maybe this could be the perfect way to keep in touch when she moved back to Hud's? Meeting him regularly for some national monument hopping?

Just because they hadn't really done anything like that before didn't mean they couldn't now. After spending a month in his house and getting reacquainted, it'd be stupid to live twenty minutes from each other and not bother to catch up again, right?

For a start, Hud would think that was weird. And secondly, they *were* friends. Even if she was more aware of him as a *man* now. Something that little Miss Blonde had brought sharply into focus.

'They even do an excellent lemon meringue tartlet,' he continued. 'Or they did last time I was here anyway.'

'Really?' Caro dragged her head back into the conversation. '*Hmm.*' She glanced at him playfully, quashing the irritation of the blonde's interest. 'I'll be the judge of that.'

Before going to the café, they stopped at the gift shop, where Caro bought some risqué fridge magnets for Hud because she knew he'd get a kick out of them and a gorgeous book on autumn foliage with blank pages where leaves could be pressed. Then, surrounded by beautiful light, outdoor views and amazing art and enjoying lively conversation with Warwick about their favourite portraits, she ate the most deliciously fragrant bowl of pumpkin soup with sourdough croutons followed by a lemon meringue tartlet.

'Not bad,' she admitted as she took her first bite, enjoying the tang of citrus mixed with the sweet melt of marshmallow-y meringue.

He lifted an eyebrow. 'Told you.'

'Mine's a little more tart,' she said as her taste buds tried to differentiate between the two like she was a judge on *Master Chef.* 'And their base is thicker.' A bit too thick for Caro's liking but only marginally.

'I didn't say yours wasn't superior,' Warwick said around a mouthful. 'Just that this one is also excellent.'

'Superior, huh?' Her chest filled with some of that sunshine from outside at the compliment. Also, his lips shone a little from the sticky cling of meringue, which was both fascinating and distracting.

Warwick rolled his eyes. 'Yes, Caroline, yours is superior.'

Caro grinned. 'Good answer.'

'Do I look stupid to you?'

Hell, no, he did not. He looked like Warwick. Only more. Older, scruffier, sexier. With a shiny mouth. Stirring part of her that had no business being stirred. 'You look like someone who really does know what side your bread is buttered on,' she said, echoing his comment from last week.

He laughed then and, damn, if a wave of goose bumps didn't sweep across her skin from scalp to shins, scrunching her nipples to tight points. 'I do,' he agreed cheerfully, oozing so much masculine confidence and charisma in his Superman T-shirt, it was making her a little dizzy.

And not just her apparently, as the blonde from earlier chose that moment to slink past their table, blasting Warwick with a smile and saying, 'Hey again.'

Caro stared at the swaying ass of the woman. '*Hey again?*' she demanded of Warwick. 'I'm *right here*.'

Warwick didn't bother to pretend he didn't know what she was talking about. He just grinned like he knew exactly the effect he had on passing women. 'Yeah, but it's not like we're an item.'

Caro dragged her gaze back to him, the words not only beside the point but also itching under skin like he, too, thought the idea preposterous. '*I* know that,' she said, 'and *you* know that but…how does *she*?'

If Warwick had been wandering around by himself, that would make him fair game, but when he was with a woman—old *friend* or not—that should make him off-limits to this blatant kind of come-on. It was as if she'd summed Caro up in a few seconds and decided that, as a couple, she and Warwick made no sense.

Which was, of course, correct. But was the notion of the two of them together really that preposterous to this woman?

'We're sharing food,' Caro continued. 'Even though we're not a thing, that's a universal signal for being together. Has she never seen *Lady and the Tramp*?'

Warwick laid down his fork and dabbed at his mouth with his napkin, wiping away every sticky trace of meringue on his lips, which was a very great shame. 'I guess she figured if she didn't try she'd never know. Fortune favours the brave and all that. Plus—' he shrugged '—maybe she's had a really shitty morning and just wants to feel good for a bit.'

His consideration for the blonde's potential circumstances made Caro feel judgemental and, in turn, defensive. 'By picking up a stranger in an art gallery?'

He laughed. 'Sure. Why not?'

Caro frowned at his amused response. 'It sounds like *you've* been picked up in an art gallery before.'

'An art gallery?' He shook his head, a small smile playing on lips that might not be sticky any more but probably still tasted sweet. 'No.'

So *not* an art gallery but some place similar, obviously. 'A museum? A stately home?' Caro wasn't sure why she was persisting but her whole brain itched and she couldn't seem to stop. 'A cathedral?'

He leaned in, that great big S in the centre of his chest strangely hypnotic. 'A gentleman never kisses and tells.'

Caro huffed out a breath as she sat back in her seat and picked up her cappuccino to take a fortifying sip and wonder what was wrong with her. None of this was her business. But she couldn't deny she was curious about his romantic history these past years. Hud had never mentioned any kind of permanent fixture but then, Hud took great care not to mention the Devlin name at all.

She eyed him over the rim of her cup. 'I suppose that happens to you all the time?'

Picking up his espresso, he said, 'What?'

'Women coming on to you.'

He snorted. 'No.'

'Oh, come on.' Caro cradled her cup in her hands. 'You're objectively...hot.' She stumbled over the word but, ex-BIL or not—it was the truth. 'You're smart. You're a doctor, for crying out loud. You own your own home, have all of your teeth and can wear the hell out of a Superman T-shirt.'

He blinked as she listed off his attributes and Caro wondered if she maybe shouldn't have been so frank about his pros. Had she shocked him by telling him he was hot? Surely he knew that, right?

'Have all my own teeth?'

Caro rolled her eyes. 'You know what I mean. Look.' She sighed. 'None of this is any of my business so if you don't want to answer then you don't have to. I'm just... I don't know, curious, I guess. I'd have thought you'd be snapped up a long time ago, especially considering Brad's on his *third* marriage.'

'Maybe I'm not as decisive as my older brother.'

A snort blew Caro's fringe back. 'I think the word you're after is impulsive.'

That was how their marriage had happened. A rush of blood to the head after her positive pregnancy test and a quick dash to the register office before anyone in their families could object to their rashness.

When Warwick didn't comment, Caro pushed some more. 'There hasn't been *anyone* special?'

Picking up his cup again, he took another sip. 'Not... really.'

Not really—what the hell did *that* mean? Almost. Not quite. Potentially. 'You care to elaborate on that?'

'I've...' he shrugged '...dated. There have been a few short-term relationships that—'

'How short-term is short-term?'

'A couple of months here, a few months there.'

'Have you ever lived with anyone?'

'It's never got that far.'

Caro was genuinely puzzled. Warwick was a great guy—good-looking, charismatic, easy to laugh, an entertaining conversationalist and fun to be around. 'I don't understand. Do you…snore? Or…pick your nose in public?'

He laughed. 'Not as far as I know to the first and no to the second.'

'Are you bad in—?' Caro cut herself off as she realised what she was about to ask. That was one hundred per cent none of her business.

An amused eyebrow winged high. 'In?' he prompted as a smile curved his lips. 'You think I can't satisfy a woman, Caroline?'

Oof…there was a silky thread to the low enquiry causing a frisson of something to zap between them as heat bloomed in Caro's cheeks. And elsewhere. Mortified at his giant leap, she met his gaze. 'I was going to say bad in *the kissing department*.'

She *had* meant that but now she was swimming down the deep end with Warwick thinking what he was clearly thinking.

Gah! How had the conversation become *this* personal?

Did she think that Warwick was a dud in the sack? Nope. The man oozed competence that she had no doubt spilled into *every* area of his life. Plus, Warwick had always put women at the centre of his attention. In conversations and in social situations. He let them talk and enjoyed listening to what they had to say. And she knew that because she'd been a recipient of this treatment, as had her uni friends.

Unlike with Brad, conversations with Warwick were two-way streets, not a catwalk.

'Ah,' he said with a grin as he eased back in his chair. 'I've never had any complaints in that department. In *any* department, actually.'

Caro had no problem believing his definitive statement. 'I guess it's just not easy being the partner of a doctor.'

'Oh, *pfft*.' Her fringe blew up again. 'You're not working the graveyard shift as an intern in an emergency department during a pandemic. You're mostly in private practice with regular hours like every other nine-to-five guy out there in a relationship.'

'Sure. But I still sometimes get called overnight or go in on weekends. And I'm heavily involved in the research project that keeps me occupied outside standard work hours and which I suspect makes me a little bit boring to a lot of women.'

'So, you don't have the time, is that what you're saying?'

'Not really. But…the truth is…' He glanced outside briefly before turning his gaze back to her. 'I'm waiting for the one. I guess that probably makes me a bit of a sap but—' he lifted a shoulder '—I want an all-in, head-over-heels love. Like…' He paused for a beat, his jaw clenching slightly. 'You and Brad.'

Like her and Brad.

The words sounded foreign to Caro's ear. She'd certainly fallen hook, line and sinker and been all-in. And they'd stayed together for three years—six months of those as husband and wife—which was a record for him. But had he really been *the one*? He'd swept her off her feet, no doubt, caught up in the absolute razzle dazzle of his charisma, but deep down Caro had known before she got pregnant that the shine was coming off.

And he'd known it, too.

Which was why he'd panic-proposed when they'd discovered she was pregnant because he hadn't wanted to be accused of being an arsehole and she'd panic-accepted because she'd felt it gave them a chance to get back to the glory days, which had been so damn good.

Because hoping a baby would repair things always worked out so well…

Looking back now at their relationship, Caro figured it had probably been more like infatuation than love. She hadn't been able to believe that someone like Brad had liked her and there'd been an addictive giddiness to that. As for him? Who knew? But she didn't think it was love.

'I want to…settle down, have some kids,' he continued, breaking into her turbulent thoughts. 'But with the right person.'

Caro wondered what Warwick's ideal woman would look like then stopped because it was surprisingly depressing. But one thing was sure—he'd make a great father. Seeing him in action on the paeds ward had confirmed that.

A little nerdy boy or nerdy girl—or both—like him with glasses and superhero T-shirts.

'So, get on a dating site. I could help you with the swiping?'

Where that came from, Caro had no idea, but she wished she'd left it unspoken. The last thing she wanted to do was get involved in finding Warwick *the one*. Even the thought of it was like a rusty fork in her brain.

But that was what friends did for each other, right?

His brow wrinkled a little and Caro got the feeling she'd displeased him somehow. Although she supposed an ex-SIL meddling in your dating life wasn't something a lot of people would welcome. His smile seemed strained when he replied. 'I'm not sure that's the place to go for love, if you know what I mean.'

'True.' Caro nodded in relief. Being Warwick's wing woman was not a role she relished and she certainly wanted nothing to do with any of his hook-ups or booty calls. Just the thought of them caused a roiling sensation in her gut.

'You know...one of the new RNs I met at orientation, she's a scrub nurse in Theatre. Her name's Willow. She's single and looking.'

Caro blinked, wondering what the hell was happening right now. She'd really liked Willow but thinking about her with Warwick hurt her brain. Thankfully, he actually grimaced at the suggestion.

'I think there's a lot to be said for if it's going to happen, it'll happen.'

Caro wanted to point out that it didn't seem to be working for him so far, but she was just pleased to be given an out from her runaway mouth.

'So, what about you?' he asked. 'What's happening in *your* dating life? Been with anyone special since Brad?'

Turnabout was fair play, Caro supposed, but she was about as reluctant to talk about her dating life as he'd been about his. 'No one special.'

'It's been nine years since the divorce. That's a long time.'

'I haven't been a nun, if that's what you're asking.'

Despite the heat in her cheeks, she held his gaze. If he thought she was still pining after Brad or had taken a vow of abstinence until she had another ring on it, he was wrong. A frown flitted across his forehead like he wasn't comfortable hearing these details but too bad—he'd asked. 'You don't approve?'

He blinked. 'What?' His expression turned incredulous. 'Of course not. It's none of my business.' But he still didn't look comfortable. 'I guess I'm just also...surprised that *you* haven't been snapped up.'

Caro didn't want to be flattered by that, but she was. Brad had outshone her in so many ways and she'd basked in his glow, but she'd always felt a little like she was the one *punching up* in their relationship.

'Do you snore? Or pick your nose in public?'

A smile played on his mouth and Caro rolled her eyes. 'Ha,' she said. 'Funny.'

His eyes danced in amusement. 'Are you bad in the... how did you say it? Kissing department?'

Arching an eyebrow, she picked up her cup. 'I am an exceptionally good kisser.'

Caro didn't know what on earth possessed her to elaborate in such a way. She could have laughed it off. She could have coyly demurred. She could have simply said *no*. But instead she'd...*bragged*.

What was *wrong* with her today?

Whatever it was, he wasn't smiling any more as his gaze drifted to her mouth, causing her lips to tingle, and for a moment neither of them said anything as Caro's head filled with the thud of her pulse.

'I suppose my point is,' he continued like she hadn't just divulged something he'd probably never wanted to know, 'I'd hate to think that, with everything that happened... Brad...the baby... you were turned off finding happiness with someone else.'

Unsurprised by Warwick's sharp insight, she folded her hands in her lap and regarded him for a beat or two. Nobody ever really talked about that time in her life—afraid she might break, or something, she supposed. But she was stronger than some gave her credit for and, right now, it was preferable to talking about intimate things like *kissing*.

'It took me a couple of years after losing the baby to really come out of my funk and start participating properly in life again.'

The emotional whammy of Brad cheating, the separation, the divorce had all happened in the midst of her grief and, as such, had been subsumed into the dark place she'd already been inhabiting. So by the time she'd come out the other side, she'd worked her way through all of it.

'I remember.'

He did?

Warwick had still been living in the share house at that time with Hud. Caro had moved back to her parents' from her and Brad's rental seven weeks after her one week stint in hospital and two days after she'd found out her husband of six months had cheated. Her mother's clucking and furious protection had been the perfect balm for her grief.

She didn't remember Warwick being around much at all. Maybe hovering in the background from time to time, which had annoyed her because she hadn't wanted him to hover, she'd wanted to talk to him about that night. Because nobody else had been. But he'd always seemed to disappear before she'd got the chance.

'By then Brad was living in Sydney and engaged again,' she continued, 'getting on with his life, so I just picked up and started again, too. I didn't think I'd want to date for a while and I definitely couldn't even contemplate being pregnant...' She shook her head, looked out of the window as her palm flattened against her abdomen. 'But then a guy I met at a party asked me out and I said yes and...' She shrugged. 'I had fun. I only saw him a couple of times but it broke the ice, I guess.'

'So, you're pleased you took that first step.'

'Yeah, it really helped me feel part of life again.'

'But no one special's come along?'

'I guess because of what happened in the past, I'm a little gun shy about rushing into anything too quickly.' She turned her gaze back to him. 'Maybe I'll never be ready.'

'Would you be okay with that?'

'Yeah.' Caro nodded slowly. 'I think so.' One thing the upheaval in her life had taught her was how self-sufficient she was. She might not be rich but she could support herself and she led a fulfilling life.

'You don't...want to have a baby?'

The question was tentative but he'd gone there when so many people in her life still avoided the topic altogether. 'I didn't,' she murmured. 'For a long time. The thought of being pregnant again, of the same thing happening again.' She shuddered. 'But the longer I work in paeds, the more I realise I would like to. One day. If the circumstances were right.'

'Is it hard working with kids? With babies? Does it... bring back memories?'

'Sure but...you know what?' She searched his gaze earnestly. 'I *want* to remember. Do you think I don't think about him every day anyway?' She shook her head. 'He was a boy—did you know that?'

'Yes.' Warwick nodded. 'I did.'

Yeah, she supposed he did, given how he'd been there for her. 'Did I ever thank you for helping me?' When she'd woken up from the operation Brad had been there and Warwick had gone.

His brows pleated into a line. 'You don't have to thank me.'

'Yeah, I do. I don't know what I would have done had you not been there.'

There'd been *so* much blood. And when she'd stood, she'd felt incredibly weak and cold and dizzy and yet she remembered being hysterical looking at her sheets, at her hand, covered in the red sticky warmth of her own blood.

'You'd have done what I did. You'd have called an ambulance.'

Caro shook her head. He was underplaying his role that

night and how his quick actions had saved her life. A lot of things were fuzzy from that time but the look of utter shock on Warwick's face when he'd burst through her door in response to her primal scream was crystal clear.

That was when she'd known something was seriously wrong. When the real hysteria had begun. *I'm losing the baby, aren't I?* That was what she'd said just before she'd passed out.

'I'm not so sure about that. I remember how hard my legs and hands were shaking. Not sure I could have coordinated myself.'

Irritation flared in his eyes as he looked out of the window and muttered, 'Brad should have been there.'

Caro wasn't sure if he was mad at his brother for shirking his husband duties or because it had put him in the hot seat. Made him deal with the blood and hysteria.

'He wasn't to know,' she murmured.

Brad had been out partying with his mates. Caro had been out having dinner with them earlier and, when it was done they'd wanted to go to a karaoke bar then hit a nightclub. But at twenty-one weeks pregnant, she'd been too tired and her back had been aching—she'd thought from twisting to grab a patient as they'd fallen the day before—and being the only sober person in a crowd full of drinkers hadn't been her idea of fun.

So she'd called Hud to come pick her up because she'd been feeling progressively worse, like she had the flu or something, and hadn't fancied waiting in the mile-long queue for a cab or half an hour for an Uber. But Warwick had answered her brother's phone, which he'd accidentally left in the kitchen on charge when he'd been called into work.

So *Warwick* had picked her up that night. Promptly. And fussed over her. Helped her into and out of the car. Pushed her in the direction of her room when they'd got back to her place and told her to go to bed. Made up a hot-water bottle for her sore back. Pulled the blanket up over clothes she hadn't even bothered to change. Told her he'd sleep on the couch until Brad got home and to yell if she needed anything.

Little had he known she'd be doing exactly that a few hours later.

'You're very forgiving, you know that?' he asked, glancing back at her.

Caro shrugged. 'It would have happened had he been there too.' Although, she suspected, he would have been far less effective than Warwick. Brad liked things being planned and controlled and tended to…flail when things went off the rails.

'Maybe,' Warwick conceded. 'But it wasn't the only way he let you down, was it?' The question was as grim as the set of his mouth. 'He cheated on you after you'd just lost the baby and you seem so… I don't know… Zen about it. You talk about him with…affection. You still send him a Christmas card every December.'

The exasperation in Warwick's voice would have made Caro laugh had it not been for the tension in his body. The erectness of his posture, the shift of his jaw beneath the scruff of his face as it clenched and unclenched. This clearly wasn't about her sending her ex a Christmas card. The card was just a metaphor for whatever *this* was.

Did he think…?

'You don't think I'm…still in love with him, do you?'

'What?' Warwick's eyes widened as he stared at her like she'd sprouted snakes from her hair. 'No.' His denial was swift—maybe too swift—the question clearly surprising him. Not, she suspected, the content, but the fact she'd even gone there.

They stared at each other for long moments before he eventually spoke. '*Are* you?'

'No.' She shook her head. 'I'm not.'

He nodded but still eyed her doubtfully. 'Okay.'

Clearly he wasn't convinced but that was his issue—not hers. She had other stuff she wanted to address. 'And I'm also not angry all these years later. I was sad and angry for two years, Warwick, and that was *exhausting* and getting me nowhere. More than that, it stopped me from realising that it takes two people to mess up a relationship and that the truth was, had I not got pregnant, I don't think we would have lasted much longer.'

Again he looked totally flummoxed. 'Really?'

'Yes, *really*. Did your brother colour himself in glory by cheating? Of course not. But the more I think about it, the more I suspect it was some kind of subliminal act of sabotage on his behalf. The only thing he could think of that gave him an out. You know Brad always did like a bit of drama.'

A grudging smile came her way as she reached across the table and squeezed his hand. 'Yes, your brother did a bad thing. But he's not a bad person. And life is too short to carry around a bunch of anger. I've moved on, maybe you should too?'

He didn't say anything for a long moment, just observed her as if he was carefully weighing up her words. 'See,' he said eventually, a smile pulling at his lips even if it did seem a little forced. 'Zen.'

Caro laughed as she clasped her hands together and said, '*Ohmmmmm.*'

CHAPTER SEVEN

THEY LEFT SHORTLY AFTER, Caro scooping up a perfect red leaf from the ground in the car park as her mind buzzed with the topics she and Warwick had just discussed.

Particularly about his romantic life.

The fact he wanted an all-in, head-over-heels kind of love was fascinating for a guy who had been pretty much single all his life. A spurt of envy rose in her chest as she opened the car door and slid inside, placing the leaf on her lap as she buckled up. She sure as hell hoped that whoever this mystery, some-day woman was, she realised how lucky she was to be at the receiving end of all that Clark Kent truth, honour and justice.

All that capability. All that take-charge energy. All that confidence.

She remembered all too well his whispered, *It's okay, I got you, you're going to be okay* that night. Yes, his arms around her, sweeping her up, had been strong but his voice—rich and sure and steady—had been a point of focus in the foggy white light that had surrounded her and she'd clung to it, using it to anchor herself to the ground when the floating sensation had threatened to unmoor her from Earth.

Whoever the future Mrs Devlin might be, Caro knew that, unlike Brad, whose personality depended so much on the shifting sand of popularity, Warwick's was hewn from rock. Warwick would always be an anchor.

The inside of the car was deliciously warm and Caro sighed as he started it up, allowing the heat to seep into her bones. The day might be bright and blue but the temperature was hovering around five degrees with a brutal wind chill factor and Caro felt like a hothouse flower unfurling as the trapped sunshine warmed the tips of her fingers, her ears and her nose.

Add to that her pleasantly full belly and drowsiness quickly tugged at her eyelids, the expensive purr of the engine lulling her to sleep until the car pulled to a halt some time later.

'Hey, sleepy head,' Warwick murmured as her eyelids fluttered open.

Caro looked around, a little disorientated. The bright sunshine had gone and they were no longer on the road. They were home, the darker environment of Warwick's garage nowhere near as inviting as the bright, filtered light outside.

She sighed. 'It's going to be cold out there. Do we have to get out?'

Rather than mention that *the house* was warm, he chuckled and said, 'I guess not.'

His laugh increased the cosiness and Caro smiled. 'I like it when you wear your glasses,' she said softly.

Why she'd decided to share that little morsel of information, Caro had no idea. It was the truth, of course, but it was probably oversharing a bit too much. Unfortunately, her tongue was as languid as the rest of her, which made it hard to drag up one single give-a-damn. Sitting here in the cab of his car, inside his garage away from the prying eyes of the world, it felt like she could say whatever she wanted.

'You do, huh?'

'Yep.' She undid her seat belt and turned on her side to face him, drawing her legs up, tucking her clasped hands under her cheek to prop her head a little. 'It's like the old Warwick. The one I met all those years ago.' Before she'd met Brad and everything that had happened. 'Do you remember how much we laughed that first day?'

'Uh-huh.' He nodded as he followed suit, pressing the button on his seat belt and half turning in his seat, the steering wheel preventing him from completely mirroring her position. 'You were at your mum and dad's sitting cross-legged on the floor with a cylinder of helium. She'd asked you to blow up hundreds of balloons for Hud's birthday party that night.'

Caro smiled at the memory, wishing suddenly she was that eighteen year old girl again, back before life had left its scars. 'And you offered to give me a hand. We sang "Teenage Dirtbag" chipmunk style.'

'I think we probably over-inhaled.'

'I was definitely light-headed once or twice.'

'Me too.' A wistful kind of smile replaced his grin. 'It's a wonder we didn't lose consciousness from hypoxia or do our lung parenchyma permanent damage.'

Caro rolled her eyes. 'You are such a doctor.' But he just laughed and she felt the warmth of it *everywhere*. 'Then you held the ladder for me while I hung them all.'

'Because *you*, on top of a hefty dose of helium, had already downed several mimosas but insisted that you could do it yourself. Even though I could have easily hung them without a bloody ladder.'

Yes, she remembered that being her first impression of him—how *tall* he was. Not that she wasn't used to tall men. Her dad and Hud were both just over six foot. But Warwick was almost six feet four—two inches taller than Brad—and she'd really had to crane her neck from her seated position on the floor to look into his eyes.

'That was a good day,' she said, snuggling a little into her seat. 'A good night.'

He nodded slowly. 'That's where you first met Brad.'

'Yes.' And he'd been at his dazzling best, like a disco ball of light and energy and magnetism and when he'd looked at her, she'd been sucked right into his orbit.

And the rest was history.

His smile and the light of laughter in Warwick's eyes slowly dimmed and Caro couldn't bear the thought that, in all this lovely lazy warmth and the glow of good memories—*their* memories—Warwick still thought she was holding some kind of torch for Brad.

'I don't, you know,' she murmured. 'I really don't.'

He raised an eyebrow. 'Don't what?'

'Still love Brad.'

Warwick regarded her for long moments. 'I was there, Caroline. I remember what you two were like. Does that love ever really go away?'

'Yes.' She nodded with absolute certainty. 'It does. Because it *changes*.'

Pressure in her chest, slow but persistent, pushed at Caro's ribs as the dull thud of her heartbeat rose in her ears. She needed him to believe her.

'I *do* love Brad. In the way you love that high school teacher who inspired you to go travelling or that pair of jeans you looked hot in that one summer when you were a teenager. He was a huge part of my life when I was young and what happened in our relationship has shaped me irrevocably. But I'm not *in love* with him, Warwick. To be honest...' Caro lifted her shoulder '...I don't know if I ever was. I was *infatuated* but that's obsession, not love.'

He regarded her for long moments and she could see the

battle going on in his eyes. Like he wanted to believe her but still couldn't quite get there.

I was there, Caroline.

Yeah, he had been. And he'd seen a teenager fixated on a gregarious, outrageously handsome guy who had the ability to look at a woman—*any* woman—and make her think she was the only person on the planet.

How could she make Warwick understand that she wasn't that person any more when it was almost like he *needed* Caro to still be in love with Brad? Despite him being his brother's loudest critic at the time, including an argument that had got physical the day before she'd moved back to her parents' house.

Surely her *not* loving Brad was what he wanted?

He opened his mouth to speak but she stalled him with a 'Don't'.

'Don't what?' he whispered.

It was then she realised she'd impulsively pressed her index finger to his lips, which meant she was now touching him. Touching *Warwick*.

Touching his *mouth*.

As she stared at her finger against the firm cushion of his lips, everything shrank down to that point of contact, the thick thud of her pulse and the roughening cant of his breathing forming a heady background beat in the ticking silence.

'Caroline?'

It wasn't much more than a gravelly whisper but it buzzed from his lips to her finger, spreading outward from there, humming along all the tributaries of her nervous system, delivering the hot breathy sensation to every cell in her body. His eyes widened a little as if he could feel it too.

'I *am not*,' she reiterated, her voice hushed, 'in love with your brother.'

With her heart rate filling her head, she let her finger slide from his mouth, her palm smoothing his cheek as it continued around to his nape, her fingers pushing into the softness of his hair. Then, because it was the only way she could think of to really convince the man she was *not* still in love with his brother, she leaned across the space between them, her eyes closing as her mouth landed where her finger had been.

And he didn't recoil in horror. Or jerk back. In fact, he went very, *very* still. His lips immobile. Just breathing. Warm whorls of it caressing her face. She stilled too. Just breathing. The scent of him flaring her nostrils.

Holy crap. She'd done this completely reckless thing with only one thought in her brain. She wouldn't kiss Brad's brother if she were still in love with Brad—*right*?

But…what now?

Because she didn't know. She hadn't thought that far ahead. And if she had, she'd have figured that Warwick would probably end it straight away. But he hadn't and here they were, still as statues as if they were both waiting for the other to make the next move.

And that was when Caro felt it—movement. Softening. The merest slackening of his mouth. Just a little. But enough. Enough for her to think maybe she hadn't ruined things with her brother-in-law.

Ex-BIL.

And maybe he wasn't hating it, either. Because she certainly wasn't. So…she softened her mouth too and suddenly it felt like a real kiss, like two people were involved. A tiny sigh escaping from the back of her throat as she sank into it a little, still not moving but not making a point any more either.

Actually forgetting why she'd even been so bold in the

first place as she tuned into the thrum of her blood washing through her veins. The vibration of the air, the sizzle of their mouths. Everything humming like an electrical current.

Oh my. She should *not* be feeling this way. This was *Warwick*. They were friends. They didn't kiss. Not even chaste ones that could barely be categorised as a kiss.

Yet, nothing about it felt friendly. Or chaste.

Which was why she finally pulled back, her pulse fluttering at her temples as they stared at each other, their breathing once again the only sound in the cab. Why they were breathing so hard when the kiss had been so light, Caro didn't know, but her mouth was tingling and she absently pressed her fingers against it, trying to quell the sensation.

'Caroline?'

It was just one word, just her name, yet it was said with such softness, such enquiry, like he was trying to make sense of it, too.

'I'm sorry.' Caro shook her head. 'I...shouldn't have...'

'It's okay,' he murmured. 'I get it.'

Caro blinked. He did? Because she didn't *get it* at all. Impulsively kissing him to prove a point she could maybe get on board with? But the way the kiss—that very chaste kiss—had made her feel? And the fact that actually, despite her knee-jerk apology, she wasn't sorry about it...

What the hell? Had she not learned her lesson about the Devlin brothers the first time around? Feeling things too quickly, acting too impulsively. She felt alarmed and overwhelmed at the direction of her thoughts, and his calm acceptance of what had just happened was like nails down a chalkboard.

'I am *not* still in love with Brad,' she repeated stubbornly, because *that* had been the whole point of this reckless exercise—nothing else.

He nodded. 'I believe you.'

Caro searched his eyes, every nuance of his expression, and found no trace of disbelief, which calmed her inner consternation. Reckless it might have been, but it seemed to have worked so it'd probably been worth it. *Probably.* 'Good.'

But, what now?

She was at a loss as to what she should be doing or saying now a line had been crossed she could never step back behind. *She'd kissed Warwick Devlin.* A tentative pressing of two mouths that could have lasted no longer than fifteen seconds yet had, somehow, managed to take her breath away.

All week—God, had it only been a week?—she'd been seeing Warwick in a very different light and this kiss was not going to help matters.

Because she couldn't give any of the complicated feelings clashing around inside her any quarter. Warwick could *never* be someone she could just fool around with for a while and see where it went. There would never be just the two of them in any kind of relationship—there would always be Brad *and* Hudson and their convoluted, intertwined history.

So, Caro, too overwhelmed by what had happened, did the only thing she could. Turning away, she reached for the door handle, opened it and stepped out of the vehicle, the autumn leaf she'd plucked from the ground at the gallery fluttering to the floor as she walked away, not looking back, not stopping until she flopped onto her bed with an audible sigh.

What the hell had she done?

Warwick was in his office later that evening pretending to be working on the research project. And there *was* plenty he could be doing. Lots of never-ending daily data to be reviewed and paperwork that could be attended to but instead he was just staring at his computer screen thinking about *the kiss*.

It was all he'd been able to think about from the moment she'd pressed her mouth to his. Over a decade now he'd thought about kissing Caroline Eastwood and it had never been like *that*. Just their mouths pressing together.

It had always been hot and heavy. Frantic. Lots of panting and groaning and tongue. But their gentle, unexpected kiss had slayed him in ways a hard and fast kiss wouldn't have.

In its quietness, in its simplicity. It had taken his heart, which had been beating for her for *so long* now, and cradled it so reverently he'd barely been able to breathe.

She'd been right. He hadn't believed her when she'd said she didn't love Brad any more. He'd thought she'd been kidding herself, burying her feelings because the memories hurt too much.

But he believed her now.

Because kissing him—Brad's twin brother—was something Caroline would *never* do if she was still carrying any kind of a torch for Brad. So, as a statement on her lack of feeling for her ex, it was a powerful one.

Still, it had been unexpected. Even as he'd watched it happen in slow motion—Caroline inching closer, her eyelids fluttering closed—he'd been shocked when her mouth had landed.

Good shocked. But still...*shocked*. His brain synapses lighting up with a feverish kind of disbelief and exhilaration as a swirling fog of lust ruffled fingers over every erogenous zone, urging him to open his mouth and kiss the hell out of her.

Staying still had been an exercise in control but he'd managed it. Because he'd not been foolish enough to believe the kiss had come from some deep, hidden well of desire. It had been entirely impulsive. An act of frustration. A form of persuasion.

She hadn't *meant* anything by it.

Not desire. Not want. Or need. It hadn't been a prelude to something else. It'd had nothing to do with romance or dating or relationships and thankfully he'd still had enough of his wits about him to know that.

So, as hard as it had been, he'd tempered himself. He'd shut everything down.

But if he'd thought for *one second* that it had been more? If there'd been the slightest hint of her *wanting* more? Well... God help them because he had twelve years of desire bottled up inside and if that had been unleashed?

He wasn't sure the car would have survived.

'I've made things weird, haven't I?'

The voice behind him startled the crap out of him and he shot a look over his shoulder to find Caroline standing in the doorway bearing a plate with a slice of lemon meringue pie. She'd changed into jeans and a T-shirt and her feet were bare and she was chewing her bottom lip as if she was worried about the answer.

Warwick wanted to roll his eyes and ask her what she'd expected. But there was no need to throw her actions in her face when she was clearly feeling bad enough. He swivelled his chair to face the door and smiled. 'Of course not.'

She gave a half-laugh, half-snort. 'You've practically hidden away in here ever since. You haven't even touched the sorry-I-kissed-you lemon meringue pie I made.'

She held it up like it was exhibit A and Warwick laughed despite the hitch in his breath at the casual mention of their kiss. At least she wasn't shying away from what had happened—or how it had gone down.

'I'm just busy,' he assured.

'Look… I didn't mean anything by—'

'It's fine,' Warwick cut in, not able to bear her dismissing the act as nothing of any consequence when his lips still tingled from the soft press of hers.

He *knew* that already. He didn't need to hear her say it.

'You were just making a point and you wouldn't have needed to if I'd believed you about your lack of feelings for Brad.' She'd done it out of necessity, really.

'Yes.' She nodded. 'But I don't want there to be any awkwardness between us so I've been thinking I should move to a serviced apartment. It'll only be for a few more—'

'Hell *no*.'

Warwick hadn't meant for his rejection to come out so forcefully but he hadn't been able to stop it, either. Shutting himself away in his office hadn't been done to make her feel unwelcome—he'd just needed a little space.

She shrugged. 'It's probably for the best.'

His pulse bumped up a little at her choice of words. Was she hinting that maybe, despite what she'd said, there had been something more to the kiss? And that scared her as much as it scared him because of how it might affect the people in their life? In which case he should graciously agree and yet…he couldn't bring himself to do it, no matter the urgent whispers from his wiser angels.

'There's no need. I'm not trying to avoid you, really, I *am* just busy with this research stuff and I lost track of time.'

Which was a giant lie. Warwick had done nothing useful this evening at all, just sitting and staring at the numbers while his brain was back in the car. But she was worrying her lip again and Warwick was suddenly desperate to convince her to stay because, damn it, he loved having her under his roof.

Talk about going against his own best interests.

'Hud would wonder why you left.' It was the only argument he knew would be persuasive enough for her to abandon her moving plans, because it was true.

'Well, yeah…' She blew out a breath that ruffled her fringe. 'He would wonder.'

'You know what he's like. A dog with a bone. He'd be pissed at me for letting you leave and highly suspicious of the reasons. And I think we can both agree what happened in the car isn't something he needs to know about.'

Warwick had already lost a sister. And had a rollercoaster relationship with his twin brother. He didn't fancy blowing up his friendship with a guy who was like a brother to him. Not over something that was…who the hell knew what?

'Oh, God, *no*.'

Her look of alarm confirmed his thinking. She might be as confused by it as him, but the kiss had been an impulse she had no desire to make public. Warwick just wished her instant recoil didn't hit quite so hard.

'Yeah, okay.' She nodded. 'I should stay. You're right.'

Her sigh was loud and glum and, now the imminent threat of her leaving was off the table, Warwick was relieved despite his conflicting emotions. So he did what he'd always done—injected some levity. 'I'm sorry?' He cupped his ear. 'Could you say that again a little louder?'

It worked, a grudging smile turning her frown upside down.

'On the weekends, I usually catch up on the lab data,' he explained, feeling the need to reiterate. 'And sometimes I get so absorbed I don't realise hours have gone by. I'm *not* avoiding you, really.'

Which *was* true. The first part anyway.

Thankfully, Caroline chose to run with the levity. 'Fun,' she murmured, a slight smile playing on her mouth.

He laughed and ignored how very much he wanted to kiss that smile right off. How very much harder it was going to be to ignore the constant push-pull of his desire now he'd had a taste of her mouth.

'Yup. That's me. The life of the party.'

Laughing at his self-deprecation, she wandered into his office. 'So, this research?' She slid the plate with the pie and a spoon onto his desk as she drew level with him, her gaze flicking to the screen that was currently full of tables of data. 'What's it about?'

He swivelled his chair around so he was facing his computer again, conscious that she was standing close enough to touch. 'It's working on a predictive blood test as part of neonatal screening that identifies infants who have a high risk of developing type one diabetes at some time during their life.'

'Really? *Wow.*' Caroline's eyebrows rose as she looked at him, clearly impressed. 'That would be…game-changing.'

'Yep.' Warwick loved that she instantly got how important and exciting this work was. The fact she was looking at him with admiration didn't hurt either. 'It's not a cure but we might be able to prevent it developing or delay it in some people by specifically targeting them with new treatments as they come on board.'

He thought about his sister and how if what he was working on now ever came to fruition, it could have prevented what had happened.

'Is it close?'

He shook his head. 'It's very early days.'

'Right.' Her nod was very matter-of-fact. Warwick didn't have to tell her medical research was a marathon, not a sprint. 'How did you get involved? You're not a researcher.'

'I read about the research happening at the ANU and knew some people that were on the project. I expressed interest and asked if I could be involved in some way and they brought me into the team as one of their clinical consultants.'

'Nice one.' She paused for a moment as she regarded him solemnly. 'You think we'll ever find a cure?'

Warwick lived in hope of such a holy grail moment. 'Who knows? Medical advances will happen so much faster now AI is in the mix. If nothing else, I hope we'll be able to develop a pill or some kind of adjunct therapy that will reduce reliance on insulin injections.'

'Well, I'm all for that,' she said with a smile. 'So, I better let you get on with it.'

He nodded. 'Thanks for the pie.'

'Of course.'

She turned to go and Warwick looked over his shoulder, watching her depart, the muscles in his neck slowly uncinching the closer she got to the door.

Muscles he hadn't known *were* cinched.

'I'll be out in about ten if you want to watch a movie or something?'

Avoiding her had only caused her to worry, so that had to stop. They were both adults and he'd just assured her everything was fine. So he needed to put on his big-boy pants and hang out with her as he had this past week. Not skulk in his office, afraid to live in his own damn house. He had to walk the walk, not just talk the talk.

So, they'd kissed. It had been a strange moment born from proximity and ancient history. It didn't have to define who they were today.

She half turned, a smile tilting her mouth, obviously relieved to be back on an even keel. 'Sure, that'd be great. I'll load something up.'

'Okay.'

He watched her as she disappeared from view, letting out a long, slow sigh. He could do this. He could sit through a movie with her and not think about the kiss.

He just needed ten minutes.

CHAPTER EIGHT

WARWICK KNEW FROM old that Caroline had never been a fan of night duty—her grumbling about it when they'd all lived together had been infamous. She apparently found getting any quality sleep during the day difficult so she was essentially tired and grumpy the entire time and it usually took her a couple of days to fully recover.

It had been a running joke in the share house to avoid her during nights and Brad had usually made himself as scarce as possible until she'd emerged from the room the afternoon/evening after her last night when she'd finally managed a proper sleep. Warwick, on the other hand, had worked out that if the fridge was stocked with chocolate, it definitely helped Caroline's mood, so he'd always made sure there was plenty to be had.

Which was exactly the tactic he employed this time.

He was gone when she got home Monday morning but he'd left out two Cherry Ripe mini bars—her favourite mini chocolates—on the island bench because he knew her post-night-shift routine was to hit the kitchen to feed the tired, hangry beast. Beside them, and rather impulsively, he'd placed a perfectly formed, bright red leaf that he'd watch fall from the maple tree outside as he'd stared into the yard while drinking his coffee.

He left a note with his offering.

Saw this fall and thought of you. Sleep well.

She probably wouldn't but that didn't mean he couldn't wish it, right?

The chocolate and the leaf were gone when he got home, which made him inordinately pleased, a state he was still in when she finally emerged from her room all rumpled-haired and grumpy about two hours before she had to leave for her shift. Thankfully her mood seemed to subsume any lingering awkwardness between them as he persuaded her to let him make her dinner.

'I'm supposed to be cooking for you,' she grumbled as she sat at one of the stools lining the far side of the central island.

Warwick knew she saw her role in his house as head chef but he hadn't got to thirty-two without being able to feed himself and he knew it would take him no time to whip up a pasta meal that would keep her warm and full for some time.

'Thank you for the chocolate,' she murmured as she sipped the coffee he'd made her and absently watched the cold butter sizzle in the fry pan. 'And the leaf. It was very thoughtful.'

Warwick smiled. 'It's begun now. The fall. It won't take long for the trees in the yard to be bare and I'll be cursing all the raking I'll have to do.'

Her answering smile was wan but he was conscious of her watching him as he salted the pasta he'd put on to boil before quickly and efficiently dicing the onions, his heart skipping all over the place at the intensity of her interest. Like a man cooking for her was a revelation.

Had his idiot brother never done something so damn simple?

'I guess they're a hazard,' she said, her voice still a little sleepy, 'and maybe I'll feel like that after a decade of Canberra autumns, but at the moment I'm that person who rolls their eyes at people who say that Venice is a hot, stinky, overpriced swamp. Like…do they have no soul?'

Warwick laughed, trying not to home in on her inference that she was planning on staying in Canberra for some time. 'Are you saying I have no soul?'

She laughed too and it was husky with tiredness, which set up an ache in Warwick's chest and had his fingers curling into his palms to stop himself from rounding the bench to slide an arm around her and pull her close.

'I'm saying beauty is pain, even in nature.'

'For the record,' Warwick said as he added the onions to the melted butter in the frying pan, 'I think Venice naysayers have no soul, either.'

She grinned as their gazes met. 'I would be heartbroken if you thought anything else.'

And if it was weird in this moment to want to whisk her away to Venice and watch her drink an Aperol Spritz in St Mark's Square, the sun on her shoulders, then, so be it. But the fact this feeling was far more than just physical attraction had him breaking eye contact for fear of giving away too much.

The mushrooms became his next target as he set about chopping them into thin slices, hoping she was too tired to notice the yearning tugging at him from every angle.

'Do I have time for a quick shower?'

Glancing up, Warwick saw the same kind of reluctant awareness in her eyes that hummed through his body and grabbed at her suggestion. 'Sure. This is about fifteen away.'

'Good.' She slid off the stool without looking at him. 'Be right back.'

And it wasn't until she'd disappeared from sight that Warwick breathed easy again.

* * *

Which was pretty much how the week unfolded. Mornings of chocolate, red leaves and sticky notes, followed by evening dinners together, him cooking for her as he ignored the attraction. Her too, he thought, but he wasn't sure so he refused to entertain such fancies.

What was the point when things were far too complicated between them anyway?

Sometimes they talked while he cooked, sometimes they didn't, depending on whether Caroline was in the mood for conversation. If she was, it was mostly about patients or the nurses she was working with and once about the fire alarm that had gone off in one of the staffrooms where some toast had been incinerated.

He'd laughed as she'd joked that one of her colleagues had suggested they do the same the following night so two engines worth of firefighters would visit their ward at four in the morning when staying awake was at its most challenging.

Warwick let her chat when she wanted and ate in silence when she went all starey-eyed, just enjoying those slithers of time in her company. A little hit of Caroline went a long way and although part of him wanted more and probably always would, this gave him the best of both worlds—nearness *and* space.

And it made him feel like he could actually do this.

Actually get through another couple of weeks living together without succumbing to the constant thrum of awareness that was stoked every night in his empty house thinking about that kiss. And smouldered during the day, thinking about her tucked up in her warm bed, Heidi—who had taken to sleeping with her—curled around her head.

Maybe he could persuade her to work all nights until

Hud's apartment was ready? Sure, no possible good could come to mankind from a sleep-deprived Caroline, but a little bit of her each day would give him his fix, his dopamine hit, that kept him functional.

The problem was, addictions grew, right? That was what made them addictions...

Friday arrived quickly and Warwick knew as he drove home from work that Caroline's run of nights had finished this morning and she had three days off now. Which was good and bad.

Pro—the world was once again safe from a tired, grumpy Caroline Eastwood.

Con—*he* was *not*.

Grumpy or back to her usual self, the fact of it was they'd be seeing much more of each other, which was a double-edged sword. On one hand, he yearned to spend more time in her company. On the other, limiting their moments together had worked well to keep his world in balance, to keep his crush in check.

Sometimes less really was more, right?

She wasn't up when he arrived home at just after five although she clearly *was* home. The chocolate and leaf he'd left this morning were gone, Heidi was nowhere to be found and Caroline's handbag and sunglasses were sitting on the couch as if she'd flopped there for a bit before hitting the sack.

Her bedroom door was shut and he hoped she was still sleeping. He remembered she always got her best sleep the morning after she finished nights—something about her body knowing it didn't have to go back to work that night.

With the house silent, he decided to go for a run by the lake then come home and cook dinner. He could put some aside for Caroline in case she woke at some point and was hungry.

Changing quickly, Warwick was out of the door within ten minutes, pulling the zip on his hoodie all the way up as the bracing autumn air slapped him in the face and he hit the pavement. He'd be shrugging out of it soon enough but for now, he hunched into its warmth.

As he ran he emptied his mind. Of his day, of the paper he was writing to present to the paediatric endocrinology symposium he was going to next month, of the data he had to review over the weekend.

Of Caroline—in his house, in his spare bed, in his life.

A lot of people he knew listened to music as they ran but Warwick liked to tune into the sounds of nature—the birds and the insects—and the slap of his feet on the pavement. Like the rhythm of a train on a track, it lulled him into a state where he didn't feel the burn of his lungs or the bitch of his muscles. He just rode the endorphins flooding his system, accessing that high runners often described.

The alarm on his watch trilled, indicating he'd done his half-hour, and Warwick slowed his pace, coming to a halt on the well-lit path beneath one of the many oaks that were planted along the banks of the lake. Looking out at the water, he stretched his hamstrings. It was black now apart from the reflection of streetlights and a thin lip of distant orange as the last rays of sun reached across the surface.

Concentrating on his breath, Warwick revelled in the dopamine buzz as he waited for it to settle and for his heart rate to recover, feeling the pulse and surge of his blood in the tips of his toes and fingers and ears. When he straightened, a leaf fell right in front of his face, fluttering down and, on reflex, he snatched it up.

Overhead light gilded the perfect yellow specimen to a deep golden hue and he smiled at it as he twisted the stem, inspecting the colour and the delicate network of veins.

Caroline's delight at the autumnal bounty all around had made him see the season in a new light. He was so used to the annual change, it was too easy to see the endless raking and the slip hazards of wet decaying leaves and completely miss the stunning beauty.

It wasn't the first thing he'd seen in a new light since Caroline had re-entered his life. Her in her nursing persona had been a surprising delight. Her no longer in love with Brad had been a freaking revelation.

A part of him rejoiced in that and, in his more positive moments, he thought *maybe* and *what if?* What if this new vibe between them could be explored rather than ignored? What if he wasn't alone in this? What if there was a chance for the two of them?

And, as he twirled the leaf, he thought about the big one. What if, in the car that day, he'd kissed her back? Fully. Properly.

What if?

Caroline still hadn't emerged when Warwick returned. Heading to the kitchen, he placed the leaf on the central island and poured himself two glasses of cold water—one after the other—and chugged them down. Then, retrieving the sticky notes from the drawer where they were stashed, he wrote a note.

It's not red but this one fell right into my hand. How could I not bring it home?

Sticking it beside the leaf, Warwick headed for the shower, thinking about dinner until the other thing took over now he'd dared give it space in his brain.

What if he'd kissed Caroline back?

He hadn't, so it was a moot point, but the thought was insidious and persistent. Would she have welcomed it? Was that what she'd meant by, *It's probably for the best*? Or would she have withdrawn in shock? Because the kiss hadn't been a *kiss* kiss and she'd only ever looked at him as Brad's brother.

As her brother-*in-law*.

Would her rejection be worse than his long-suffering denial? Worse than her *for sure* leaving for a serviced apartment? Worse than potentially screwing up their friendship for ever?

Because if they ever did *kiss* kiss, they'd *never* be able to go back to what was before.

To their long-standing friendship. To their amicable brother/sister-in-law relationship. To him just being her brother's best friend.

Was he prepared to risk all that on the maybes and what-ifs?

The bottom line was *no*. He wasn't. Not when he could also potentially screw up a couple of other relationships in his life. Which was depressing as hell and made him want to scream at the shower head until he had no breath left in his body. Instead he turned off all the hot and made himself stand under the freezing spray.

Shock his system. Shock himself out of thoughts of things that could never be until he could stand it no longer and flicked the tap off.

Warwick pulled his T-shirt on over his head as he walked to the kitchen, faltering a little as he emerged from the head hole to see Caroline standing at the central island, leaf in her hand, looking at him. In fact, he'd go as far as to say staring.

At his chest.

Pulling his shirt all the way down seemed to break the spell, her eyes jerking from his body to his face, confusion clouding her gaze as their eyes met. Like maybe she'd been checking him out but knew she shouldn't be? Or maybe it was her just-woken-up expression.

Because that *had* to be it. Jesus, dufus, *get a grip*.

'Hey there,' he said as casually as he could considering the jitters crackling through his system as he entered the kitchen.

'Hey,' she returned as she quickly dropped her gaze to the leaf she was twirling between her fingers, just as he had done only half an hour ago.

She was in her pyjamas—at least he thought they were. Striped flannelette bottoms, an oversized long-sleeved T-shirt, a pair of Uggs on her feet. A crease from the bedclothes marked her cheek and her feathery locks were in complete disarray, both sides pushed haphazardly behind her ears. She looked wild and tangled and it might be some kind of perverse part of his personality but he liked that she didn't care how she looked around him.

There was nothing knock-out sexy about any of it—not that being sexually alluring for him had been her purpose *obviously*—except he was fairly certain she wasn't wearing a bra, which did things to his libido that made him wish he'd stayed in the cold shower.

But the bigger problem was Caroline all sleepy-eyed and cosy, looking perfectly at home standing in his kitchen, did things to his *heart*.

'Yellow,' she murmured, looking at the leaf as if she was drinking it in with her eyes and truly appreciating the beauty and simplicity of nature.

It made Warwick smile despite the quagmire of his thoughts as he crossed to where she was standing, propping a hip against the bench, leaving some space between them. 'Why should red get all the kudos?'

She nodded as she lifted her gaze, blinking at him blearily. 'Right?'

Tired eyes. Warwick remembered the sensation well, having done more than enough brutally long night shifts before moving into private practice. The feeling right at the back of the sockets, like the eyeballs have been soaking in formaldehyde all night.

'Did you manage some sleep?'

'Crashed for a couple of hours, got up to pee then tossed and turned until about three, when I finally managed to crash, only to have Heidi miaowing in my face ten minutes ago to be let out.'

'Oh God, sorry.' Warwick glared at the cat, who remained unconcerned as she cleaned her whiskers after consuming whatever Caroline had put in her dish. 'Shut her out of your room next lot of nights. Your sleep is more important than her dictates.'

'It's fine. I get to sleep all night tonight. Besides…she miaows at my door if I don't let her in.' She smiled at the contrary cat. 'And I like the way she wraps herself around my head and purrs.'

Maybe that explained Caroline's hair—wearing a cat like a pair of headphones with fine hair that tended to tangle probably wasn't the best combination. 'Yeah. She does that so you forget about her bossiness.'

Caroline laughed, her eyes brightening. 'She is very bossy.'

He smiled. 'It's like this is her house and she's just letting me live in it because I supply the food. God help me if she ever develops opposable thumbs and can open a tin. I'll be hunted out for sure.'

'She might let you sleep in the garage.' And then she laughed again, this time slightly maniacal. Clearly she was in that *so-tired-everything-is-hysterical* stage of sleep deprivation. She was laughing so hard, she dropped the leaf and Warwick stepped forward and scooped it up off the floor before Heidi, who'd watched the leaf fall with interest, could pounce.

He straightened and handed it to Caroline in one movement, realising they were much, *much* closer now. Maybe only a hand's breadth from each other, his fingers on the bench only a quick slide to where her fingers were resting, her warm, soapy scent enveloping him, wrapping him up in her space as she took the leaf, her eyes still shining with laughter.

Absently she lifted it to her face and brushed it across her nose before drifting it across her cheek and rocking her head from side to side as if revelling in the texture, a little hum of satisfaction growling from the back of her throat.

It was utterly hedonistic and stole his breath.

'Soft,' she murmured as their gazes met, hers smiling and dreamy.

But not for long, the smile slipping, the leaf lowering, her eyes widening as if she, too, was aware of how close they were standing. About as close as they had been in the car, but the last thing Warwick needed was to think about the car right now.

It was too late of course because that was *all* he was thinking about, his gaze drifting to her mouth as her lips parted slightly.

Lips he'd already tasted. But not yet explored.

Warwick's pulse washed through his chest and his neck and his head, the urge to close the distance between them surging with every beat of his heart. The urge to just step right in. Pick up where they'd left off almost a week ago now.

Because she wasn't stepping back or looking away. In fact her eyes were on his mouth—*fixed* on his mouth—her breath falling between them a rough kind of pant that was infecting his own lungs.

Was she thinking about the car, too? About what they'd left unexplored?

But that would mean the kiss really hadn't been about proving a point and he couldn't wrap his head around that possibility. The possibility she might have kissed him for other reasons even if she hadn't been aware of them. The possibility she might want him to kiss her right now.

Was that what she wanted? What she was waiting for? Him to make that move? Because she wasn't standing down. She wasn't moving back. She wasn't breaking eye contact. And every part of him itched to lean in and push that boundary.

His libido was screaming at him to *just kiss her already* but his head was blaring out a warning—*don't do it, man*. They were, after all, in a weird forced-proximity situation and she was massively sleep-deprived.

Thankfully, a very loud, very bossy *miaow* saved Warwick from himself and they both started, two ragged audible intakes of breath loud in the air between them as they each took a step back.

Heidi wound herself around his legs, oblivious—or maybe not—as Warwick's pulse beat like a gong in his chest.

'I was thinking of doing—'

'Did you want to get—?'

They spoke over top of each other then stopped. 'You go,' Warwick said, gesturing for Caroline to talk.

'I was thinking Chinese takeaway?'

Yes—*food*. Food was good. Food was not kissing. In fact, food was something to do with the mouth that *wasn't* kissing. Something much safer. 'Sure.' He nodded and then, needing activity, he grabbed his phone from his pocket and scrolled to a delivery app. 'Beef and black bean still your favourite?'

When she didn't answer Warwick risked a glance to find her looking at him. 'You remember that?'

Warwick shrugged. 'I remember everything.'

Caro was hyperaware as she listened to her two-year-old sleeping patient's chest through a stethoscope on Wednesday afternoon that Warwick would be doing his rounds soon. There were a few kids on his patient list to see as well as Didi, who had been moved into the six-bedded bay Caro was in charge of today and was all set to go home later this afternoon if Warwick gave the okay.

Had she requested this bay today so she could see Warwick? No. She saw him every morning and every night. In fact she saw him way too much for her own sanity, especially since that strange moment in the kitchen after her nights.

Just one of a cascading amount of strange moments.

She'd requested this bay because she'd developed a real rapport with Didi and her family and continuity of care, particularly in paediatrics, was important for patient and parental welfare. There was also her own professional satisfaction. Following a patient through from admission to discharge was highly gratifying.

The fact she got to see Warwick as Dr Devlin again? That was just a bonus.

Also she knew how to handle *that* Warwick. They were

in their professionals roles and she had a playbook for that scenario that allowed her to treat him like any other doctor she'd assist during rounds.

The Warwick she lived with? *That* Warwick? The one she didn't see as her ex-BIL any more. Didn't see as Hud's friend any more. The one she'd kissed in the car. The one she'd been pretty sure had been about to kiss her in his kitchen. *That* Warwick?

She didn't have a playbook for that one.

She'd always been aware that Warwick was sexy and attractive. In a much less brash way than his twin, for sure—but still there. And she'd always felt a connection. Except she'd thought that was a friendship-group thing, their lives closely entwined, what with them all sharing the same living space and the way they all intersected beyond that.

But Warwick's *I remember everything* had struck a chord. Because it was true—he'd always been attentive. Even back in the beginning when Brad was still putting sugar in her coffee after they'd been together a year, Warwick always got it right. Or like how he used to stock the fridge with chocolate when she was on nights just as he had this past week.

It had been like…having another Hud in her life. Someone who knew her well and had her back. Another person she could call if she'd needed help moving furniture or painting her house or advice on which lawnmower to buy.

Or calling an ambulance in the middle of the night.

But none of what she was feeling since she'd moved into his spare room was remotely brother-ish or friend-ish. She'd been aware of him as a man from the get-go, thanks to him being in nothing but a towel.

And in her dreams? Heidi had *not* interrupted any kissing in her dreams.

Her patient coughed in his sleep and stirred but settled

without opening his eyes. Caro removed the earpieces of the stethoscope and noted in his bed chart the scattered wheezes she could still hear on both lung fields.

'How does it sound?' his father asked.

'The wheeze is definitely reducing and he's not using his intercostals to help him breathe any more, so his three-hourly bronchodilator is holding him.' When Albie had come into the emergency department a couple of nights ago, he'd been on half-hourly therapy. 'They'll probably knock it back to four-hourly later on or tomorrow and see how he goes.'

'But if he gets worse?'

'We'll put him back to three hourly again. Don't worry.' She smiled as she crouched beside the chair and squeezed his arm. 'We won't let him struggle. He's in good hands here.'

Standing, she moved to the next bed, smiling at Didi, who was bright-eyed and bushy-tailed and raring to go home. Her usually curly mass of hair was confined in two sleek topknots, her cheeks were a lovely pink, she'd put on weight and she'd returned to the lively, chatty three-year-old her parents recognised. With no more tussles over four-times-a-day finger pricking, she was a whole different child.

'She looks like she's going to miss us,' Caro joked.

Leesa laughed. 'She mightn't but we sure will.'

Caro could tell that Leesa was still a little anxious about cutting the umbilical cord and she didn't blame her. A young child not fully yet able to communicate with a serious chronic condition was a potentially fraught situation. Especially when the family lived in a regional location.

But with the CGM now a part of their everyday lives and Leesa and Gary quickly mastering counting carbs and calculating insulin doses, they were well equipped to move back home and start living their new normal.

Helen had come earlier with all her usual bolstering assurances. The fact that *she* had confidence in Leesa and Gary's ability to manage their daughter's condition had given *them* confidence, too. She'd also made an appointment next week for them to see the rural diabetes educator who visited their area monthly.

Crouching beside Leesa's chair this time, Caro said, 'You're nervous.'

'A little.' She blew out a breath. 'It just feels like a big step.'

'I get that.' Caro nodded. 'But you and Gary are all over this. Just…try not to think too far ahead, yeah? That can be overwhelming. Take it one day at a time.'

Leesa smiled and sniffled a little just as a voice behind them said, 'Where is my magic girl?'

The fibres in Caro's belly slid warm and languid against each other at the oh-so-familiar tone. Didi's face brightened and she giggled as she announced, 'Here.'

'Oh, that can't be possible.' Warwick pulled up beside Caro, who noticed both the superb tailoring of his dark trousers and the way he wore them just before she stood. 'The girl I'm after is all pale and sleepy and sad with wild, knotty hair.'

Another giggle. 'It's me.'

'I don't think so.' He shook his head. 'Wait, let me see.' He reached over then and plucked a coin from behind her ear, doing a dramatic double take. 'It *is* you!'

Didi held out her hand for it and he obliged. She had quite the treasure chest of magic coins now. Acknowledging Caro with a quick nod, he turned to Leesa. 'How are you doing?'

'Good.'

'Gary with Harrison?'

'Yep. Took him across to the accommodation for his afternoon nap.'

Warwick turned to his usual entourage and invited one of his junior doctors to go through the updates. When it was done he held out his hand to Didi for a low five. 'Well now, gold-star girl, are you ready to go home?'

She nodded vigorously, all teeth and big round eyes as she slapped his palm. 'Yes!'

He presented his fist. 'Lay it on me.'

Didi presented her fist and they bumped them together, both waggling their fingers as they pulled their hands away to simulate exploding bombs. Warwick laughed before he returned his attention to Leesa. 'Are *you* ready?'

She sucked in a breath and let it go noisily. 'As I'll ever be.'

'You're going to do just fine.' He smiled at her and Caro didn't know about Leesa, but the faith projected in that smile made her feel like *she* could leap tall buildings in a single bound. 'And tomorrow Cheray from my office will call and check in with you and she'll call every week to see how you're going, okay? We want to make sure you feel well supported.'

Leesa nodded, her eyes misty again. 'Thanks.'

'Good, then. We'll just get your paperwork sorted and as soon as Gary is ready to pick you up, you guys can head home.'

'Is that it?'

'You thought there'd be more fanfare?' He grinned. 'A pipe band?'

Leesa laughed. 'Trumpets at least.'

'We usually save the bells and whistles for admission.'

She bugged her eyes. 'I remember.'

* * *

Half an hour later the paperwork had been completed and Gary had arrived with Harrison to help Leesa, Didi and the assortment of stuffed animals and balloons, and other treats that had arrived from family and friends over the course of the past two weeks, down to the car. Then before Caro knew it, she and Warwick were accompanying the family down the corridor and watching them walk out of the door. Didi was grinning and waving, clutching the latest coin Warwick had pulled from her ear. Leesa was smiling, her eyes glassy, and Gary looked like a man who'd had the weight of the world lifted from his shoulders.

'They're going to be okay,' Caro said, staring after them through the glass panels of the doors as they made their way to the lifts.

'They are.'

Once the lift doors closed, Warwick stirred. 'Well, I gotta get to the clinic. They'll be wondering where I am.'

Caro nodded. 'Sure. I'll see you tonight.'

About to respond, he was cut off by a frightened, 'Help. *Help!* She's choking.'

A spike of alarm jettisoned adrenaline into Caro's system as she and Warwick dashed into the closest bay where a woman was ineffectually bashing an infant on the back in one of the toddler cots. 'Wanda Sykes. Twenty months,' Caro said as they got to the cot, her brain coming into sharp focus. 'Admitted last night with a suspected UTI.'

'I've got her,' Warwick said, stepping in to take over from the mother, who was wild-eyed and frantic.

'It's a grape,' the woman supplied as Warwick delivered a more effective blow between her shoulder blades and Caro hit the call emergency button at the back of the cot before grabbing the sealed plastic bag of emergency equipment next to the wall oxygen and suction outlets, which she quickly flicked to *on*.

'She's eaten a half-dozen just fine,' the mother said, tears coursing down her cheeks as she tried to reach past them to comfort her distressed child. 'But a balloon popped and she got a fright as she put this one in her mouth and I think she inhaled it.'

Haley and Glenda arrived in the bay in response to the alarm as Caro rammed the Yankauer sucker into the suction tubing. 'Choking on a grape,' Caro said without looking up. 'Can someone grab the trolley and take care of Mum?'

Wanda's lips were alarmingly dusky, her big eyes round and frightened as she clutched at the air and screamed. Or attempted to, anyway. But no air came out—the grape had obviously occluded her airway.

'It's okay, baby,' Warwick crooned, calm and steady. 'You'll be okay.' Then, as his repeated attempts at delivering blows between the shoulder blades failed to dislodge the grape he calmly said, 'Suction?'

Caro was only vaguely aware, as Warwick placed a flailing Wanda on her back, of the things in her periphery. The low hum of the wall suction, the roll of the trolley wheels as it arrived, Glenda placing a bag mask apparatus on the head of the bed, Haley comforting a sobbing mother. The quiet terror of onlookers as the emergency unfolded in front of them.

She zoned them all out as she inserted the sucker into the child's mouth. Unfortunately, all she managed to suck up were oral secretions that were rapidly pooling in the back of the throat and Wanda's lips had gone from dusky to blue.

Glenda quickly taped an oxygen saturation probe on the infant's foot, the instant low *booping* of the monitor a cause for alarm. 'Fifty-three per cent,' Glenda murmured.

As frightening as that number was, it was something they needed to know as everyone's hyper-focus was on Wanda. 'You want a laryngoscope and a Magills forceps?' Caro asked.

'Yes, please,' he said, still composed despite the *booping* tone dropping lower.

'Forty-eight per cent,' Glenda said as Warwick flipped Wanda over again, delivering more blows while he waited for the items.

Caro checked the light was working on the scope and placed it and the angled forceps on the mattress as Warwick placed the panicked child across the bed. 'Hold her still,' he murmured.

Caro laid her body across the legs and torso of the child, who wriggled desperately against the restraint as she reached for air, tears running out of her eyes. Glenda, who was at Warwick's side, clamped her hands around Wanda's head.

Quickly, as the *booping* went lower, Warwick tilted the child's head and inserted the blade of the scope past her teeth and along the tongue, which shone the light directly down her airway.

'Forty-one per cent.'

Caro could feel the wild shift of the child's muscles as she bucked at the invasion, straining against her hold. She was surprisingly strong despite the situation, which was better than the alternative—Wanda growing floppy and unresponsive.

'I can see it,' he muttered, his voice steady.

Caro slapped the forceps into his Warwick's palm just as he said, 'Magills.'

He glanced at the instrument as if surprised how it got there so quickly, shooting her a quick look of admiration and gratitude as Glenda said, 'Thirty-eight per cent.'

There were a tense two or three seconds that felt more like thirty as he held the scope in one hand and inserted the forceps with the other, angling them around, his elbow high in the air as he manoeuvred. Then a triumphant 'Gotcha' as he pulled out the scope and the forceps bearing the grape.

The infant took a huge breath, coughing and gagging then bawling at the top of her rapidly re-oxygenating lungs. '*Wanda!*' her mother cried as she surged forward, the tone of the saturation monitor rapidly picking up.

It was chaos then as the entire bay erupted in applause and a pale and sweaty Wanda, screaming blue murder in between coughing, was passed to her hysterically sobbing mother. The child was not happy at all about the cheering crowd or Haley trying to place a mask on her face for a few minutes of supplemental oxygen, but she was pinking up nicely, her bawling lungs filling with much-needed air.

Glenda let out a sigh of relief as she strode to help Haley and Caro sagged a little against the cot, her legs trembling now as the emergency abated and adrenaline whooshed out of her system.

'All's well that ends well,' she said, glancing at Warwick, who was still holding the forceps, the intact grape cinched between the spoon-billed jaws.

'Thanks to your efficiency and experience,' Warwick murmured.

She cocked an eyebrow, flattered by his praise despite knowing emergencies such as this one required a team effort. 'I'm not the one who pulled out the grape.'

'But you anticipated what I needed, which saved valuable seconds.'

Sure, she had, and seconds mattered when a child couldn't breathe, but Warwick's confidence had been the clincher. He'd been in control from the get-go. Exactly how he'd been that night with her—stay calm, take charge, do what had to be done.

'Anyway... I have to get to the clinic. Tell Glenda I'll come back and write it up after I'm done.'

Caro nodded as he strode to the resus trolley and placed the Magills into a green plastic kidney dish before he swaggered out of the bay without a backward glance.

And every woman with a pulse who'd witnessed the emergency—including Caro—swooned a little.

CHAPTER NINE

Two days later, Caro was sitting on the sun lounge in the back garden, braving the wind chill factor on the breezy afternoon. She had three days off before a run of three night shifts—*ugh*—and she intended to make the most of them. Like spending most of today wandering in and out of various shopping centres and familiarising herself with the Civic precinct. She wasn't someone who could shop all day but every now and then she enjoyed some mindless browsing.

A frosty gust blew a chunk of Caro's hair across her face and she pushed it back, tucking it behind her ear, which was freezing. She should really be going in now the temperature was starting to drop and night would soon be upon them. But she was dressed warmly and had a cat draped across her feet.

And she was enjoying the display of falling leaves too much. The wind whipping at the dried stems easily separating them from their branches. The leaves, varying shades of red—russet, vermillion and scarlet—twirled as they fluttered to the ground joining piles of their brethren on the ground. Every now and then the wind ruffled through the piles, stirring them a little, dispersing a few to the lawn, before they settled again.

In a matter of a few days, the fine but windy weather had denuded the maples by about fifty percent and Caro followed the bare outline of branches poking heavenwards in every direction. She plucked her phone off her lap and snapped a picture, her brain enjoying the contrast of gnarly old wooden fingers pointing at the vast arc of softening sky.

She'd taken so many pictures of these trees since she'd arrived, a veritable time lapse of their change was splashed across her camera roll. Caro suspected if she stayed around in Canberra longer than she'd stayed in other places more recently, she'd get blasé about this annual spectacle. Maybe even get on board with the grumbles about the amount of raking and how slippery wet fallen leaves could be on footpaths.

But, as she'd told Warwick, not this year.

Her first real autumn had been such a visual feast she'd enjoyed every moment of it. From the trees in Warwick's back yard to the ones lining the lake and those planted around the hospital grounds, Caro had been utterly delighted.

She smiled to herself thinking about the leaves Warwick had gifted her since realising they'd become a bit of an obsession. They were just leaves, dying ones at that, but it was further evidence to support his bald statement last week.

I remember everything.

Not only did he remember but the fact he had to be thinking about her to pick one up made her smile even harder. Made her chest expand in a way that sent jittery sensations in tiny spirals through her body.

Yeah, he remembered. But he also *got* her and that was a whole other thing.

He didn't dismiss her obsession, or belittle it or even just tolerate it—he indulged it. And that? Well…that made her feel like she was nineteen again and high on helium.

Light and airy and just a little bit dizzy.

She cautioned herself against it, trying to temper the flurry inside her chest, excruciatingly aware that she'd already rushed in too quickly with one Devlin brother. And this one was very much off-limits.

But the dizziness persisted.

Then, as if she'd conjured him up, the sliding door opened and she rolled her head to the side as he stepped out, her pulse fluttering as long legs encased in dark trousers ate up the distance, the wind tousling his hair. The round neck of his navy sweater sat low enough at the front to see the knot of his tie and tight around his shoulders. It didn't exactly look warm but her belly lurched a little at the perfection of the fit.

'That looks snug,' he observed as he came to a halt in front of her.

Dressed in layers, Uggs and thick polar fleece, her hair a tangle of knots and cocooned in a couch throw, Caro figured *slug* emerging from a chrysalis was more apt. Heidi, lifting one eyelid to investigate who was disturbing her peace, perked up as she spotted Warwick.

Smart cat.

Lifting to her paws, she stretched before jumping to the ground and greeting him, winding herself around his ankles.

'You're early.'

'Last appointment of the day cancelled.'

He didn't look sad about it and Caro laughed. 'That's a nice TGIF gift to you.'

A grin warmed his face. 'I'm not complaining.' He shoved his hands in his pockets. 'Is there a reason why you're out in this cold wind communing with nature when the house is nice and toasty?'

'Just enjoying the show,' she murmured, tipping her chin at the trees as more flashy twirls of red fluttered to the ground.

Casting an eye over the scatter of leaves, he sighed. 'That's my job tomorrow. Raking all those suckers up and disposing of them.' He returned his attention to her. 'If you want any of that lot you better grab them before they get mulched.'

And there went her breath again at his thoughtfulness. 'Good idea.' Caro kicked off the blanket and swung her feet to the ground.

'I didn't mean now,' he said as she pushed upright and he took a step back.

Caro grinned. 'I know but, here—' She unlocked her phone and opened her camera as she offered it to him. 'I've been meaning to get a pic of me with leaves falling all around. If I throw a bunch in the air would you mind getting a couple of snaps as they fall down? I've got it on live so I should be able to bounce and loop them as well.'

'Of course.' He smiled as he took the phone. 'Go play.'

And that was what it felt like, Caro almost clapping her hands like a little kid as she hustled to the closest pile and kicked, the leaves lifting and scattering even more as the wind picked them up and twirled them around again. She wished the mounds were ten times higher and wider and she could just face-plant in them.

Bending over, she scooped up an armful and turned to face Warwick, who was already snapping away. 'Ready?'

He was standing casually with his feet planted evenly apart, a Siamese cat at his feet, her phone held out in front of him, a smile warming his face and, damn, if her belly didn't feel as floaty and swirly as the leaves. 'Yep. Go!'

Caro grinned as she threw the leaves in the air then posed with her arms extended as they twisted and swished in the wind on their way back to earth. 'Was that good?' she asked.

'Amazing.' He walked over and showed her.

Caro grimaced at the screen. The falling leaves were spot on but her eyes were huge and round like someone had surprised her and her mouth was open mid maniacal laugh. Nothing like the picture she'd had in her mind. 'That is terrible.'

'What? No.' He shook his head as he looked at her. 'You look cute.'

Oh, dear Lord. Being called cute when she decidedly *was not* shouldn't make her stomach flip. But it did. 'Take it again,' she bossed.

So he took it again and again as she decided maybe a series of pics was a good idea—plenty to choose from. And she had fun, tossing leaves in the air as Warwick called, 'Work it, work it,' and she laughed as she threw a bunch at him and he laughed as he tried to dodge them and tossed some back and then the cat decided it wanted in on the action so Caro obliged, scooping her up for some pics.

And then they did a selfie of all three of them, a leaf of bright vermillion landing on Caro's head as Warwick tossed a bunch behind them with one hand and took the photo with the other just as the phone rang, interrupting the glow from the sheer *nearness* of him.

'It's the engineer,' Warwick said as he passed it over.

Which was a sharp pin to their bubble of fun. 'Hi,' she greeted. 'This is Caro.'

The call didn't require much input or last very long. Just a few *uh-huhs* and *okays*. The apartment foundations had been fixed and passed inspection and all residents were free to move back in from tomorrow morning. Something about signatures from each apartment owner and they'd been in contact with Hud but all she could think was—this was it.

Her time at Warwick's was up.

A few weeks ago, when having to temporarily move out

of the apartment in the middle of the night, she'd have loved this phone call, but right now it left her feeling...empty. Ending the call, she glanced at Warwick, who was watching her intently. Forcing a smile to her face, she said, 'I can move back in from tomorrow morning.'

'Oh.'

Which pretty much summed it up. *Oh.* Two letters and yet they were as weighty as any line of literature. He looked as gazumped as she did, which she didn't really know how to interpret. She was moving twenty minutes away—she could see him any time she wanted. But the plain fact of the matter was that living under his roof because of *circumstances* seemed much more...acceptable then dropping in to visit him *just because*.

One had not been her choice, the other very definitely *was*.

Glancing around her absently, she noted the destruction they'd wrought. What had been a few mostly neat piles was now leaves scattered all over the lawn. 'Oh God. I'm so sorry.' She rubbed her forehead, aghast. 'I've made a huge mess for you. I'll rake them before I leave tomorrow.'

He laughed but it sounded harsh and grated on her nerves like nails down a chalkboard. 'It's fine,' he dismissed. 'It won't take me long.' Then he reached across and plucked something from her hair, presenting her with a stunning example of an autumn leaf.

Despite how depressing the thought of moving out made her feel, she smiled as she accepted the offering. It felt like they had their own secret code now as she lifted her face to his, to find a smile playing on his mouth.

'Hot chocolate? Or...' he waggled his eyebrows '...a cheeky wine?'

If there was one thing Caro knew in this moment when

the thought of not seeing him every day was stabbing like nails into her bones, it was that she should say hot chocolate. It was definitely the weather for it and she should *not* be imbibing alcohol in this mood.

But it was Friday, right? Probably the last Friday they'd spend in each other's company. *Which was a good thing.* She knew that. But it didn't stop the pulse of recklessness washing through her veins.

'Wine,' she said and smiled.

One glass of wine became two as they cooked together in the kitchen laughing and chatting as they chopped and diced and prepared. He made spaghetti bolognese while Caro made an apple pie for dessert from the Granny Smiths she'd bought at the market earlier today. Two glasses of wine became three as they sat in front of the TV, side by side on the couch, watching a movie, their bellies full, their feet up on the coffee table, the lights dimmed as the fire glowed orange in the grate.

Caro was definitely not drunk—three glasses of wine over two hours was hardly a binge session—but she felt loose and relaxed. Slightly…buzzed, she supposed as the movie credits rolled. Also a little melancholy. It was hard to believe that there'd be no more nights like this—her and Warwick in front of the television, relaxed in each other's company.

She'd enjoyed these past three weeks. Maybe a little too much…

'Thank you,' Caro said as Warwick turned down the volume, which had increased several decibels as the last track played.

He rolled his head to the side. 'For what.'

Their gazes met, his dark eyes lit with the glow from the

fire, and her breath caught in her throat as an overwhelming urge to touch him rose up. To push her hand into his hair, to trail her fingers down his cheek, to trace his lips.

Bad Caro.

Ignoring the slow slug of her heart, she curled the fingers of the hand closest to him into her palm—just in case. 'For this.' She gestured around the room with her other hand. 'For giving me a temporary roof over my head.'

He shrugged. 'What are friends for?'

'Is that what we are?' she asked before she could stop herself or think better of it. Maybe it was their proximity. Maybe it was the mood. Maybe it was the fire. Maybe it was that recklessness that still had her in its grip. 'Friends?'

He'd taken his sweater and tie off a long time ago, rolled up the sleeves on his business shirt to expose forearms that made her a little weak in the knees and undone the top two buttons of his collar. Which made it very easy for her to see the thick bob of his throat before he said, 'Sure.'

'Okay.'

His brow pulled down. 'Are we not?'

'Yes. Of course. Sorry, I just—' Caro shook her head and huffed out a laugh. She couldn't say that.

'Just, what?'

Caro's face grew warmer. 'I… I don't know. Maybe it's just me but things feel…different between us now.'

Her pulse thudded thicker through her veins as she moved very slowly in a direction she wasn't sure she should be taking. One she probably wouldn't have had her tongue not been a little loosened by the wine. But she didn't seem to be able to turn back either, because things *had* changed between them.

And while that had been overwhelming a few weeks ago,

on the eve of her leaving it felt more overwhelming to keep it to herself. She'd be gone tomorrow, after all.

'You...' he hesitated as if he was also treading carefully '...feel it, too?'

A slow husky breath slid from her mouth at the *too*. She wasn't in this alone. Much as she'd done that day in the car, she turned on her side, her cheek pressing into the warm leather as she murmured, 'Uh-huh.'

There. It was out now. Not named or identified but acknowledged anyway. They were both aware of the elephant in the corner even if they weren't up to giving it a name just yet.

And it felt big. But also good. A relief.

He turned to mimic her position, their heads level, his eyes drifting over her face, inspecting every inch, brushing across her mouth before returning to lock on hers. 'So, where to from here?'

Well, that was a very good question. And one she didn't think she was capable of answering. Just articulating this *thing* had been enough.

'I don't know,' she whispered. Dropping her gaze to the nervous fidget of her fingers, she said, 'I don't know if I can think beyond what I just said.'

She huffed out a breath. Caro didn't want to think about the broader implications of her admission, especially when she didn't trust feelings that had sprung up so quickly—not with her track record.

'So don't.' His finger slid under her chin and tilted it up, the uncertainty of her gaze meeting the steady, dark potency of his. She could feel the thready flutter of her pulse against the pad of his finger and wondered if he could feel it too. 'Don't think beyond it,' he murmured as his hand fell away. 'Just think about right now. What do you want right now?'

She shook her head. There was no way she could speak aloud the things she wanted right now. That stuff belonged in the twisted, forbidden heat of her dreams where their whole complicated dynamic didn't exist and she could burn off her sexual frustration in privacy.

Sidestepping the question, she said, 'I wish...'

'What do you wish, Caroline?'

Her breath hitched as the truth welled up, pushing to get out. 'I wish you'd kissed me back that day in the car.'

There it was. The truth. She'd told herself at the time the kiss was to prove a point, but she'd been lying to herself, trying to stop herself from being dragged into another Devlin whirlwind.

'Oh God, Caroline.' It came out on a low kind of groan, his eyes closing briefly before opening again and piercing her with a sudden intensity. His hand slid to her face, cupping her cheek. 'On a scale of one to ten, how drunk are you right now?'

She was breathless and floaty and giddy but it had *nothing* to do with the wine. Was she one hundred per cent sober? No. But she was fully in charge of her faculties. 'Three.'

'That's good enough,' he muttered.

He bridged the distance between them then, which was, admittedly, small anyway, pressing his mouth to hers on a deep guttural groan that stiffened her nipples to tight buds. And this time he was not passive, he was not still, and neither was she as a rush of all the things she'd been denying—every hitched breath and hot flurry in her belly—broke through a wall and pure unadulterated lust flushed through her body.

No, it was more than lust. It was something much more compelling. Deeper. More abiding. They were doing this.

They were actually doing this. *Kissing.* Warwick was kissing her—for real. This man who remembered. Who knew her. Who indulged her.

Caro opened to him on a moan that felt like it had been coming for a very long time and he opened to her, too, his tongue licking inside, her pulse singing in her ears, drowning out anything other than him.

Warwick.

The taste of him. The smell of him. The feel of him. The frantic suck of his breath as if he was trying to inhale her body into his. The firm, sure slide of his hand to her hip, to the back of her thigh, to her ass, urging her closer as he kissed her deeper and deeper, urging her over until she was straddling his lap, their mouths still fused.

Until she felt it—the long, hard length of him. Pressing into the soft, slick give between her legs and she broke off on a gasp, it felt so indescribably perfect. She stared down at him wide-eyed. '*Warwick,*' she panted, staring down at him. 'I...'

She didn't know what to say, a pressure of words in her brain roaring around and around somehow all inadequate to describe the sensations gripping her body. So she let her hips do the talking, grinding against him, shuddering at the eye-rolling pleasure of it.

'I know,' he muttered, his lips hot on her neck as his hands clamped on her hips, holding her as he did some grinding of his own. 'I know.'

Caro whimpered as her clitoris pulsed in response. 'I want... I need...'

His lips left her neck, his hands left her hips, his palms sliding to her cheeks as he gazed into her face. 'Are you sure? We could slow this down.'

Caro liked that he wasn't pretending he didn't know

where this was heading. And she admired that he was giving her an out. But she didn't need it. This had been coming since she'd seen him in nothing but a towel. Since her blinkers had been ripped off and she'd realised Warwick was a man—not just her ex-BIL—and she didn't want to deny it any longer.

Not tonight anyway.

Tomorrow was a new day. Tomorrow she moved away. But they had right now and that was all she was thinking about.

'No.' And she kissed him again, his hands falling back to her hips as he met her lips with a passionate kind of fury.

Heidi, though, had other ideas, two paws landing on Caro's shoulder as she miaowed *loudly*, causing them to break away again. Panting hard, Caro stared at the cat, nonplussed for a moment, the pulse at the side of her neck thrumming wildly.

Warwick let out a husky chuckle. 'Maybe that's the universe warning us to stop?'

Caro raised an eyebrow. 'Do *you* want to stop?' This was, after all, his second offer of an out.

He blinked, then shoved his hands back on her cheeks again, his gaze meeting hers and holding it for long intense seconds. 'I want to be inside you so badly I'm bursting out of my skin with the need.'

Caro smiled as a flood of relief joined the flood of hormones stirring hot in her blood. 'Then maybe it's the universe telling us we should get a room and shut the damn cat out.'

He grinned. 'I like that version better.'

His room was closer so they hurried there, hand in hand, laughing as they stumbled in their haste but finally, finally stepping over the threshold and shutting the door. Shutting the cat out. Shutting the world out.

Shutting all the reasons they might regret this tomorrow out.

He kissed her then—hard. The force of it pushed her back against the door as his hands slid under her shirt—sliding up, up, up—his thumbs brushing over her nipples on their way over her breasts causing Caro to cry out his name.

'Warwick!'

But he didn't linger, not yet, he just kept going upwards, urging her shirt off over her head, his gaze falling to her breasts as his fingers reached for the clasp at the back, making short work of it, sliding the straps off her arms.

'Oh, *yesss*,' he muttered as he filled his hands with the spill of them, kissing her again as his thumbs toyed with her nipples.

Caro cried out again as the sensation rippled *everywhere*. Then his mouth was on them and Caro lost all track of time and place. Hell, if it hadn't been for the firm hold of his body against hers, she'd have slid to the ground utterly boneless as his tongue flicked back and forward between her nipples.

So engulfing was the sensation she didn't even realise his hand was smoothing down her body until the snap of her jeans released and his hand pushed inside her underwear, his fingers finding the slickness of her in seconds. He groaned so deep and low she felt it in her toes. 'God, Caroline,' he panted into her neck, 'you're so wet.'

'Warwick.'

Her pulse thumped an erratic drum beat as she reached for his trouser snaps, needing to touch him, too. To feel him. To explore the hardness that had pressed against her so urgently on the couch. But he grabbed her hand.

'If you touch me,' he muttered, lifting his lips from her neck, his blazing eyes meeting hers, 'I'm going to explode.' His gaze went dark and hot and earnest, like he'd peeled back the layers and she was seeing down into his soul. 'I've wanted you for too long.'

Wanted *you*. Not this. Not sex. *You*. He'd *wanted* her?

But Caro barely had time to register what he meant before his mouth was back on hers and his fingers slid inside her, his thumb finding the hard knot of her clitoris and stroking and there was no room in her head for any coherent thought—just the blinding need to ride this all the way to the end.

She gasped against his mouth, her head falling back, *thunking* on the door, her eyes closing as his deft fingers worked her from the inside and out, turning her body into one giant throbbing pulse that echoed in her chest and her lungs and her head and beat thick and heavy between her legs. Legs that were as useless as two pieces of string.

His mouth slid down her throat, licking a hot river of pleasure all the way to her breasts until he once again sucked the hard point of a nipple into his mouth and Caro almost fainted at the wash of pleasure. At the low undulations that were pulling everything taut inside her as muscles deep and low contracted with every spear of his fingers, every circle of his thumb, every swirl of his tongue, her lungs grabbing for air as they cinched tighter and tighter and tighter.

Until they couldn't contract any more and they released in one starburst of bright light that popped Caro's eyes open and arced through her system like a lightning strike.

'I can't,' she said on a gasp, clutching at his shoulders as fireworks spun and danced and fell around her like neon leaves and she stood on the precipice, panicked by the pull and the power.

'Yes, you can,' he muttered, his lips returning to hers, whispering words of encouragement against her gasping mouth as his fingers continued their devastating invasion.

'*I've got you,*' and, '*Let go,*' and, '*That's it...yes, that's it,*' and, '*I always knew you'd be this magnificent when you came.*'

Low, hot urgings that prolonged her pleasure, that held her fast through the twisty, bone-drilling spiral at the eye of her stormy release.

Caro seemed to coast for ever in sensations that left her in a much more gentle manner than they'd arrived, petering off, getting less and less until she collapsed against him, dragging in much-needed air. He withdrew his hand from her pants and Caro moaned as her internal muscles released him in a delicious shivery shudder.

She tipped her head back to look at him, her breathing still coming in ragged pants. He was smiling as his eyes roved over her face and she laughed.

Now he was smug. And had every right to be.

'Well... I certainly picked the wrong brother.'

Caro wasn't sure she should be making that kind of joke right now—or any time really—but when there was *too much* to say sometimes comic relief went a long way.

He grinned. 'You sure as hell did.'

Then he was swinging her up in his arms and Caro clutched his shoulders for the half-dozen paces it took for him to reach his bed and toss her down on top. She must look a mess, her boobs wobbling from the mattress bounce, her jeans half undone, her hair doing God knew what, but his gaze was hot, looking at her like she was his to do with as he pleased and he was trying to decide where to start.

'Take off your jeans,' he said as his fingers went to his belt.

Caro watched as Warwick stripped it off then pulled his shirt out of his trousers and, instead of undoing the buttons, yanked it off over his head and tossed it on the ground. His bare chest and abs were firmly muscled and covered with a light smattering of hair that, God help her, she wanted to feel rubbing against her nipples asap.

'Caroline,' he muttered, his voice low and dark as he unzipped. 'Jeans.'

The sound of his fly being yanked down stirred her to action as she wiggled and squirmed out of the denim, taking her underwear down as well, kicking out of the confines of her clothes the same time he stepped out of his trousers. And then they were both staring at each other—naked— eyes roving, taking in every square inch.

Strangely she didn't feel self-conscious even as her nipples scrunched tight at the way his gaze lingered between her legs. Maybe because Warwick had literally just been right there—with his fingers while his mouth had turned her nipples as hard as they were now.

Or maybe because she was just too damn distracted by the magnificence of *him*, his erection surging out from the dark thatch of hair, thick and potent.

She swallowed against a suddenly parched throat. '*Wow.*'

He chuckled as she stared at his dick like she'd never seen a naked man before, but Warwick Devlin with no clothes on was a sight to behold. The hard jut of flesh and steel dominated *everything* and Caro wanted to touch more than her next breath.

Pushing to a sitting position, she reached for him, tentatively sliding her fingers onto the taut flesh of his shaft. It bucked at the stimulus and he sucked in a noisy breath as if he was in actual physical pain when she wrapped her fingers around him and slowly slid her hand from root to tip.

'God, Caroline.' He shut his eyes as his hand stilled hers and heat flushed her body at the intimacy of their combined grip. 'Have some mercy.' He opened his eyes and Caro met his gaze that was burning fever-bright. 'I promise to let you play after but I'm too close right now. I just need to be inside you.'

The fine crack in his voice was dizzying. He sounded in pure agony and that shouldn't make her feel so damn smug, but it did. Warwick wanted her badly.

I've wanted you for too long.

Well, he didn't have to wait any longer. She slid her hand from him and eased herself against the mattress, bending one knee and placing her foot on the mattress, flashing him a peep in wanton invitation. 'What are you waiting for?'

Warwick's gaze cut straight to the apex of her thighs, his nostrils flaring as he leaned down and yanked the bedside drawer open. Not taking his eyes off her, he groped around for a few seconds before producing a little foil packet. Quickly he tore it open and suited up, which caused a stirring between Caro's legs, both from the intensity of his gaze and watching him touch himself.

When he was done, she held out her arms, dropping her bent leg to the side, opening completely for him, moaning in satisfaction when he joined her, covered her, his body hard and hot and heavy—but good heavy.

The way it should feel to be under a man and know he'd soon be thrusting inside.

He lowered his mouth to hers, Caro meeting him halfway, her pulse thudding a crescendo through her head as their lips clashed in greedy haste and he guided himself to her centre. The thick head of him nudged at her entrance once, twice, then pushed home, all the way in, Warwick hunching over her, gathering her close as he groaned in deep, *deep* satisfaction.

Caro shuddered in his arms at his overwhelming possession, stretching her so damn good, the embers of her orgasm already flaring to life. But it was the utter rightness of *him* that stole her breath. Washing over her like truth serum flooding her veins.

This *man*, this *place*, this *time*. Everything in her life felt like it had been leading to this moment. With *Warwick*.

But then he moved again, withdrawing, and the thought was torn from her throat before she could voice it, escaping with her gasp at the sheer ecstasy of the friction. And then the rhythm took over and Caro let herself get lost in it, lost in the play of his mouth and the thrust of his hips, the surge and retreat of him as each stroke took her higher and higher, revelling in the harsh pull of his breathing, the fine sheen of sweat on his back and the tremble of his muscles just beneath his skin.

Revelling in the heat and sweat and mayhem of her own body. Her breathing as erratic as his, her heart thumping in time with his, one-on-one through the walls of their chests, her orgasm building again, rolling back around with every pass of his erection over the hard knot of her G-spot, hitting it just right *every single time*.

Then, just as it flared to life and she moaned, Warwick buried his face in her neck and gasped, '*Yessss*,' as his release took him, reigniting hers in the wake, and they shuddered through their mutual release, riding it to the very, very end.

CHAPTER TEN

Warwick woke some time in the middle of the night, wrapped around Caroline, the big spoon to her little, her ass snuggled in his lap causing quite a lot of interest from an area of his body he would have thought more than satisfied by now. They'd made love twice more since their first quick releases, dozing off in each other's arms in between.

Yes. *Made love.* Not sex. Not for him anyway.

He'd spent over a decade telling himself that what he felt for Caroline was just a crush. An infatuation that stuck around because of their forced proximity. An inconvenience for sure but something he could easily dismiss.

Except he never *had* been able to dismiss it or her and he knew why, the second they kissed. Properly kissed. Not pressing mouths together to make a point. *Passionately kissed.* He was in love with her. He'd spent a lot of years lying to himself about it but he couldn't deny it any longer.

Didn't want to.

He was in love with Caroline Eastwood. His brother's ex-wife. He'd been in love with her from the moment she'd greeted him with a chipmunk voice sitting cross-legged on the floor surrounded by balloons. Had he ever thought in a million years that she'd come back into his life twelve years after that first meeting and they'd find themselves in a situation where those feelings would finally crystallise and be explored?

No.

But here they were. And he'd opened himself to the truth. *Finally.* And he wasn't going back to pretending that he didn't have feelings for her.

So, he'd put every ounce of those feelings into their lovemaking. And it had been everything he'd dreamed it would be—and more. After all this time, and all the yearning, he'd given himself carte blanche to show her with his body what he couldn't put into words.

Not yet, anyway.

I picked the wrong brother. That was what she'd said. In jest, yes, but he was going to prove her right. It should have been him and her. It *always* should have been him and her.

But he knew he couldn't just come out and say that—as much as he preferred a direct approach. He might only have allowed himself tonight to open the box inside labelled *Caroline, do not open*, but he'd been sitting with these feelings brewing for a very long time.

She had not.

While he didn't know for sure, he was fairly certain that rushing in with a declaration of love was a good way to freak her out. Giving into their sexual attraction tonight was one thing, opening up and letting it all out was another. Because he didn't want just one night. He wanted all of her nights. All of her days. All the seasons.

He wanted to be bringing her fallen leaves for all the autumns of their lives.

But what he wanted didn't matter. It was what *Caroline* wanted. Maybe she wouldn't have an issue with exploring something more? She had, after all, kissed him to prove she was over his brother and she'd been in relationships with other guys.

But Warwick knew he wasn't just any other guy. That there was a *third person* who'd have to be taken into consideration in any potential relationship they might have. He also knew that being *over* Brad didn't mean that her entering into a relationship with ex-husband's twin brother wouldn't have blow-back.

For both of them.

Warwick didn't have a problem with him and Caroline being together. But he suspected Brad would because Brad. Which might make Caroline extra skittish.

So, he had to take this slow. Tread carefully. One day at a time. Et cetera, et cetera. And hell, he'd waited this long, he could wait some more.

If she felt the same.

She stirred and Warwick suppressed the urge to groan at the delicious friction of her ass cheeks against his groin. 'Are you awake?' she whispered.

Warwick smiled as he dropped a kiss on her nape and rubbed his erection against her buttocks. 'What gave it away?'

She laughed. 'I didn't think your dick required you to be awake to go rogue.'

He chuckled, his breath ruffling the fine hairs at her nape. 'True.'

She turned in his arms and Warwick fell back against the mattress, drawing her in close, her front smooshed to his side, her head snuggling into the crook of his shoulder, her arm slung across his chest, her thigh slung across his thighs, his fingers absently stroking up and down her arm, neither of them speaking for a bit.

Lying with Caroline like this was something Warwick

had never dared let himself imagine but tonight, it was a reality, her hand warm and heavy over his heart, every beat pulsing with his love for this woman.

'What are you thinking?' she asked eventually.

Warwick's belly gave a little kick. This was an opening. He could be flippant or he could test the water. 'I'm thinking...' his fingers stilled in their movement, tension cranking as he chose his words carefully '...how *not* weird it is that we...ended up here?'

There was a pause before she answered. It felt excruciating but was probably only several seconds. 'Yeah. It is strangely *not* weird.'

Every muscle in Warwick's body suddenly unclenched on a rush, his fingers resuming their caress. That was very good news. She hadn't rejected his statement or tried to diminish what had happened or pretend that she didn't know what he was talking about.

'What are *you* thinking?' he asked.

Another pause, which had Warwick wondering if it was a good thing or a bad thing. Maybe she was just feeling her way, too. Or maybe she was preparing to deliver a speech about being one and done? 'Do you...feel something for me?'

Warwick relaxed even further, a buzz surging through his system. It wasn't a 'one and done' speech. Nor was she doing some kind of damage control, trying to make excuses about how they ended up in bed together. She was opening a conversation about *feelings*.

That had to be good, right?

But that didn't mean Warwick knew how to answer. He didn't want to scare her away with *all of the things* he felt. This love he'd been carrying around for so long was expanding rapidly now he'd let it out of the box but he'd been here, or close to it anyway, for a long time. He'd had time to adjust.

Do not use the L word, dude. Do not.

'I do,' he said, talking to the ceiling. 'And, if I'm being honest, which... I think we probably *should* be right now, I have for a long time.'

It was the closest to honest he could get anyway at this stage, with them both being so tentative. There was no point making a declaration of love, laying all his cards on the table only to discover she wasn't interested in playing with them past tonight. Because that could irrevocably sink their relationship and some of Caroline every now and then was better than none of Caroline for ever.

'That's what you meant last night when you said you'd wanted me for a long time?'

Okay. So she had remembered that. 'Yes.' Even though his feeling were far deeper than physical want. 'Do you? Feel something for me?' Warwick steeled himself for the answer. But knowing where he stood was better than not knowing.

She shifted, rolling up onto her elbow, their eyes meeting in the darkened room as she regarded him solemnly. 'I feel like something's...happening here. Between us.'

Warwick didn't dare move, not wanting to scare the horses, but his pulse leapt at what she was saying. It wasn't just him in this. 'Uh-huh.'

'And yet...there are a lot of reasons, like your brother *and* mine, that complicate things happening between us.'

Warwick hadn't really thought about her brother being part of this equation. Hud was his best friend, for crying out loud. He knew Warwick was an honourable, upstanding guy so he should be thrilled that his sister might find happiness with someone as great as him. Even if Warwick did say so himself.

But Hud *was* protective of Caroline, especially since another Devlin had already screwed her over. The unfairness of that was like a pike being shoved into Warwick's brain.

'Right. But…' He tried not to let his frustration show but, *ugh*, this sucked. 'It really is none of their business. I mean, we're both grown adults who are allowed to be with whoever we want to be with.'

She shot him a reproachful look even as a smile touched her mouth. 'Yeah, but it's different for us and I think you know why without me having to explain it.'

He shut his eyes. She was right, of course. To Brad and Hud he and Caroline weren't just any two people they knew talking about getting into a relationship. The Venn diagram of their interpersonal relationships resembled something more like a spider's web than a few overlapping circles.

It was convoluted.

Opening his eyes, he found her watching him, her teeth worrying her bottom lip. 'If this becomes…something, it'll alter more than *our* relationship. It'll alter our relationships with both of them.'

'Maybe for the better.'

She smiled. 'Maybe. But, what if it's for the worse? What if they react…*not* well? What if it causes arguments or even a rift between you and your brother?'

'It wouldn't do that.' It was different circumstances than last time.

'Really?' She quirked an eyebrow. 'I remember what it was like there for a while after Brad cheated on me and you and Hud were so angry with him for a couple of years. I remember what a knock-on effect that had on the rest of your family. And what if Hud stops talking to you because of us? I don't want to be the cause of an uproar in your life.

Or mine, for that matter. I don't want to be the cause of another ruined Christmas.'

Warwick's jaw tightened. 'Damn it, Caroline.' He slid a hand onto her cheek. 'You weren't the cause. *Brad* was. Him and his actions.'

She sighed as she slid her hand over his and brought their joined hands down to his chest. 'Whoever was the cause, it was the same end result. And I don't want to be the woman that drives a wedge between you and the people close to you.'

Warwick realised he should be cheered by that. Caroline didn't want to be a wrecking ball—that was a good thing. Memories of how upset she'd been that he and Brad had been at loggerheads all those years ago filled his brain.

The thing was, he was in love with *her*—not Brad, not Hud. One was his twin and one was his best mate and he loved them but he wasn't *in* love with them and *could* live without them in his life if that was what they chose.

But he couldn't live without Caroline. Not now he'd admitted to himself the true depth of his feelings and not if she reciprocated.

'Hey,' she said with a smile as she slid her elbow down and leaned in, dropping a light kiss on his mouth. 'I'm just saying…we need to be sure about this.' She stayed close, her mouth temptingly near, the warmth of her breath fanning his face. Near enough for his ardour to stir again despite the depressing topic of conversation. 'So maybe I move back to Hud's and we could, I don't know…go on a couple of dates. See where it leads? But keep it all on the down low. If it doesn't pan out, we've embarrassed ourselves and we'll have to work out how to navigate that, but no one else is involved.'

Warwick had to stop himself from pumping his fist. He'd been prepared for slow and steady so the fact she'd suggested it was a win-win. She wanted to date for a while—in secret or otherwise, he was fully on board. He wanted to do this right, do the dating thing, the getting-to-know-you thing. They'd kinda skipped straight to the good part but that didn't mean they couldn't reverse this car and start from the beginning.

'I'm *totally* on board with that.' He stroked a finger down her arm. 'As slow as you like. As long as you like. As secret as you like.'

'Thank you,' she murmured and dropped another kiss on his mouth.

This one was *much* more lingering and Warwick was dizzy when she pulled back. 'So…you're going back to Hud's in the morning?'

Man, he was going to miss having her so close.

'*We-e-ll-ll…*' She smiled, and it was dizzying too. 'I *can* move back in from tomorrow. Doesn't mean I *have* to…' Her hand slid slowly down his stomach. 'I *could* stay until you leave for work on Monday morning?'

Warwick shivered and his belly muscles twitched as her fingers trekked south. He grinned. 'I like the way you think.'

They could leave the car in park for a couple of days, right?

When her hand hit pay dirt, he groaned and shut his eyes, hot fingers of need sinking talons into his ass as she squeezed then stroked the burgeoning length of him. 'Condoms in the drawer,' he muttered as he opened his eyes.

But she just shook her head, a wicked smile on her pretty mouth. 'I'm not going to need a condom for this.' And she wriggled down his body until her *mouth* hit pay dirt…

The debauchery lasted until almost eleven Sunday morning when it came to a crashing halt with Warwick's bedroom door being reefed open and a booming voice with a slight American accent ripping Warwick out of the most satisfying sexually exhausted slumber of his life by the roots of his hair.

'Jesus, brother, what kind of a time do you call this?'

Warwick sat dead upright, his pulse leaping at the intrusion, his brain scrambling to put a bunch of signals together as he stared incomprehensibly at Brad for long seconds, vaguely wondering why he'd ever given him a key as *Caroline* stirred beside him mumbling, 'What time is it?'

Oh crap. A very bad feeling took hold of Warwick's gut as time slowed right down, unfolding like a car crash happening before his eyes, and he was powerless to stop it.

'Oh, Jesus, sorry.' Brad laughed, shooting Warwick a *you sly dog, you* look. 'Didn't mean to interrupt your—'

'*Brad?*'

Warwick's eyes shut briefly as Caroline pulled herself up beside him, blinking disbelieving at his brother—her *ex*—the sheet clutched to her naked body.

Jesus. This was not good. So much for slow. So much for secret.

It was Brad's turn to blink. '*Caro?*'

He looked between the two of them like he couldn't quite compute what he was seeing. In fact, there was a moment where all three of them just stared at each other like they had no clue what to do next.

Caroline recovered first. 'Get *out*,' she yelled.

Unfortunately, Brad seemed as glitched as Warwick felt but Caroline was now fully animated as she glared at their unwelcome bedroom invader. 'Get the hell out. *Jesus.* Haven't you ever heard of knocking?'

Brad recovered then, looking between the two of them before scowling at Warwick. '*Outside,*' he snapped. 'We need to talk.' Then he turned on his heel and marched out, slamming the door behind him.

Anger roiled in Warwick's gut, blood hot as burning oil rushing through his head. He was incensed at his brother for this and every other thing he'd ever done to hurt Caroline all over again. Throwing off the sheet, he stepped out of bed and into his trousers that were still on the floor from where he'd discarded them on Friday night. He didn't bother with a shirt.

'Warwick?'

'Stay here,' he muttered. 'I'll handle this.'

'Warwick!'

But he didn't hear the warning in her voice. The plea. The worry. He didn't ask her if she was okay. All he could hear was the pound of his blood through his chest and his groin and his head as a red mist descended because, *goddamn* it, Brad had been privileged to have Caroline's love and devotion and he'd squandered it in ways that still enraged Warwick.

And now he had the goddamn *nerve* to be all Neanderthal about her living her life?

'I'll be back,' he muttered.

Warwick also slammed the door as he left, striding out to talk to Brad although the desire to punch him in the face was a close second. 'What the hell are you doing here?' he demanded, glowering at his brother, who was pacing back and forth near the couch.

Seriously, why wasn't he in LA catering to B-grade movie actors and wannabe influencers?

Brad ignored the question throwing back one of his own. 'You're *screwing* my wife?'

An explosion of red flashed inside Warwick's head and he was surprised Brad couldn't see it flaring in his pupils. There were so many things wrong with that statement Warwick didn't even know where to start. 'Are you *shitting* me?'

Brad's expression became bullish, his chin jutting. 'So, you're *not* screwing her?'

'She's *not* your wife. Remember? You pissed that against the wall when you cheated on her.'

'And you were there for her, huh?' he sneered. And then, as if the true meaning of that thought hit him, Brad blinked. 'Jesus. Have you two been doing this behind my back for bloody *years*?'

Warwick's harsh laugh cut across the insulting suggestion. 'Oh God, you are *un*believable. Still looking for some kind of moral out for your despicable behaviour.'

Yes, he had forgiven his brother and moved on because Caroline had and their rift had distressed her, but that didn't mean he'd forgotten.

'Nice sidestepping, brother.'

'If you think for a second that Caroline would have had any truck with that, then it really does prove you never did know her at all.'

'So, *Caro*, no, but—' Brad pierced him with a look that peered right inside Warwick's head and every guilty fantasy he'd ever had about his brother's wife. 'What about you, huh? My *brother*?'

Warwick's blood pressure shot up, his temples pulsing with the hot rich blood of indignation. But the worst part was, he couldn't look at Brad, the person he'd shared a womb with, and deny the accusation. If Caroline had come to him during her marriage and propositioned him—which she would *not* have—*would* he have gone there?

He'd like to think he wouldn't have. That he had more honour. But he'd already proven that where Caroline was concerned—he just wasn't that strong. And did that make him any better than Brad?

So he obfuscated. 'This is none of your business any

more, dude. None. *Zero.* What Caroline does, who she sees, who she *sleeps* with is none of your concern.'

'What he said.'

Warwick had been so involved in the heated argument with his brother, he hadn't heard Caroline storming into the fray. But there she was, in the clothes he'd peeled off two nights ago, hands on her hips, her hair pushed back behind her ears, glaring at both of them.

Brad's eyes cut to Caroline. 'Is this you getting back at me?'

'Brad.' She shook her head, clearly exasperated. 'I don't know if you know this, but my life does *not* revolve around you any more.'

'You expect me to believe that you and Warwick just suddenly decided to start something?'

She took a deep breath like she was trying to deliberately calm herself. 'I know this is a shock. If it helps, it's a surprise to me too. But, honey, we've been divorced for almost nine years—you don't get a say any more.'

Her voice gentled, which made Warwick twitch. As did her calling Brad *honey.* She'd always called him that. Even after the divorce. It was just her chosen form of endearment. Hell, he'd heard her call patients that. So he needed to take a goddamn breath.

'Does Hud know?' Brad demanded.

'Does Hud know what?'

All three of them turned to the front door, where Hudson was standing, his eyes moving between them all, his brow crinkled.

'I knocked,' he said, 'but nobody heard.'

Warwick blinked. What the hell? What was *Hudson* doing here? Wasn't he in the wilds of South Australia somewhere? And how in the hell had he found himself in some kind of bizarre family circus? 'Hud?'

'*Hud?*' Caroline repeated.

'Does Hud know that his good buddy—' Brad swept his hand towards Warwick, ignoring everyone's confusion and answering the question '—is *screwing* his sister?'

'*What?*' Hud said as Caroline gasped.

Warwick, ignoring Hud's response, was *done* with Brad's crudity. 'Hey.' He took two paces towards his brother. 'Knock it off. This is *not* that.'

Brad glowered and gave Warwick's chest a shove. 'Oh, really?'

'Stop it,' Caroline snapped, also stepping forward.

His vision nothing but blood red now, Warwick didn't even register Caroline's objection. He was too furious at the cheapening of what was happening between him and Caroline. 'Yes.' Warwick shoved back. *Harder*. 'Really.'

'*Stop it!*' Caroline repeated, reefing his arm away from Brad's chest.

'So you weren't both naked in your bed right now?'

Warwick had never used his two-inch height advantage over his twin before but he sure as hell did now as he glowered down at his brother. 'Some of us don't just use sex for recreation.'

'You're sleeping with my sister?'

Warwick flicked his gaze to Hud, who was storming towards him now, staring at him like he was some kind of monster. His best friend in the world was looking at him like he was *some kind of monster*. Which was like a drill into his brain. He freaking worshipped Caroline. Surely Hud must know that Warwick would *never* treat his best friend's sister with any kind of disrespect. He'd never *play* with her.

'You're *sleeping with my sister*?' Hud repeated as he

pulled up close to Warwick, taking his turn to poke two fingers into Warwick's chest.

Okay, well…obviously not.

'Stop it.'

Caroline all but stamped her foot, her angry command like a whiplash into the fray, dragging everyone's attention as her eyes radiated spitting, fiery anger. 'I'm going to Hud's place,' she announced. 'But I hope you're all really happy here in your mutual circle jerk of guilt and recriminations.' She stormed over to the couch where she'd left her bag on Friday afternoon and scooped it up. 'I don't want to see or hear from any of you—' her gaze stabbed into Warwick's '—for a bit. I need some space to think about things and decide if *I* want any of *you* in my life.'

'I'll come with you,' Hud said.

'You will not.' She speared a finger at her brother. 'I don't know why you're back all of a sudden but, right now, you are as bad as them. Stay here in your little patriarchal cabal. I don't want to see any of you until you can apologise about treating me like I wasn't right here the entire time and realise that I'm not some Jane Austen heroine who needs some man to look out for me. Screw you all.'

Alarmed as she turned away, Warwick stepped towards her, touching her arm. They'd been so close, how had it fallen apart so quickly? 'Caroline?'

'Don't,' she hissed, yanking her arm away. 'I can't be dealing with all this testosterone bullshit right now. I'm leaving.'

CHAPTER ELEVEN

Warwick watched her go—they all did—her spine straight and steely, leaving him gut-punched. Wanting to go to her but not wanting to ignore her wishes. Knowing he'd let his insecurities about their relationship and goddamn *Brad* get under his skin. He'd ignored her entreaties and as good as pushed her out of the door.

Given her a reason to run.

He didn't know what an acute breaking of the heart felt like but he'd bet his last dollar it felt a helluva lot like *this*.

Turning to Brad and Hud, he said, 'Now look what you've done.'

'What *we've* done?' Hud hissed. 'You're the one who screwed with her.'

'It's *not* like that.' Warwick shook his head, feeling more bereft than angry now as he strode to the couch and sat down, cradling his head in his hands. 'I love her. I've *always* loved her. From the moment I saw her sitting on your parents' floor blowing up balloons for your birthday.'

Brad sat opposite staring at Warwick, nonplussed. '*What?*'

Hud also sat, looking between the brothers. He didn't say anything but Warwick could tell he was thinking about the situation.

'And then *you* come along.' Warwick glared at his brother.

They were the same age and yet Brad already had some work on his face. Warwick supposed that was an occupational requirement. Brad's patients probably wanted a doctor who personified their fountain-of-youth dreams.

'Being all *Brad*,' he continued. 'And she was totally dazzled and...' He shrugged. 'I knew I'd lost her.' He locked eyes with Brad. 'To you.'

As if Warwick's being raw and honest had tripped something in Brad, he said, 'Well, jeez, man. I didn't know you felt like that.'

Warwick gave a half-laugh and shook his head. Of course his brother didn't. Brad was utterly egocentric and had never pretended otherwise. 'Well, now you do.'

'I did love her,' Brad said, almost defensively.

Warwick nodded. 'I believe that you believe you did.' But the truth was, Brad loved Brad first and that was not how love—true, deep, abiding love—between two people worked. Each had to love the other more than themselves.

Warwick knew that.

He scrubbed a hand over his face then glanced at Hud. 'I'm sorry. I tried to keep a lid on it. I really did. But things... *shifted* between us while she was here...and I'm done with denying that I'm in love with your sister. So you can huff and puff and be all *get-your-filthy-hands-off-my-sister* as much as you want, but you know she deserves the best of men and if you don't think I'm *that* then why the hell are we even friends?'

Hud nodded, raising his hands in an expression of *yeah, yeah*. It seemed kinda grudging but, to be fair, this whole mind-altering thing had just been dumped on him. 'That's a fair enough point.'

'I need you to know that I will worship her for the rest of my life. If that's what she wants.' At the moment he wasn't sure she'd ever talk to him again.

Hudson was clearly still processing everything as he fixed Warwick with an uncompromising look. 'I seem to remember another Devlin—' he glanced at Brad then back at Warwick '—making similar claims a decade ago.'

'Sure. But *I* mean it.' Warwick met his best mate's eyes. 'And you *know* me. You know I wouldn't be saying any of this if I didn't mean it.'

He nodded again, not remotely grudgingly this time. 'Yeah. I know.'

A cooling flood of relief charged through Warwick's system. He didn't need Hudson's approval—he needed only Caroline's. But this was his best friend. Knowing Hud had faith in him, trusted him with his own sister—that meant everything.

'So what now?' Brad asked.

'One thing I know for sure,' Hud said. 'If my sister wants space, give it to her.'

Warwick wished that weren't true but he knew Hudson was right. 'She's also starting nights tomorrow night.'

'Oh, Jesus.' Hudson's recoil would have been funny at any other time. 'Then *definitely* stay away until after she's done with them.'

Warwick gritted his teeth. He didn't *want* to stay away; he wanted to rush over, knock down the door if he had to. But she had asked for space and the one thing he could do, after ignoring her pleas and getting into an affray with Brad and forgetting that this was about *her* as well as him, was to give her the space she asked for.

She'd be finished her nights on Thursday morning. That

was only five days and four more nights away. He could wait until Thursday evening.

Even if it did kill him.

Caro wished she could say her nights flew by. Alas, they did not. An unusually quiet spell made each night feel like twenty hours instead of the actual ten. Not even the massive offering of chocolates—split into three parcels, one for each shift—that Leesa had sent to the ward on Monday afternoon with a note thanking them for the care of Didi had helped ease the terrible toll of night shift.

Not when the days were full of sleepless hours where that last testosterone-laden clash between the three men in her life played over and over. She supposed some people might get off on three angry men fighting over her, but she was not one of them.

Frankly the fact that they'd all acted like they had some kind of ownership over her—Warwick included—had been the last damn straw. It had been bad enough that her fears about driving a wedge between Warwick and his other relationships—Brad and Hud—had come to fruition before her eyes without the whole thing almost devolving into fisticuffs.

All of them, she noted, had been conspicuous by their absence these past few days. Yes, she'd asked for space, but she hadn't expected any of them to comply. But, she supposed, they were the only three guys in the whole world who knew what she was like on night shift, so she couldn't really blame them, either.

Hud had texted her to apologise for what had gone down and to tell her he'd come back to check on the apartment and sign some forms and was leaving again next week and that he'd dropped her bag in the parcel room. She had no idea where he was sleeping although she assumed he was at Warwick's.

Brad had also messaged an apology and to tell her he'd come back for a seminar in Sydney in a couple of weeks and had decided to surprise his brother and he'd like to *catch up* with her properly before he left. Whatever that meant.

And Warwick? *He* hadn't texted at all.

She should be fine with that. Happy, even. She'd specifically asked to be given space and he—unlike them—had complied. But, perversely, she was *miffed*.

Because night duty.

Or that was what she told herself anyway as she crashed into bed on Thursday morning, so tired she could barely see straight. But it was also the first thing she thought about when she woke nine glorious hours later, the apartment dark at just after five in the evening according to the luminous dials of her bedside clock.

Why had he not texted her? And how had things changed so rapidly? She'd come to Canberra a month ago looking forward to starting a new chapter of her life. House-sitting for her brother. A new workplace. New faces. New friends.

And catching up with her old friend Warwick.

And now here she was with everything turned upside down. Her house-sitting gig turned on end, just like her relationship with Warwick.

God…she'd *slept* with Warwick. And it had been *good*. And they'd agreed they'd start seeing one another because there was something happening between them but that had been before her brother and her ex had shown up and everything had gone south.

Could she be with him knowing there might be bad blood between him and Brad? Him and Hud?

Sticking her hand out from the duvet, she dragged her

phone under the covers, hoping Warwick had sent her a text—because, apparently, she was hopelessly contrary—and she'd been too comatose to hear the chime. There wasn't a text but her phone did that thing where it showed her a random pic from her camera roll and, of course, it was the selfie Warwick had taken with her and him and Heidi under the tree, leaves falling all around them.

She realised she hadn't really looked at it properly, seeing as how she'd been rather…occupied since it had been taken, and her heart clenched as she did so now. They were laughing, but not at the camera. At each other. Grinning like loons. Like two people really comfortable in each other's company.

No…not like that. Her heart gave a *thunk* as she took in the way they were looking at each other, intently, their gazes light and flirty and honest. The truth there for everyone to see. Their love there for everyone to see.

Oh *crap*. Was it possible to have fallen in love with him? For this *thing* she'd cautiously mentioned that was happening between them to already be so far advanced?

It couldn't be. Brad was furious. Hud was pissed. This was the worst timing.

The phone rang, startling her. *Hudson*. Taking a breath, she tapped the screen. 'Hey.'

'You're awake, then. And human.'

Caro rolled her eyes. 'Yes. To both.'

'Good. I'm ringing to apologise for my behaviour on Sunday. I was…shocked. I had no idea that Warwick had feelings for you and it was just sprung on me and after the way things ended with Brad… I just had this nightmare scenario of your heart being smashed to smithereens by another Devlin and—'

'He's your best friend, Hud,' Caro interrupted. Her feelings might be all up in the air right now, but she knew Hud judging Warwick against Brad's example was terribly unfair. They might be twins but the only thing the Devlin brothers had in common was that for nine months, thirty-two years ago, they'd shared the same womb.

'I know. I know.'

Hud's tone was contrite and Caro could tell he *did* know that Warwick shouldn't be judged by his brother's standards. Just as she did.

'I'm sorry. I was a little freaked out and I kinda lost perspective there for a bit. Warwick is the best man I know. Why wouldn't I want that for the best woman I know?'

Stupid, post-night-duty tears pricked at the backs of Caro's eyes. That was possibly the nicest thing her brother had ever said to her. She knew she didn't need her brother's approval to be with anyone but his recommendation was welcome.

'So, I'm really sorry and hope you can forgive me for being such a dick.'

Caro laughed. 'Don't I always?'

They talked about other things then, catching up on Hud's plans for the next few days. They arranged that he'd come back to the apartment tomorrow when the worst of the night-duty crank should be done and dusted and Caro hung up feeling better about *their* relationship at least.

Getting out of bed, she pulled on her fluffy dressing gown and padded out to the darkened living area on her way to the kitchen to find something to fill her growling stomach. She didn't bother to turn on the lights. It was a similar layout to Warwick's living area in a lot of ways, just much smaller.

Which made her think about Warwick all over again…

But before she could go down the rabbit hole of what she should do next where he was concerned, her phone rang again. This time it was Brad. She hadn't had a phone call with him in such a long time it seemed odd seeing his name flashing on her screen.

'Hey,' she said as she answered.

'I'm an idiot.'

'Yes,' she said as she opened the fridge, throwing some light into the kitchen, screwing up her nose at the lack of chocolate.

He laughed. 'You always were hard on the ego.'

Probably why they'd already been flagging before their baby surprise. Brad had been quite high maintenance. 'Sorry.'

But she wasn't.

She shut the fridge, plunging her into the dark again as he said, 'It was just…the last thing I expected to find when I walked into Warwick's room was you. I was…surprised and I had a dumb knee-jerk, caveman reaction, which I had no right to be having.'

Yep, that pretty much summed it up. 'Well…if it's any consolation,' she countered as she wandered in the dark to the couch, easing herself down, 'him and me is the last thing I expected, too.'

'He's in love with you, you know?'

Her knuckles whitened around the phone. She was starting to think it might just be so. That she might also be in love with him. 'You don't have to do that.'

But Brad wasn't finished. 'I should never have pursued you, all those years ago. I really am sorry. About everything. Not just the other day.'

More dumb tears threatened. 'I know.'

And she did know how remorseful Brad was, although it was the first time she'd heard him lament his pursuit of her. If he hadn't would she and Warwick have been together? She thought back to that night blowing up balloons together. The fun. How he'd made her laugh. How he'd made her feel, in the chaos of the party prep that had been all about Hudson, like it was her birthday.

They talked for a bit longer, Brad being his best Brad as he regaled her with stories of his LA adventures. When she hung up she was glad that she'd seen him again—despite the circumstances. Glad they'd talked.

He's in love with you, you know.

Was it strange that coming from her egocentric ex she was more inclined to believe it? Her pulse fluttered at the thought as she flopped back on the couch. A month ago she'd have counted Warwick as one of her closest friends. And now not only were they lovers—*gah*, lovers!—but she was starting to think she was in love with him, too.

Her phone rang again and she didn't have to look at it to know it was Warwick. Fingers trembling, her pulse tapping wildly at her temple, she tapped the screen. 'Hey.'

'Hey.'

'I…miss you.' It hadn't been what she'd planned to say but when she heard his voice in her ear, it just spilled out. A giant wellspring of *missing him* surged up.

'Open the door. I'm outside.'

Caro blinked, her pulse also surging now, a feeling that the rest of her life was on the other side of the front door, which felt wild and just *too soon*. How did she even trust her emotions when they'd been so wrong in the past?

She didn't know about those things, but she did know she couldn't *not* see him.

Stumbling from the couch on suddenly wooden legs, she crossed to the door and flicked on the light switch, blinking against the sudden brightness. Her hand shook a little as she reached for the deadlock and opened it to find him standing there looking haggard and hassled, his hair haphazardly finger-combed, but looking better than any man had a right to in his business shirt, his tie pulled askew, holding a block of dark almond chocolate.

Caro sucked in a breath as she snatched it out of his hands then grabbed him by the tie and yanked him inside. Kicking the door shut with her foot, she backed him against it as he'd done that night to her in his bedroom before he'd stripped her clothes off.

She kissed him then—hard—because she'd missed him so damn much. And he groaned and ploughed his fingers into her hair and kissed her back, the hot swipe of his tongue more addictive right now than the chocolate being squashed between their bodies.

When he broke the kiss off, Caro mewed in displeasure, but he didn't go anywhere, just held her face in his hands as he held her gaze.

'I'm sorry for being such a Neanderthal the other day.' He was panting, so was she, in the aftermath of their kiss. 'For ignoring you every time you tried to get my attention. I was so furious with Brad swanning in like that, acting all butt-hurt, but that's *no* excuse. I want you to know that I'll never do that again.'

Caro believed him. Not just because he looked so damn earnest and angry at himself, but because Warwick had never been *that* guy. He'd always been the one that calmed a situation, not escalated it.

'Thank you,' she said as she stepped out of their embrace, needing to think coherently for this next bit.

He stayed where he was, shoulder blades to the door, as she wandered to the couch and leaned her butt against the back of it, folding her arms as she faced him. 'Brad said…' he stiffened a little and she felt her heart rate speed up, not quite believing what she was about to say but knowing this was the time to be really honest '…you're in love with me. Is that true?'

He swallowed but he didn't bother denying it. 'Yes.'

The answer was quiet but hit like a sledgehammer. Oh God. Warwick Devlin—her ex-brother-in-law, her brother's best friend—*loved* her.

'And you?' he asked.

Which was a fair question. 'I want to,' she said, trying to answer it as honestly as she could. She really did want to. 'But…isn't it just…too soon?'

He shook his head with utter assuredness. 'No.'

'I fell too quickly for Brad and look where that got me.' Got *them*.

'You think what you're feeling now…' he pushed off the door and ambled in her direction '…how this thing has unfolded between us, is *anything* like you and Brad?'

There was a note of incredulity in his voice, which Caro had to admit was warranted. 'No.' She shook her head. He was right about that—it was chalk and cheese. Night and day. But… 'It's been a month, Warwick. Isn't that a little… wild?'

He halted in front of her, his physicality as overwhelming as usual, and she wanted nothing more than to slide her arms around his waist, lay her head on his chest and shut her eyes. But this was cards-on-the-table time.

Shaking his head slowly, he said, 'It *hasn't* been a month, Caroline. It's been *twelve years*. I've been in love with you for twelve years. Through all the highs and lows. And I told myself it was just a crush because it was the only way I could be around you and not give away to anyone, including myself, how deeply I felt. But it was all a lie and I think you have feelings for me too that might be newer and might feel very different from what you've experienced concerning me before but doesn't make them any less important.'

Caro swallowed as his words resonated deep in her soul. He was right. They'd known each other for years. This thing between them hadn't just happened. It wasn't this surface, floaty, giddy thing making her want to scream it out in performative excitement.

It was a marrow-deep *knowledge*. A realisation. Like maybe it had always been him. The truth was she and Warwick weren't a whirlwind, they were a long, slow burn.

And all she had to do was say the words.

'Yeah.' She nodded, her voice husky. Then she smiled. 'Yeah.'

'Yeah what?'

'Yes. I love you, too.' And it did feel, standing here in front of this man she'd known for ever, that she *had* loved him for ever, too.

He smiled as well and then they were both grinning at each other. 'So if this is *wild* then sign me up,' he said. 'We've already wasted too many years putting other people between us and I don't want to waste another second.' He held out his hand. 'What do you say?'

Her heart brimming, Caro took his hand. 'I say yes.'

And she stepped into the wild with the man she loved.

EPILOGUE

Five years later...

A LUMP THE size of Australia lodged in Warwick's throat as two sweet little fairy girls, identical in every way from their fluffy, flyaway strawberry-blonde hair to their brown eyes and the birthmark behind their left knees, threw rose petals from small, beribboned baskets as they tottered down the aisle towards him.

The entire congregation let out a simultaneous *'Aww'* at the sight and his beautiful daughters—Mabel and Maeve—in their matching wings, petal-skirted dresses and floral wreaths, lapped up every second of the adoration. At just over two years old, they already knew how to play to an audience.

Hudson, standing beside him in a matching tux, leaned in. 'Cutest kids ever, man,' he whispered.

Brad, also in a tux and standing beside Hud, agreed. 'You're a lucky man.'

Warwick smiled at his daughters doing their flower-girl job so diligently. He *was* lucky, even if life hadn't been smooth for him and Caroline. A miscarriage and several rounds of fertility treatment had tested their bond to the limit. But it had never shown a single sign of breaking. If anything it had forged the bond in steel as they'd leaned on each other, carried each other, *loved* each other.

And as he stood here today, his girls looking at him like he hung the moon, waiting for his bride to come down that aisle, he knew he was truly blessed.

Two paces from their final destination, the girls gave up any pretence of decorum, tossed their baskets and ran, arms open, towards him, earning a fresh round of *'Aww*'s.

He swung them up in his arms, one on each side, kissing their foreheads. 'You guys did such a good job,' he murmured.

'We're fairies, Daddy,' Maeve—the younger by five minutes—whispered loudly.

'You are,' he agreed with a grin. 'Fairy princesses.'

'Mummy is a *real* princess,' Mabel said, her tone hushed as if a little in awe.

Then the music changed to the bridal march and he turned his attention to the end of the aisle and understood his daughter's awe. He sucked in a breath, his heart so full it felt like he was choking—Caroline was indeed a princess.

Caro swallowed a lump the size of Australia as she walked steadily, her arm hooked through her father's, towards her destiny. Her beautiful baby girls and her husband-to-be. The man who had loved her since the day he laid eyes on her, who had been there for *all* the hard moments in her life—recent and past—and loved her bigger and harder every time.

Just as she had loved him bigger and harder.

And today they got to celebrate it—formally—this wild, *wild* love that made her feel like the luckiest person in the world. Like she was the only woman in this chapel.

Caro blinked back the tears as she neared the end of the aisle where all that she held dear was waiting for her to begin the rest of their lives. She wouldn't cry on this perfect day, not when her heart was singing.

'I told you she looked like a princess, Daddy,' Mable said as she and Maeve held out their arms to her and Caro unlinked from her father and walked straight into the open embrace of her precious family.

'You ready?' Warwick asked after a long moment, his voice muffled in the huddle.

Caro nodded as she pulled back to look into her three favourite faces, two earnest little cherubs and one devastatingly breathtaking man. 'I am.'

She was more than ready for the rest of her life.

* * * * *

If you enjoyed this story, check out these other great reads from Amy Andrews

Forbidden Fling with the Princess
Harper and the Single Dad
Nurse's Outback Temptation

All available now!

DOCTOR BOSS WITH BENEFITS

JC HARROWAY

MILLS & BOON

To heroes everywhere,
for being brave enough to fight for love.

CHAPTER ONE

Over the span of Dr Greer Thorn's twenty-year career in emergency medicine, the night shift had become her favourite. It enabled her to prioritise raising her daughter. And while tonight was clearly going to be a busy one, she shared the shift with one of the more competent and experienced registrars, Dr Nate Hunter.

Ten minutes earlier, a code blue alert signalled the arrival of the occupants of a car involved in a head-on motor vehicle collision. Both had been critically injured. Knowing Nate assessed the front-seat passenger nearby allowed Greer to focus solely on the driver, a man in his thirties named Dave.

'I need another dose of morphine,' Greer told the staff nurse. 'And anti-emetic, please.'

Dave groaned in pain. The monitors sounded their invasive alarms. Greer could hear the same hurried energy from the other side of the curtain where Nate treated Dave's girlfriend.

'Lie still, Dave,' Greer urged, quickly administering the pain medication via the cannula in his arm.

Her patient's injuries weren't life-threatening. A fractured right clavicle from the seat belt and a fractured right ankle from the brake pedal. That said, he would need admission to the orthopaedic ward. He would, most likely, need surgery. He might even end up under the care of Greer's orthopaedic surgeon ex-husband, who also worked at Kensington Hospital.

As the painkillers worked to ease Dave's discomfort, he quietened and stilled.

Greer poked her head through the curtains into the next resuscitation bay and asked Nate, 'How are we doing over there?'

'I have a fractured sternum and pneumothorax,' Nate replied, his voice calm but pressing.

They'd only worked together for a month but Greer trusted Nate's clinical skills. Greer might be his senior and technically his boss, but, at thirty-two, Nate wasn't far off becoming an emergency medicine consultant. It seemed his patient was clearly the more urgent of the two.

'Blood pressure is falling,' he added. 'It's beginning to tension. I could use your help with a chest drain.'

Leaving her lower-priority and stable patient in the care of Harry, one of the junior emergency doctors, and the nurses, Greer quickly washed her hands and then ducked into the adjacent bay to join Nate.

'What do you need me to do?' Greer asked, their eyes meeting for a second. With one quick glance at the patient's chest X-ray on the computer monitor Greer confirmed Nate's diagnosis. The woman's right lung had collapsed and was at risk of being compressed by the free air inside the chest cavity, which without an escape route would build in pressure and eventually cause a cardiac arrest. A tension pneumothorax, if left untreated, was life-threatening, as evidenced by the piercing alarms recording the woman's pulse, blood pressure and oxygen level.

'Can you draw up some local anaesthetic?' he asked,

then, to the nurses, said, 'Where's that chest tube kit? I need it now.'

The atmosphere was tense, everyone rushing to assist, bodies dodging each other in the limited space. While Greer and Nate hurriedly pulled on sterile gloves, a nurse quickly opened the sterile kit, tipping a scalpel, plastic chest tube, clamps and syringes onto the wheeled tray. Nate had already tried to decompress the pneumothorax by inserting a large-bore needle between the ribs on the anterior chest wall, but the definitive treatment was a tube thoracostomy.

'Kathy, I need to put a drain between your ribs to help that collapsed lung expand, okay?' Nate explained to the patient, his voice soothing despite the sense of urgency and time pressure.

The patient's monitor alarms sounded once more, telling them all what they already knew: her blood pressure was dangerously low and they needed to act fast.

Greer drew up the local anaesthetic into the syringe. Nate swabbed the skin with iodine. While he injected the local anaesthetic and then made a small incision between the ribs under the patient's arm, Greer peeled open the chest tube from its sterile wrapper and connected the tap that would allow the air compressing Kathy's lung to escape.

Working quickly but expertly, Nate guided the tube through the incision with practised ease, and as Greer released the clamp and the air in the chest could finally escape, relieving the pressure on the collapsed lung, Kathy gasped.

'Well done, Kathy,' Nate told the woman, glancing at the monitor where the blood pressure had now stabilised. 'That should help ease your breathing. I'm going to suture and tape the tube in place and then we'll repeat your chest X-ray, okay?'

The woman nodded gratefully. Greer too breathed a sigh of relief as her stare met Nate's once more. She gave him a nod she hoped conveyed praise for his competence and quick thinking. As ED doctors, they were used to operating under adrenaline-charged conditions, but they were still human. Sometimes, it was impossible to be unaware of the life-or-death stakes of their work.

With the immediate danger over, Greer and Nate finished up with their patient and headed to the computer terminals to write up their notes, review test results and organise referrals.

'Well, the night is off with a bang,' she said, seeing from Dave's notes that her patient had already been admitted to the orthopaedic ward. Well done, Harry.

'I like the adrenaline, don't you?' Nate asked, shooting her a confident smile she couldn't help but return.

She'd noticed that when it came to his work, he liked to be right but wasn't overly arrogant.

'Sometimes,' she said, his curious expression making her pulse accelerate. 'Although nights are generally a bit quieter than this.'

And while she loved her job, she also loved parenting Lily, a role she intended to fiercely cling to until her daughter left home for university after the summer.

'Thanks for your help with that chest drain,' he said. 'Sometimes you just need an extra pair of hands.' He glanced up from the computer screen, his dark brown eyes holding her gaze for a little too long, as they often did.

Maybe that was another confidence thing.

'That's my job,' she said. 'Not that you really needed me.'

Nate shot her a curious smile. 'I guess I do know my strengths. And weaknesses, for that matter.'

Greer looked away, both certain that his weaknesses were few and embarrassed that she often felt uncertain of her self-assured, handsome registrar. At six-foot-three with an athletic build, dark hair and eyes and a charming smile, he'd been an instant hit with most of the single nurses and with the patients alike. Charm and charisma most definitely featured on Nate's list of strengths.

But for Greer, older, supposedly wiser and sadly cynical since her divorce, her intense awareness of him complicated their every interaction and felt wrong. Dangerous. Forbidden. It made no sense, but, in his company, she simply couldn't fully relax. He had this way of looking at her that made her feel as if he knew what she was thinking. As if he knew she found him very attractive just like those single nurses his own age. Hopefully she was mistaken. Because lusting after a colleague eleven years her junior who was also under her supervision must be a sackable offence.

Greer sighed, focused on checking her patient's lab results. Maybe she'd been alone for too long… After all her ex had moved on. And on and on. She'd lost track of his girlfriends.

'And I appreciate your help all the same,' Nate said, his voice tinged with amusement. 'Not every consultant is as…collaborative with juniors as you.'

Taken aback by his compliment, Greer looked up to find that his dark stare had turned inquisitive as he watched her in that undaunted way of his. As if he found *her* fascinating.

'Aren't they?' Greer concealed a small flustered shudder, easily dismissing the idea he was interested in her beyond their working relationship as she'd been doing for the past month. 'But I'd hardly call you a junior. You have your exams, right?' she asked about the professional postgrad qualification required to apply for a consultant post.

He might be younger than her, but, career-wise, he wasn't far off being her professional equal. Greer wasn't one to pull rank, not when a registrar like Nate could very soon become a consultant colleague.

'Yeah, of course,' he said, his fingers flying over the keyboard as he typed.

Greer glanced his way again, something about the set of his broad shoulders telling her his comfort level had slipped. 'So are you applying for any consultant posts? I hear St Mary's has a vacancy.'

Nate finished typing his sentence and turned to face her. 'Not right now. Maybe in six months' time.'

Greer frowned, surprised at his reluctance to apply for the top job. 'Most registrars can't wait.'

'I'm happy to do things my way. What's the rush?' he said with a careless shrug. 'I'm enjoying gaining the extra experience. I like to be good at my job.' He smiled again, obviously confident in his decision as he was in everything.

Greer scoffed softly. 'I don't think anyone could find you lacking there, Nate.'

Within two minutes of meeting Nate Hunter, Greer had known exactly what kind of doctor he was. Calm, self-assured and decisive, he had the precise personality required for a career in emergency medicine, which could be fast-paced, unpredictable and often high-stakes. If he was something of a perfectionist, that could only be a strength in their profession. But he tempered what might be perceived as arrogance with an appealing degree of humility and maturity. Combined with his natural charm, keen intelligence and tall good looks, he had an innate knack of putting patients at ease.

Greer glanced down at his feet, wondering if his popularity with patients was in part also influenced by his penchant for colourful food cartoon socks. Today's were lime green and decorated with watermelon slices.

'You like these, huh?' he asked, lifting the leg of his scrubs slightly to show them off. 'My nephew bought this pair.'

Greer glanced back at her computer screen, flustered that he'd caught her checking out his socks. 'Your burger socks are my favourite,' she said, with a straight face, ignoring his charming smile and the way his dark brown eyes sparkled when he was pleased with himself.

She shouldn't be noticing his wacky sock collection, his expressive brown eyes or the way his scrubs showed off his muscular build and tight backside. Just because she found him attractive there was no need to lose her very sensible and mature head. He didn't wear a wedding ring, but he must be taken. He probably had a sexy girlfriend of his own age. Or maybe he played the field, used dating apps for steamy hook-ups she was too terrified to even imagine. Whereas she was a single, forty-three-year-old divorcee with a demanding job with unsociable hours and a strong-willed teenaged daughter as her main priorities.

'Noted, boss,' he said with a playful mock salute, his grin widening as if she'd said something hilarious. 'I'll wear those next time we share a shift.'

Unsettled by the intimacy of his promise, Greer cleared her throat, which had tightened the minute she'd started thinking about her gorgeous colleague's sex life. 'Right, back to it,' she said as she stood and logged out of the computer, slipping on her usual professional demeanour, before he thought she was flirting and reported her to HR for harassment.

Just then, Sally, one of the young, pretty nurses, approached.

'Dr Hunter,' she addressed Nate, blushing slightly because she obviously fancied him too, 'we're expecting a patient with status epileptics in Resus any minute.'

'I'll see the patient,' Greer said to Sally and then, to Nate, 'You finish up what you're doing.' She tucked her chair under the desk as if to draw a line under their earlier playful conversation about socks and her ridiculous imaginings.

Of course Nate Hunter wasn't interested in her, not when he could have his pick of women his own age. Just because today was the four-year anniversary of her divorce, a day that marked the years of solitude—no dates, no sex, no romantic connection—was no reason to fixate on her incredibly hot registrar. Or to imagine that sometimes, when he looked at her in that inquisitive way, *he* might be flirting.

'You're sure?' he asked, a curious look in his intense eyes as he watched her gather her stethoscope and phone.

'Absolutely.' Greer nodded, grateful to have a legitimate reason to escape him and that tension that must be all in her head. 'You'll probably have chance to pay me back later.' She tried to smile in a friendly manner. 'It's obviously going to be one of those long and busy nights. Not that I'm complaining. I like it busy.'

Less time to imagine fictitious flirtations with a younger man. To dread the prospect of *empty nest syndrome* once Lily left home. To face her fear of dating, something that, unlike her ex-husband, she'd successfully avoided since their divorce.

'Maybe I can also make you a coffee later,' Nate called as she headed back to Resus to await her next patient.

Greer continued walking, offering him a casual thumbs-up over her shoulder, telling herself his looks and compliments and thoughtful gestures were simply friendly and respectful.

Because even if the flirtation was real and not imagined, it was also irrelevant. Greer was a mature professional woman with an almost eighteen-year-old daughter. Lily had been through enough heartache and change in recent years without Greer introducing new men into her life. Attractive, confident Nate Hunter was either already in a relationship or playing the field where there were, no doubt, many eager hopefuls. Whereas she had the emotional baggage from her own upbringing, an ex-husband who worked at the same hospital to provide the near-daily reminders of the guilt and regret she carried over her failed marriage. And more importantly, she was Nate Hunter's boss, responsible for his ongoing medical education and professional supervision.

For all his sexy good looks, nothing could ever happen between them and that suited Greer just fine.

CHAPTER TWO

IF REQUIRED, NATE COULD compile a whole list of reasons why he was deeply attracted to his very sexy boss. Aside from her beauty—long, dark hair, big brown eyes, gorgeous curves and a stunning smile—she had an elegant way of carrying herself that appealed. Combine that with her intelligence and a dry sense of humour he'd barely glimpsed and, for him, Greer Thorn represented the epitome of seriously attractive femininity.

And sometimes, when she looked at him and then quickly looked away, often blushing slightly, he knew she fancied him too. Knew she felt the chemistry that was obvious during every non-urgent conversation they had. The chemistry that had been there from day one when he'd joined Kensington Hospital and they'd been introduced.

Of course, instinct told him she'd likely never do anything about it, but as the weeks passed, Nate found it harder and harder to ignore. These days, he went after what he wanted. Because he'd learned the painful way that life was often too short to harbour regrets.

Just before dawn, during a quiet moment in the department, Nate headed for the doctors' office to make Greer the promised coffee. He was pouring boiled water into two mugs when the door opened and she appeared, her stare appearing a little fatigued, but her hair neat as if she'd brushed it.

'Just the person I was about to come looking for,' he said, adding a splash of milk to her coffee, just as she took it. 'The coffee I owed you.'

'Oh, thanks.' Greer smiled tiredly, taking the drink and sinking into a comfy chair with a sigh. 'Are things still quiet out there?'

'Yeah,' he said, choosing the seat but one to her right. 'I'm awaiting blood results and X-rays on my last two cases. And there aren't too many obnoxious drunks in tonight, which makes a nice change.'

He flashed her a playful grin, grateful that Greer was the perfect consultant, exhibiting a balance of support and trust in his abilities. He hated the ones who constantly hovered, checking up on his every move as if he were a freshly minted medical student in a pristine white coat. He worked hard to prove himself good at this career. He needed to.

'There's always at least one,' she said with an answering smile.

Kensington Hospital wasn't far from Kensington High Street and its collection of bars, pubs and restaurants. On any given night there were usually a handful of people who'd overindulged, lost their balance and fallen, wandering into the ED with cuts and sprains, impaired judgement and righteous belligerence.

'I prefer my night shifts a little busier than this though,' Greer said with a sigh as she sipped her coffee. 'Boredom is a killer. Too much time to think...'

Nate nodded in agreement. 'Keeping busy is an excellent coping mechanism,' he said, wondering from what unwanted ruminations Greer suffered.

Fortunately Nate's shift work, his free time spent with his nephew, kept him pretty exhausted. Because in those quiet moments… That was when the regrets came. The memories, good and bad. The grief.

'Feel free to get your head down for a couple of hours,' he offered Greer, because there were on-call rooms with beds for the extremely rare possibility of time to rest. 'I'll call if I need you.'

Some consultants made themselves scarce unless there was a serious case. But not Greer. She mucked in with the junior doctors, took her share of cases and not just the easy ones. She also took every opportunity to supervise procedures and educate those in training. Maybe that was another reason he found her so…intriguing. She was a definite team player and while Nate needed to be good at his job, he also appreciated Greer's support and years of experience.

'Thanks, but I'd rather push on through,' she said. 'I've spent years retraining my circadian rhythms for night shifts. Can't mess with the sleep patterns now.'

'Fair enough,' he said, curious about her personal life, of which he only knew the talk he'd overheard—that she was divorced and had a teenaged daughter. 'Is that why you stick to night shifts?'

Where Greer was concerned, he'd paid attention. While Nate, like the other registrars, worked a rotating shift pattern, Greer worked only nights. And he looked forward to those nights when they worked together.

'I've grown to enjoy them over the years.' She nodded, looking at him with answering curiosity. 'Especially now that my daughter is older. They weren't quite so easy when she was young.'

'How old is she?' he asked, certain that Greer would

tell him if she wanted him to mind his own business. She could be firm but fair. Always clear and direct.

'She's almost eighteen,' she said on a mock sigh that made him laugh. 'She's in the middle of her A level exams. I'll just have time after our shift to rush home, make sure she's awake and wish her luck for today's.'

Nate winced, recalling years of exam stress. 'What's the subject?'

Fortunately exams were years away for Callum, although Nate's sister-in-law, Maggie, was already dreading the teenage years without Dylan. Nate would continue to be there for his late brother's son, but no amount of excelling at his job or helping out with childcare could atone for missing the signs that his brother was sick. Dylan should be the one spending weekends with his eight-year-old, hanging out, going to the park or playing computer games.

'Further mathematics,' Greer said, drawing Nate away from his guilt and shame and grief. 'She wants to study astrophysics at uni next year.'

'Wow,' Nate said, impressed. 'She sounds like a very smart cookie.'

Greer nodded, her stare filled with pride. 'She studies hard, too. Do you have kids?'

Her voice rose in pitch as if he made her nervous. But her curiosity about his personal life gave Nate a rush of satisfaction. He might not be able to bide his time much longer before he asked her out. 'I don't. But I have a nephew I'm close to, Callum.'

'How old is he?' she asked, glancing at him with interest, as if she'd made assumptions about him and he'd surprised her.

'He's eight going on sixteen.' He crossed one ankle

over his other knee, flashing the watermelon-slice socks she'd noticed earlier. 'Thinks he should be allowed a phone like some of his friends.'

She laughed and Nate immediately knew he could get addicted to that rare sound. It drew his attention to her parted lips, to their curves and apparent softness, the pronounced cupid's bow he wanted to trace with the tip of his tongue.

'So what are you trying to avoid thinking about?' he asked to distract himself from the dangerously strong impulses. His attraction to Greer had been instantaneous. Violent even, only strengthening when he'd found out from the nurses that she'd been divorced from the tall, commanding Mark Thorn, an orthopaedic surgeon at the hospital, for four years. Rumour was she hadn't dated since.

'Oh, just life,' she said with a casual shrug. But her smile dimmed. She obviously hadn't survived the divorce unscathed.

'How it sometimes fails to pan out the way we expect?' he gently suggested, able to relate.

Being an identical twin meant he'd grown up never knowing life without his brother. Until the worst had happened and Dylan had died, snatched away at the age of thirty after a brief illness Nate hadn't spotted soon enough. Not a day passed when he didn't regret that he'd been too distracted by work and professional exams to see the signs. When he didn't berate himself both for letting Dylan down and for Nate's grief-stricken error of judgement months after the funeral.

She looked up, surprised. 'Yes.'

Nate shrugged. 'We all have sorrows and regrets,' he said quietly, his own mistakes a bitterness on his tongue.

The memory of the night he'd slept with Maggie while they'd both been grieving for Dylan, both comforting the other, both immediately certain after it was over that it had been a terrible mistake, still brought him shame. 'Or circumstances we find challenging.'

'Or circumstances we've partly created,' she added with a resigned twist to her mouth.

'That too.' He nodded, holding her stare. 'But for what it's worth, I admire you. You work hard. You're an inspirational consultant and I know you're well respected by everyone here. And it sounds as if you've done a great job of raising that incredibly smart daughter of yours.'

She stared, blinking, as if shocked to hear such praise. 'I don't know about that...' She glanced at her lap. 'Divorce messes kids up. Today is my divorce anniversary, actually. Four years,' she scoffed bitterly and raised her coffee mug as if in a toast.

Nate touched his mug to hers, holding her stare as they both sipped. 'I'm sorry about the divorce.'

'Oh, don't be sorry,' she said, shaking her head as if flustered. 'My regrets are more to do with how long I allowed the marriage to limp along rather than its inevitable demise.'

'So you ended it?' he asked, understanding her regrets more clearly now. She obviously put her daughter's needs first, probably why she was still single. Whereas if the rumours were to be believed, Mr Thorn had dated extensively since their divorce.

But there was no way Nate could be similarly open with Greer. His ex, Mia, the last woman he had told about his mistake with Maggie, had been horrified. Unable to tolerate his ongoing close relationship with his brother's widow, she'd broken things off with Nate, compounding the paralysing guilt and failure he'd already felt by betraying Dylan.

'The decision to split was mutual,' she said carefully. 'We're trying to stay on good terms for Lily's sake. My parents are divorced, so I know the impact it can have on family. I never want my daughter to feel trapped in the middle.'

Nate nodded, his attraction now a persistent buzz, demanding more and more attention. 'Well, cheers to that.' Nate touched his coffee mug to hers once more. 'To fresh starts.'

She watched him curiously. His pulse surged with excitement. Now seemed the perfect moment to ask her out. He went after what he wanted and despite Greer's attempt at humour, to downplay the impact of her marital breakdown, this was the closest they'd come to a personal conversation.

'I don't know if you're seeing anyone at the moment,' he said, 'but would you like to grab dinner some time?'

Her cheeks immediately flushed, and he hid a smile of satisfaction. 'With you?' she croaked, her composure slipping slightly. Obviously he'd surprised her again.

Nate smiled and shrugged. 'Yeah, of course with me. Who else? I'm not asking for a friend.'

'I... I...' she stuttered, as if dumbfounded by his interest in her.

'I'm assuming we're both single,' he continued. 'We have heaps in common. Why not get to know each other better?'

'Because...' Her stare held his but she swallowed hard as if preparing an answer. 'I'm not sure it's a good idea.'

'Why?' Nate turned and leaned a little closer, witnessing the telling dilation of her pupils. Part of her liked the idea. 'Because we work together?'

'Yes, that,' she said, her breathing speeding up as her stare flitted over his face, to his mouth and back. 'And I don't really do dating. That is, I haven't bothered since my divorce.'

'Well, you said it earlier: it's been four years. Perhaps it's time to start thinking about yourself.' Like her ex-husband.

She shook her head, looking away. 'I work full-time. And if I'm not working, I take care of my daughter. That's really all I have time for.'

'But Lily will be leaving home soon.' Surely she was running out of excuses and she hadn't explicitly said no. Otherwise he'd have immediately backed off.

'I couldn't possibly...' She shook her head again as if convincing herself, but she didn't move, only continued to stare. 'I mean, I'm technically your boss.'

Seeing the excited flutter of her pulse in her neck, Nate leaned closer and lowered his voice to a playful whisper. 'I won't tell anyone if you don't.'

She gaped, but not before he witnessed the definite flicker of interest in her eyes.

'Look, in all seriousness, Greer,' he said, pushing his case, 'I'm man enough to handle our boss-subordinate power dynamic. I promise to voice my consent or lack of, so you don't have to worry about taking advantage of me, if that's what's stopping you.' He playfully raised his eyebrows.

She was obviously intrigued. And flustered, maybe even a little turned on by the idea. Oh yes, she felt this too—the driving forces of two people who just clicked, regardless of logic or convention.

'I'm certain HR would have something to say about it,' she said, her voice croaking as if her throat was tight.

'Are you?' His pulse surged at her expression of wavering hesitation. 'There's no explicit rule that I'm aware of against hospital colleagues dating.'

She opened her mouth to argue and closed it again.

'I've seen the way you look at me, Greer. I know that, like me, you've felt this connection between us. It's been there from the start. Since my first day.'

He'd obviously been right about their chemistry; she did fancy him back. She simply wasn't used to putting her needs first or she was hung up on their age gap or scared it might break a hospital management rule.

She sucked in a tiny, telling gasp of shock. 'But I'm older than you. A *lot* older.' Her breathing sped up, her breasts rising and falling as if daring him to lower his stare.

'That doesn't bother me.' Nate leaned closer, his arm on the chair's armrest only a hair's breadth from hers. 'We have insane chemistry. We've ignored it for a month, and we can continue to do so, but, until we stop working together, it isn't going to go away.' And they were still negotiating. She hadn't dismissed him outright and walked away. 'You're a beautiful woman. I like you. Respect you. It's just a date. We could have a good time.'

'A good time?' she all but whispered as if the concept was foreign or her mind was going to some X-rated places.

Hell, yeah… Fighting his own heated imaginings, Nate nodded, the soft pants of her breaths drawing his attention once more to her entirely kissable parted lips. It had been a while since he'd dated. Maybe too long, because, as inappropriate as it was while at work, he really wanted to kiss Greer. To see if she'd moan his name, run demanding fingers through his hair, press her gorgeous body to his as they tried to get closer.

She sighed. 'I—'

But before she could finish what might have been another feeble argument and before he'd need a cold shower to calm down, the department's code blue alarm sounded.

Without hesitation, both he and Greer abandoned their coffees and took off running for the resuscitation bay, led by the flashing lights and deafening alarm.

'Seventy-nine-year-old brought in by a friend with chest pain, collapsed on arrival,' the nurse told them as everyone present acted swiftly to follow the cardiac arrest protocol.

'He's in VF,' Nate said, after glancing at the cardiac monitor.

'You defibrillate,' she told Nate as she relieved the nurse who'd been doing the chest compressions, taking over while calling for intravenous adrenaline.

With another nurse inflating the patient's lungs, Nate fired up the defibrillator. 'Do we have venous access?' he asked Harry, who'd initially seen the patient.

'Yes,' someone said as the anaesthetist arrived and quickly intubated the man and took over inflating the lungs.

'Shocking,' Nate said. 'All clear.'

Greer stopped the chest compressions and stepped back. Nate placed the defibrillator paddles on his chest to deliver a shock.

'Still in VF,' Greer said, recommencing the CPR.

'That's three minutes,' Nate informed the team, tracking the time elapsed. 'Administering adrenaline.' He flushed the drug through the patient's intravenous cannula and recharged the defibrillator to repeat the cycle.

At the next pause, the next shock to the heart returned it to a normal rhythm.

'I have a pulse,' Greer said, her relieved stare meeting his as if she was seeking confirmation.

'Sinus rhythm,' he said calmly, a surge of euphoria holding his stare to Greer's. 'Let's take bloods,' Nate instructed Harry, the patient more pressing than his connection with his boss. 'A chest X-ray and an ECG.'

'I'll call the medical registrar,' Greer told Nate, 'if you take a history from the friend who brought him in.'

Nate nodded, his head firmly back in work mode following their moment of honesty in the staffroom. Their conversation would need to be postponed but not indefinitely. Nate refused to see Greer's objections as obstacles. If she'd wanted to say no, she'd have done so. Obviously she, too, felt this thing between them, which wouldn't be silenced for much longer. And Nate had enough regrets without adding a missed chance to explore something with a woman like Greer. But for now, until he could once more get her alone and press her for a real answer, he'd need patience.

CHAPTER THREE

THE FOLLOWING AFTERNOON, after wishing Lily luck for her maths exam and then heading to bed for a few hours' sleep, Greer awoke still confused by Nate's shocking invitation.

There had been no time after the cardiac arrest to discuss it further. Greer had spent the remainder of her night shift busily admitting a steady stream of patients: one with an acute asthma attack, an unstable diabetic in ketoacidosis and two elderly women with falls who'd both sustained a fractured neck of femur requiring orthopaedic referrals to her ex-husband's registrar. And Nate had been similarly occupied with his own cases.

But now, as she stepped under the shower to fully wake herself, their exhilarating conversation was all she could think about.

For the past four years she'd focused on raising Lily after the upset of the divorce and having to split their assets and move to a much smaller place. What with guiding her daughter through her teens while also working full-time, there had been little time to analyse her feelings of loss over the relationship, or the emotional, physical and financial upheaval of the split. She certainly hadn't been ready to face dating again or meeting men who might have their own emotional baggage. Because who didn't at her age?

But maybe four years without any romantic contact was a mistake because, despite her many objections, she found Nate's sexy proposal, his resolve that the age gap didn't bother him, more tempting than she should. It would be easy to reason that if it didn't bother him, why should it bother her? And he was right about their chemistry and how much they had in common. He'd even surprised her when he'd talked about his close relationship with his nephew.

But…

Lily was still her priority. Her daughter had dealt with enough change. Having to move homes, being shared between her parents, Mark introducing her to a new girlfriend every few months. Greer had no intention of competing with her ex on that score. But Nate had only suggested dinner. It needn't go any further than that and they could keep it a secret, especially at work.

Emerging from the shower still torn, Greer brewed tea, reaching for a second mug when she heard the front door open and knew it would be Lily.

'How was it?' she called from the kitchen, trepidation hollowing her stomach. Maths was Lily's strongest subject, but you could never tell which way an exam would go. And no matter how well prepared Lily was, Greer had still had to deal with the inevitable tears and bouts of doubt.

'Terrible…' Lily muttered, slinging her backpack onto the floor in the hallway.

'Really?' Greer asked, her heart thudding. She hated to see Lily dejected, especially when there was little she could do to fix things. 'Was it genuinely terrible,' she asked, keeping her voice calm, 'or just standard terrible because it was an exam?'

'I don't know.' Lily flopped onto the sofa dramatically and stared ahead at the blank TV screen, clearly exhausted. 'Probably the latter...'

Greer placed a mug of tea and a half-eaten packet of chocolate Hobnobs in front of her daughter and sat beside her on the sofa.

'Well done.' She tapped Lily's knee. 'You're almost halfway there. I'm sure you did better than you think. Best not to dwell on it now that it's over.'

Lily sighed just as her phone pinged with an incoming text. She pulled it from her pocket and scanned the screen, her thumbs flying as they typed a rapid reply.

'That was Dad asking how it went,' Lily said with another long-suffering sigh, sliding her phone onto the coffee table. 'It would be really good if you two could communicate, then I wouldn't need to repeat everything twice.'

Greer nodded and silently counted to five. 'We do communicate about you. All the time. But yes, I can imagine how tedious it must be to have to repeat yourself. I'm sorry.' She concealed a wince of guilt, certain that Lily was simply lashing out, a hypothesis that was confirmed when her daughter wordlessly turned to Greer and hugged her tightly.

Greer hugged her back, stroking her curly hair the way she'd done since Lily was a baby. 'Everything is going to be fine,' she said in her soothing motherly voice. 'You've worked so hard for so long. I promise you that it will all be over soon. That all your preparation will pay off. Then you'll have a wonderful summer holiday and university to look forward to.'

Lily nodded mutely, her arms squeezing Greer's waist a little tighter. Funny that, even now, she still occasionally needed a mum-hug.

'You just need to keep going a little longer,' Greer said, 'jump these last few hurdles and in September you'll be leaving home for new adventures in Manchester.'

Lily nodded again and then looked up, her wide blue eyes full of concern. 'And what about you?'

Greer frowned, taken aback. 'What do you mean? I'll be fine.'

'Will you?' Lily asked, her own frown deepening. 'Because I don't want to have to worry about you being here alone when I'm in Manchester.'

'Why would you worry about me?' Greer said. 'You absolutely mustn't. It's my job to worry about you, not the other way around.'

'Because—' Lily chewed her lip and glanced at her lap, telling Greer something else was bothering her. 'I... I didn't know if I should tell you this... If you'd even want to know... But... Dad is engaged to that physio he's been dating.' She looked up uncertainly. 'He told me when we went for brunch at the weekend.'

Greer swallowed, desperately trying to hide her annoyance from her face. Why couldn't Mark have saved his happy announcement until after Lily's A levels? It was so self-absorbed of him to put his own excitement above their daughter's peace of mind.

'You don't have to keep secrets from me, darling,' she said softly, hating that their divorce had inevitably put Lily in the middle, despite Greer's best attempts to keep things amicable. Because she knew exactly what that felt like from her own upbringing, from her own parents' long-winded marital troubles. Her father's cheating then swearing he would change. Her mother repeatedly forgiving him but never able to trust him again. The endless tension in the home that, at Lily's age, Greer had been desperate to escape.

But no matter how hard Greer tried not to succumb to one-upmanship with her ex, Mark was selfishly putting his needs first.

'I didn't want you to be upset that he's getting remarried,' Lily said, still staring at her lap.

'I'm not upset about that,' Greer insisted, trying to calm down. 'Dad and me have been over for a long time. We both walked away from the marriage, which was simply no longer working for either of us. If he's met someone else and is happy, then I'm happy for him, okay. Don't you give it, or me, another thought, especially not now that you have so much else going on.'

This was exactly what she'd spent the past four years protecting Lily from. The breakdown of her and Mark's marriage, their divorce, were nothing to do with their daughter. After several years of dysfunction and resentment, they'd both agreed that, on reflection, they probably shouldn't have rushed to get married when they'd fallen pregnant with Lily after only a year of dating. They'd tried their best to make a marriage work and had succeeded for a while. But eventually with Greer's hang-ups, her tainted expectations of marriage and men in general, and with Mark's propensity to shut down his emotions and withdraw when challenged, the unpredictable demands of their careers had led to too many arguments and they'd drifted apart, existing side by side rather than as a loving team.

'I can't stop thinking about you, Mum,' Lily said quietly. 'It's been four years and you haven't been on a single date. Unlike Dad...'

Greer laughed off her daughter's accurate observation. 'I've been busy. Working, being a mum, spending time with my girl.' She brushed a stray curl from Lily's cheek. 'But you should be focused on your own life.' Not dealing with the dramas of her parents' love lives. Or sad lack of one in Greer's case.

Lily looked up, hesitation in her stare. 'Dad's been doing those things too, but he's managed to find time to date and move on and get engaged.'

Greer nodded, furious with Mark for his thoughtless timing. 'And just because I'm single right now doesn't mean you need to worry about me. I've had other priorities up to now, but that doesn't mean I'll be alone for ever. In fact, someone invited me out to dinner only yesterday.'

She wasn't sure she'd bother getting married again, but maybe she should be open to casually dating the right man.

Lily's eyes widened. 'They did?'

Greer nodded and gripped Lily's hands. 'Yes. And I promise that if I meet someone I'm really serious about, you will be the first to know, okay? But until then, your job is to pass your exams, enjoy your holiday in France, leave for uni and have a wonderful time making new friends and meeting new challenges. Not to worry about the love lives of your parents, who've already had their time as carefree youngsters.'

'Okay.' Lily nodded, appeased. She hugged Greer once more, her upset seemingly easily forgotten. 'Love you, Mum.'

'Love you too,' Greer replied, flashing a brave smile, relieved that Lily, despite her parents' divorce, was so resilient and determined. She was going to miss her daughter when she left home, but would also enjoy every bitter-sweet second of watching her spread her wings.

'So are you going out for dinner with this man?' Lily asked, looking mildly uncomfortable, despite her concerns and her attempts to encourage Greer to date.

Greer flushed, as taken aback by Lily's question as she had been by Nate's. 'I um... I'm not sure yet.'

Long term, Nate obviously couldn't be the right man for Greer to take seriously. But he was charming and attractive. He understood the demands of her shift work and seemed genuinely keen on a date. Maybe the universe was trying to tell her something. Maybe dinner with Nate would be a toe-dip into the daunting world of dating without having to take it too seriously or trawl through the icky profiles of a million strangers.

Lily sighed with relief. 'Well, I'm glad to hear you have offers. Go you, Mum.' She stood, scooped up her tea, the biscuits and her backpack. 'I'm going to hit the physics books.'

Greer nodded and watched her go, her stomach sinking as it once more hit home how much everything was about to change. Soon, the affordable little nest she'd feathered for her and Lily after the divorce would be empty. Greer's life had been all about work, her marriage and motherhood for so long, Lily's absence would leave a massive hole. But it also presented an opportunity. Maybe it was time for Greer to re-evaluate. To rediscover exactly who she was as a single woman with a grown-up daughter.

With the first flutters of possibility dancing in her stomach, she pulled up her shift roster on her phone, scanning the days ahead to find when Nate would be working another night shift. Friday, three days from then.

The hollow disappointment she felt spoke volumes. He'd been right about their chemistry. Right about the way she looked at him, because he returned those same lingering, confidence-boosting stares.

Maybe what she needed, rather than a new hobby—wine tasting, a book club or hiking—was to stop hiding behind her work and her mum duties and start meeting people the way her ex had done. And maybe Nate Hunter, a man she liked, respected and fancied rotten, was as good a place to start as any.

It was three days later before Nate and Greer's night shifts coincided again. Nate had just finished suturing a scalp laceration in a fifty-year-old man he'd discharged with painkillers and instructions to see his GP to have the stitches removed, when he saw Greer at a computer terminal in a deserted corner of the ED. His pulse accelerated excitedly. She'd been constantly on his mind since their last shift. More than once he'd kicked himself for not giving her his number that night before they'd got too busy again.

'How are the exams going?' he asked, pulling up a seat next to hers and logging into an adjacent computer terminal.

'As well as can be expected,' she said with a hesitant smile and excited eyes that told him she'd been thinking of him too. 'I'll be secretly relieved when they're all over.'

He smiled and raised his eyebrows. 'So will she, I imagine.'

Greer nodded. 'I'm getting tired of saying "keep going; it will be over soon",' she said, sounding a little breathless, 'so I'm sure she's tired of hearing such useless advice.'

'But you're making all the difference by simply being there for her.' Nate tilted his head, entranced by her eyes and their long lashes. 'I'm sure she appreciates that, even if she doesn't always tell you. Does she have any plans for the summer, after exams?'

Greer observed him thoughtfully. 'She's spending a fortnight in France with her father. Then she has a summer job lined up for when she returns.'

'Nice. Saving for uni?' Nate asked, wishing he could read Greer's mind. But maybe he could. She'd already outlined all of her misgivings about dating him when he'd asked her out.

'More like for all the cute outfits she can't live without.' Greer rolled her eyes indulgently so he understood she and Lily had a close relationship.

They smiled together and Nate glanced around to make sure they were alone. 'We didn't get to finish our conversation the other morning,' he said, noting the way her breathing sped up as he wheeled his chair a fraction closer.

'No.' She held her ground, her chin tilting up. 'But I'm not sure there's anything new to say.'

'You could answer my invitation to dinner,' Nate said, relieved when she glanced down at his mouth, then met his stare once more. 'I promise that, aside from my terrible taste in socks, I'm good company.'

She pressed her lips together as if holding in a smile, amusement lighting her eyes. 'I'm very pleased to see my favourites tonight.'

'I wore them just for you.' Nate winked then raised the leg of his scrubs and flashed his burger sock.

Greer shook her head, but her lovely lips twitched with amusement.

Nate smiled and waited, knowing she was too direct to leave him hanging again.

'Listen, Nate,' she said, scooting closer, her voice low, as if she didn't want to be overheard, 'I'm not really looking for anything serious right now. Once bitten, twice shy and all that. And I have…priorities. Responsibilities.'

'You said that the other day,' he pointed out, excitement a rush through his system. 'And casual works for me.'

She swallowed as if her throat was dry, but she held his eye contact. 'What do you imagine could happen between us?' A steely glint of sharp intelligence he found incredibly sexy shone in her stare. Greer would never tolerate any games.

Nate raised an eyebrow, a playful smile tugging at his mouth. 'I have a very good imagination, Greer. But zero expectations.' He sobered. 'I find you very attractive. I enjoy your company. Why don't we start with dinner and just take things from there?'

'I'm still not sure,' she said, looking away, her colour rising as if her mind might also be imagining what might come after dinner.

He should be so lucky…

'But you want to say yes,' Nate pointed out, smiling. 'You think I'm attractive too. It's okay to admit it.'

When she looked up, he winked again.

'That's irrelevant,' she said, pressing her lips together, her face barely managing to stay straight as she slowly shook her head in mock disappointment.

Triumph surged through him at her confirmation she was tempted to say yes.

'You were doing so well up until that point,' she said, tutting teasingly. 'I'd almost convinced myself you had none of the arrogance of so many of our counterparts.'

She gathered up her stethoscope and one of the department's tablets they used for accessing patient records, preparing to leave. She pushed back her chair and stood and Nate rose too.

'So is that a yes? I'm willing to wait,' he said, reaching for the pen she'd left on the desk and holding it out to her. 'It's just dinner, Greer. No big deal. If my socks of the day offend you, we can call it quits and forget it ever happened. No harm done.'

She glanced down at the pen and slowly reached for it. As she took it from him, Nate released his grip, his hand deliberately grazing the back of hers.

Her eyes flew to his, her lips parting on a gasp. Nate froze, certain she'd felt it too. The magnetism? The heat? The sizzle of really strong chemistry?

'I'll think about it and let you know,' she said, visibly swallowing and tucking the pen into her breast pocket. But her eyes were bright with excitement and her lips curved into a small, private smile that gave him another surge of hope she'd eventually capitulate.

Nate nodded and stepped back. 'Like I said, some things are worth waiting for.'

And he had no doubt that Greer Thorn was one of them.

CHAPTER FOUR

Two hours later, Greer was about to head to the break room for a drink and mull over exactly how she would tell Nate she'd finally decided to say yes to dinner, when a blue-light emergency arrived. She rushed to the resus room, arriving before the patient to find Nate was already there.

'What's happening?' she asked him, the thrill of their secret adding to the surge of adrenaline a blue light always caused.

'A four-year-old with fever and possible seizures,' he told her, his expression tense with concern.

'He'll probably need a lumbar puncture,' she said, her mind racing. 'I usually perform one in cases like this, just to be on the safe side.'

Nate nodded, looking focused.

'Want me to stick around?' she asked, sharing his obvious clinical concern although he was capable of handling this case alone. A diagnosis of meningitis or encephalitis, both serious, life-threatening infections, would need to be excluded.

'Sure,' Nate said. 'If you're free, that would be great.'

They headed outside just as the ambulance backed into the unloading bay.

'This is Toby,' the paramedic said as she wheeled the

boy from the rear of the ambulance. 'He's pyrexial, temperature thirty-nine-point-two, GCS thirteen out of fifteen. No seizures observed but mum and dad give a good history of a convulsion lasting two minutes, thirty minutes ago.'

Greer and Nate introduced themselves to the boy's parents and, with the help of a nurse, Nate manoeuvred the stretcher into the resuscitation room while Greer spoke to the boy's concerned parents to ascertain any relevant medical history, allergies or current medications.

'Toby,' Nate called the boy, who was drowsy but somewhat rousable, opening his eyes for a second or two before falling back to sleep even while Nate examined him.

'Seizures in young children with a high temperature are relatively common,' Greer explained to the parents. 'We call them febrile convulsions and they affect around one in twenty kids between the age of six months and six years.'

While Nate performed a neurological examination on Toby, Greer tried to reassure mum and dad. 'One short-lasting seizure in a child Toby's age, with his high temperature, doesn't mean there's anything more serious like epilepsy going on. But we do need to exclude some things. The most common cause of the fever is something like an ear infection or tonsillitis or a urinary tract infection,' Greer explained, questioning them further about any additional symptoms that might have accompanied the fever.

'There's no ear infection,' Nate added, having completed his exam. 'So we like to run some tests. Take a sample of blood and urine and also perform a lumbar puncture to exclude a serious infection like meningitis, although that's just a precaution as there are no other signs to suggest that diagnosis.'

'He's very drowsy at the moment,' Greer said, 'which is common after a febrile convulsion. So he might not even feel the tiny needle we use to take blood and give local anaesthetic for the lumbar puncture.'

'You're welcome to stay with Toby if you want,' Nate added, 'or you can go to Reception with the nurse and fill out the admission forms, by which time it will all be over.'

When the parents had reluctantly left, Greer and Nate washed up at the sinks.

'Aside from the temperature and tachycardia, examination is normal,' Nate told her, his mind clearly working through the possible causes of Toby's symptoms.

'I'll insert a butterfly and take some blood,' she said, pulling some latex gloves from a box beside the sink. 'You do the lumbar puncture.'

'Sure.' Nate nodded decisively.

After Greer had taken blood for testing, she and the nurse repositioned Toby on his side, tucking his knees under his chin to flex the lumbar spine and open up the space between the vertebrae.

Wearing sterile gloves, Nate located the spinous process of the fourth lumbar vertebrae, cleaned that area of skin, and injected local anaesthetic while Greer supervised. Using a spinal needle, he carefully accessed the spinal canal and extracted a small sample of cerebrospinal fluid for testing.

'CSF looks normal,' she said, glancing over his shoulder as he removed the needle and covered the puncture wound with a dressing.

'Yes.' Nate nodded, peeled off his gloves and rested his hand on the boy's sleeping head. 'Well done, young man.'

Greer's throat tightened. It was one thing to know Nate was an excellent doctor—competent and dedicated and a hit with patients—quite another to see his compassionate side so openly on view.

'I'll organise the blood tests if you speak to the parents and call Paediatrics,' Greer said, silencing her pager, which displayed a summons to Minor Injuries.

'You're sure you're okay?' she asked Nate, who watched the nurse cover Toby with a blanket and wheel him, still sleeping, from Resus to an observation bay.

He met her stare, a slightly vulnerable look on his face. 'My nephew used to suffer from febrile convulsions at a similar age. They're pretty scary from a parent's perspective.'

Greer nodded in understanding, moved by his closeness to his nephew. She wanted to press him on the relationship. To probe the sadness in his eyes, which seemed greater than his comment would warrant. To reach out and touch him. But she could do none of those things here and now.

'I'll speak to Toby's parents,' he said finally, collecting his stethoscope from the desk and looping it around his neck.

'Okay. Talk later,' she replied, unaware that the rest of their shift would be so busy that she wouldn't cross paths with Nate for the rest of the night.

By the middle of the following week, after several night shifts with another of the emergency registrars, Greer seriously regretted her previous reluctance for Nate's dinner invitation. Checking the staff roster for his name with the giddiness of a schoolgirl, despite being a medical professional and a mature divorcee with a teenager, was something of which she wasn't proud. If only she could stop thinking about him—the hunger in his stare when he looked at her, his charmingly sexy smile, the exhilaration of finally saying yes to their date and starting her journey of empowerment and rediscovery as a single woman.

Sighing after a long busy night in the ED, Greer finished with her final patient, an elderly woman who'd suffered a stroke leading to a fall in which she'd fractured her hip. She washed her hands and stood at a computer terminal to write up her notes. If she sat down she might fall asleep, although her feet were throbbing hard enough to make that possibility highly unlikely.

Glancing up at the clock on the wall, she saw that her shift had officially ended forty minutes ago. Dreaming of a long hot bath and her cool, clean bed sheets, she logged off the computer and headed for the doctors' office to collect her bag.

She rounded a corner and froze in her tracks. Across the department stood Mark. And he wasn't alone. He stood close to a woman dressed in a navy physio's uniform, presumably the fiancée Lily had mentioned.

Mark smiled sexily down at her, resting one hand on her waist as he dipped his head to murmur something that made her laugh. Greer tried not to stare at the couple, but she couldn't seem to look away. Mark, who sported a new, shorter haircut, was clearly smitten with the younger woman, openly flirting in the middle of the ED, and all before eight o'clock in the morning.

His fiancée, who appeared to be in her late twenties with long brown hair and dark eyes, was very attractive. Clearly forty-five-year-old Mark felt deserving of a second chance at love, another shot at making it last for ever. And unlike Greer, he had no qualms about their age gap.

Squaring her shoulders and running a hand over her hair, which thankfully she'd brushed an hour ago while taking the opportunity between patients to freshen up and clean her teeth, Greer approached the love birds.

'Mark,' she said, dragging his attention from his companion. 'Are you here to review Mrs Philips? Fractured neck of femur? I spoke to your reg.'

Mark's name had been on the orthopaedic surgery roster for referrals today.

Mark straightened guiltily, the look he shot her petulant. 'Yes, I was passing on my way to clinic, so thought I'd take the case,' he said, slinging his hands in the pockets of his smart suit trousers, his white shirt taut across his lean torso. He'd lost some weight to go with his new haircut and looked good. Happy and healthy.

'Greer, this is Cara Atkins, my fiancée,' he added with only the barest hint of smugness. 'Cara, this is Lily's mother, Greer Thorn.'

Greer stuck out her hand and smiled warmly at the woman, who, on closer inspection, was strikingly beautiful. But then who wasn't at her age?

'Good to meet you, Cara,' she said, 'and congratulations on your engagement. Lily told me last week. Have you set a date?'

Greer didn't want to end up bitter. She bore Mark no ill will. As far as she'd known, and despite her suspicious nature over the years, he hadn't cheated on her. As long as his new relationship didn't impact on their daughter in any negative way, she was happy for them both. And if Cara was to become Lily's stepmother, Greer wanted to get to know the woman better.

'We thought at the end of the summer,' Cara said, shyly. 'Before Lily leaves for Manchester. We've asked her to be bridesmaid.'

'I'm sure she's excited by that.' Greer smiled, unable to locate a single iota of envy. In fact she'd spent the last five years of their marriage surprised it had endured as long as it had, concluding that they'd each clung to the wreckage for their daughter's sake. 'I'm happy for you both.'

Cara, perhaps finally feeling awkward, muttered something about seeing a patient and departed.

'Mrs Philips is in bay nine,' Greer told Mark, preparing to leave, too.

She was bone-tired and emotionally wrung out. Not from jealousy or regret over losing Mark, but from the growing realisation that, with Lily leaving home soon, with Mark having moved on and about to be remarried, Greer had a duty to begin prioritising *her* needs. To re-assess her dreams and wants and hopes. To be a whole and stronger person. To thrive. After all, she'd ignored her personal life for too long. She too deserved to be happy one day. Deserved for now to have a good time, to flirt and laugh and bask in the feeling that someone found her attractive.

'Tell Lily I'll see her Saturday,' Mark said as she turned away.

When she looked back, the eager smile he'd worn for his fiancée had vanished.

Greer nodded. 'I will.' Then she paused as another thought occurred. 'Is it still just the two of you going to France?'

She didn't really want to know his business, but she wouldn't want Lily to be blindsided if she had to play gooseberry to the newly engaged couple on what was supposed to be a dad and daughter holiday planned long ago.

'Yes, of course.' His stare narrowed, his defences clearly building. 'Why do you always do that? Assume the worst of me? Assume I'll let our daughter down or that I don't care about her as much as you do?'

Greer scoffed, refusing to play this game with him any longer. The one where he put his work, his priorities first and shut down emotionally when challenged. Where he accused Greer of being paranoid and unreasonable. Where he refused to see her point of view at all. She could admit that, because of her past, seeing the fallout of her father's repeated cheating on her parents' marriage, she'd sometimes allowed her unfounded suspicions of Mark to cloud her judgement. But knowing what she'd grown up with, he never seemed to be able to bring himself to communicate openly or reassure Greer.

'You're newly engaged,' she said, calmly. 'It's a fair assumption that Cara might want to join you on holiday. Anyway, have a wonderful time in France and take care of our girl. I'm off home for some sleep.'

And with that, she walked away, not for the first time grateful that at least, alone as she was, she'd achieved an invaluable sense of peace and no longer had to participate in the emotional game-playing that had become her marriage by the end.

CHAPTER FIVE

NATE ARRIVED TEN minutes early for his day shift. He dropped his backpack in the doctors' office and had just clipped his name tag to his scrubs when the door flew open and Greer appeared, out of breath and clearly a little unsettled.

'Hi.' Nate smiled, his pulse accelerating as it always did when he saw her. 'This is unexpected. I thought you'd probably already gone home.' They hadn't worked together for days. Plenty of time for his need to see her to build into a frenzy.

'I'm heading off now,' she said, glancing down as she calmed her breathing. 'I got…held up with a patient.'

'Busy night?' Nate asked, wondering what might have upset her, because his day was already a little brighter from this chance meeting.

'Yes, very,' Greer said, staring at him as if she wanted to say more.

Nate waited, looping his stethoscope around his neck while she watched his every move.

'About dinner,' she blurted suddenly, her voice high-pitched. 'If you can wait until next week when Lily is in France, I… It's a date.'

Nate's smile was automatic, excitement pounding through his blood as he stepped closer. 'I told you I'd wait, Greer. But what's brought on the change of heart? You seemed upset just now when you walked in.'

She shook her head, her stare determined. 'Not upset. Just…distracted. I ran into my ex-husband. Not an ideal end to a busy night. Unfortunately he still knows how to press my buttons.'

'I can imagine that must be awkward,' Nate said and inched closer, intrigued that she'd changed her mind about the date and not remotely jealous of the ex, for all the other man's charm and intelligence.

'More frustrating than anything else,' she admitted breathlessly, still standing with her back to the door. 'Although I think his new fiancée felt pretty awkward. She fled not long after he'd introduced us, poor thing. Taking on an older man with an ex-wife and a teenaged daughter is a lot.'

Nate inched closer still. Her stare darted from his to his mouth and back as if she expected him to kiss her. So he'd been on her mind too…

'Well, I'm glad you changed your mind about dinner,' he said, catching the light coconut scent of her shampoo.

Her breathing sped up, her breasts rising and falling under her scrub top as she looked up at him with fiery desire in her eyes. She wanted him, maybe as badly as he wanted her.

'Of course,' he continued, 'I'd have preferred that your acceptance was unrelated to seeing your ex and his new woman.'

'It *is* unrelated.' Greer stayed against the door, raising her chin to look up at him with resolve and challenge. 'I wouldn't have said yes if I didn't want to go out with you. It never works out when you do something because you think you should.'

'That's good to know.' Triumph surged through Nate, energising him way better than his morning coffee. 'Although you seemed pretty against the idea the other night.'

He dipped his gaze, lingering on her parted lips as he imagined their taste and softness. The moans and pants that might emerge if he were to kiss her right now, to press his body against hers and unleash the passionate woman he instinctively knew was underneath her layers.

'All those reasons I stated still stand, Nate.' Her dark eyes shone as she tilted her chin another defiant notch. 'I'm still older than you. I'm still your boss. But you're right about our attraction.'

'I know I am.' Nate smiled, his heart thudding as he stepped closer still so he heard her soft gasp, felt the heat from her body and the thrill of excitement her closeness caused. While he understood the long list of fears she'd articulated, he wanted her ready to admit the things he saw when she looked at him. He knew with all certainty that if they ever touched, ever kissed, they'd be utterly explosive together.

She was breathless now, some internal constraint—maybe her hang-ups about being older or the fact they were at work—keeping her static, when everything else in her seemed desperate to act, to break this unbearable tension, to buckle and kiss him.

'Shouldn't you be out there?' she whispered, her stare flicking to the clock behind him. But she didn't move from the door, which she knew was his only means to escape the room.

'I have three minutes before my shift begins,' he said, resting his hand above her shoulder, fingers curling around the edge of the ajar door as if he might open it. 'And I'm suddenly in no rush. I'd rather enjoy the way you're looking at me a little longer.'

He was so close now, the scent of her, warm and tempting, tickled his nose. She licked her lips and looked up at him with obvious, unfiltered desire. Finally the truth. Answering need, surprisingly insistent, thrummed through his system, tightening his muscles, heating his blood, sharpening his focus to just Greer.

'How am I looking at you?' she asked, her bold eyes locked to his, her professional mask on the floor so he glimpsed the passionate, sexual, undaunted woman for the first time.

'Like you want me. The same way I'm looking at you.' He held her stare and dipped his head, his lips mere centimetres from hers so he heard the sharp inhale of her breath and felt the crackle of electricity between his body and hers.

'Can you feel it?' he asked, her breath brushing his lips, her scent a warm perfumed cloud luring him towards temptation.

She nodded, transfixed. Beyond them, the noises of the department waking up grew: people coming and going, phones ringing, voices droning. They could be interrupted at any moment, but Nate couldn't bring himself to care. The sound of his blood rushing through his ears drowned out every noise, even his own internal voice of reason.

'Believe me, I want nothing more than for you to kiss me right now,' he said at last, staring into her eyes as his body strained to put them both out of their misery and close the gap.

'What makes you so sure that's my intention?' Despite her denial, she was panting now, her big eyes blinking up at him, hungry with need.

And it would be so satisfying to give them both what they so obviously craved. But when she finally surrendered her last remaining internal battle and kissed him, he wanted to be the only man on her mind.

'I think the time for pretending is over between us, Greer.' When she didn't argue, only glanced down at his lips, so close to hers, he added, 'But I'd rather you kiss me when it's only about us and not him. I said I'd wait for you, but I do have some ego. When you moan my name, I want you thinking only of me and the way *I* make you feel.'

'I—'

He pressed the tip of his index finger to her lips, cutting off further explanations or excuses. 'Tell me another time. I have to go. But our time will come.'

Using every scrap of his willpower, Nate dropped his hand to the door handle and stepped aside, his regret and responsibilities at odds. Looking as turned on as he felt, Greer moved into the room, freeing up the door. She gripped her arm across her chest.

'Sleep well,' he said with a regretful smile, aware of the tiredness around her eyes. 'I'll see you back here Sunday night.'

If she was surprised that he'd memorised their shift rosters, she didn't show it, only gave a shaky nod and a smile tinged with disappointment.

With one last look her way, he locked down the need that had been background noise since the day they first met, left the room and the physical temptation of Greer behind and began his work day, one hundred per cent certain she, and their unfinished business, would be constantly in his thoughts until their next night shift.

CHAPTER SIX

THAT SATURDAY GREER had a rare luxury—an entire day and night off. In preparation for her holiday, Lily was eager to do some last-minute shopping for outfits, so they set off for trendy boutiques lining Kensington High Street, the sun baking the crowded pavement under their feet.

Lily chose her favourite shop, leading Greer into the cool interior.

'I'm going to try these on,' Lily said after ten minutes of browsing, adding a couple of minuscule bikinis to the pile of promising garments draped over her arm. She passed her bag to Greer and wandered off to find the fitting rooms.

While Greer waited, she idly perused the racks near the door where the stream of cool air from the air-conditioning unit was strongest, raising delicious goose pimples over her bare arms and billowing the hem of her skirt around her calves. Not that she was seriously considering any of the garments for herself. This boutique was more appropriate for Lily's age group than her own. Greer kept in shape, but her minuscule-bikini days were sadly over thanks to her Caesarean section scar.

As she had since the morning she'd last seen Nate, the

morning she'd almost kissed him in the doctors' office, Greer wondered for the thousandth time what she'd been thinking. In respect of both saying yes to a dinner date and the almost kiss. Aside from the risk she might face a slap on the wrist from hospital HR for dating a more junior doctor, or getting steamy with him on the premises, she hadn't been on a date with anyone other than Mark for over twenty years.

What if the rules of engagement had drastically changed? What if she messed up, acted too keen or not keen enough? And what on earth was she going to wear for a dinner date with a thirty-two-year-old that could, for all she knew, be anywhere from a burger restaurant to the Ritz Hotel? Certainly nothing to be found in this trendy shop.

Greer had just identified a cute strappy sundress that Lily might like, when someone called her name.

'Dr Thorn.'

Greer turned to see Nate standing there, his charming smile wide with delight, his stare showing only a fraction of the heat from their last encounter, most likely because there was a small boy at his side.

She smiled back, her pulse flying and her knees trembling with excitement and lust at the sight of Nate in casual clothes rather than scrubs: worn jeans and a navy T-shirt, sunglasses perched on the top of his head.

'We were just passing and I spied you through the window,' he said in explanation, his gaze sliding the length of her body down to her toes and back. He licked his lips, a knowing look on his face.

There was now an understanding between them. An honesty she couldn't deny and no longer wanted to. Their chemistry was a massive elephant in the room. An elephant painting itself red, waving a flag and banging cymbals, clamouring to be seen and heard.

'Hi,' she said, instantly overheating at the memory of how easily he'd sensed she'd wanted to kiss him that morning. No doubt he also knew how turned on she'd been by his closeness and the intent look in his eyes and the thrilling things he'd said.

Because she didn't want him to know that he inspired a perpetual state of excitement, she dragged her stare from his and glanced down at the child.

'This is my nephew, Callum,' Nate said, smiling down at the boy and adding, 'Dr Thorn works at my hospital.'

'Nice to meet you,' Greer said to Callum, who looked uncannily like his uncle. Same hair colouring, same nose, same deep brown eyes.

'Hello,' Callum said politely, his face lighting up with surprised delight when Nate pulled his phone from his back pocket and handed it over.

'Just that one game you're allowed,' Nate said with sexy authority, 'and only for two minutes while Uncle Nate talks to Dr Thorn about work, okay?'

Uncle Nate... Even that was sexy.

Callum nodded eagerly. He took the phone as if he'd been handed a pile of gold treasure and sat on the floor just inside the door to enjoy his few minutes of screen time.

When they were alone, Nate stepped closer and dropped his voice. 'It's good to see you. You've been on my mind all week.' His stare shifted lazily over her body, warming the places it landed as if he'd touched her skin. She might have complained if she hadn't appreciated his moments earlier.

'Have I?' Greer asked, her mouth awash with saliva

at how hot he was and how he stared so intently, as if he wanted to devour her. But she needed to play it cool. She didn't want him to think he could read her like a book.

'Mm hmm.' He smiled confidently. 'And you've been thinking about me.'

He stepped another inch closer so she felt the heat from his body and detected the subtle spice of his aftershave. His words from that last morning at work slithered through her mind like a falling silk scarf grazing sensitised skin.

I want nothing more than for you to kiss me right now. I'd rather you kiss me when it's only about us and not him. When you moan my name, I want you thinking only of me and the way I make you feel.

She'd been too turned on by his closeness in that moment to explain that her apparent change of heart over the date had been less about her ex and his fiancée and more of a reflection of how tempted she'd been to say yes from the start. She'd needed time to come to terms with the very inconvenient attraction. Time to rationalise her needs. Her internal battle between *want* and *should* still raged. And Lily would always be her priority.

Reminded that she had bigger concerns than what to wear on their date, this insanely fierce attraction for one, Greer felt her nerves multiply.

'About the other morning,' she said, clearing her tight throat, saying her piece before Lily returned and she missed her chance. 'I'm sorry if my accepting your invitation seemed reactive. It wasn't. I was tempted to say yes the first night you asked me.'

'That's good to know.' His gorgeous smile widened and he inched closer still, his stare nowhere near professional or friendly. 'I'm glad. And there's no need for an apology. Actually I'm the one who's sorry. I should have let you kiss me that morning after all. I deeply regret being so...principled.'

Bitterly recalling how much Mark had loved to hear *I'm sorry*, Greer squashed her excitement. 'Too late now,' she said smugly while she hid her smile. 'You missed your chance.' She tilted her head towards Callum.

Nate grinned, his stare alive with heat and challenge. 'I hope there'll be others.'

Greer concealed a shudder. How could he turn her on with just a look or the way he spoke her name? How was it possible that every time they interacted, her attraction grew and her resolve to play it cool disintegrated? Yes, she was rusty at flirtation, but she was a mature woman. Only he made her feel...light-headed.

'So if it wasn't your ex that made you change your mind,' he said, 'what was it? I don't usually have to beg women to go out with me.'

Greer pretended to consider his question. 'I'd like to have seen the begging, actually. It might have swayed me sooner.'

When he only smiled as if delighted by their banter she continued. 'Your invitation made me realise that, after four years, it might be time for a casual date. Turns out, you were right. This is about us.'

Nate's stare darkened. Then he cupped his hand around his ear and said, 'Sorry, could you repeat what came after "turns out"? I didn't quite catch it.' He smiled triumphantly.

Greer bit her lip to hold in the return smile that threatened. His gaze fell to her mouth as she sucked in a ragged breath that seemed too low in oxygen. Was he thinking about kissing her? Did she imagine she might kiss him here, in a busy shop with his nephew close by? She was so out of practice with this stuff, but now she couldn't scrub the idea of kissing him from her mind.

'I like the dress,' he said, glancing down to where she still clutched the garment she'd picked out for Lily in her fist.

He looked at her as if he wanted to see Greer in the strappy creation. Or even out of it. And her knees quivered with lust. It had been so long…

Greer swallowed hard. How did he manage to make nearly every word that came out of his mouth when they were alone sound sexy? That was another concern—what if all this chemistry they shared led to kissing on their date and then to sex? It had been more than four years for Greer and even then, for the previous twenty years, with the same man.

'It's for my daughter,' she said, refusing to be anything she wasn't. 'She's in the changing rooms. I'm most comfortable in jeans.'

And she didn't need to overthink the sex thing today. Even if she wanted to peel him out of those clothes, they each had plans.

'Where are you two off to?' She glanced over at Callum, who was still engrossed in the phone.

'We're going to the park and then the movies,' Nate said. 'On my Saturdays off I often hang out with Callum to give his mum a break.'

'That's…awesome,' she said, trying and failing to hide her surprise.

'Is it?' he asked, amused.

Greer flushed. 'I just assumed, after working a sixty-hour week, that your weekends would be filled with… social events.' She'd imagined wild parties and numerous dates and casual hook-ups, because Nate was in the prime of his life, hot and single. 'He looks like you,' she added to cover her body's overheated reaction to the idea of Nate's sex life.

Nate's confident smile faltered, a sadness shifting behind his eyes. 'His father and I were identical twins. My brother, Dylan, died two years ago. Hodgkin lymphoma.'

Greer gasped, her hand automatically reaching for his arm. 'Oh, Nate, I'm so sorry,' she whispered, her heart aching for little Callum and for Nate. When he'd mentioned giving Callum's mum a break, she'd assumed the woman was Nate's sister rather than sister-in-law. But this explained why he was so close to the boy.

He shrugged and Greer dropped her hand, the palm tingling from the illicit heat of his skin, the softness of his arm hair and the firmness of his defined forearm muscles.

'Thank you,' he murmured. 'So do you have any plans for when Lily is away?' he asked, changing the subject. 'Are you taking any time off? I hear we're in for a summer of heatwaves.'

'I haven't planned to go anywhere. I'm not sure I can face all the traffic. I might take a few days' leave and just stay home, read all the books I'm normally too busy for and enjoy London and having the flat to myself.'

He nodded and just then, as Nate continued to stare, his smiling eyes doing the talking, Greer became aware of another person joining them.

'Lily,' she said, stepping back from Nate as guiltily as if she'd been plastered all over him, which in her head she had. 'This is a work colleague of mine, Dr Hunter. Nate...' she bumbled, overtalking to cover her embarrassment. She'd completely forgotten about Lily.

How could she? And would her super-smart daughter notice that she and Nate were…friendly?

'The budding astrophysicist,' Nate said calmly, shaking Lily's hand. 'Your mum's been telling the emergency staff how hard you've worked for your A levels. I bet you're glad to have them behind you.'

'Hi,' Lily said, smiling distractedly. 'Yeah, I am. Now it's just a waiting game for the results. Oh, I like that dress. Is it for me?'

Greer nodded and Lily took the garment in exchange for the two tiny bikinis and an armful of tops and shorts that had clearly passed the try-on test.

'Do you mind waiting a while longer while I try it on?' Lily asked Greer, obviously unsuspecting of her and Nate, maybe because of his age.

But then why would Lily suspect anything? While it was socially acceptable for Mark to marry a twenty-something, society was unfairly less forgiving of an older woman, younger man dynamic. Not that Greer was eager to marry again, anyway.

'Of course,' Greer said. 'I'll wait here.'

Lily rushed off and when Greer once more caught Nate's eye, she sighed. 'I haven't told her about you,' she confessed with a wince. 'I've mentioned that someone has invited me out to dinner, just not who or that I've said yes.'

Nate shrugged. 'Hey, it's fine.' He flicked a glance towards Callum. 'We all have our secrets. I don't mind being yours. In fact—' he stepped closer once more '—it's flattering. Kind of sexy in a taboo kind of way.' He waggled his eyebrows suggestively.

Greer flushed and then frowned, curious as to what Nate's secret was and guilty that she'd made him hers.

'It's just that Lily has a lot going on at the moment, what with her father getting remarried. I want her to enjoy her holiday.'

Nate nodded in understanding.

'I…' she went on, 'well, I promised myself when I got divorced that I wouldn't play games of one-upmanship with my ex. I don't want Lily to ever feel like she's trapped in the middle. That her loyalties are torn between her father and me. I grew up like that with my parents and I don't want the same for her.'

'Of course not.' Nate frowned. 'I understand that she's your priority, Greer. We haven't even been out yet so there's nothing to tell anyway. And it's just our business, right?'

Relieved that he was so emotionally mature and articulate, Greer nodded. 'I meant to ask where you had planned for dinner, just so I know what to wear. Jeans or fancy.'

'What's your favourite type of restaurant?' he asked, his eyes smiling as if he couldn't wait.

'Oh, I like everything.' She waved her hand dismissively, flustered because her nerves were back. Would they have anything to talk about? Would she come across as desperate if she kissed him at the end of the night? Would it be awkward at work the next day?

'That's not an answer, Greer,' he said softly, his stare once more penetrating hers. 'Why don't you pick your favourite restaurant close to where you live? Because I'll eat anything, and I'm happy to travel from Shepherd's Bush.'

'My favourite is Greek,' she said. 'There's a taverna called Diamanto's off the Cromwell Road that's really good. I took Lily there for her birthday last year.'

'Sounds perfect.'

As Callum ambled over and passed Nate the phone, his time clearly up, Greer stepped back, away from the delicious heat and scent of him and the bubble of intimacy they'd created among the racks of clothing.

'Thanks, mate,' Nate said, taking the phone from his nephew. But rather than return it to his pocket, he held it out to Greer, his stare full of secret, grown-up, unspoken communication. 'I only have your work number.'

Reading his meaning, Greer quickly typed her contact info into his phone, the illicit thrill of simply giving a man her private number after all this time making her belly tremble.

'Thanks,' Nate said, his voice low and husky. 'Now we can decide on a day that works.'

Greer nodded, certain her eagerness must be written all over her face. 'Bye, Callum,' she said. 'Enjoy the movies.'

After that sexually charged interaction, she needed a second in order to pull herself together before Lily came back.

'I'll see you tomorrow night for our shift,' Nate said, the parting look he shot her hot enough to melt the tarmac on the road outside.

Shaking inside, she watched him leave, his hand on Callum's shoulder as they smiled at each other. By the time Lily returned from the changing rooms for the second time, Greer had almost brought her excited breathing under control enough to act normally. But when her phone pinged a moment later, his text, the two simple words, Nate's number, were enough to shunt her back into a state of frantic excitement. So much for playing it cool…

CHAPTER SEVEN

Sunday night the emergency department was frantically busy. Nate and Greer had no opportunity to speak, as case after case rolled through the doors. But as frustrating as it was to have no time alone with Greer, Nate had the memory of their almost kiss and her messages to keep him warm.

She'd been the one to initiate contact after he'd sent that initial text, suggesting Thursday evening for their dinner date at Diamanto's. They'd even chatted about their Sundays, Greer's enjoying a quiet day at home alone and walking in the park and his playing social five-aside football in Shepherd's Bush before heading into work.

By 4:00 a.m., Nate was in the middle of treating his latest patient—a seventy-eight-year-old man with dizziness and fainting spells due to bradycardia or a slow heart rate—when the man went into cardiac arrest and the heart monitor sounded an ear-splitting alarm.

'Call the crash team,' Nate called, quickly commencing chest compressions while a nurse inflated the man's lungs with a bag and mask.

Within seconds, Greer and a few others arrived, looking to Nate for a history.

'He came in with dizziness and was in complete heart block,' Nate told her, maintaining the rhythm. 'I set up transcutaneous pacing and was just about to insert a central line when he collapsed. Now in asystole.'

Greer nodded and, in keeping with the protocol, administered a dose of intravenous adrenaline. When they paused CPR to check for a pulse, Greer's stare met his.

'I've got one,' she said just as the anaesthetist arrived to monitor the patient's breathing.

'Let's get that central line in and a temporary pacemaker before he collapses again.' Nate moved to the head of the stretcher and quickly established venous access in the right side of the man's neck. Using ultrasound guidance, Nate then passed the cardiac pacing wire through the venous catheter in the internal jugular vein, advancing the tip of the wire until it was situated in the apex of the right ventricle, where it could stimulate the heart to beat at a more effective rate.

'That's a good position,' Greer said, watching his progress on the monitor.

Nate nodded, satisfied with the procedure. With the temporary transvenous pacemaker set to eighty beats per minute, Nate peeled off his sterile gloves, relieved to have successfully resuscitated and treated his patient in spite of the cardiac arrest.

'Call the radiologist back for a repeat chest X-ray,' he told Harry. 'I'll call Cardiology and make a referral.' The man would need a permanent pacemaker fitted under anaesthetic.

With the patient now stable, Nate called the cardiology registrar on call, looking around to find Greer at his elbow.

'Well done,' she said, her eyes saying more than her words. 'For keeping your cool in that situation.'

'Thanks for your help.' As usual, Nate appreciated her support.

'I'd better get back,' she said, regret in the minute tightening of her mouth. 'I was in the middle of admitting another patient.'

'Of course.' Nate nodded, his adrenaline following the emergency draining away so he wished they could snatch a moment to themselves.

'Maybe we'll get a chance for a break soon,' she said, her shift clearly as hectic as his.

'We can hope,' he said with a small smile, his mind on his patient and the test results.

Before she stepped away, Greer hesitated, her lips pressed together as if she wanted to say more but was holding back. Clearly they both were. Looking forward to their date on Thursday, Nate watched Greer leave and then got back to work.

By 5:30 a.m., the rush of new patients had slowed to almost nothing. Needing to wake herself up after a long hectic night, Greer visited the bathroom, splashed cold water on her face, cleaned her teeth and brushed out the tangles in her hair, feeling instantly more awake. In the moment of quiet, she pulled out her phone and reread the messages she'd received from Nate earlier that day, scouring each promising word as she allowed her excitement for their date to finally spill free.

Hope Lily arrived safely in France.

Thursday night works for me.

Looking forward to my next night shift.

Dragging in a shaky breath that did nothing to settle the flutters in her chest, she pocketed the phone and was just heading for the doctors' office to make a reviving cup of coffee, when Nate came around the corner, obviously headed for the same destination.

'How's it going with you?' she asked, her voice catching on a breathless thrill and her fatigue from moments ago evaporating.

How could she be so pleased to see someone she saw all the time? How could a simple smile from him affect her so strongly? If she wasn't careful, a beady-eyed colleague would pick up on how much she fancied Nate. And what then? Would she be called to HR? Would word spread to Mark and then to Lily? She needed to be really careful.

'All good,' he said, following her into the room. 'My pacemaker patient is stable on Cardiac Intensive Care. Since then it's just been cuts and sprains.'

'That's good news,' she said, flicking on the kettle to cover her awareness that the last time they were alone, in the shop yesterday, there was some full-on, non-verbal, X-rated communication happening.

'I couldn't say it earlier,' he said, staring with sincerity, 'but I always appreciate your calm guidance. If no one has told you lately, you're a great emergency doctor and an astounding colleague. I'm lucky to work with you.'

'Thank you.' Greer warmed at his compliment, even as shame for her unprofessional thoughts heated her cheeks. Needing to say something else to break the unspoken tension, she glanced at his feet. 'It's been so busy tonight, I haven't even had a chance to check out today's socks.'

She was nervous again, deflecting, struggling to be vulnerable with him because the last time she'd been that way with a man she'd been let down, hurt, the relationship abandoned.

But this flirtation with Nate was helping her to feel more resilient, hopeful for the future. Certain that as a single, soon-to-be-childless woman, she could one day have a relationship on her terms. With Lily gone to France, she'd had a taste of what her future would look like. The flat was too quiet, but Greer also had space to put her own needs first. To play *her* music and enjoy uninterrupted long soaks in the bath and to find her wardrobe unrifled.

'Hot dogs.' Nate grinned and raised the leg of his scrub trousers, showing the socks off.

'Stop,' she teased, her stomach rumbling. 'I could murder a hot dog right about now. Somehow an apple just won't be the same.' Because she knew he took his coffee the same as hers, she made two mugs and slid one over to him.

'Thanks,' he said, with the same secret smile he'd worn yesterday. 'But now that you've raised the idea, I'm starving for a hot dog, too. What have you done to me?'

She laughed. 'Maybe we should cancel Diamanto's,' she suggested playfully.

'No way. I'm looking forward to it.'

Greer's nervous smile faded when, instead of taking his coffee and sitting down, he stepped closer so her pulse leapt wildly.

'I'd like to pick you up for our date, if that's okay,' he said, his voice low and intimate-sounding.

How...gallant.

'But I'm happy to meet you at the restaurant if you prefer,' he finished, that intense look back on his face.

Greer shuddered and hesitated, her heart banging against her ribs. 'You can pick me up if you want. I live in South Kensington, flat two, Willow Gardens.'

'Great.' He glanced down at her mouth. 'I'll be there. Seven fifteen.'

Greer inhaled a slow shaky breath and nodded, desperately trying to keep her eyes on his and not slide them to his lips and lower, to that triangle of manly chest exposed by the V of his scrub top, and on to his broad shoulders and well-defined pecs… How would it feel to be held in those strong arms? To be desired again? To burn with first-time lust?

'I'm warning you now,' she said, her voice catching, 'I haven't been on a first date for a long time.' While she was excited to dress up and confident that she could maintain suitable over-dinner conversation, her biggest concern was whether she should kiss him at the end of the date.

'I'm not worried about that,' he said, unmoving but for the rapid surging of his carotid pulse. 'Are you nervous?'

'A bit,' she admitted, blinking up at him. 'But I'm looking forward to it, too.' She wanted the time between now and Thursday to fly. She wanted to enjoy this undeniable chemistry between them away from prying eyes. To forget she needed to keep them a secret, from work, from Lily, even from Mark, who would no doubt have something dismissive to say if he found out.

'I'm pretty sure that when it comes to dating nothing's changed,' he said with a playful smile. 'We eat, we talk, I ask if I can see you again.'

Greer fought a smile. 'How do you know you'll want to see me again?'

He tilted his head, a *don't be stupid* expression on his face. 'I'm already looking forward to our second date.'

Greer inhaled. He looked at her with hunger and heat. His height made her feel feminine. His hypnotic hold over her felt dangerous, but she didn't want to come to her senses.

They'd been staring for so long now she dared not move a single muscle. Her heart jerked with trepidation as she weighed the risks—stepping away and wasting this rare and precious moment with him versus staying locked in such intimate proximity that she could see the desire in his stare, hear his accelerated breathing, feel the heat of his body, so close but not quite close enough.

'Do it,' he said quietly, as if he'd read her mind.

Dazed by lust, her pulse roaring through her ears, Greer looked up from his lips, his intent stare luring her closer to reckless surrender. He looked as if he wanted to devour her. The door was closed but not locked. Anyone could walk in in search of them. But she couldn't find the energy to fight the forbidden temptation a second longer.

Ignoring the war between right and wrong, she stepped forward. Nate's hands found her waist as hers curved over his shoulders. He pulled her close. She surged up onto the balls of her feet. With a sigh of released anticipation that almost emerged as a groan, she pressed her lips to his, all the fight she'd battled for weeks draining away.

The thrill of her lips on his struck her like a blast, violent in its intensity. Every one of her former reservations popped like bubbles. Nate pressed one hand between her shoulder blades, his other cupping her face as he deepened the kiss. Greer yielded, her lips parting when his demanded it, her tongue sliding against his as he groaned, her backside hitting the edge of the counter as he stepped forward, his hard thigh between her legs causing all sorts of below-the-waist fluttering.

Panting hard, he broke free of their kiss to stare down at her. 'I've waited so long for this,' he said, sliding his lips along her jaw to her earlobe so her body all but incinerated.

'Me too,' she said on a sigh as her head swam with dizzying exhilaration. She slid her fingers around the back of his neck and into his hair, needing to touch him to confirm he'd feel as good as she'd imagined.

'Can I touch you?' His stare blazed into hers, full of sexy confidence and undeniable promise.

'Yes,' she said, almost begging as she drew his mouth back to hers. Yes, yes, please, yes!

His hand snaked around her waist under her top, his fingertips dancing over the skin at the small of her back, setting off mini explosions along her tingling nerves. While their tongues duelled, their kisses ravenous, his other hand cupped her breast through her bra.

Greer choked out a strangled moan of euphoria. His touch felt so good. And so forbidden. She shouldn't be doing this. Not here. But she'd lost any ability to be rational. She could barely stand, kissing Nate was so hot.

Nate pulled back, watching her hungrily as his thumb rubbed back and forth across her peaked nipple sending tingles of delight radiating throughout her body. 'You are so sexy.'

'So are you.' She slid her hands down his muscular back to grip his waist to shunt his hips closer to where she ached to feel him, hard and thick behind the fly of his scrubs.

His desire for her darkened his expression so she barely recognised him. But she barely recognised herself. It had been so long since she'd felt so liberated. And wanted.

Nate cupped her backside and hoisted her onto the counter, stepping into the space between her spread thighs. 'I knew we'd be this good together.' He pressed his hips to hers, his erection between her legs so she rocked her hips and sighed. 'I knew it the first time we touched. When we shook hands on my first day.'

'This is crazy. We need to stop,' she said, in a desperate attempt to control the way he made her feel attractive and desirable. But in the same breath, she chased his lips with hers once more, seeking another life-affirming kiss as she held his waist so he couldn't escape.

'Not yet,' he said, trailing his lips and the wet tip of his tongue down the side of her neck. 'You're too sexy. You taste too good. Not yet...' He kissed her again, deeply, ravenously, clearly as on edge as Greer.

She slid her fingers through his hair, holding him close as their kisses deepened wildly, tongues surging together, their need escalating quickly out of control, as if they were each desperate and determined to squeeze in one more kiss before they'd have to break the spell and stop.

He slid her hips forwards to the edge of the counter, drawing them closer, grinding them together, the friction sublime. Simultaneously too much and too little. Greer moaned and tore her mouth from his, panting as she met his darkly aroused stare.

'Nate... We shouldn't be doing this,' she said in a half-hearted attempt to bring this madness to a close. But powerless to her own needs, she curled her fingers around the back of his neck and brought their lips back together, spread her thighs wider, craving more and more as pleasure erupted and engulfed her.

She was lost. Aroused and abandoned. Her need for him obliterating all else.

Nate groaned against her neck. 'I know... I just... I want you so badly.' His hips bucked against hers, sending more heat to pool in her pelvis. His hands cupped her face, fingers sliding into her hair, which must have been horribly dishevelled as he peered down at her, unmistakable craving on his face.

'Me too,' she admitted, kissing him again. Just one more kiss. Last time.

'Tell me to stop again and I will,' he said, bending his head to kiss her collarbone, her chest, down into her cleavage, groaning when he exposed a glimpse of black lace.

'I can't...' Her body molten with need, Greer struggled to breathe let alone speak or issue orders. Instead she kissed him again, determined this would be the very, very last time even as she slid her hands to his backside to press his hips closer so they moaned in unison at the gratifying contact.

But Nate clearly had more willpower than Greer. After one final searingly hot kiss where she feared she might never be able to stop this, that she might actually have sex with him, right there in the doctors' office, he pressed his forehead to hers and slid his hand from under her top.

'I've never wanted anyone as badly as I want you,' he said hoarsely, breathing hard as he eased his hips back, obviously mining impressive reserves of discipline.

Breathless, Greer could only stare and nod. Every inch of her body was alight with need. The past few wildly passionate minutes had shattered her every reservation about this reckless relationship. Her principles and professionalism were ground to dust. And she didn't care.

'I'm sorry. I shouldn't have done that,' she said, coming to some of her senses. Swallowing hard, Greer slid from the counter and ran a trembling hand through her tangled hair, trying to put herself back together.

'Don't apologise.' Nate helped, one hand still on her waist as he pushed her hair over her shoulder and smiled regretfully. 'That was even hotter than I'd imagined and I've been thinking about it a lot.'

Greer smiled, relieved that they'd got away with a serious lapse in judgement on her part. 'Still, we're at work.' Their shift didn't end for another hour. There would be more patients to see, and anyone could come in search of either of them and find them flushed and panting and still staring hungrily at each other. 'I should have controlled myself.'

'Well, I'm glad you couldn't.' Nate retrieved his name tag, which must have become dislodged during all the frantic kissing, from the floor and clipped it back on. 'How do I look?' he asked, catching his breath, a guilty but still hot smile tugging at his kiss-swollen mouth.

With her heart still tripping, Greer ran her fingers through his silky dark hair, straightening the strands. 'Like some woman has just ravaged you senseless in the doctors' office.'

'Cool.'

They smiled together, the tension breaking.

'Your coffee is probably cold,' she said, crossing her arms over her chest. 'Sorry about that.'

'Are you kidding?' he asked with an incredulous smile as fire once more flickered in his stare. 'Who needs coffee with you around?'

Greer smiled, pressing her lips together to hold in a giggle. She knew what he meant. Those kisses had rejuvenated her more effectively than an intravenous caffeine infusion.

'I need to get away from you,' Nate said, pressing his lips to her forehead, breathing into her hair. 'Get a hold of myself.'

Greer dragged in another shaky breath and stepped back, away from the temptation to kiss him again or keep touching him.

At the door, he paused and turned to shoot her another heated look. 'I don't think you need to worry about our date or be nervous. After that, I think our only problem will be avoiding setting Diamanto's ablaze.'

Greer nodded in agreement. 'If I don't see you before I head home, I'll see you Thursday evening,' she said, watching as he gave her one last smile then disappeared, leaving her to wonder how on earth she'd stop herself from ripping his clothes off the minute he knocked on her door for their date.

CHAPTER EIGHT

'So how come you're single?' Greer asked that Thursday evening, unable to put off the burning question a moment longer. She glanced guiltily around Diamanto's. They were one of only two couples still seated as the staff discreetly cleared up. But she didn't want the date to be over.

For the first time that evening, Nate's expression became guarded. 'My last relationship ended about a year ago.'

She nodded and twirled the stem of her near-empty wine glass, her gaze drawn to Nate's across the flickering candle flame at the centre of their table as it had been all evening while they'd talked about everything from their careers to the films and books they loved and their dream holiday destinations.

'We were only together three months,' he added, 'so it wasn't that serious.'

'Just didn't work out, huh?' she prompted, her curiosity burning bright. The closer the time came to leaving Diamanto's, the more nervous she felt, despite the lovely meal and abundant light and flirty conversation. Not to mention the heated looks. Because now she knew Nate was right. They were good together. Better than good. If they ever went further than some serious heavy petting, she had no doubt they'd be...utterly glorious.

'Kind of,' he said, his stare unflinching but no longer relaxed. 'It was good at the start. But after the first few weeks she became quite jealous. Not a great combination with a partner who works unpredictably long hours the way we do.'

Greer nodded in sympathy and understanding, aware that the same issues had arisen in her marriage. 'Did she…have any reason to be jealous?' Greer asked, her face hot because cheating or sneaking around was a definite trigger for her. Ironic, then, that she was sneaking around with Nate both at work and by hiding the relationship from Lily.

'I'm not a cheat, if that's what you're asking,' he said, his stare glittering. 'But yeah, she struggled with my close relationship to Maggie, Callum's mother.'

Greer winced. 'That's not good.' Especially when Nate was understandably supportive of his twin brother's widow and son.

Nate shrugged it off. 'Eventually we came to the joint realisation that it wasn't working out. What about you?' he asked, changing the subject. 'Was there any cheating in your marriage?'

Greer shook her head, her throat tightening with shame as she reluctantly sipped the last of her wine. 'My ex always denied it, but that didn't stop me having plenty of suspicions over the years. My father cheated on my mother so I grew up witnessing the fallout of a trustless marriage. I guess that shaped me.'

'I'm sorry.'

Greer shrugged. 'I was determined that I would never tolerate that in my own relationships. But it's like you said. Our work is often unpredictable, our hours long, especially in surgery. My ex and I argued a lot, too. My suspicious nature combined with his propensity for emotional withdrawal when he felt challenged was not, it turned out, a match made in heaven.'

'How long were you married?' he said, his expression intensely watchful.

'Fourteen years. I think the final five were mainly for Lily's sake. We probably shouldn't have rushed to get married in the first place, but I got pregnant after a year of dating and on some level we obviously both thought it was the right thing to do.' One of her biggest fears about dating seriously again was that history might repeat itself. She might get it wrong again. Rush into something that wasn't right for her. Maybe that was why she'd put off dating for so long.

'Not that I regret it all, of course,' she continued. 'My marriage gave me my daughter and there were many happy times over the years, especially in the beginning.'

Nate nodded thoughtfully.

'Anyway...' Greer said, hating that they'd have to bring the date to an end. 'We should probably call it a night. If you haven't noticed, they're clearing up around us.'

'Yeah, I guess we should,' Nate said, standing and pulling out his wallet, clearly intent on paying the bill. 'Would you like to walk home? It's probably still warm out. I can walk you home then take the Tube.'

'Sure.' Greer nodded, slipping on her lightweight cardigan over the short-sleeved dress she'd worn, shivering slightly because Nate was so considerate and gentlemanlike.

Now that the end of the evening was here, her nerves crept back. That kiss at the hospital had proved their sexual chemistry wasn't going to be a problem. And as much as she wanted him physically, she still had mental reservations. She didn't want to lead him on or for there to be any awkwardness at work. And if a kiss goodnight led to more, was she ready to be intimate with another man?

Nate insisted on paying for dinner, and as they left the restaurant, he reached for her hand, sliding his fingers between hers and tugging her close so they could walk hand in hand. Greer shuddered, both elated and unsettled by the illicit and intimate contact that still felt…forbidden. After weeks of keeping their flirtation a secret, the public gesture felt odd. But then he'd also given her the hottest kiss she'd experienced for years so there was no point denying how much she craved his touch.

'How was your first first date in years?' he asked, shooting her that sexy playful smile of his. 'Clearly you weren't put off by the cartoon socks.'

Greer laughed, her heart light. 'I had a lovely time. I was particularly thrilled to glimpse today's very appropriate socks—olives. Well chosen.'

'Thought you might like those,' he said, grinning.

'I'm impressed by your sock collection,' she said, to keep her mind off the dwindling minutes until they reached her place. 'You must own enough pairs to wear a different set every day, because, with the exception of my favourites, I've yet to see the same pair twice.'

'I'm glad to hear you've been keeping track.' He shot her another flirtatious look. Then his smile became tinged with sadness. 'Dylan started the trend. I was doing my Paediatrics rotation when he bought my first pair—pizza slices—as a Christmas gift. When I told him I'd worn them to work and one of the sick kids I'd treated that day had noticed them and smiled, he continued to buy more and more pairs, every birthday and Christmas. And sometimes just because he'd found a pair that stood out.'

Greer smiled, her heart thudding painfully for his enormous loss. 'You must miss him terribly. I can't even imagine what you and your family have been through.'

'I do miss him, of course,' Nate said, looking straight ahead as they walked. 'We were really close. His death left a massive hole in the family, not just in my life. That's why I try to spend time with Callum, so we can talk about Dylan whenever he wants. I'd hate for him to grow up feeling he couldn't mention his dad in case it upset people. Because his dad was amazing. I would never want him to forget that.'

'You're amazing, too,' she said, her throat tight with emotion. 'Callum's lucky to have such a dedicated uncle.'

'I don't know about that.' He looked straight ahead. 'Most of the time I just feel guilty. Dylan should be the one raising his son. He should be the one making memories, watching his football matches and talking about the issues at school.'

'I'm so sorry that he's gone,' Greer said, fighting the urge to hold him. But they weren't a couple. This was about lust and fun. About Greer finding her feet and jumping the first hurdle on her journey of self-rediscovery.

'Me too.' He glanced her way and shrugged. 'But that's why I haven't applied for a consultant job yet,' he said, volunteering information. 'I need to be good at my job, but I'm in no hurry to work longer hours or take on more responsibility. Callum is only eight and life is tough for kids these days. He needs positive role models now more than ever.'

Greer nodded, her heart pounding because he kept on showing her new parts of his personality and passions.

And so far there was nothing she disliked. Not a single red flag to be seen.

They walked the last street in increasingly edgy silence. When they were standing on Greer's doorstep, Nate confidently tugged her hand, stepped close and dipped his head to hers, brushing a soft restrained kiss over her lips.

'I really enjoyed our date. Thanks for saying yes,' he said, his fingers holding hers. 'I wanted to ask you out the first day we met, as soon as I clocked the bare ring finger.'

Greer smiled, her heart leaping at his playfulness and confidence, her mind whirring suddenly because when she'd prepared for tonight, she hadn't planned to invite him in. But now she wanted more.

She slid her hand to his waist and pressed her mouth back to his, parting her lips when he kissed her harder, sliding her tongue against his, moaning when his arms encircled her, his hand pressed between her shoulder blades so there was no space between their bodies. Only heat and sparks and burning need she could no longer fight.

'Come inside,' she whispered after pulling back, her breathing tight and her heart racing.

Nate stared down at her, his eyes dark with desire, his erection a flicker against her stomach. 'Are you sure?'

'Yes.' Their chemistry was insane. She liked and respected Nate. They understood each other's priorities and she didn't have to worry about this becoming serious. It was just sex.

Before either of them could change their minds, she reached for his hand, turning to fumble for keys in her bag and unlock the outer door. Her flat was on the ground floor but they only made it inside the communal foyer before Nate pressed her up against the wall, his hands in her hair as he kissed her deeper, trailing his hot mouth down her neck.

'Greer,' he groaned. 'You are so sexy. I haven't been able to forget that kiss. Haven't stopped thinking about you since.'

'Come on,' she said, galvanised into action by the molten need making her legs unsteady.

Within seconds, they'd charged inside Greer's darkened flat, where he reached for her again. She shrugged off her cardigan, now too hot. His kisses grew more determined, his hands restlessly skimming her body, her breasts, waist, hips and backside through her clothes, his sexy groans unrestrained. Nate was honest about what he wanted and he wanted her.

All but levitating with lust, Greer tangled one hand in his hair while the other explored his bunched shoulder, his hard chest, the ridges of his steely abs and the long hard length of him behind his fly.

He groaned once more and she smiled. Every inch of him felt magnificent. A gloriously sexy man in his prime.

'Bedroom,' she said when they paused for breath. She led him down the hall and pushed open the door, grateful that she'd put her clothes in the laundry basket earlier rather than tossing them onto the bed or leaving them in a heap outside the shower.

'Tell me what you like,' he said, one arm banded around her waist as he kissed her while walking her backwards towards the bed, then pulled back, waiting.

What she liked? Greer's brain synapses shorted out; his demand was so sexy.

'You,' she said, embarrassed that she couldn't come

up with something more sexually sophisticated like a favourite position or kink.

As if doused in chilly water, she stared up at him. 'Why? What do *you* like? Because... I haven't done this in a very long time.'

'I don't care.' He chased her lips with his, murmuring, 'That's hot. *You're* hot. And I want you, too.'

'But...' She swallowed again, already so turned on from his pretty simple touch, she felt sure she would reveal herself as too vanilla. Perhaps he expected dirty talk, some exotic position she'd never heard of. Perhaps he had a sexual fetish. She'd heard they were all the rage these days.

He gripped her face between his palms, his lips brushing hers. 'What's wrong, Greer? Tell me what has you suddenly overthinking this.'

Greer hesitated, her heartbeats now painful throbs in her chest. 'I'm worried there's a whole sexual subculture I knew nothing about. I'm worried that I'll disappoint you. I'm worried we won't click.'

Nate frowned and froze, staring wordlessly down at her for several long beats. Greer's stomach plummeted and her feet turned to stone, every doubt she'd thought she'd dismissed roaring back to life. Maybe she couldn't do this after all.

Nate breathed through the firestorm of his arousal burning him up, through the urge to kiss her, to tongue every inch of her body and pleasure her into incoherence. 'I'm sure there *is* a sexual subculture you know nothing about, but I'm sure I'm just as ignorant as you.'

He hadn't expected to be invited in tonight, but he wasn't about to miss this opportunity. He felt feverish with wanting her, as if this moment—standing in the dark in her bedroom—had been building since the first time they met.

He pressed his lips back to hers, smiling into their kiss when she sagged against him with relief, peppering her face with more kisses. 'Just so we're on the same page, I'll tell you what I want.' He pulled back to stare at her. 'I want to kiss you and touch you and see you naked,' he said, sliding his palms up and down her bare arms. 'And you have my consent to do the same to me.'

She nodded, her hands sliding around his waist, her body restless against his as if, despite her wobble of confidence, she was as turned on as Nate. 'I do want.'

'Thank God.' Nate groaned, his lips desperately tracing her skin. 'I want to make you come and make you smile, make you laugh,' he continued, pressing her body against his. 'I want us to explore and enjoy each other and discover if this chemistry is as good as I know it's going to be.'

'Nate…' Greer gripped his upper arms, her doubts clearly appeased. 'I want that too.'

'So you'll tell me if I do something you don't like or don't want. And I'll do the same. Okay?' Nate cupped her breast with one hand while the other slid under her dress and slowly grazed her outer thigh.

'Yes.' She shifted against him, seeking friction. He ran his nose along her jaw to the place beneath her earlobe where her natural scent was strongest.

'You are the sexiest woman I've ever met, Greer,' he said. 'Just talking to you turns me on. I want you so badly, I'm scared this will be over too soon, before I've had a chance to do all the things I've imagined doing with you.'

Greer moaned, dropped her head back so his lips could

glide wherever they wanted along her neck as he breathed her in and learned the sensitive places that made her sigh and twist her fingers in his hair.

'So are you still sure about this? Do you want to stop?' he asked, his fingers curling into the fabric of her dress at her waist as he held himself in check, waiting.

'No! I want to see you.' She slid her hands under his shirt where his skin was surely scalding hot, her hands roaming, his muscles tensing everywhere she touched as she shoved up his shirt and stared at his naked torso, her bottom lip trapped under her teeth.

Nate kissed her once more and reached for the zip at the back of her dress. The metallic scrape echoed in the silent room, the only other sound but for their increasingly ragged breathing. He pushed the dress from one shoulder, taking her bra strap too until he'd exposed her breast. Desperate to taste her and deliver on his promises, he leaned down and covered her nipple with his mouth, sucking and flicking it with the tip of his tongue so she gasped.

'Nate,' she said on a half-sob, watching him for a few seconds. Then with renewed determination, she pushed his shirt up, removing it, sliding the tip of her tongue over his chest, and up the side of his neck as if in retribution.

'Greer…' Nate crushed her semi-naked chest to his, skin to skin until he felt coated in the heady scent of her perfume. They kissed, intermittently breaking free for Greer to run her hands and her stare over his torso, for Nate to expose the other breast and take that nipple in his mouth until she moaned louder.

'You were right,' she said, sliding her arms free of her dress, allowing it to pool at her feet, removing her bra and kicking both items aside before stepping back into his arms. 'This is definitely about us and we are good together.'

'Better than good.' He smiled, satisfied, groaning when she kissed him deeply, her fingers unbuckling his belt and unbuttoning his jeans.

'Greer,' he said in warning as she stroked him through his boxers, her lips gliding along his collarbone.

Then her tongue headed south as she dropped to her knees and pushed his jeans over his hips, looking up at him with a feline smile.

'Great idea.' Nate reached for her elbows and drew her to her feet, walking her back towards the bed, following her down when she lay in the middle. 'I want to taste you.'

Kicking off his shoes, he leaned over her, his hips between her spread thighs, and poured all the need that had been building these past few weeks into their frantic kisses.

She sighed as he kissed and licked a trail down her belly, sliding off her underwear as he went.

Pausing, he knelt between her legs and stared, his hands gliding up and down her thighs. 'You are so beautiful,' he choked out, arousal boiling his blood. 'Definitely worth the wait.'

'So are you,' she said when he stood and removed the rest of his clothes, and they stared at each other's naked bodies unashamedly.

He retrieved a condom from his wallet and then rejoined her on the bed, starting at her ankle and kissing a path up her leg until he was where he wanted to be.

'Yes,' she gasped as he covered her with his mouth, pleasuring her so all he heard were her cries and moans and chants of *yes*.

She speared her fingers through his hair, her moans

building with every swipe of his tongue until she cried out and came, sobbing his name.

Before she could come down from the high, Nate tore into the condom and covered himself.

'Come here.' Greer reached for him, pulling him into the cradle of her hips, gripping his waist with her thighs as he slowly slid into her warmth.

'Are you okay?' he asked, holding still, biting his tongue against the flood of pleasure radiating throughout his entire body.

'More than okay,' she said, smiling, brushing her lips over his, tilting her hips so he sank deeper and groaned against her neck. 'Let me go on top,' she whispered.

'No problem,' he said, gripping her waist to roll them, still locked together as one.

She was magnificent. Flushed from her orgasm, her hair dishevelled, her smile satisfied as she braced her hands on his chest. Staring down at him, she began to rock, riding him, her breaths panting as she found her rhythm and showed him her fearless passionate side, the one he'd been desperate to see.

'Still worried that we won't click,' he asked, one hand leaving her hips to cup her breast and toy with the nipple.

She laughed joyously, the sound shifting into a low moan as he thrust upwards when she rocked down. Nate found some hidden reserves of stamina, desperate for Greer to be in no doubt of their chemistry. Desperate to give her the time of her life so she had zero regrets.

With another broken cry she came again, tossing back her head to expose her neck. Nate sat up, crushed her in his arms, held her through every spasm and then finally let go, the high of being with Greer definitely worth the wait.

CHAPTER NINE

GREER'S HEAD GREW heavy on Nate's chest as she basked in the afterglow of astounding sex.

'How was that?' he asked, his voice smiling as he ran his fingertips lazily up and down her spine.

'Are you kidding?' she mumbled. 'I can't believe I waited so long...' She'd genuinely enjoyed every moment of their date. He'd made her laugh so many times over dinner and goodness knew it had been a long time since anyone apart from Lily and her girlfriends had done that. Not to mention the sex... She was definitely hung up on the sex.

He chuckled and reached for her hand, sliding his fingers between hers, the gesture so intimate—ridiculous she should think that after what had just happened—that her mind began to race.

They'd agreed this was casual, but did that mean they were done? She hadn't planned to invite him in tonight, but now that they'd slept together, she wanted to do it again. How could she not? Nate was a perfectly endowed god well acquainted with a woman's body.

'What happens now?' she asked, her hand on his abs so she felt him tense beneath her touch.

'Now I catch the Tube home,' he said, his fingers gliding through her tangled hair, 'and let you get some sleep.'

He pressed a kiss to the top of her head in another sweet gesture that left her even more panicked. Part of her didn't want him to leave. But nor did she really want him to stay the night. She needed to analyse every second of what had happened. Alone. To recall and overthink every word of conversation, every moaned utterance and desperate touch until it all made sense and she'd clarified exactly how she felt about it all.

It was one thing to want to bravely rediscover yourself. Another thing entirely to navigate the rules of casual sex with a younger man. Because as much as she still wanted him, she couldn't become too addicted.

She and Nate were at different stages of life. She'd done things—marriage, a child—that he still had ahead of him. She wouldn't lead him on, not when this could never be a serious or long-term thing.

'Okay,' she said, unmoving, because part of her wanted him for a little longer.

'I'm taking Callum to the dentist first thing tomorrow,' Nate explained, 'because Maggie has an early start at work. Then dropping him at school after his appointment.'

Greer nodded, grateful that Nate too had obligations. She'd planned to organise Lily's surprise eighteenth birthday party tomorrow. Hire caterers, message all of Lily's friends, order a couple of cases of champagne.

'Has your sister-in-law begun dating again?' she asked, her mind returning to their earlier conversation in the restaurant. The one where he'd expressed guilt that it was him and not Dylan parenting Callum.

'Yeah, a bit.' Nate's slow even breaths stalled. 'Don't think she's met anyone serious though.'

'It's great that you help out with childcare,' Greer said,

picking up on a feeling that he was hiding something. That she'd touched a nerve earlier and again just now.

Or maybe he simply wanted to leave now that the sex was over.

'I do it for Dylan, mainly,' he said quietly. 'I've never really wanted kids of my own, but if I had one and the roles were reversed, if it was my child left fatherless, I'd want my child to know their uncle.'

'Of course,' Greer said, a part of her needing him to be a bit less wonderful. But it was obviously just the sex talking. She'd left it too long and now she feared she'd want more and more despite her current massive hangover. It had been that good.

'For what it's worth,' she said, finally raising her head to look at him, 'I think you're doing your brother proud.'

Rather than take her compliment, he froze, his body tensing under hers. Sensing his discomfort, Greer sat up, drawing the sheet up to cover her nakedness. Nate rose too, turning away from her to sit on the edge of the bed, his forearms braced on his thighs.

'I'm not so sure about that,' he muttered, reaching for his boxers from the floor before pulling them on.

What? This wasn't the confident, self-assured man she'd come to know.

'Why not?' Greer asked, shivering from the sudden chill in the atmosphere.

'I'm a doctor,' he said, standing and pulling on his jeans with hurried movements, making all her lovely post-orgasm endorphins drain away. 'I of all people should have spotted the signs of Dylan's illness sooner, don't you think?'

'No, I don't. You weren't *his* doctor. It wasn't your fault.' Her voice was flat because she wasn't sure he was even listening. This conversation was obviously a trigger for him. He couldn't seem to get dressed quickly enough.

He smiled mirthlessly, shaking his head. 'Technically you're right, but that doesn't change the facts that by the time he sought help for his symptoms, he already had stage four disease and was dead within a year.'

He disappeared for a second inside his shirt. When his head emerged, he'd withdrawn behind the determined expression of his. 'It makes no difference now, but there's a part of me that can't help but wonder if I'd been less self-absorbed, less busy chasing the next job and passing the next exam, I might have noticed something was wrong with my twin brother. Been there for him when he needed me most, when it might have made a difference.'

Greer nodded, sadly, knowing nothing she said would likely change Nate's flawed thinking or the way he felt irrationally responsible for his brother. And it wasn't her place to try and fix Nate. He was a smart man. He'd figure this out for himself in time.

And their…relationship was just a bit of fun. A brief fling at best.

'I'm sorry that's the way you feel,' she said quietly. 'Is that why you need to be good at your job? To prove something to yourself?'

Nate stared. 'You know, up until this moment, I've always admired your directness. But yes, the part of me that let him down, the part that's scared to forget Dylan, needs to be good at my job. I couldn't help him but maybe I can help others.'

Greer glanced down, ashamed that she'd overstepped the mark. 'Sorry. It's none of my business.'

Uncertain how to proceed, she watched him pull on his socks. Maybe she should end things on a high. Send him off with a *'thanks for the date, for the orgasms, but let's resume business as usual'*. Only the pinch of disappointment in her stomach told her she wanted more.

'I'm going to head out.' He looked up and levelled his guilty but guarded stare on her as if waiting for more trite advice. When she stayed silent, merely nodding that she'd heard, he braced his hands on the bed and leaned over her, kissing her lips. 'Despite this last conversation, I had a great time tonight.'

'Me too,' Greer said, feeling irrationally hurt that he was leaving on a sour note. 'I'll see you out.' She flung off the sheet, rose from the bed and donned her robe, which had been hanging on the back of the bedroom door.

When she looked up from tying the belt around her waist, Nate's stare blazed with hunger.

'I want you again,' he said starkly but unmoving, as if he now resented the hold she might have over him.

'I thought you were leaving,' she replied, fresh heat sliding through her limbs to settle in her core, because she wanted him too. One time wasn't enough. Not when they'd clicked so magnificently.

Nate prowled closer, his stare locked to hers. 'I only had one condom,' he said, scrubbing a hand over his face. 'And you haven't invited me to stay the night.'

She squared her shoulders, determined to set some boundaries. 'Maybe now is a good time to address our expectations for this.'

He nodded, tension pursing his sexy mouth. 'I want more than a one-time thing. I'd like to see you again. What do you want?'

'So I'd be your boss with benefits?' she asked, liking the idea more than she'd imagined possible. 'I can handle that.' Why not? Nate was fun and respectful and the sex… How had she gone without for so long?

A hint of amusement tugged at his lips. 'If you like.'

'Obviously that's all it can be: a fling,' she pointed out, because Nate could have his pick of women his own age and Greer wasn't ready for a real relationship. 'Neither of us wants anything serious.'

She wasn't sure she ever wanted to be married again. In fact, the idea of being so romantically vulnerable again made her want to change her mind, end this now before either of them could get hurt.

'Whatever you want, Greer.' He stepped closer still, his gaze flicking to her lips so her heart galloped, her wants a confusing jumble among her desires.

'Lily's home from France in nine days,' she said, breathlessly, deciding that might be a good place to draw the line. 'When she's home, I won't really have time for sneaking around or keeping secrets. We'll be preparing for her move to Manchester.'

'Okay,' he said, his expression unreadable. If he was disappointed, he kept it hidden.

Greer dragged in a shaky relieved breath at such smoothly negotiated terms. 'In that case, I'll buy a jumbo box of condoms tomorrow,' she said, lingering fear forcing her not to reach for him, not to kiss him, to drop to her knees and take him into her mouth until he growled her name and forgave her for overstepping the mark before.

His face slowly split into a sexy smile. 'Good idea. I will too.'

He reached for her waist, but she ducked away, shooting him her best seductive look. She left the bedroom and breezed her way down the hall to the front door, her silky robe billowing.

This, him leaving, them both hungry for more, was the perfect finale to their date. She could come to terms with her reawakened physical desires while sending the right message that they shouldn't get too used to each other because this had temporary stamped all over it.

She opened the flat door and stepped aside while he put on his shoes. Looking up, his stare darkening, he closed the distance, scooped one arm around her waist and kissed her hard and deeply, pressing her against the wall with his hips.

Instantly and impossibly needy given the two orgasms she'd had, she clung to his shoulders, kissing him back, her resolve forgotten. Hooking one leg around his thigh so his hardness prodded between her legs and he groaned into their kiss.

He pulled back, panting. 'Do you have plans for the weekend?' His hand cupped her backside, holding their hips snug as they rocked together teasingly, mini aftershocks of pleasure spiralling out from her core.

Greer shook her head, too turned on from the heat of that kiss and the possessive look in his eyes to make any sense or put up another fight.

'Can I see you?' He pushed her hair back from her flushed face, the pad of his thumb tracing her cheekbone as his stare turned a little vulnerable.

'Okay,' she said. 'I'll meet you in Covent Garden, at the Seven Dials monument, Saturday afternoon, four p.m.'

A small satisfied smile tugged the corners of his mouth, a mouth that had wreaked sublime havoc on every part of her body. 'See you there.'

With a final swift kiss, he released her and stepped out into the foyer. 'Sleep well, Greer.' Then he turned and left.

'You too,' she called, closing the door before he disappeared out onto the street, when all she really wanted to do was watch him until the last minute, a dreamy smile on her face.

But just because she'd had life-altering sex didn't mean she could forget herself. She still needed to be professional at work. Her priority was still her daughter. They could enjoy a few stolen moments until Lily arrived home but beyond that it wouldn't do to become addicted to him or forget that long term, for many reasons, they were a highly unlikely match.

CHAPTER TEN

IT HAD BEEN easy to swap his Sunday early shift with one of the other emergency medicine registrars so Nate could work the Friday night shift with Greer. Not that he'd told Greer his plans or seen her since he began the shift an hour ago. But this way, he could enjoy their second date Saturday afternoon without having to think about an early start the next day.

He'd just finished helping one of the junior doctors to reduce a dislocated shoulder and was checking some results at the computer terminal, when Greer appeared from one of the patient bays.

Dressed in their usual navy scrubs, her dark hair, which had been sexily dishevelled the last time he'd seen her, was pulled back in a neat ponytail. Her eyes lit up when she saw him, her ready smile falling as the shock and delight drained away and she quickly glanced around the department in case someone might be looking.

'What are you doing here?' she asked in a suspicious whisper, taking the seat beside his and trying to act normal. But her cheeks flushed as if she was recalling the last time they'd seen each other. The things they'd done to each other. The way that they'd slotted so perfectly together in the bedroom. For the entire journey home on the Tube, Nate had cursed his lack of preparation on the condom front.

'I swapped shifts with Dr Beynon,' he said, his heart pounding and his smile uncontrollable. 'Turns out I've developed rather an addiction to night shifts recently.'

And also an addiction to Greer. Thursday night had been... Wow! And right up until the moment where she'd prodded him to talk about Dylan, he hadn't wanted to leave. He'd had such an amazing night, had been half sex-comatosed, that he'd relaxed too much. Let his guard slip so when she'd probed, he'd revealed something he might otherwise have kept to himself. But he needed to be careful. If this was only casual, if they had only a matter of days left to enjoy each other, he needn't tell her his other guilty secret.

'You ought to see a doctor for that,' she quipped, flashing him a playful smile. 'But as you're here, you can take the ingrowing toenail in bay two.' She cast him a straight-faced look.

'No problem.' Nate grinned, gratified to have her play with him after his minor freak-out Thursday night. That, despite their hot night together and the subsequent rather clinical discussion of their romantic expectations, he still had the power to affect her and vice versa.

Just then, before he could ask her if she'd thought of him after he'd left her place, the way he'd obsessed over her, Michelle, one of the senior nurses, appeared.

'Dr Thorn, thanks for the books,' she said. 'I really appreciate it.'

'Oh, no problem, Michelle,' Greer replied. 'I hope your son finds them helpful. Lily no longer has any use for them so they might as well go to someone else.'

'I'm sure he will,' Michelle said. 'Maths is his least

favourite subject but he needs to pass the A level next year if he's hoping to study engineering.'

Greer smiled warmly and Michelle rushed off to answer a call buzzer. Nate waited until she looked up at him then raised his eyebrows questioningly.

'I gave Michelle Lily's study guides for her son who is in lower sixth.' She touched the mouse on the desk to wake up the computer, before logging in, ignoring Nate, who continued to stare, mesmerised.

'That was very thoughtful of you,' he said, his gaze tracing her profile, the elegant slope of her neck, a place he'd explored with his lips and tongue until she'd moaned.

Greer gave so much of herself to others, through her job, to her colleagues, to Lily. Nate couldn't help but wonder what she needed for herself. And with that question came stirrings of doubt. He'd agreed to a casual fling. That was the safest option, the one Greer wanted, too. But a part of him was already addicted to her physically. Addicted to her quiet strength. Her sometimes dry sense of humour. Her unguarded smile and joyously throaty laugh.

'What?' she asked, because he was still staring.

Nate shrugged. 'I just like that you know who you are. How you handle things. It's…attractive,' he whispered the final word and her gaze darted around the department once more.

'Stop,' she said, a small knowing smile tugging at the corner of her mouth. 'Go and discharge that ingrowing toenail if you've got nothing better to do.'

'Whatever you say, Dr Thorn.' He stood, and paused, stooping to add another playful whisper. 'I love it when you boss me around.' He made his way towards the patient, her startled gasp ringing in his ears. He unleashed a satisfied grin. It was good to know that, after their incredible date, he still had the power to surprise her.

Greer watched Nate walk away, her heart pounding erratically. His tall swagger, the clench of his gorgeous backside, the way he'd whispered that last comment close enough that his warm breath had slid down her neck like honey, igniting her erogenous zones... She licked her lips and released a happy sigh, snapping out of her dreamy state when Nate was intercepted by Kaz, one of the junior doctors working the shift.

'Nate, can I ask you a question?' Kaz said, blinking up at him with obvious awe.

'Of course. Any time,' he replied, glancing down at the department's tablet Kaz held.

Greer stopped listening, trying to focus on the computer screen, on the patient notes she was typing up, but her gaze kept returning to Nate and Kaz, who were now side by side, each looking at the tablet while they talked.

Greer half listened, half squirmed, catching phrases that made it obvious they were discussing a patient... basal crepitations...congestive cardiac failure...diuretics... Maybe it was in Greer's imagination that Kaz, a pretty twenty-something, was standing a little too close to Nate. Smiling a little too much. Nodding too enthusiastically when Nate advised her on appropriate tests and a management plan.

Feeling uncomfortable spying and unsettled by the intensity of her feelings of jealousy, Greer typed a few more lines of her notes. But when she looked up again, Kaz and Nate were still talking. Only now Kaz wore a wide smile, the tablet clasped to her chest, the patient discussion clearly over.

'Thanks so much for your help,' Kaz gushed on a tinkle of nervous laughter. 'I completely understand now that you've explained it. I actually like working with you. The other registrars always act too busy for my silly questions.' Kaz smiled and twirled the end of her long ponytail.

Sharp stabs of jealousy pricked Greer's skin, leaving her hot and itchy. It was irrational. Greer had no claim to Nate. They weren't a couple. They weren't seriously dating. She'd even voiced as much the night before when she'd insisted all it could be was a fling. But maybe because Kaz was so much more suited to Nate, age-wise, Greer couldn't seem to dismiss her feelings as easily as she would have liked.

'No worries,' Nate said. 'Come find me later when you have the results back, yeah?' He stepped back, glancing over Kaz's shoulder to see Greer watching the interaction.

Mortified, she ducked her head, resumed her typing, aware of Kaz departing. Hopefully Nate would continue towards the ingrowing-toenail patient and Greer could pull herself together in peace.

No such luck.

'Hey, you okay?' Nate asked from beside her.

Greer finished typing her sentence then looked up from the screen. 'Of course.'

Of course Nate would be popular with the ladies. He was gorgeous and evolved and fun. Not that in answering Kaz's patient query he'd done anything more than his job. But Greer couldn't seem to move past her instantaneous but irrational spike of possessiveness.

'Did you send the toenail home?' she asked coolly, desperately trying to hide her uncertainty and embarrassment that she'd not only been listening in to his conversation but also gone right back to a place of distrust, a pathway she knew well.

'I'm on my way now,' he said, a small frown tugging at his mouth as he hesitated, obviously eager to say more or call Greer out on her attitude.

'Great,' she said, turning back to the screen as shameful heat blazed through her. Was she really pulling rank with Nate just to manage her unexpected feelings of jealousy? When she'd insisted this was only a fling?

Just then, before she could examine her behaviour more closely, the code blue alarm sounded. Greer ran to Resuscitation, aware that Nate followed close behind.

'Suspected ectopic pregnancy,' Michelle said as the nurses hurriedly prepared for the emergency admission. 'Patient twelve weeks gestation, first pregnancy confirmed by her general practitioner.'

'Call the obstetrics registrar,' Nate instructed Kaz, who'd also responded to the emergency alarm. 'We'll need cross-match for a transfusion just in case and blood work in preparation that the patient needs surgery.'

There was no time for Greer to rationalise her earlier envy. With an emergency like this it was all hands on deck. Within seconds, the patient was wheeled through the doors from the ambulance bay, and everyone present sprang into action.

'Latest blood pressure one hundred over sixty,' the paramedic said, stepping back from the stretcher to give the team access.

While Kaz drew blood to cross-match for a transfusion if required, Nate quickly examined the patient. Greer observed her vital signs. She had tachycardia and hypotension. With a history of abdominal pain and positive pregnancy test, the signs added up to a ruptured ectopic pregnancy and internal bleeding.

'Helen, we're going to run some tests, okay?' Nate said to the patient while Greer inserted a second intravenous cannula.

'Let's get more fluids going,' Nate said to Michelle, who hurried to start a second intravenous infusion of saline.

'Have you had any vaginal bleeding?' Greer asked the young woman, to which Helen nodded.

'A little,' she said shakily, her voice thick with tears. 'Then the pain started. It got so bad that I fainted, so my partner called the ambulance.'

Having examined the woman's abdomen, Nate glanced at Greer, their stares meeting. 'She's tender in the suprapubic region with guarding,' he said, describing definite signs of peritonitis.

'Helen,' Greer said, 'we need to perform an ultrasound scan. You have signs of internal bleeding, so we just need to see what's going on.'

The woman nodded tearfully and Nate reached for the mobile ultrasound they kept in Resus. He squirted gel onto the end of the probe, sliding it over her lower abdomen where the woman was tender.

Greer stood beside him so they could each see the screen. While Nate oriented himself, adjusting the resolution of the grainy scan images, Kaz approached.

'Obstetrics are on their way,' she said.

Greer nodded. 'Thanks. Can you chase up the urgent blood results, please?'

'There's free fluid in the pouch of Douglas,' Nate told Greer, pointing out what they'd already suspected.

There was some internal bleeding causing some of Helen's symptoms.

'I agree,' she said, watching over his shoulder as Nate repositioned the probe.

He paused, the image on the screen showing Greer the empty uterine cavity. He looked up, their eyes meeting. She gave a tiny nod, acknowledging the significance of the finding: there was no embryo inside the uterus.

Nate shifted the probe again towards the right fallopian tube and ovary.

'What are you seeing?' Greer asked him, taking the moment to test his clinical acumen.

'There's a four-centimetre adnexal mass here,' he said, once more meeting Greer's stare.

Greer gave a small nod, silently communicating that they were on the same page when it came to their clinical suspicions. Evidence of internal bleeding and a mass involving the right fallopian tube most likely represented a ruptured ectopic pregnancy.

As Nate finished the scan, and gently wiped the gel from Helen's abdomen, Greer gave him an encouraging nod, letting him know she agreed with his diagnosis and was there to support him when it came to breaking the sad news to the patient.

'We've asked our colleague from Obs and Gynae to see you, Helen,' Nate said. 'Our concern is that the pregnancy is ectopic. It looks like the embryo implanted outside the womb in the fallopian tube and as it's grown, it's ruptured. You have some internal bleeding, so you'll most likely need surgery, I'm afraid. Did your partner come with you?'

Helen nodded, a confused frown on her face. 'He's outside calling our parents.'

From beside him, Greer added, 'Unfortunately, there's nothing we can do to save the embryo. I'm so sorry.'

Tears seeped from the corners of Helen's eyes. 'Can't we wait and see what happens?'

'We'll take advice from the specialist who is on his way,' Nate said, 'but you're already bleeding internally so the risk of further bleeding is high. Your blood pressure is low, so waiting might not be an option, I'm afraid. We have to put your safety first.'

The patient nodded bravely and Nate touched her shoulder. 'I'll talk to your partner and send him in to be with you while we wait for the obstetrician.'

'Thank you,' Helen said, obviously in shock.

Greer followed Nate away from the bedside, speaking in a hushed voice. 'I'll check the blood work and wait for the obstetrics' reg. Why don't you get what additional history you can from the partner?'

He nodded distractedly and Greer's empathy swelled. The job of breaking bad news like this was never easy. But it was an inevitable part of their work.

'You did good,' Greer said, resisting the urge to touch his arm. 'You know where I am if you need me.'

And then she walked off, determined to stay busy for the rest of the night. Because busy meant there'd be no time to question what she was doing with Nate or how inappropriate it was on multiple levels. No time to examine her jealousy and what it meant. No time to conclude that she was playing with fire and needed to be very careful so no one got hurt.

CHAPTER ELEVEN

By five in the morning, Greer had barely seen Nate. She'd been granted her wish. A constant stream of walking wounded and inebriated patients had kept all three doctors on duty occupied. But after checking in with Kaz, who was in the process of assessing a woman with a minor scald, Greer finally sloped off to the doctors' room to freshen up and rehydrate.

She downed half a bottle of water and had just emerged from the bathroom, where she'd cleaned her teeth, brushed her hair and splashed cold water on her face, when Nate appeared, obviously also headed for the office.

He came to a sudden halt. 'Hi.' There was a hint of a smile in his eyes but also a wariness for which she was responsible after her coolness earlier.

'How's it going out there?' she asked, trying to act normal as she stashed her bag in the lockers.

'It's quietening down,' he said with a small frown. 'How about your end?'

'Same. I planned on grabbing a quick coffee. Want to join me?'

'What's going on, Greer?' he asked in an exasperated tone of voice. 'I saw you watching me earlier with the junior. Now you're acting distant.'

Flushing, Greer swallowed and glanced down at her

feet, scuffing her toe over the linoleum. 'Nothing is going on. I just... I didn't mean to watch you. It struck me that you and Kaz look very good together.'

'Are you jealous?' he asked, his frown deepening as if he was stunned and disappointed rather than flattered.

'No. I mean she was so obviously flirting with you, which was hard to watch.' Greer looked away, her entire body flushing, hating how uncertain she now felt of Nate in the wake of her jealousy.

Rather than respond, Nate quickly scanned the empty corridor and then took her arm and led her into the on-call room a few doors down from the doctors' office.

'What are you doing?' Greer asked, her pulse so fast it hummed in her head. They couldn't be caught together in here.

'This.' He cupped her face and fiercely kissed her, pressing her back against the closed door.

Unable to stop herself because it felt like an age since they'd kissed goodnight yesterday, Greer kissed him back, her lips parting, her tongue stroking his, her hands gripping his waist to drag him close so his hard body pressed against hers from chest to thigh until her doubts fell silent.

'I've waited all night to do that,' he said when he pulled back, breathless, dragging his lips over her jaw, her cheek, pressing kisses to her eyelids. His lips left her skin and she opened her eyes to see desire on his face but also the return of his irritation. 'I don't care how we looked together, Greer. I didn't flirt back. I don't deserve the cold shoulder. You have nothing to be jealous about.'

Greer nodded, her body aflame from both Nate's touch and her confusion. 'I... I know.'

'It was nothing,' he emphasised. 'A harmless comment I wouldn't have given a second thought but for the look on your face.'

As if he couldn't stop touching her despite his annoyance, he tunnelled his fingers into her hair. 'I've thought about you constantly since I left your place last night. I've waited all night for the chance to kiss you. I know you have trust issues, but it was one work-related conversation.'

She nodded again, her throat tight. 'I'm sorry.'

His frustrated stare searched hers. 'Have you even thought about me at all since last night?'

'Of course I have,' she said, her fingers clenching at his waist. 'I woke up thinking about you. I could barely walk. I've struggled to think about anything else but what happened last night, anything but you and how you made me feel.'

As if satisfied with her answer, Nate groaned and kissed her again. More desperately this time, as if trying to prove her jealousy was unfounded. Greer clung to him, uncaring that they might be discovered together, eager to show him that her desperation matched his.

'Nate,' she said when he pulled back from their kiss. She dropped her head back against the door, absorbing every sensation of his touch: his hot breath on her neck, the scrape of his stubble against her skin, his wandering hand delving under her top to cup her breast as if he couldn't stop himself.

'Tell me how I made you feel,' he demanded, peering down at her while he stroked her nipple.

'Alive,' she said on a gasp, so instantly turned on, she forgot about the world beyond this room. 'Liberated. Desired. Accepted for being myself.' Unwilling to drown in desire alone, Greer cupped his erection, stroking him through his trousers.

His lips returned to hers, nibbling, tasting, buzzing as he released an agonised groan of pent-up need. 'I want you,' he said, his lips grazing her jaw and the side of her neck. 'I can't stop wanting you. I can't wait until this afternoon when I'll see you again.'

Mindless from pleasure, Greer fumbled at her back for the door lock and gave it a twist.

Nate pulled back, his aroused stare full of questions.

'I want you too,' she said, her throat tight. 'I wanted you last night when I was alone and again when I woke up this morning. I wanted you the minute I saw you tonight.'

Nate pressed his forehead to hers, breathing hard as if trying to pull himself together.

Greer slipped her fingers into her pocket and pulled out the condom she'd stashed there earlier in the bathroom, pressing it into his hand. 'I thought we needed to be better prepared after last night. I've stashed condoms all over my flat. We'll have to use them all before Lily gets home, don't want her traumatised if she finds one.'

There was just enough light entering through the crack under the door to witness the surprise and then growing arousal on his face as he considered her suggestion. 'That is the best plan I've ever heard,' he said, settling his lips over hers once more, his tongue surging and retreating, his kisses deepening until she was dizzily high.

'Hurry,' she said, kicking off her shoes, shoving down her trousers and underwear. 'We might not have much time.'

'I don't want to hurry,' Nate said with a trace of a sexy smile. He braced one hand on the door above her shoulder, kissed her again, his other hand sliding between her legs where she was beyond ready for him.

In near total darkness, all she could see was the gleam

of his eyes as they kissed and stroked each other into a frenzy of need. Greer bit back every moan that wanted to escape and swallowed every gasp. But his touch stoked her entire body, heat racing along every nerve as he stroked her clit and watched her increasingly desperate reactions.

When he raised the hem of her top and peeled down the cup of her bra to suck her nipple, Greer shattered, her orgasm weakening her legs as she covered her mouth to hold in her cries so no one passing would hear.

Then he picked her up, deposited her backside on the room's desk and shoved down his clothing to put on the condom.

'What are you doing to me?' he asked rhetorically, kissing her again and again so she couldn't possibly respond even if she'd had the answer. Because whatever it was, he was doing it to her too.

Greer wrapped her legs around his hips and held his shoulders as he slid her to the edge of the desk and slowly pushed inside her and then froze for a second, each panting and staring as if in wonder.

'This was your idea,' she said, sliding her fingers through his hair. 'For me it's a definite disciplinary action.' But she couldn't seem to find the energy to stop or care.

'Only if we get caught,' he said, his fingers rubbing over her still exposed nipple as he started to thrust. 'Do you want to stop?'

'No!'

He smiled, his lips recaptured hers, his tempo building as their tongues surged together wildly. Greer crossed her ankles and clung to his shoulders, lost to everything but the way he and this fling made her feel free and powerful and reborn. Stronger and ready to face whatever her future held. There was life after divorce. Euphoric, wonderful life.

She tore her mouth from his as her second orgasm hit, staring into his eyes as wave after wave stole her breath and her mental capacity so she was pure joyous abandon.

'Greer,' he groaned, crushing her to his chest as he bucked and stiffened and breathed heavily against the side of her neck, holding her tight, their hearts thudding side by side.

After, they held each other in the dark for what felt like long minutes, their breaths easing.

'You okay?' he asked eventually, cupping her face, brushing her lips with his in that tender way.

Greer nodded, choked, and he withdrew. Finding a box of tissues on the desk, he dealt with the condom and pulled up his clothes. Greer held his waist, uncertain she'd be able to stand. That was when the giggles began.

'I can't believe we just did that,' she said from behind her hand.

Nate pressed his lips to her forehead. 'I can't believe how incredibly sexy you are. I'm only human.'

He took her hands as she slid from the desk, stooping to collect her clothing from the floor.

'Nate, I'm sorry about earlier. I'm ashamed of how easily I slipped into old habits.'

He held out her clothes, then gripped the back of her neck and pressed his lips to her forehead. 'It's okay. We all have our triggers.'

Nodding, Greer pulled on her underwear and then her scrubs. 'You leave first,' she told him, slipping on her shoes. 'If the corridor is clear, tap the door twice and walk away. I'll wait a minute and follow.'

'Whatever you say, boss.' Nate snaked an arm around her waist, kissing her again. 'Just one more kiss to tide me over until this afternoon.'

'You might want to find a mirror,' she said when he released her, his light-hearted jibe touching a guilty nerve. 'Check that you're presentable.'

He smiled. 'If I look a fraction as good as I feel I'll be a happy man. If I don't see you before you leave, I'll see you later in Covent Garden.'

Greer nodded, watched him leave, heard his two taps on the door, her heart surging in her chest. As she waited a moment, her high drained away. That was the hottest, most reckless thing she'd ever done. Not that she had a single regret beyond her silly jealousy.

But as she straightened her hair, her stomach quivering, only now in trepidation, not pleasure, she lectured herself to calm down. She needed to be careful with Nate. Just because he made her feel twenty-something again, she wasn't. This fling was fun, but it could never turn into a serious relationship. Greer clearly wasn't ready for that and Nate needed someone his own age, someone without an ex-husband and a teenaged daughter. Someone without Greer's emotional baggage.

Deciding she had nothing to fear as long as she reined in her possessiveness and stuck to the deadline they'd set, she returned to the emergency department to see if any new patients had arrived.

CHAPTER TWELVE

LATER THAT MORNING, after watching Callum's football match, Nate used the key Maggie had given him to unlock her front door, allowing Callum to enter ahead of him.

'Don't forget to take off your muddy boots,' he told the boy. 'Remember the trouble I got into last time you forgot.'

Callum dutifully did as he was told, shouting a quick hello to his mother before running into the back garden where he'd recently discovered tadpoles in their small ornamental pond.

Nate headed for the kitchen and dropped Callum's bag in front of the washing machine. 'Hi,' he said to Maggie, who came in through the back door carrying a laundry basket.

'Did his team win?' Maggie asked, flicking on the kettle and reaching for a couple of mugs from the wall cupboard.

'Lost, two goals to one,' Nate replied, 'but, to be honest, he seemed more upset that the tadpoles might have grown legs while he was out.'

Maggie smiled indulgently and said, 'Coffee?' She added two heaped teaspoons to her mug and glanced up at Nate expectantly.

'No, thanks. I don't have time.'

'You sure? You look tired.'

'I worked the night shift last night.' Surviving on caffeine, the tepid shower he'd grabbed at the hospital before he'd left and the anticipation of his date with Greer later, Nate planned to forgo sleep today.

Maggie's eyes widened with shock. 'Then go home and sleep. What are you doing watching Callum's football match?'

'I promised him,' he said, simply. 'And I'm actually heading back out later. I'm meeting someone. I um… have a date.'

Maggie's eyes rounded with surprised delight. 'A date? That's awesome. Who is she?'

Nate shrugged, uncomfortable to discuss this with her. Not because of the mistake they'd made by sleeping together—that was in the past—but because he didn't want to upset his sister-in-law, who, despite going on a couple of token dates this summer, was still grieving Dylan's loss.

'Just someone from work,' he said, momentarily reliving that hot quickie in the staff on-call room. 'It's early days.'

Although all his instincts about Greer had proved accurate. They had fun together, respected each other, aside from her minor wobble last night. And the sex *was* explosive. She was…incredible. Although that moment of distrust had given him pause. If Greer was jealous over a harmless conversation, how would she react to his relationship with Maggie once he told her about their mistake?

'But…' Maggie said, peering at him over the rim of her mug, waiting for more.

'But, yeah... I really like her.' So much so that ever since she'd suggested the expiry date when Lily returned home, he'd been racking his brains for ways he could persuade her to extend their fling. He understood that her daughter was her priority, but why end a good thing if it was working? Surely Greer would agree and they could be discreet.

'So what's she like?' Maggie pushed, her eyes only slightly shiny with repressed emotion.

Nate took a deep breath, grateful to have someone he could tell about Greer, because Dylan would have been his first choice. 'She's smart and kind and...you know, all the things.'

Career-driven, self-assured with a great sense of humour. And so sexy he couldn't think straight when they were together.

'How does she feel about you?' Maggie asked, sliding onto a bar stool and blowing the surface of her drink to cool it.

Nate shrugged one shoulder, not sure he wanted to know that Greer saw him only as a good time for now, because his feelings for her were, he suspected, so much more...complex. Why else would he have reacted so viscerally to her jealousy? 'It's going in the right direction for now.'

He understood her reservations about their age gap. Knew that her divorce and her past had impacted her ability to trust men. But right then, he couldn't imagine them simply walking away from this in a few days' time. But if he wanted Greer for more than a fling, that came with a big risk. He'd have to tell her about Maggie and risk that she'd react negatively like his ex and walk away.

Maggie nodded knowingly. 'Well, don't play it too cool, will you? A woman likes to know she's exceptional.'

'Yeah...' Nate half-heartedly agreed, not because Greer wasn't exceptional—she most definitely was—but because where he feared his addiction to Greer was growing stronger day by day, she was already plotting the end of them. Maybe her trust issues were bigger than he'd realised.

'Have you...discussed your pasts?' Maggie asked carefully.

'Yeah, a bit. I mean, she's divorced so...' Nate dragged in a sigh. 'But I haven't told her everything.'

And the longer he kept his secret from Greer, the harder it was to just casually mention it, especially after last night. He didn't want it to become an issue between them, though. If there was any chance she might want to keep seeing him after Lily returned home, he'd have to tell her soon. Then again, if she saw no future in their relationship, he could keep his secret to himself.

Maggie nodded, looking guilty. 'I know you had that bad experience with Mia, but maybe this time it will be different.'

He nodded again, his doubts unfurling. He'd never given Greer any reason not to trust him. She was a mature woman who knew her own mind and was comfortable in her own skin. Two things he really admired about her. But, like his ex, she might well care about his close relationship with his sister-in-law once she knew the whole story.

At that moment, Callum ran inside. 'Uncle Nate, Mum, come see. One of the tadpoles has turned into a frog.' He took Nate's hand and led him outside, Maggie following behind.

Caught up in Callum's wonder and joy, Nate shoved aside his doubts about Greer and recalled his priorities—being there for Dylan's son if required. Excelling at his job. Deciding that he should take one day at a time with Greer, enjoying whatever time they had together, he gave Callum his full attention, knowing that if Dylan were there, that was exactly what he'd have done.

Saturday afternoon after a few hours' sleep and an invigorating shower, Greer had felt uplifted as she'd set off in the sunshine to meet Nate at the Seven Dials monument in Covent Garden. Waiting for her when she'd arrived, he'd smiled as if he hadn't seen her for weeks and kissed her as if they were alone before taking her hand in his as they ambled along the cobbled streets of the Seven Dials towards the colourful and trendy Neal's Yard.

'Did you get much sleep?' she asked, because he looked a little tired. As she'd awoken in her own lonely bed two hours ago, there'd been a big part of her that had wished he'd been asleep at her side.

As if she was too far away, he wrapped his arm around her shoulders and drew her close. 'Nah... I promised Callum I'd watch his football match so I went there straight from work this morning.'

'You should have cancelled me,' she said, partly glad that he hadn't. After her silly wobble last night, she was determined to enjoy every last second of their time together. Because she couldn't help but be aware of the ticking clock. They had one week before Lily returned from France. Then Greer would need to focus all her time and energy on Lily's last weeks of living at home. Ensuring she had everything she'd need for uni. Helping her pack. Taking some time off to see Lily settled in Manchester.

'And miss the chance to see you away from work?' Nate said, smiling playfully. 'Are you kidding? If I'd cancelled I wouldn't be able to do this.' He stopped walking, flexed his arm, bringing her lips to his, and kissed her deeply, in the middle of the street. A deliciously decadent kiss she felt all the way down to her flip-flopped toes.

Greer shuddered against him, delicious tendrils of desire snaking along her nerves as she basked in the freedom of touching him whenever she liked.

'You make a good point,' she said when they broke apart, and Nate laughed, pressing his lips to her temple as they ambled on.

'Fancy a gelato?' he asked, pointing out a hole-in-the-wall ice-cream shop with a small queue.

'Always,' she said, laughing, her arm around his waist as they perused the flavours on offer and made their very different selections. A scoop of pistachio topped with another of milk-chocolate pretzel for her and Limoncello and custard cream for Nate.

They sat on a bench in the sun to watch the world go by, his arm around her waist and her hand on his thigh.

'Mm, mine's delicious,' she said, swiping her tongue through the rich creamy flavours, a dreamy state of contentment leaving her relaxed and languid.

'Can I try?' he asked, licking his lips as he watched her eat.

'Sure.' She held up her waffle cone for him to try but he ducked his head, bypassed the ice cream and kissed her lazily, his tongue gliding against hers.

'You're right,' he said when he pulled back and licked his lips the heated look he gave her turning her into a puddle of lust. 'Delicious.'

'Oh, very smooth.' Greer rolled her eyes, secretly delighted that he couldn't seem to keep his hands off her. Because she felt the same way.

They smiled goofily at each other, chat turning to Lily's escapades in Provence and Callum's latest obsession: tadpoles.

'You said you never wanted kids of your own,' Greer said hesitantly, 'but you're clearly a great uncle-figure for Callum. He must adore you.'

Even when their marriage had been good, Mark had rarely attended Lily's extra-curricular activities. He'd always had a surgery, or a private patient to see, or simply relied on Greer making the time because of her shift work.

'I try my best.' He licked a smear of ice cream from his top lip. 'He's so funny. If he could sleep with the tadpoles on his pillow, he would.'

She laughed and leaned her head on his shoulder, his proud smile warming her as effectively as the evening sun.

'He obviously gets that from Dylan,' Nate said quietly. 'He was the same growing up. He loved hard and fast, always flung himself into the obsession of the moment, whether it was a girl at school or his BMX bike or learning the keyboard so he could join a boy band.'

'Was Dylan the oldest?' she asked cautiously, so he didn't shut down again. He obviously wanted to talk about his brother and Greer was intrigued to know how they were similar and different.

'No. I was older by eight minutes.' His sigh was so quiet, she might not have heard it if she'd been sitting any further away.

'What about you and girls and your passions?' she asked. 'Were you similar in that way too?'

Nate shrugged. 'I try to make time for hobbies even though I need to be good at my job. And I'm no slouch when it comes to dating. I've had my fair share of girlfriends.'

Greer chuckled. 'I've no doubt.'

Nate fell silent for moment, then went on. 'But as soon as Dylan met Maggie that was it for him. He'd met the one. That's what makes it harder to accept that he's gone. He had it all, you know. A job he adored, married to the love of his life, a family. He had everything to live for.'

Greer nodded, scared to look up, scared to say the wrong thing again. 'Is that what you want, too?' she asked, telling herself her interest was selfless. Nate was too young, too sexy and had too much going for him to be alone. She understood why Callum was his priority, but he must one day want similar happiness for himself.

'I've already got the job. As for the love thing…' he said quietly so Greer held her breath, 'maybe one day. But Callum is enough for me when it comes to kids.'

Greer raised her head, a small frown tugging down her brows. 'Don't forget about your own needs and happiness though, will you? I know you have a loyalty to Callum, that you obviously adore each other, but your well-being is just as important as those of the people you love.'

His dedication to his brother's son was admirable. But as a mother, Greer understood how easy it was to prioritise the needs of others above your own. Easy but not always healthy.

His mouth flattened, his stare searching hers. 'You sound like you speak from experience.'

Greer glanced at her lap. 'I guess I do.' She inhaled and met his stare, trying to be more open. 'I've spent the past four years focused on Lily and work, too busy to put myself first, which is easy to justify when you're someone's parent or carer. That doesn't mean it was emotionally healthy.'

'Maybe you were just too nervous to put yourself out there and meet people,' he said softly, his expression devoid of judgement, because she'd already confided as much in him.

'That too.' She nodded, taking a deep inhale. 'Until you came along and asked me on a date, I couldn't really find the energy for worrying about my personal life or meeting someone new. To be honest, thinking about a serious relationship feels terrifying and exhausting, you know? I have enough baggage of my own without taking on someone else's too. And what man in his forties has no baggage?'

Nate nodded thoughtfully, a small smile kicking up his mouth. 'Even us men in our thirties have some. But you do so much for others, Greer. You deserve to think about yourself. You've raised an incredible young woman while being an amazing doctor. And you're too young to just give up on relationships because one went bad.'

Greer looked up, surprised that he saw her so clearly. 'Yes, I am. But I'm not sure I'd bother to ever get married again.'

Nate tilted his head and frowned. 'Even if you were in love?'

'I don't know.' Losing her appetite, Greer tossed what was left of her cone into a nearby bin and wiped her fingers on a napkin. 'With Lily leaving home after the summer, it seems like the perfect time to rediscover myself. To figure out who I am now after divorce and what I want from the rest of my life. To build on the inner strength I had to find when my life crumbled and re-evaluate my boundaries so my next relationship is more...satisfying. On my terms. Know what I mean?'

'I do. And that sounds very healthy,' Nate said, an encouraging smile dancing on his lips. But it quickly faded to be replaced by a frown. 'But maybe you might get remarried, if you met a man you could trust.'

'Maybe.' She ducked her head, the old shame returning, because she'd obviously disappointed him last night. 'I know not all men cheat.' She met his stare. 'And I'm ashamed to say that there was some part of me, even a subconscious part, that went into my marriage almost expecting it to fail because that was my frame of reference.'

Nate nodded sadly. 'Healthy relationships are about mutual respect and good communication. They're always a two-way street. Maybe now that you've been able to analyse some of your past triggers and behaviours, you can go into your next relationship safe and comfortable enough to know you'll be heard.'

Greer nodded, in awe of his emotional intelligence. 'Well, I'm definitely a work in progress,' she laughed, swooping in to steal a kiss because they had veered into some heavy territory. 'Come on.' She stood and pulled him to his feet. 'It's cocktail hour. I'm going to buy you a drink.'

Nate binned his unfinished gelato and slung his arm over her shoulders once more. 'Can I have beer instead?'

'Of course.' Greer nodded, reaching up to grip his fingers and smiling up at him as they left Neal's Yard and headed towards the Crown and Anchor pub and their delightful beer garden.

CHAPTER THIRTEEN

After the pub, where the conversation returned to lighter topics: the football teams they supported—him Arsenal, her Chelsea—the common music they loved, how they each adored everything about Christmas, they headed for the Tube.

Outwardly, Nate smiled and laughed and pulled her close for a kiss whenever the urge arose, which was often, but inside he couldn't help but be unsettled by their conversations these past twenty-four hours. He could understand Greer's trust issues; they made sense given what she'd experienced growing up. But while he craved her trust as much as he craved her kisses, could he expect her to fully trust him when he was hiding something? Or would him telling her his secret only give her another reason to form an unfounded jealousy?

Her reluctance to remarry shouldn't bother him, given this was just casual. But he felt restless, as if, on some level, he needed to prove to her that some men were different. That they could give as much as they took, could communicate effectively, be respectful and considerate and listen.

Inside Covent Garden Underground station, they paused between the eastbound and westbound platforms where they'd need to part. But despite his fatigue and his lingering unease over Greer's ability to handle his revelation if and when he made it, he wasn't ready to say goodbye.

'Come back to my bachelor pad,' he said, smiling roguishly and taking both her hands while his need for her simmered beneath the surface. 'I know Shepherd's Bush isn't Kensington, but I promise I'm fully domesticated. I'm actually a bit of a neat freak and I'm also a whiz in the kitchen. I could make you dinner.'

For a moment she looked as if she might refuse. But then she nodded. 'Okay. I'd love to. If you're sure you're not too tired.'

'Never.' Nate scooped his arm over her shoulders as they alighted the Piccadilly Line train north, exiting one quick stop later at Holborn, before changing to the westbound Central Line. It was standing room only, so Nate held the grab pole with one hand, his other arm around Greer, holding her close so he could enjoy the feel of her body against his as the train carriage rocked.

She clung to his waist to keep her balance against the back-and-forth movement. It was too crowded to have a conversation, the clack of the train on the tracks too loud, but they simply smiled at each other, clearly equally relaxed.

After three stops along their journey, Nate suddenly felt Greer stiffen, her hold on his waist loosen as she glanced down at her feet.

'You okay?' he quietly asked, glancing around the carriage to see a young woman was blatantly staring at them, when everyone knew one of the unspoken Underground rules was to avoid eye contact with fellow passengers.

Greer nodded and looked out of the window at the tunnel walls speeding by. Obviously something had bothered her. As soon as they were outside, he'd ask.

At Shepherd's Bush, they disembarked and climbed the stairs to street level. Near the top of the last flight of stairs, an older woman ahead of them, tightly clutching the hand of a girl who was most likely her granddaughter, slipped and fell onto her knees, crying out in pain and shock.

Greer reached her first, bending to take the woman's elbow. 'Are you okay?'

Nate moved in front and offered her his hand. The woman, who was clearly in some pain, nodded up at them, her embarrassed gaze flicking to her granddaughter.

'I've got arthritis so I can't move quickly.' She reached for the handrail and slowly found one foot on the stair below.

'Just take your time,' Greer said. 'There's no rush.'

But the impatient passengers behind them formed an irritated bottleneck, many offering dirty looks Nate was only too happy to ignore as they streamed around them without offering to help.

'Lean on us,' Nate told the woman as she slowly tried to stand. He positioned his body as a barrier to the flow of passengers rushing to get on with their evenings, shielding the other three from being jostled as best he could.

'Grandma, you're bleeding,' the little girl said, her face pale with worry.

'It's okay. We're doctors,' Nate told them both, glancing at the graze on the woman's knee and the trail of blood dripping down her shin.

'Let's find a member of staff,' Greer said, leading the woman and her granddaughter towards the exit. 'They should have a first-aid kit.'

Finding a customer service assistant, who led them to a chair and produced the first-aid kit, Greer gently cleaned up the woman's knee wound with gauze while Nate tried his best to make the granddaughter smile.

'Doesn't look like it needs stitches,' Nate said, to which Greer nodded in agreement.

'I'll cover it for now,' she said to the woman, 'but when you get home, gently clean it with some disinfectant and replace the dressing.'

'I'll be fine,' the passenger said. 'Thank you, both. How lucky am I falling in front of two doctors?' She turned to her granddaughter and added, 'Silly old Grandma.'

'It could happen to anyone,' Nate said as Greer stuck a dressing over the graze. 'Can I call you a taxi?' he asked as they exited the station.

'We only have a short walk, but thank you.'

They watched them leave, then headed in the opposite direction towards Nate's flat.

'Some people,' he said, once more resting his arm on Greer's shoulders and holding her hand. 'The dirty looks some of the passengers shot us because they were slowed down for thirty seconds.'

Greer nodded. 'Yeah. Some people...' she agreed, but to Nate sounded distracted and tense.

'You're kind,' he said, pressing his lips to her temple.

'So are you.' She smiled up at him.

'We make a good team, then,' he said as they crossed the road and headed for his flat.

Nate's 'bachelor pad' turned out to be a bright and stylish two-bedroom apartment on the top floor of a charming Edwardian red-brick mansion overlooking Spencer Green, a leafy urban park popular with families, dog walkers and joggers. The large sun-drenched reception room gave way to an open-plan dining room and kitchen where Nate was clearly very much at home. Sexily so, although Greer was obviously biased.

'Red wine or white?' he asked, retrieving two glasses from a sleek-fronted modern wall cabinet.

'Red, please,' she answered, taking a seat at the island to watch him pour the wine while she tried to brush off what had happened on the Tube.

She'd been having a lovely evening, enjoying the sunshine and bustle of the city. Enjoying Nate's uplifting company and frequent touches. Holding hands, his arm around her shoulders, the way he seemed as addicted to their kisses as she was. Then she'd looked up and caught someone staring at them on the train and all her doubts had resurfaced like repeated blows from a heavyweight boxer.

'Is pasta okay for dinner?' he asked, filling a pan with water, adding a pinch of coarse sea salt and placing it on the ceramic hob.

'Great,' Greer said, although she wasn't particularly hungry. Nate was observing her cautiously as if he knew her fears and doubts. As if she were made of glass. She didn't want to hurt him or make him feel as if she didn't want to be there, so she smiled brightly as he turned from the stove.

'To summer dates and gelato,' Nate said, touching his glass to hers.

'Cheers.' She held his eye contact as they each sipped.

Nate reached for her hand and led her to a comfy sofa, where she kicked off her flip-flops and leaned into his side, her head resting on his chest. He'd put some music on when they'd arrived and she listened for a few moments, trying to rediscover the contentment she'd felt earlier.

'What happened on the Tube?' he asked after another moment's silence, his heart thudding under her cheek. 'I noticed you became uncomfortable suddenly.'

Greer swallowed, wishing she could hide the truth or dismiss his concern, but she respected him too much to even try, especially after how she'd behaved last night.

'Just a silly moment. *My* silly moment,' she said, looking up and brushing his lips with hers. 'Someone was staring at us and it suddenly hit home why. That it was most likely because I'm older than you. I'd kind of mostly forgotten that this past week, believe it or not.' But the staring woman on the train was just another reminder that, as great as he was, Nate wasn't the man for her.

Nate slid his thumb over her knuckles. 'I *can* believe it, Greer. When I look at you, when I'm with you, I'm not thinking about the numbers and the arbitrary norms acceptable by society. I'm just in the moment with you, a woman I enjoy spending time with, can laugh with and who I also find as sexy as sin.'

Greer chuckled softly. She felt exactly the same about him. Then she fell serious. 'I haven't been thinking about our age gap this whole time either. I guess her staring today made me question it again. We're at different life stages, you and I. I've been married and you have that to come. You have time to test out relationships until you find the one. Whereas I don't have the luxury of making another big mistake. I almost have an adult daughter and—'

'I have Callum,' he interrupted, clearly uncomfortable with her comparisons.

'Yes.' She nodded again, lowering her stare from his.

'I guess, up until today, I've convinced myself that our handful of stolen moments during the night shift, our conversations, our first kiss, even that incredibly hot sex we had in the on-call room… It's all felt like a dream. A very sexy, forbidden dream that makes me want to stay asleep a bit longer.'

'I get that,' he said, a thoughtful frown pinching his brows together.

And yet for all her maturity in years, sometimes, like now, he made her feel inexperienced somehow, vulnerable and afraid of the power of their connection. When they were alone, when she was caught up in him, the rest of the world, her worries and hang-ups just disappeared. But they were there beneath the surface. And they were real.

'Come here.' Patting his lap, he urged her to sit astride his thighs. He cupped her face, his stare locked to hers. 'This is just about us. You and me. No one else matters.'

'I know.' Greer nodded, awash with embarrassment that she'd allowed such an irrelevance as the judgement of a stranger to get into her head. 'How is it that sometimes you seem like the mature one?' Open and communicative and dauntless.

He smiled sadly, as if he'd expected her to be over this issue by now. 'We don't just make a good team,' he went on, 'we're also good together, aren't we? Is it just me who feels it? Because from where I'm standing, what we have is pretty special.'

She nodded again. 'I feel it too.' But just because they were a great team at work and clicked in the bedroom, shared a sense of humour and were comfortable with each other, didn't change the facts.

Nate was in his prime. He deserved all the things

Dylan had had. And Greer wasn't sure she was ready to look for love again.

'Our private life is just that, Greer: private. We don't owe anyone an explanation or justification. We don't have to apologise or make ourselves smaller to make strangers feel comfortable in their narrow beliefs or opinions.'

'You're right.' She nodded once more, her breathing tight because he seemed to see and understand her so clearly.

'And aside from the fact that we're not engaged,' he went on, 'that this is a fling, what's the difference between you and me and your ex and his fiancée?'

'Nothing,' she agreed. 'I don't want to feel this way... I just...' She faltered, scared that her unhelpful thinking might simply be her fear at play. Because when she was with Nate, it sometimes felt so right she had to catch herself and remember that it wasn't a serious relationship. That it couldn't go anywhere. That it would soon be over.

'Maybe it's because the patriarchy runs the world,' he said, his expression sardonic. 'It's okay for a man to date a woman half his age, but not the other way around.' He smiled sadly as if taking the responsibility of every man on his shoulders, and Greer smiled back, loving that he cared so passionately.

'I mean, it's not really okay,' she said, feeling lighter for having shared her thoughts with him. 'If Lily brought home a forty-year-old boyfriend I'd have a lot to say about it, but I appreciate your point. Thanks for talking me down from the ledge. I guess I've just been so engrossed in this sexy guy I'm seeing, a part of me isn't ready for the bubble to burst.'

Nate searched her stare, his turning serious. 'Why does

it have to burst? Can't we keep it intact a while longer and see how it goes?'

'Yes.' Greer nodded, her heart thudding because part of her wanted exactly that. 'I'm sorry I freaked out. Again. I told you it was silly.'

Nate shook his head. 'Nothing you feel is silly.'

Sighing, she leaned down and pressed her lips to his, sliding her fingers into his hair, tilting his head back as she touched her tongue to his, kissing him freely and deeply, exploring him until his hands fisted gently in her hair and he groaned. Desire for him bloomed anew, crushing all other feelings until she forgot about the world outside, forgot her responsibilities. She even forgot to play it cool and simply lived in the moment with Nate.

'Turn off the pasta water,' she said, when, panting, they broke apart.

Nate stared up at her with desire-darkened eyes and nodded. 'Hold on,' he said, cupping her backside and standing, carrying her to the kitchen, where she reached down and turned off the hob, before he strode to his bedroom and lowered her to the bed.

They stripped in silence, their stares hungrily roaming each other's naked bodies, their constant need for each other clearly matched. When they lay face to face, their palms gliding over skin, their legs entwined as they kissed and kissed, Greer closed her eyes, basking in the perfect moment of connection with this incredible man. A man who'd given her back a part of herself she hadn't realised was missing.

Nate cupped her cheeks, stroking her hair back from her face as he pressed kisses over her closed eyelids. 'I see you, Greer. I know you've been hurt before. I know you've struggled with trust because of your parents and your past. But I'm not the kind of man to cheat or mess around.'

Greer opened her eyes and swallowed at the honest vulnerability she saw in his. 'I know,' she whispered, wishing she could feel this certainty for ever.

'If I wanted anyone else, I wouldn't be here with you,' Nate said, staring deep into her eyes.

Greer nodded, emotion welling in her throat as she held him close. 'I want you too, Nate. I don't think anyone has ever seen me as clearly as you do. It's...scary.'

Because he'd shattered every assumption she'd made about him. Showing her over and over again his emotional depth and complexities. His incredible strength and empathy. His maturity and dependability.

He nodded, sighing. 'I know. I... I feel it too. I... I want you all the time.'

'I'm right here.' Determined to look no further ahead than today, Greer slid her fingers into his hair and brought his mouth back to hers. His kisses, deep and drugging, silenced her doubts. His fiercely possessive touch soothed her fears. In his arms, free to be herself, anything seemed possible and she knew exactly who she was. Knew that he wouldn't hurt her just as she wouldn't hurt him.

'Nate,' she moaned as he captured her nipple with his mouth, sucking as he stroked between her legs, drowning out everything but the clamour of sensation and need.

Reaching for the condom he'd tossed on the bed earlier, she covered him and pulled him on top of her, parting her thighs to accommodate his hips, kissing him again as he slid his fingers between hers and pressed their joined hands into the mattress.

'Do you trust me?' he asked, peering down at her, his eyes determined and dark with desire.

'Yes.' Greer nodded, her lips chasing his once more as he pushed inside her and she groaned, crossing her ankles in the small of his back.

'Look at me,' he demanded, his hips beginning to move so all she could do was cling to him and ride out the surges of pleasure and obey. She gasped at the dark possessive look on his face.

'This is about us, Greer,' he said, his expression fierce. 'Just us.'

She nodded, too turned on to speak, too lost to do anything but grip his hands and stare back as he drove them both higher and higher, his thrusts faster and harder.

'Nate,' she gasped, her orgasm all but tearing her apart as he groaned, reared up and, with a final jerk, his face twisted in blissful release, came too.

CHAPTER FOURTEEN

'WHY DON'T YOU stay the night?' Nate asked sleepily as Greer hunted the bedroom floor for her underwear. The twenty-four hours without sleep was finally catching up with him. His eyelids felt made of lead. He couldn't even muster the strength to properly admire naked Greer, who was gorgeously dishevelled, her skin still flushed from her orgasm. He wanted to shower with her, wash every inch of her body and then fall asleep with her in his arms, waking her up with morning sex until she was too pleasure-drunk to overthink what was happening between them, too consumed by this to care about other people and had to rely solely on feelings. Because when they were together, he too forgot his doubts and fears.

'I can't. I have a ton of things to do tomorrow, including cleaning the flat. Lily is home Saturday. It's her birthday. I'm throwing her a surprise eighteenth party.'

'Okay.' Nate rose too and pulled on his boxers, certain from the hollowness in the middle of his chest that his addiction to Greer had reached new heights and that he already had feelings for her. The idea of simply walking away from this the minute her daughter returned from France made him want to throw up. But Greer, despite her assurances that she trusted him, despite their growing connection, hadn't mentioned revising the plan.

'Next Saturday...' he mumbled, knowing that if he weren't so tired he'd seize this moment to discover Greer's thoughts. 'That's come around pretty quickly.'

Every bone in his body ached with resistance at the arbitrary cut-off she'd set. But since when had he been passive? If he wanted something, he went after it, fatigued or not.

Greer pulled on her jeans and looked up with uncertainty and a flash of guilt. 'I... I wondered if you'd like to come to the party,' she said with only a hint of hesitancy. 'I've invited my ex and his fiancée, Cara. She's asked Lily to be her bridesmaid and if she's going to be my daughter's stepmother, I'd like to know her better. And some of the ED nurses too. The ones who've met Lily over the years.'

Nate picked up her T-shirt and held it out to her, his heart leaping with excitement even as he told himself to calm down. 'I'd love to come, if you want me there.'

It was a small step but maybe it meant she was ready for them to step out of the shadows. To stop all the secrets and sneaking around. To have a shot at making this fling a real relationship.

'Of course,' Greer said, pulling the shirt on, 'it's just a barbecue with Lily's school friends and plus ones mainly. Very casual.'

Because she was distracted and acting flustered, as if already stressing about the event, Nate snaked an arm around her waist, pulled her body flush to his and kissed her, slowly, lazily, deeply. She sighed, crossing her arms over his shoulders, pressing his head closer with her forearms so the kiss deepened and she moaned.

Holding her waist, he pulled back. 'I know we agreed to stop seeing each other when Lily returns, but I don't want this to be our last week together.' His pulse buzzed in his ears as he held his breath.

'I know.' She winced, her eyes darting away. 'I just… We need to be careful. I don't want Lily to be confused or hurt by this. Us. I don't want to act like Mark, forcing her to meet all his casual conquests as if it legitimised the relationships that obviously weren't destined to last. I haven't even told her that I'm dating someone. I need to tread carefully, because she'll be gone again in a matter of weeks to Manchester.'

Nate nodded in understanding, relieved that they were on the same page, that neither of them was ready for this to end, even as unease tensed his shoulders at the idea of Greer dating a string of men after him. 'You'll tell her in your own time. Don't put any pressure on yourself. Just know that I'm here if you need me. For anything. Minor freak-outs. Dinner I promise to finish next time. Mature advice dressed in cartoon socks.'

Nate understood this relationship was difficult for her. In addition to her previous trust issues, she feared judgement over their age gap and professional embarrassment because he was her registrar. But if they wanted to make this work, he knew she'd work through all of that in time. And he'd give her that time. After all, she was worth waiting for.

'Thanks.' She looked up and smiled with shining eyes. 'I'm going to go,' she said, pressing her mouth to his in a restrained kiss. 'You need to sleep before you collapse.'

'Can I see you after work, Monday?' he asked. 'Before you start the night shift?'

She smiled and nodded. 'Absolutely. Just come round to Willow Gardens when you finish. We've barely made a dent in that jumbo box of condoms.'

'Challenge accepted.' Nate grinned and shot her a flirty wink. 'It's a date.'

At the door to his flat, she pressed her lips to his one final time, her hand cupping his bristled cheek. 'Sleep well.'

And then she was gone, taking a small slice of his peace of mind with her, because no matter what they'd said to reassure each other, no matter how strongly his feelings were when they were together, once apart Nate too felt the pressure of his doubts.

His secret grew heavier. He didn't want to let Greer down. He didn't want to fall for another woman who might not tolerate his relationship with Dylan's family. But stronger than either of those was his fear of once more failing someone he loved. And when it came to Greer, to the feelings he was desperately trying to untangle, he might already be headed in that direction.

By Friday, a new work-life pattern had developed, one for which Nate could develop a serious addiction. He'd finish his day shift at the hospital and race straight around to Greer's place. They'd spend an hour in bed, the sex intense and desperate because of the time restraints and the fact that their freedom to see each other as much as they wanted would end once Lily arrived home. Then they'd shower together and walk hand in hand to the Tube station, where they'd part, Greer headed for the hospital and her night shift and Nate headed home to crash.

Energised to repeat the pattern and see Greer later that evening, Nate arrived early for his day shift and got straight to work. His first patient of the day was a thirty-nine-year-old man with chest pain and shortness of breath. As the nurses wheeled the patient into Resus, adjusting the oxygen flow through his mask and attaching him to the cardiac monitors, Nate quickly spoke to the paramedic for some history.

'He's an oncology patient here,' the paramedic said. 'Had an orchidectomy for testicular cancer eight weeks ago. Had his third round of chemotherapy last week. He's tachycardic, respiratory rate of twenty-two and his blood pressure is low.'

Nate listened, while he began his observations of the patient, noting the man's blue lips, a sign of central cyanosis, and corresponding low oxygen saturations.

'Hi, Matt, I'm Nate, one of the emergency doctors here. I need to examine you and run some tests.'

He fitted his stethoscope and listened to the patient's heart, noting that his ECG appeared normal apart from sinus tachycardia. Some chemotherapy agents could be cardiotoxic, causing heart failure or arrhythmias.

'Do we have the notes?' Nate asked Harry. 'Check the chemotherapy agents he's received and call his oncologist and Radiology. We need an urgent chest X-ray.'

Needing to exclude pneumonia or a pulmonary embolism, Nate listened to the patient's breath sounds, closing his eyes to focus amid the noises of the room: shoes squeaking on the linoleum, the beep of monitors, the whoosh of the door swinging open and shut. Nate could hear crackles at the lung bases when he listened, telling him the lungs were waterlogged because the heart was under strain, but there was another sound too. A subtle creaking on auscultation of the chest, a sign called a pleural rub, an indication of an infarcted lung grating on the pleura.

'Is Dr Thorn still here?' Nate asked Sally, one of the nurses, when he'd completed his examination. His suspected diagnosis was a pulmonary embolism. He felt confident he was right, but it wouldn't hurt to have a second opinion, especially in a case like this that was complicated by a recent cancer diagnosis and chemotherapy.

'She's with a stroke patient next door,' Sally said, apologetically, and Nate nodded. 'I haven't seen Dr Huxtable yet this morning,' Sally said about the consultant on the day shift today. 'Do you want me to page him?'

Nate nodded. 'Thanks, Sally. But first let's start an anticoagulant infusion.' Nate reached for a syringe to take an arterial sample from the man's wrist to measure his arterial blood gas levels.

Just then the radiologist arrived and, using the portable X-ray machine, quickly took a chest X-ray.

'Order an urgent V/Q scan,' Nate told Harry, who rushed to the computer to do just that. The ventilation-perfusion scan would definitively identify a pulmonary embolism.

While everyone present rushed to treat the life-threatening condition, the worst happened. The patient slumped and fell unconscious. The cardiac monitor alarms sounded, and when Nate tried to find a pulse, there wasn't one.

'Call the crash team,' he said, reaching for an oropharyngeal airway and a manual resuscitation bag. 'Start CPR.'

Sally began chest compressions. Nate glanced at the cardiac monitor. The patient's heart was in asystole or flat-line. Just then, the crash team arrived, the anaesthetist taking over the patient's breathing so Nate could administer the adrenaline.

Greer too arrived, looking tired as she glanced at Nate for an explanation.

'Suspected massive pulmonary embolism,' he told her, flushing the adrenaline that might restart the man's heart into his IV. 'He's a post-op chemotherapy patient, stage two testicular cancer.'

Greer nodded, her expression grim but determined as she took over chest compressions from the nurse, while Nate kept time, monitored the heart's rhythm and administered more adrenaline.

After ten minutes, the heart rhythm was unchanged, the prognosis poor. At some stage the patient's oncologist had arrived, the woman warily watching the resuscitation attempts from the sidelines. Nate looked to her now for her guidance.

She pressed her lips together, her expression similar to every other person's in the room. Resignation tempered by a glimmer of hope. It seemed no one was ready to make the call to stop CPR, least of all Nate. But it was his job to make such calls. Yes, the outlook for this patient was poor given the diagnosis and the prolonged period of resuscitation. The potential for the patient's recovery without permanent neurological consequences was dwindling as time went on. But Nate refused to give up on someone so young. Someone not much older than him, someone like Dylan.

'Is everyone happy to keep going?' Nate asked, making the judgement call and his position clear.

Everyone nodded, Greer included.

'Get me a central line kit,' Nate told Sally, quickly washing up and pulling on sterile gloves. 'I need an rtPA infusion.'

Administered directly into a major vein, the clot-dissolving drug might be enough to treat the embolus in the man's lung and allow his heart to function once more. It was certainly worth a shot with other options dwindling.

Standing beside the anaesthetist who'd intubated the patient, Nate inserted the catheter into the man's jugular vein and attached the infusion. With his last-ditch attempt complete, Nate looked up to find Greer staring at him with sympathy. She knew him, knew what he was thinking: that if there was any chance of recovery, Nate would do what he could. And she also knew why he was fighting so hard, because he'd confided in her about Dylan and his regrets. But he couldn't be distracted by that now.

The CPR continued for another fifteen minutes, during which Nate became increasingly despondent. Then, suddenly, just as he thought he might have to re-evaluate the decision to keep going, the heart rhythm changed and everyone immediately felt for a pulse.

'I've got one,' Greer said, looking to Nate with relief.

'Me too.' He kept his fingers on the man's carotid artery, never more relieved to feel the rhythmic beat of life against his fingertips.

'Call ICU,' Nate instructed Harry as some members of the crash team departed, their roles over now that the patient had been resuscitated. 'And chase the chest X-ray results.'

Sally, next to him, touched his arm and said quietly, 'Well done, Dr Hunter.'

Nate nodded, relieved that his efforts to resuscitate the patient had succeeded. He looked around for Greer, but she'd already left too, replaced by Dr Huxtable. The consultant on the day shift.

It was only hours after the emergency that Nate realised that Greer would normally have offered him a secret look or word of approval after they'd worked on a case together. It shouldn't bother him. He could do his job without her support. They were busy medical professionals for whom the job, the patient, always came first. And she would be at home asleep by now after her night shift.

But as he went about his work day with Greer constantly at the back of his mind, Nate realised how deeply he was in this. He ached, constantly craving her, addicted to her smile, her support and whatever scraps of her time he could get. Fearful that, despite what she said, she didn't fully trust him. Certainly his feelings seemed to eclipse hers, and if he wasn't careful, if he laid himself bare, told Greer his secret shame and opened himself up entirely to her and she didn't feel the same way, he'd be devastated.

With only her message on his phone to tide him over—*meet you at Spencer Green after your shift*—Nate shoved away the thought that maybe the time had come to tell Greer about Maggie and focused on work.

CHAPTER FIFTEEN

Later that day, Greer awoke to find a message from Nate saying he'd be home at 4:00 p.m. Unsettled by what she'd witnessed earlier at the hospital—Nate's heavy emotional investment in his patient—Greer packed her work bag and headed over to his place on the Tube.

She pressed the buzzer to his apartment, her stomach knotted with apprehension. She understood how easy it was to be affected by some cases. Doctors were only human. For Nate, this morning's cardiac arrest patient had most likely reminded him a little too closely of his brother. But for Greer it had been a sign that, while he took pride in being good at his job, there were clearly underlying emotions that drove Nate, who maybe wasn't as far along in the grieving process as she'd assumed. Her need to make sure he was okay even eclipsed the niggle of lingering jealousy she'd experienced when nurse Sally had touched him after the arrest.

'Come up,' Nate said through the intercom, the buzzer sounding and the front door lock disabling with a metallic click. When she reached his floor, Nate stood in the open doorway of his apartment, looking tired, his stare a little wary.

'Hi,' she said, sliding her arm around his waist as she pressed her lips to his. 'How are you doing?'

'I'm fine,' he said, leading her into the kitchen, where she placed her bag on a bar stool. 'Do you want a cold drink?'

She nodded and he fixed them each a tall glass of tonic water with ice and a slice of lemon.

'Shame there's no gin in it,' she said, trying to be playful then taking a sip to calm her nerves.

He gave her a small smile then watched her carefully, his expression guarded. Maybe he was expecting another jealous cold shoulder.

'I'm sorry about this morning,' she began. 'Sally came looking for me saying you needed help, but by the time I got there the arrest was in full swing. Any idea how the patient is doing?' Because there was too much distance between them, she abandoned her drink and stepped close, wrapping her arms around his waist and resting her head over the reassuring thud of his heart.

'He's still unconscious in ICU,' he said flatly, his arm around her shoulders and his chin resting on the top of her head as he held her close.

'You did everything you could, Nate. Now it's just a waiting game to gauge his recovery.'

Nate nodded, the tension in his body palpable so she could tell he was in no way convinced.

'I'm really sorry I wasn't there for you when you needed me,' she said softly. 'After the arrest, I had no legitimate reason to hang around the emergency department on the off chance we'd have a moment to speak. You were busy. I didn't want to arouse suspicion by waiting for you.'

'It's okay,' he said. 'I understand, Greer. Although right now, I'm struggling to care about suspicions that we might be more than colleagues. But I understand you feel a degree of professional responsibility, given our positions.'

'Of course I do.' Greer blinked, shocked by his candour, feeling uncertain of him in this mood. 'I'm not sure I'm ready to simply announce us to the world.' In fact as the days passed, as Lily's return approached, she was less and less sure of everything beyond the fact that she couldn't seem to control her physical addiction to Nate.

'Don't worry.' He scrubbed a hand over his face. 'I'm just tired. It's been a long day.'

Greer winced, watching him closely. She cared about him the way he cared about her. She couldn't simply stand by and see him struggle with his guilt over Dylan.

'Listen, I know it's hard to be objective sometimes,' she continued, stepping back to face him, 'especially when patients are young. When they remind us of someone we know or we can put ourselves in their shoes or those of their loved ones. I've been there, too.'

When he stayed silent, watching her with an expression more haunted than when she'd first arrived, Greer pressed her lips together. She seemed to be making things worse, not better. He clearly didn't want to talk about this.

Suddenly, as if coming to a decision, Nate stepped forwards and reached for her, kissing her hard and fast and desperately as if he'd waited too long or wanted to halt further conversation. Aching for him and the demons he was so clearly still struggling with, Greer kissed him back, her hands sliding under his shirt, her tongue sliding against his as she became engulfed in familiar desires.

'I missed you,' he said desperately, his lips gliding along her jaw, his fingers sliding into her hair. 'I know it's crazy because we see each other all the time. But… I don't want this to be over.'

'Nate,' Greer moaned as his hand slid along her thigh under her skirt. 'I missed you too. It's not over.' Not yet, although maybe Nate could hear the same ticking clock she could hear. And as much as she was trying to trust him, her demons weren't silent either.

He pressed her back against the counter, hoisting her up onto the edge and standing between her spread thighs to deepen their kiss and then pull back.

'I need you,' he said, their eyes locked as his fingers delved inside her underwear, stroking and teasing and sending spirals of delicious pleasure along her legs down to her toes.

'I need you too.' She pulled at his T-shirt and he tossed it away. Then she reached for his fly, popping the button of his jeans and shoving them and his boxers over his hips to free his erection.

'Condom in my bag,' she mumbled as he kissed her again. While she reached for the bag, Nate peeled her underwear down, his hand back between her legs, his fingers sliding inside her so she gasped.

'Hurry,' she said, handing him the condom, desperate now to reaffirm their connection to banish the emotional day and silence all the noisy doubts.

While he put it on she kissed his face, his neck, his shoulders and chest, sliding her tongue over his skin, breathing in the comforting scent of him to hold it like a memory. He was such an incredible man. She could hold onto this, take one day at a time. Show him she did trust him.

She gripped his shoulders. He wrapped one arm around her hips and held her in place, pushed inside her, while they kissed and moaned.

'Yes, Nate,' she said, clinging to him as they moved,

fast and frantic. She wrapped her thighs around his waist and he held them in his hands, chasing her mouth as if he couldn't bear for one part of them to be separated.

They came together, her with a blissful cry and him with an agonised groan he uttered against the side of her neck as his breaths heaved and his arms tightened, holding her close.

As they caught their breath, Greer stroked his back, surprised by his tight grip on her. Something subtle had changed between them. Nate seemed withdrawn, as if, despite what he'd said about wanting more time, this was coming to its natural end. Or maybe he recognised both her lingering trust issues and her growing doubts, saw how conflicted she was, desperate for him one minute, hardening her heart the next because it surely had to end some time. And she didn't want either of them to be hurt.

'Are you okay?' she whispered, remembering what he'd been through and why, for him, today might have been a tough one.

He nodded, looked up and slowly withdrew, helping her down from the counter. 'I'll be back in a second. Don't go anywhere. I need to talk to you.'

While he was in the bathroom, Greer pulled on her underwear and ran her fingers through her hair, her stomach hollow with the idea she was responsible for their situation. Yes, Nate had asked her out on a date. But she could have shut him down. Made it clear that she wouldn't tolerate such a lapse in professional judgement on her part. But it was too late now. She'd been flattered and weak. She'd allowed herself to know him, to see him as clearly as he saw her. And now she wanted him to be happy and fulfilled regardless of how long this relationship could last.

'I want to talk to you, too,' she said when he came back from the bathroom.

He reached for her hand and led her to the sofa, where he pulled her down to sit at his side.

'You go first,' he said, a frown pinching his brows together.

She squeezed his fingers, his strange mood and her guilt for her possessive thoughts over Sally leaving her uncertain where to begin. She didn't want to overstep again and make him withdraw, but after today nor could she stay silent. 'I wanted you to know that, just like you see me, I also see you,' she said softly. She could sense he was holding back. Throwing all he had into his job and Callum when he had so much more to give for the right woman.

'It struck me this morning after the cardiac arrest,' she said, 'that the reason you were maybe not as objective as at other times is because of Dylan.'

He frowned deeper and Greer rushed on. 'I think you're struggling to forgive yourself for not spotting that Dylan was sick. Maybe you're even telling yourself that you don't deserve to be happy because you let him down or because he's not here to feel the same way. But that's not true, Nate. You do deserve that. You—'

He began to shake his head, dismissing her observations before she'd even finished.

She gripped both his hands, urging him to hear what she had to say. 'What happened to Dylan wasn't your fault. Just because we're doctors, doesn't mean we're not also human. It doesn't mean we can fix everyone. And I'm sure Dylan wouldn't want you to feel guilty or hold yourself responsible. He loved you like you love him. He'd want you to be happy, too. You have to let this guilt go and forgive yourself so you can be fulfilled. So you can have the things Dylan had and loved, if you want them.'

She wasn't sure how long they could continue this relationship, how long it would meet both their needs, but, like Nate, part of her wasn't ready to walk away. If she could help him see that his guilt wasn't healthy, maybe she'd have no regrets when it did end.

'I know I can't fix everyone,' he said, his voice strained. 'And I appreciate your concern. But—' He broke off and exhaled loudly, looking away. Wordlessly, he got to his feet and paced over to the window, turned and paced back, coming to stand still before Greer.

'You're right. I do feel guilty,' he said, a frustrated edge to his voice. 'I always will. Blaming myself for missing my brother's diagnosis isn't rational, I know. But I've felt responsible for him my whole life. I let him down. I was the eldest. Those eight minutes mattered to me and part of me is terrified to forget Dylan. But there's something else, Greer. The thing I want to tell you. Something I'm not proud of. Something I wish I could undo but can't.'

'It's okay. Whatever it is. You can forgive yourself for that, too.'

He shook his head, scrubbed a hand over his face then met her stare, his almost pleading. 'I…really like you, Greer. I'd like to keep seeing you. I think we could have a real relationship, but I have to tell you this first.'

'So tell me.' Dread knotted in the pit of her stomach. 'Is it to do with Sally? I noticed how close you two were this morning.'

'What? No.' Nate scowled, confused and obviously hurt by her assumption. 'It's nothing to do with anyone but me. I… Can you just listen for a moment?'

'Okay.' Her heart was beating so fast she wondered if she might be sick.

Nate retook his seat and reached for both her hands. 'After Dylan died, I was a mess.'

She nodded, her heart sore. Of course he would have been a mess. She wouldn't expect anything else.

'I kept waiting for it to get easier the way they say—that rubbish about time healing. But it didn't work. Every morning I'd wake up struck with the same sickening shock that I'd awoken to a world where he no longer existed. The only thing that helped me back then was Callum. I had to be strong for him. If he wanted to cry, I had to simply sit with him, hold him. If he had questions about his dad, I tried to answer them as honestly as I could. Maggie was in a state too. I began spending so much time at their place, Callum would ask me for a bedtime story, because that had been his and Dylan's thing.'

Greer nodded, her eyes stinging for their loss.

'Then one night, months after the funeral, Maggie and I were talking about Dylan and crying after Callum was asleep as we often did over a glass of Dylan's favourite beer, and out of nowhere we were kissing.'

Greer froze, the swallow she took painful as she tried to keep her expression neutral.

'I know,' he said, his jaw clenched. 'One thing led to another and we slept together. I hated myself immediately after, and so did Maggie. We instantly regretted it, cried some more and each swore that would never happen again. But even if I'd wanted to put some space between us, I couldn't abandon Callum, not when I'd somehow partially filled this void Dylan had left behind.'

'That was why your ex got jealous,' she said, the pieces

slotting into place. 'Why she couldn't tolerate your close relationship with Maggie. You told her, didn't you?'

Hot spikes of jealousy she wished she didn't feel stabbed at her chest. Nate and Maggie were still close.

Nate nodded. 'And why I've wanted to tell you, wanted to explain why my grief and my guilt is so…complex. Why I push myself to be good at my job so me letting my brother down isn't in vain. I messed up, Greer. I let Dylan down twice. Once when he was sick and then again by acting out and trying to numb the pain of his death. I was his older brother. It was my job to never let him down.'

Greer nodded, numbly. 'You could have told me sooner, although I understand why you kept it from me.' She winced, hearing the unfair accusation in her words.

Nate frowned. 'I didn't *keep it* from you. I didn't want it to be an issue between us but nor did I know where this relationship was going.'

Greer nodded, unable to sift through the mix of her feelings as a sickening sense of déjà vu clouded her thoughts, transporting her back in time to a hundred other moments when she'd struggled to trust and doubted her instincts.

'Part of me didn't want you to judge me,' Nate went on. 'My ex tried to make me choose between her and Dylan's family.'

'That wasn't fair of her,' Greer said, realising how close she'd come to judging him too because of her issues. 'You made an error of judgement before you met her. It was unreasonable for her to expect you to cut ties with your family, especially when you and Maggie were over.' But despite her seeing his ex's behaviour rationally, there was still a part of Greer that could relate to the jealousy element.

'Me and Maggie were never a thing,' he said, firmly. 'It

was a grief-stricken moment of madness. An unhealthy coping mechanism like binge drinking.'

'I know...' Greer nodded in understanding even as her stomach rolled again at the idea of Nate and Maggie's relationship, those old demons of hers close to the surface. Nate wasn't her father, wasn't Mark, but she couldn't help the shudder of doubt that skittered over her skin like a shiver. She'd opened up to this man, been vulnerable with him, despite her former misgivings for beginning a romantic relationship. It was only natural to feel unsettled by his revelation, especially when he'd kept it a secret all these weeks.

'I was scared that if you knew it might push you away,' Nate said, cupping her face and pressing a swift kiss to her lips, his expression hopeful and relieved. 'But I no longer wanted to keep it a secret from you. I even told Maggie about you. She's excited to meet you.'

'You told Maggie about me?' Greer's stomach tightened, sickeningly. If Nate had confided in Maggie about their fling, the two of them obviously had a *very* close relationship. And if it was definitely over between him and Maggie, if there was no longer anything to tell, if it was all harmless, why keep it a secret at all?

'Yes, because I care about you, Greer. I was excited and told her I had a date. But I haven't told her your name or any specifics. I wouldn't do that.'

'I know.' Greer nodded, ignoring his declaration. She had feelings for him too, but it was clearly time for a reality check. Would she feel that old familiar wavering of trust if she was ready for a real serious relationship? Over Sally's innocent pat on the arm and now the idea of Nate and Maggie? Clearly her recent misgivings and doubts about taking this beyond a secret fling were justified. Warnings she should perhaps heed before she got hurt again. Before this went any further and became another mistake.

Aware that Nate was waiting for a response, Greer swallowed past her dry throat. Her chest tightened, her stomach swirling. She needed space. Air. She needed to get away from him so she could think clearly. So she could untangle how she truly felt. Because maybe Nate was right. Maybe she couldn't fully trust him.

Greer's discomfort was obvious in the set of her mouth and her lowered gaze as she stood up. Nate's fingers curled into a fist and he released a frustrated sigh as he felt her slipping away. 'Do you know that about me?' he asked, frowning. She'd said she trusted him and now she was looking at him as if he were a stranger.

'Yes, of course...'

The lack of conviction in her voice sent his mind spiralling. 'You've heard every word I've said? Because I know you've struggled with trust in the past, but me and Maggie... It's not like that. Nor is there anything going on with me and Sally, for that matter. Tell me you understand that, Greer? I thought you trusted me.'

He couldn't hide his hurt and frustration. He'd assumed they'd moved past bouts of unfounded jealousy, but maybe Greer wasn't as invested in him as he was in her. Maybe he was falling for another woman who might not support his relationship with Dylan's family.

'I do understand,' she said. 'I've heard everything you said. Thanks for telling me about Maggie. I... I'm sorry I can't stay longer.' She stood, her gaze flicking towards the door. 'I need to go. I said I'd start an hour early tonight to cover for Dr Jameson.'

She sounded fatigued and resigned. Distant.

'Wait.' Panicked, Nate reached for her hand and stood too, confused that he'd poured out his heart and Greer was simply leaving, although he understood that she needed to work. 'You look like you don't believe me. You're acting like it's an issue for you.'

Greer shook her head. 'No. I do believe you. I just... I'm surprised, that's all. I wasn't expecting that revelation. I understand how grief affects people in many ways. What you've told me doesn't make me think any less of you, Nate.' She placed her hand on top of his, giving him hope. 'I hate to rush off but I have to go to work. I can't really think about this right now. Can I call you tomorrow?'

Nate pressed his lips together in frustration. 'Of course.'

Greer nodded and headed for the kitchen to collect her bag. 'I'll call you when I get home from the hospital tomorrow morning.' She walked to the door, as if desperate to get away.

Nate followed her, leaned in to press his lips to hers in a kiss that felt pleading and frantic. Irritation and panic swirled in Nate in equal measure. It felt as if he were losing her when he'd not only made himself vulnerable but had also hoped they were past mistrust.

Before she could leave, he asked, 'Do you...do you still want me at the party?' He held his breath anticipating her answer, which might go either way.

'Of course,' she said, and Nate winced at the wobble of uncertainty in her voice.

'And if I do come,' he pushed, hating their polite distance, 'how will you describe me to people? A work colleague?'

'I... I hadn't really thought. But yes...' She flushed and glanced down. 'I guess a friend is the safest option.'

She looked up, her stare vulnerable and so full of fear Nate felt sick. 'You've met Lily before. And some of the ED nurses will be there.'

Nate nodded, biting back his feelings and the things he wanted to say.

As if she sensed his turmoil, she raised her chin, her stare hardening. 'Tomorrow is all about Lily, Nate. I don't want to make it about me or us. I hope you understand.'

'Of course I do,' he said, hurt that she felt the need to remind him of her priorities and his place in them.

She stepped close and pressed a kiss to his cheek. 'See you tomorrow.'

Then she was gone without a backward glance, leaving Nate alone with his conflicted feelings. Leaving him to wait and wonder if history might be about to repeat.

CHAPTER SIXTEEN

THE GEORGIAN BUILDING housing Greer's ground-floor flat boasted a small communal garden at the rear that was available to the flat owners for private hire. When Lily returned home from France Saturday evening to find most of her friends and loved ones gathered on the patch of lawn, birthday banners and pretty lanterns strung between the trees, she instantly burst into delighted tears of surprise.

She'd worked so hard for her exams, she deserved this celebration. But with results day looming, Greer only had a few more weeks of having her daughter home before she left for University.

'A private toast to our gorgeous girl,' Greer said, topping up Lily's and Mark's flutes with bubbles and trying to hide her nerves. 'Happy eighteenth birthday. To adulthood and the next phase of your life.'

Lily laughed and Mark added, 'Cheers,' as they clinked glasses, taking a sip.

Mark glanced down at his phone. 'Oh, Cara is here. I'll just go let her in.'

Greer watched him step inside the flat and disappear, her stomach tight with anticipation. She'd slept longer than she'd planned after her busy night and had awoken to several missed calls from the caterers. What with last-minute preparations for the party and the arrival of some horribly early guests, there'd been no time to call Nate, who hadn't yet arrived. Not that she knew what to say. She'd hurt him last night and hoped to find a private moment to apologise. But they both needed to remember that the evening was about Lily.

'So, tell me all about France,' Greer said to her daughter, who looked sun-kissed and happy, her eyes bright with excitement.

At least with Nate a no-show so far, Greer could relax and not have to act *normal* in front of her daughter, Lily's friends and her ex.

'The gîte was stunning, with beautiful views of the vineyards and olive groves and lavender farms,' Lily said. 'I spent so much time in the pool, and Dad hired a car so we could explore all the quaint villages, the beaches and coastal towns.'

'Sounds like you had a magical time. I'm so glad.' Greer gulped some champagne, a part of her sad that once upon a time they'd have taken holidays like that as a family.

But after four years alone, after embracing a fling with Nate, she finally felt strong and resilient. Even if she never fell in love again, she would be okay. She could go to Provence alone—drink wine, sit in cafés, walk on the sand and through fields of lavender.

Just then, as one of Lily's friends joined them, throwing her arms around Lily, Greer looked up to see Mark reappearing from the flat, stepping out into the sunshine with a smiling Cara in tow. And behind them was Nate.

Greer froze, her heart in her throat as her past and present collided. As she'd expected, Nate looked so handsome in chinos, a T-shirt and dark sunglasses, his hair sexily ruffled and his jaw sporting a day's worth of sexy stubble. Longing built like pressure in Greer's chest as she fought the urge to go to him and kiss him as if last night hadn't happened. As if they were alone in the garden. Wouldn't Provence be a little more magical with Nate by her side, the wine a little sweeter, the coffee richer, the walk on the sand more uplifting with her hand in his?

But could they truly have a future? Greer had no desire to go back to being the suspicious and jealous one in a partnership and there would always be younger women who fancied Nate. She was forty-three. She didn't have the luxury of time to make another big mistake. And would Nate even want a future with her? The fact that he couldn't seem to forgive himself left Greer to think that he, too, wasn't quite ready for more than a fling. Could she allow herself to develop feelings for someone when the odds were so steeply stacked against them as a couple? She didn't want to end up making a fool of herself, becoming a cliché when it inevitably came to an end because neither of them was quite ready to make it last.

As Mark and Cara paused to speak to Mark's younger sister and her husband, Greer's stare met Nate's. Greer inhaled sharply as a slam of desire struck. And something else, that familiar bitter taste of fear. Could she possibly already have deep feelings for Nate? He'd declared he might have them for her, but was she ready to put her emotional well-being on the line again so soon? For a man who might not be sure, who might be scared to allow himself to be happy because of his past and his unresolved grief?

As if they were the only two people in the garden, Nate sent her a hesitant smile, his eyes lighting up as he headed her way. Greer overheated, her heart fluttering with a mix of excitement and panic. This, inviting him to Lily's party, had been a mistake. What had she been thinking? How would she pretend they were just friends and colleagues in front of all these people, many of whom knew her better than anyone? When all she wanted to do was kiss him and try to explain her conflicted feelings to them both. When if he stepped too close, she'd crave his touch, want to sneak him away from the party and forget everything apart from the way he made her feel when they were together.

'Hi,' she said, her pulse so fast her head spun. He stepped close, as if he might swoop in to kiss her cheek in greeting, and Greer stepped back. 'Can I get you a drink?'

Her voice sounded off. High-pitched. Guilty. As if she was trying way too hard to be casual.

'Sure,' he said, his smile fading. 'A beer would be great.'

She couldn't make out his expression behind the sunglasses but his posture stiffened slightly, telling her she'd hurt him again with her withdrawal. Of course she had. She was acting as if they were strangers, because suddenly this all felt too serious. Too real. Too terrifying.

Greer turned to the drinks table and selected a can of pale ale, Nate's favourite, pouring it into a tall glass. Her hands trembled. A huge part of her wished they were still in their bubble, wished she could send everyone else home and spend this beautiful summer's evening in bed with him until they laughed together again, until her feelings became clear, and matched by Nate's. But now that there was a sliver of hurt and mistrust between them, now that Lily was home, that was no longer an option. Greer needed time. Time to figure out how she really felt about

Nate. Time to know if she wanted a real relationship with him. Time to talk to Lily and the other people she loved to let them know she might be ready to move on.

Wearing a strained smile, Nate took the beer she held out to him. 'You didn't call me.'

'I know…' Greer winced at the justified accusation, her stomach knotted by what she should do and say. 'I'm sorry. I slept in then had last-minute party things to sort out. I figured we might get a chance to talk tonight.'

He watched her carefully, taking a sip of beer as he kept his emotions hidden. 'I met your ex and his fiancée on the doorstep,' he said, glancing casually around the garden so to the unobservant their conversation might appear friendly. But the distance between them had never been greater. Greer felt the tension rolling off him. Felt the same in herself. Torn. Wanting him. Feeling guilty that she'd hurt him. Certain that if she wasn't careful, her secret fling would be exposed to everyone there for Lily.

'What did you tell them?' she asked with a nervous croak, certain that Mark would likely press Nate on who'd invited him because Nate was too old to be a friend of Lily's.

'I told them we just worked together.' He met her stare, his expression blank. 'That you'd invited some of the staff from the emergency department.' His expression hardened and Greer almost reached out to touch his arm. 'Isn't that what you wanted?'

'Yes. Thank you.' She nodded, feeling remorseful and confused. She'd done this. Created the mess she now found herself in. She'd begun this relationship in spite of her reservations. She'd allowed her trust issues to resurface. She'd hurt Nate last night and again today by foolishly inviting him there.

Nate sighed and held up a small gift bag, changing the subject. 'I brought this for Lily.'

Greer smiled as if her face were carved from wood, her heart pounding with both longing and unease at his gesture. 'That's so thoughtful... She's here.'

They joined the small group of young women, who were excitedly talking about their results and which place at uni they were going to select.

'Lily,' Greer said, her chest tight and heart racing, 'you remember Nate Hunter, my colleague in the emergency department.' The words felt awkward as she articulated them but she couldn't seem to make this situation she'd created any better. She just had to hold it together and see it through. Pretend. For Lily.

Lily smiled, despite being so obviously a little taken aback that Nate had been invited. She was probably wondering who this man was, and Greer knew there would be questions later. She'd have to explain herself and hope that Lily wasn't too appalled that her mother had been dating a younger man. That this didn't ruin their last few weeks of them living together.

'Happy Birthday,' Nate said, breezing over the moment. 'I got you a small gift.'

'Thank you,' Lily said with a smile, glancing questioningly at Greer before peering into the bag. She pulled out two items. The first was a small, framed star certificate depicting a celestial constellation with Lily's name at the centre.

'You named a star after me?' Lily said, her eyes wide with delight and surprise as she grinned at Nate.

Nate shrugged. 'Every lover of the universe needs their own star.'

Greer's pulse jerked. A week ago she'd have loved

Nate's thoughtfulness, but now she couldn't help but feel that his gift was also an obvious declaration that they were more than friends. Would everyone at the party notice when she'd asked him to keep tonight about Lily and not them?

When Lily opened the second item, a small velvet box, Greer saw a delicate gold chain with an unusual hexagonal pendant and a wave of nausea struck even as she tried to smile for her daughter's sake.

'It's part of a meteorite,' Nate said. 'There's some information in the bag about its structure and where it was found.'

'It's beautiful. Thank you,' Lily said, handing the box to Greer so she could remove the necklace and fasten it around Lily's neck.

'I'm going to show Dad,' she said, rushing off, her friends in tow.

Greer glanced at her feet, a metallic taste in her mouth. 'That was… Thank you.' Greer looked up to see the flicker of hurt in his stare now that he'd pushed his sunglasses up onto his head. 'Of course, it puts me in a tricky position. I hadn't planned on telling Lily about us tonight but she's too smart not to connect the dots.' She winced and dropped her gaze from his, too strung out to think beyond the implications for her and Lily.

'I'm sorry,' he said stiffly. 'I didn't think it would be an issue, given you'd invited me to her birthday party. I didn't want to turn up empty-handed and I see other people also brought gifts.' He tilted his head towards the table near the flat where people had deposited gifts and cards.

Miserable, she nodded and glanced at the other guests to see who might be watching their conversation. 'Maybe this wasn't my finest idea…' she muttered. 'I don't think

I'm ready to answer questions about us.' She met his stare, her throat tight. 'I didn't want to hurt you. I guess, on some level, I thought that if Mark was bringing Cara, I could bring a plus one too.'

Nate nodded, his disappointed stare not quite meeting hers. 'I wondered if you'd told Lily you were dating. Now I see that you haven't.'

Greer swallowed the lump in her throat. 'Nate…' She flushed, unable to find the right words to make this better. 'I did plan to tell her. I just haven't had the right moment yet.'

'I understand.' His voice was flat.

Behind Nate, Lily summoned Greer over, and she reached for the lifeline. 'Listen, I can't do this right now. Lily wants me. Mingle for a while, and I'll be back as soon as I can. We will talk. I promise.'

But as her fears built—fear of hurting or disappointing Lily, fear of making another mistake with Nate and hurting him too if the relationship became any more serious, fear that she should have known better than to think she was ready for another relationship so soon—Greer's stomach sank. Maybe she was better off alone after all.

An hour later, after too much small talk where he'd had to repeat the lie Greer had told her friends and family, that they were just work colleagues, Nate numbly stepped inside the cool shade of the flat out of the evening sun. He'd arrived at the party hoping to find a quiet moment with Greer to declare his feelings, face to face. All of his feelings. But the moment their eyes had met across the lawn, he'd seen the growing divide between them so clearly.

Where he was certain he wanted more than a fling, that he wanted a real relationship, Greer was clearly miles behind. Not that they'd had more than that initial moment to themselves this evening. It was almost as if she was avoiding him purposely.

Leaving his unfinished glass of beer on the kitchen counter, he moved through the flat towards the bathroom and Greer's bedroom beyond, catching sight of her re-applying her lip gloss in the mirror above the chest of drawers to the side of her bed.

'I might head off,' he said, when she spotted him and started as if guilty as sin. 'Thanks for inviting me. I hope Lily enjoys the rest of her party.'

His stomach sank. He understood her obligations. He even understood her fears. But feeling the way he did about her, watching her smile and laugh and not being able to be with her, he couldn't stay and pretend for a second longer.

'Really?' Greer frowned, her eyes darting down the hallway behind him. 'Well, thanks for coming.' Obviously satisfied that there was no one watching, she stepped closer and touched his arm. 'And thank you for your thoughtful gifts. Lily loves them. I'm sorry that we haven't had much chance to talk.'

Nate shrugged, her touch both food for a starving man and a reminder that when it came to their connection, to their willingness to be emotionally vulnerable, to their desires for a real relationship, they were clearly poles apart. For Greer, the 'work colleagues' explanation wasn't a lie. They *were* just colleagues. Colleagues with benefits. Whereas Nate had started to develop feelings for her, convincing himself that she might return those feelings. That she respected him as much as he respected her. Trusted him. But if he was honest, he'd seen the truth in her eyes the day before, after he'd confessed his secret.

Sensing his discomfort, Greer dropped her hand. 'Maybe we can find time to talk tomorrow night at the hospital. We're on the night shift together.'

She offered this as consolation when Nate saw it all too clearly. He might have finally confided his greatest mistake, opened himself up to her judgement because he trusted Greer, wanted to keep dating her and see where this could go, but for Greer, he was just her shameful secret. Someone else she couldn't fully trust.

'Maybe…'

'Or…' she went on, looking uncomfortable, 'maybe we should pause things for a while. Pick up again once Lily has left for Manchester.' She couldn't quite meet his stare and for Nate this was the final blow.

Aching for the return of her touch, but determined to protect himself, Nate pulled back his shoulders. 'Actually, Greer, I'm not sure this is working for me any longer,' he said, recalling her horrified expression when he'd told her about Maggie, her jealousy and withdrawal. Her embarrassment tonight. He'd laid himself bare to her, and Greer was busy retreating. She'd enjoyed the sex but clearly wasn't ready to take this relationship or him seriously.

'Okay…' She frowned, glancing behind him once more to make sure they were still alone. 'I mean, we agreed it would be temporary so…that's fine.'

'Fine?' Nate snorted out a bitter laugh. 'Just like that, huh? You give up on us so easily. But then I think you gave up before tonight. As if I meant nothing to you. As if everything we've shared meant even less.'

She raised her chin defensively. 'You're the one ending it. I told you I needed time. Some space.'

'Because I have feelings for you, Greer.' Nate winced. She looked confused and hurt but most of all guilty. Because he'd been right in his suspicions. 'And I know you can't return those feelings. You don't even trust me. If you did you wouldn't be jealous over nothing. You wouldn't be so ashamed of us. You'd be ready to tell your daughter, your ex, our colleagues about us.'

'That's not true… I do care about you… I just… This isn't the time for this. I have to think about Lily right now. I have a flat full of guests and only a few weeks before she leaves home. I thought you understood.'

Nate nodded in defeat. 'I do understand. I know she's your biggest priority. Just like I know I'm not even a consideration or an afterthought. I'm just a secret you're ashamed of.'

'I'm not ashamed of you… I—'

'Then you're scared,' he said, needing to leave before his humiliation crushed him. 'You think that if you admit our relationship is more meaningful than a fling I'm going to hurt you. When you said you trusted me. But your repeated jealousy proves you don't trust me one little bit.'

'I'm trying my best.' She swallowed and Nate realised he'd struck a nerve. 'But you did keep a secret from me.'

Nate sighed heavily in defeat, her words like a slap. 'Only because I was ashamed of my actions, because it's my biggest regret. I was scared to let you down, the way I let my beloved brother and myself down. Scared to see your judgement, to lose you because you can't handle my relationship with Maggie and Callum. I tore myself open for you, Greer.'

She shook her head, her cheeks red. 'I didn't mean to judge. But part of me couldn't help but think if there's nothing to tell between you and Maggie, why hide it, especially when I've confided in you about my trust issues? I've opened up too, Nate.'

Nate closed his eyes, his devastation building. He was losing her, every word of this conversation he should never have begun pushing her further away. Or maybe he'd never truly had Greer in the first place.

When he looked at her once more, saw her fear and determination, he knew it was over. 'Until today, I was willing to wait for you, Greer. To take this relationship at your pace, because I understood those trust issues. Just like I understood your obligations to your family. But today I saw that I was kidding myself that you could care about me. I don't think you were ever going to tell Lily about us. I don't think you ever had any intention of giving this relationship a real chance.'

'That's not true… I just… This is all new to me. I panicked…'

Nate nodded, hardening his resolve. 'You say you don't want to let Lily down, but you're letting yourself down instead. You're just scared to put yourself first. You said that *I'm* scared to allow myself to be happy because of Dylan, and you're right. But you're scared, too, Greer. Scared to be fully vulnerable with me or any other man. Scared to embrace what we have and make it work.'

'I…' She reached out to touch him again then let her arm fall to her side, deflated.

Nate stepped back. 'Your trust issues have already played a part in the demise of one relationship. I don't want to be the second casualty.' Nate winced because his impulsive mistake with Maggie had now also cost *him* two relationships. 'I don't want to fall in love with you only to lose you, too. Fall in love with you and then feel as if I should choose between you and Dylan's family.'

Greer gasped. 'I would never ask you to choose me over your family. Now who's too scared to trust?'

Just then, the approach of heels tapping on the hardwood floor made Nate turn in time to see one of the guests, most likely a friend of Lily's, round the corner from the living room and head into the bathroom.

'I'll let you get back to the party,' Nate said with a guilty wince. 'Apologies for my timing. I shouldn't have come today. I thought you inviting me, insisting yesterday that you still wanted me here, was a step in the right direction for us, but now I see I was at most just your plus one.'

'Nate, I...'

'Don't worry about it, Greer. There's no point either of us pursuing something that just isn't going to work. I'm sure you'd agree.'

'I'm sorry,' she whispered.

'Me too,' he said, aching for her even as he stepped further away. 'Bye, Greer.'

Forcing himself to leave before the feelings he'd had for her could cut any deeper, he turned and let himself out of the flat.

CHAPTER SEVENTEEN

Greer rinsed the last of the champagne flutes and placed it upside down on the drainer, her head filled with images of Nate. His hurt and disappointment and devastation. His words, accusations, the raw honesty of his feelings.

Shame washed over her in hot waves, stealing her breath and making her cringe inwardly until she braced her hands on the edge of the sink, her shoulders hunched and her head hung. After he'd left, after she'd emerged from under the weight of what she'd said and how she'd behaved, she'd shut herself in her bedroom and tried to call him to apologise again. When he hadn't answered she'd sent a frantic message: I'm sorry that I hurt you. That wasn't my intention.

She wanted him to see her message even though she needed to spend time with Lily tonight and time figuring out what she should do next. Telling herself that the dark empty place inside her was only a temporary feeling and a result of having hurt Nate, Greer dragged in some deep breaths and slapped on her brave face.

In the hallway, Lily called goodbye to the last of her friends and shut the front door. Greer hurriedly wiped her hands on a kitchen towel and squared her shoulders, pretending, when Lily found her a moment later, that everything was normal.

'Did you enjoy the party?' Greer asked as Lily walked over and held Greer in a tight hug.

'It was amazing. Thanks, Mum. I had no idea you were planning that. Dad said you did everything. That his only contribution was get me there on time.'

'You're welcome.' Greer inhaled a shaky breath, her doubts that she'd done the right thing in breaking it off with Nate building. 'It wasn't difficult to gather people who wanted to help you celebrate becoming an adult. You have a great group of friends.'

Lily's life, her future, were rich and joyful and full of adventure. But what about Greer? She'd acted cowardly today. That was no kind of way for a role model to behave. She'd allowed her fear of being hurt again to stop her from seeing what was right in front of her face. What had been there for days, maybe even weeks. She had feelings for Nate. Huge feelings.

Lily collapsed onto the sofa with a tired sigh and a content smile. 'An adult… That sounds serious. I've asked work for some extra shifts so I can earn as much money as possible in the next few weeks.'

'Good idea…' Greer said distractedly.

Lily nodded and twisted to rest her folded arms on the back of the sofa and her chin on top. 'Are you okay, Mum? Was it hard for you having Dad and Cara here together? I was a bit concerned.'

'It was fine.' Greer gingerly took a seat beside her daughter, feeling as if one wrong move might shatter her into jagged shards. 'If she's going to be your stepmother, I want to get to know Cara better, because I only really care about you and your happiness.'

Lily winced. 'I don't think I'll ever call her my stepmother, given I'm an adult, but I'm glad you feel that way. Will you…come to the bridesmaid-dress fitting with me Tuesday?'

'Of course. If it's okay with Cara.' Greer nodded bravely, knowing Mark and Cara's wedding would be a trial. Not because she was jealous of Cara, but because, having hurt Nate and let him walk away, she'd sabotaged her own chance at a relationship that had made *her* happy.

Because that was what Nate had brought to her life: optimism, laughter, joy.

'Listen, darling,' she said, 'we need to talk.'

'Okay.'

'About Nate and me,' Greer began. 'For a long time after Dad and I split I wasn't feeling brave enough to think about moving on. But, well, the truth is, he's been more than a friend and colleague these past few weeks. That's why I invited him today. We've been seeing each other. Dating, I guess. Just casually.'

She broke off, a wave of grief hitting her square in the chest. And now it was over. And it was Greer's fault. Nate was right. She'd clung to her mistrust, her fear of being hurt again, and all it had brought her was this vile sense of failure and shame and an understanding that she'd ruined the one thing she'd wanted. The one thing she deserved. A second chance at a serious, committed, emotionally mature relationship.

No game-playing. No miscommunication and obligation. Just passion and connection and being present in the relationship because there was nowhere else she'd rather be.

Lily glanced down, fingering the pendant around her

neck. 'I kind of guessed as much, Mum. I love them both, but his gifts were way too generous for someone who feels casually about you. He obviously cares deeply. So are you a couple, then?'

Greer shook her head, fresh pain stealing her breath. 'No, in fact I think it's actually over now.' Which was ironic because clarity had come at a terrible price. Of course Greer had developed deep romantic feelings for Nate. He was the best man she'd ever met. Their relationship, before she'd messed up, had been the most mature one she'd ever been in, despite their age gap. He gave her space to be herself, to rediscover herself. He liked her just the way she was, warts and all. He believed in her and cheered at her triumphs. And she'd hurt him, allowed him to believe she couldn't trust him and didn't care. She'd ruined a special thing because she was scared.

Lily frowned, looking uncomfortable. 'I'm sorry about that. He seemed really nice.'

Greer glanced up, stunned. 'You talked to him?'

'Yeah,' Lily said, 'mainly about university. He went to Manchester. Did you know that? But he also talked about you a lot.'

'He did?' Greer asked, her voice a hoarse whisper, her throat aching.

Lily nodded. 'It was obvious he really likes you. Even Dad noticed. He said something dismissive in front of Cara and me. That's why they left suddenly, because it started an argument between them.'

Greer gaped. Her silly attempts to hide how she felt about Nate had obviously failed. Clearly everyone else saw what she'd failed to see: how she felt about Nate.

'So why did you break up with him?' Lily asked. 'Is

it because he's younger than you? Cos that's a bit shallow, Mum.'

Greer shook her head, ashamed that she had worried too much about that. 'He broke up with me, actually.'

'Oh… I'm sorry.' Lily winced. 'How do you feel about that?'

Greer searched her feelings, allowing them to all spill free for the first time since Nate had walked out. 'I… I don't blame him. I hurt him, for which I'm very ashamed. I've got hang-ups, obviously. It's not easy to make yourself vulnerable again after a divorce. But I no longer want to be that scared woman I've been for the past four years.

'With you about to leave home, it's forced me to re-evaluate my priorities. I feel stronger now, resilient, ready to face new adventures and challenges, just like you. I'll always be here for you, of course, but it's time I started putting myself first a bit more.'

'I agree.' Lily nodded. 'Do you…? Does he…? Is Nate someone you could be serious about? You'd said that if you met someone you'd tell me.'

Tears stung Greer's eyes but she sniffed them away. 'I… I care about him a lot. I thought maybe he might be…' Before she'd clung to her fear, allowed Nate to think their connection was trivial, hadn't put up a fight for him or shown him how much she cared.

'How would that have made you feel?' she asked, eager for Lily's honest opinion.

'It's not about me, Mum, but I appreciate you asking.' Her expression became determined and Greer realised that Nate had been right about that, too. She had raised an exceptional young woman. 'I want you to be happy. I'm proud of you for working on yourself and embracing a scary change. You're amazing and I know that when you do find another serious relationship, it will be the right one for you. Because that's all that really matters in relationships, isn't it?'

'Yes, it is.' Greer nodded bravely, blinking away her tears. 'I'm proud of the woman you are, too.'

Lily smiled. 'It's how you taught me to be.'

Greer chuckled. 'Yes, I did, didn't I?'

'So what are you going to do?' Lily carefully asked, as if she understood the implications Greer was only now waking up to. That Nate might not give her a second chance.

'I'm not sure,' Greer said, her mind racing. 'But whatever happens, I will be fine. I'm strong, like you. I'm excited to rediscover myself now that my daughter will soon be flying the nest. I might want a relationship, but I'm also okay being alone, which sounds lonely but is actually an important life skill. We all have to love ourselves first. And whether I'm alone, or in a relationship, I'll always be your mum. I'll always be here for you and be there to cheer you along.'

'I know that.' Lily nodded, tears building on her eyelashes. 'Love you, Mum.'

Greer smiled, feeling as if she'd reached an important parenting milestone. She was ready to let Lily go. But was she ready to lose Nate without a fight?

By seven the next morning, after a sleepless night, tossing and turning through the lonely hours of darkness, where he'd replayed every word of his argument with Greer, Nate couldn't stand another hour of his own company. Donning his running shoes, he jogged all the way to Callum and Maggie's place five miles away. He needed to see friendly faces. Needed to hear Callum's laughter so he could get out of his own head and hopefully make sense of the way he was feeling: as if he'd been hit by a bus. A feeling that reminded him of grief. But obviously, by grieving for Greer, he was grieving a relationship he'd never actually had apart from in his own imagination.

Arriving at Maggie's place exhausted, his lungs burning because he'd pushed himself so hard as if he could outrun his feelings of loss and devastation, he knocked on the front door.

The curtains twitched and Maggie's haggard face appeared at the living room window. 'Use your key,' she called through the glass. 'I've got a horrible cold.'

Nate used his key to unlock Maggie's front door and stepped into the hallway.

'Stay away from me,' she moaned from the living room, her voice thick and nasal-sounding. 'I'm horribly germ-ridden. I don't want you to catch it.'

Nate poked his head into the room to see Maggie flaked out on the sofa, her eyes and nose red and used tissues scattered over the floor. 'Where's Callum? Is he okay?'

'He's fine,' she said, waving her hand. 'My dad has taken him to the park to burn off some energy. That kid bounces back from a cold after one day whereas I'm poleaxed for a week.'

Nate's stomach sank. Looked as if he'd be alone with himself after all.

'Can I get you anything while I'm here?' he asked, keeping his distance. 'I was out for a run and thought I'd pop in to see my favourite nephew.'

'I'm out of tissues,' she said, sniffling. 'There's a new box in the cupboard under the stairs. You can toss them to me so you don't have to come too close.'

Nate located the box and did as she asked, hesitating in the doorway as if he had no idea where to go next.

'What's wrong?' Maggie asked, blowing her nose and then pushing herself up on her elbows.

'Nothing,' Nate automatically replied. 'I—' He couldn't even find the words to describe the sickening emptiness he was feeling.

'Oh no, Nate,' Maggie said. 'It's over, isn't it? You and your work colleague. The "nice lady with the big smile", as Callum calls her.'

Nate shrugged, weariness slumping his shoulders. 'Yeah... I think it is.'

'Really? Why?' Maggie sat all the way up now, the balled-up tissue sliding from her lap onto the floor to join the others. 'I thought you really liked her.' She looked appalled, personally affronted, as if she was invested in Nate's happiness, counting on the relationship to restore her faith in romance after her own loss.

'I did. Do. But... Well, it's just not going to work out.' And maybe it was for the best. Relationships took time and effort. Better to know now that Greer wasn't interested and couldn't trust him before his feelings got any deeper. Although he'd never felt this crushed after a break-up before.

'I'm so sorry to hear that,' Maggie said softly, blinking away tears.

'Hey, it's okay,' he said, feeling sick because his heartache had obviously reminded Maggie of her own over Dylan. 'I'm going to be fine, just like I know you are too, one day. When you're ready. There's no one like Dylan, but nor is he the only awesome man out there. We're both going to move on eventually and find love again and—'

Nate stopped abruptly, nausea burning the back of his

throat as realisation struck. They weren't simply feelings he had for Greer. He wasn't simply at risk of falling in love with her or headed in that direction. He *was* in love with her. Utterly and completely. That explained why he currently felt like half a man. Why he couldn't stand his own company. Why, if he prodded his devastation too closely, he knew he'd find fear that he might not survive.

Realising what he'd done and, more importantly, what he hadn't done, Nate gripped the back of his neck and stared blindly at the wall, his vision tunnelling. Greer was right; he was scared to allow himself to be happy. Because Dylan wasn't around to feel the same. Because Nate loved Dylan and it hadn't been enough to save him. Not only was he scared it might happen again, that he'd lose Greer and be broken once more, he was also scared to rip himself completely open and tell her exactly how he felt and what he wanted. Otherwise he'd have realised his feelings sooner and confessed them last night.

Nate swore under his breath, his mind reliving their break-up. He'd been so scared to chase happiness he'd thought he didn't deserve that, when she'd wobbled over her jealous impulses, he'd convinced himself he couldn't give Greer the time she might need to break the news of their relationship to Lily and ended the thing he wanted the most. Before he could get hurt again.

'It's not too late to tell her,' Maggie said, tears spilling freely from the corners of her eyes as, somehow, she managed to understand the realisations Nate had just come to before him.

He frowned in confusion, but of course Maggie understood his feelings better than he had. She was still deeply in love with Dylan. She knew all about loss and regret.

But Maggie and Dylan had known deeply committed love. The kind Nate knew he could no longer live without. The kind he knew himself capable of with Greer, if only he could forgive himself his regrets and tell Greer exactly how he felt and what he wanted.

'I have to go,' Nate said, turning towards the front door. He had to tell Greer. Now. Had to beg her to give him another chance.

'Yes. Go!' Maggie waved him away, calling after him, 'Be brave. Tell her everything. Chances are rare and so is love.'

Too desperate to reply, Nate let himself out of the house and raced towards the Tube station. Then, deciding it was better to keep on the move, that he had no patience to wait for the train, he bypassed the station and carried on running the two miles to Greer's flat, praying that she'd be home when he got there. That she'd talk to him. Give him an opportunity to say everything he'd been too scared to say the night before. He hoped it wasn't too late.

Twenty minutes later as he turned into Greer's street, his heart pounding with fear and sweat stinging his eyes, Nate spotted Greer at her front door.

Dressed in exercise clothes and wearing trainers, headphones around her neck, she was obviously on her way to the gym or going for a walk. Just going about her day as if unaffected by the loss and devastation Nate felt now that their relationship was over.

He watched in horror as Greer withdrew her key from the lock and walked down the path towards the pavement. Nate sprinted the last few metres to get to her before he missed his chance. Maybe it was already too late. Maybe she'd moved on. Maybe he might pour out all of his heart and she still wouldn't want him. Either way, he owed it to himself, to the transformative relationship they'd had and to Greer, to find out.

CHAPTER EIGHTEEN

Pausing on the path from her front door, Greer tried to breathe through the pain and panic tightening her chest as her key dug into her palm inside her clenched fist. She'd dressed for a walk, hoping a brisk round of the park in the sun might help her put everything into perspective, help her escape her sickening thoughts and fears and brutal recriminations. But it was no use. No amount of exercise or reasoning would banish how she felt—bereft, helpless, untethered. The only way to stop the pain was to see Nate and apologise. To ask him to give her a second chance. Not tonight when they'd be working the night shift together. But now.

Resolved to head for the Tube instead of the park, she paused to open the gate, looked up and sucked in a harsh breath. 'Nate… What are you doing here?'

He stood on the street, his hair and T-shirt damp with sweat and his chest heaving as if he'd run the London Marathon.

'I…need to talk to you,' he said, catching his breath. Reaching for her hand as if she might flee.

Greer nodded frantically as hope surged. 'Come inside. Lily is at work. I… I was just going for a walk to clear my head but changed my mind and decided to go to your place. I need to apologise to you, Nate.' Desperate to get him inside so she could say all the things she wanted, Greer shoved her key back into the lock.

'Wait,' he said, gripping her shoulders and spinning her to face him. 'I need to tell you this. Now. It's important.'

Greer nodded, her stomach twisted with fear. He was really there. Surely that meant she had a chance.

'I'm in love with you, Greer,' he said, exhaling a ragged sigh of relief. 'That's what I should have told you last night. But I freaked out and got scared and sabotaged us instead.'

Greer blinked in disbelief, her eyes stinging with unshed tears. Could he mean it? Could she finally be honest with him and herself and earn a second chance?

'You were right about me,' he went on in a rush. 'I have been scared to allow myself to be happy. Scared to forget Dylan. I… I felt responsible for him as I always had. I let my little brother down, twice, and I don't think I'll ever stop grieving for him. But I *do* forgive myself. I can't let what happened, the mistake I made, hold me back any longer. Not when it's holding me back from you. Dylan wouldn't want that and I don't want it either. I want *you*. I don't want us to be over. I'll wait for as long as it takes for you.'

'Nate…' she choked out, her throat aching.

'I know.' He shook his head as if shaking out the memories of the hurt. 'I said terrible things last night that I regret.' He pulled her closer. 'Of course, I'm willing to wait for you to feel comfortable with us. You have every right to tell Lily about us in your own time. My gifts were too much. Just please…give me another chance to be with you. I'm in love with you. I'm crazy about you as you deserve and I will be for the rest of my life if you'll let me.'

Greer reached up and cupped his face between her

palms. 'Nate—' Her voice broke. 'I think I love you too,' she blurted, feeling foolish that she hadn't realised the depth of her feelings sooner. Because of course she loved him. Desperately. He was everything she wanted and deserved. And she was no longer afraid of being vulnerable with him.

'You do?'

Greer nodded. 'And I know I deserve you. I was stuck when I met you. Afraid to focus on myself because starting over emotionally felt so…enormous. But you wanting me, pursuing me, it jolted me out of my inertia. You are a wonderful man. In every way.'

He frowned as if he didn't believe her, and she took his hands in hers, smiling a watery smile. 'You were right about me, too. I am scared. The power of this, of us, the connection we've had from the start…it terrified me. I convinced myself that I was okay alone. That I had peace of mind and needed to focus on raising my daughter, but I was hiding behind that. I needed more. I needed *you*. This is the most mature and mutually respectful relationship I've ever had. Real grown-up stuff. I didn't know how I would ever be this vulnerable with someone else after my divorce, but you made it easy. I don't want to be scared any longer. I want to put my needs and passions first. I want to embrace my strengths and love again with every part of my heart. I want you, too, Nate.'

A fiercely possessive expression came over his face as he cupped her cheeks. 'I love you so much.' Then his mouth covered hers, lips parting, breaths sighing, tongues duelling as they clung to each other in the street with the morning sun streaming through the filter of the plane trees lining the pavement.

'Come inside,' she said when they came up for air.

With her hand in his, she quickly unlocked the outer door and the flat door and pulled him inside, her heart soaring with joy.

'I told Lily about us after the party last night,' she said, everything she wanted him to know rushing out. 'I'm so sorry for my jealousy or if I made you feel you weren't a priority or that I was ashamed of you. You were right. I allowed my trust issues from the past to blur everything I was feeling for you. But after you left, after I thought it was over, those feelings became so obvious.'

He shook his head, reaching for her once more. 'I gave up on us, too. Some part of me obviously realised I was falling in love with you. I got scared to lose you. Scared that I'd tell you about Maggie and lose you or that I'd love you so hard, I'd lose you another way. But I promise you I won't ever give up on us again, Greer,' he added, kissing her lips, her cheeks, her eyelids. 'I won't let you down or hurt you. Ever. I want you exactly as you are—strong and compassionate and smart and sure of yourself and sexy and funny.'

'I know you won't,' she said, holding him tight. 'I trust you, Nate.' Flinging her arms around his neck, she tugged his mouth down to hers. She slid her fingers through his hair and deepened her kiss, smiling when he crushed her body to his.

'We're going to have such amazing adventures,' she said when he released her.

'And amazing sex,' he said, filling his hands with the cheeks of her backside. 'We're going to have lots of sex.'

'Definitely,' she agreed, laughing when he slid his lips down the side of her neck.

'What time is Lily home?' he asked, his hand slipping under her top to caress her breast.

'Four,' she said, mentally calculating how many hours they had between now and then.

'Could you put your hands on one of those stashed condoms?'

'Yes. On more than one if you're up to it.'

'Hold on,' he said, hoisting her from the floor so she wrapped her thighs around his waist and held on as he carried her to the bedroom. 'I need a shower,' he said and he detoured to the en suite bathroom where they quickly discarded their clothes and, laughing, both stepped under the spray.

'I love you,' Greer said, rubbing shower gel over his chest, spreading the scented suds everywhere her hands glided as Nate groaned and clutched her close, his lips roaming her neck and face. 'I'm ready to bring our relationship into the daylight. To embrace it and love every minute of being with you.'

Nate pressed her slippery body to his hard one, his arms steely bands around her. 'Do you believe that I'm all for you? That I'm a one-woman man? That you are everything I could possibly want? Almost too hot for me to handle?'

She smiled, laughed, pressed her lips to his as the water cascaded over them, washing away the suds. 'Yes. I know you. I know your strength and compassion. I know your heart and your passion. I know I'm safe with you and that this is the place I want to be.'

She wrapped her arms around his shoulders and kissed him as he turned off the shower. After the briefest of rub-downs with a towel, they hurried to Greer's bed. Every touch and caress felt like a promise. Every kiss reaffirmed their connection. Every groan and moan and whisper brought them impossibly closer so when, finally, hearts racing and breath panting, Nate pushed inside her, Greer knew that their happiness as a couple was in their hands.

Nate dragged in deep breath after deep breath, the powerful aftershocks of his orgasm tensing every muscle in his body. Turning his head, he buried his nose in Greer's silky hair and sucked in the scent of her skin. With him still buried inside her, it was impossible for them to get closer physically, but still he craved that, as if he were still scared of losing her.

'I love you,' he whispered against her ear as their hearts banged side by side. 'I never want to let you go.'

'I love you, too.' Greer pulled back and smiled with satisfaction, pressing kisses all over his face as the euphoric high lingered.

After a quick trip to the bathroom, Nate returned, sliding into Greer's bed and drawing her back into his arms. 'How did Lily take the news about us?' he asked, his heart rate accelerating once more. 'Is she okay?' He didn't want to ever be a source of conflict between Greer and her daughter, who had such a close bond.

'She took it like the intelligent mature woman she is,' Greer said with a proud smile as she lazily ran her fingers through his hair. 'Said she liked you and just wanted me to be happy. She said she knew I'd only enter into another relationship if it was absolutely right for me, which this one is.'

Nate nodded, his chest tightening. 'So we're in a real relationship, then?' He flashed her a sexy grin, elated.

Greer laughed and nodded, her smile breathtaking. 'You make me happy,' she said, cupping his face. 'You give me a safe space in which to heal and find myself and be strong.'

'And you give me everything I've ever wanted.' He cupped her chin and kissed her softly.

'Are you sure you don't want kids of your own?' she asked when she pulled back, her beautiful stare shining with love but also the last glimmer of fear. 'Because I think I'm too old now. Past that phase of my life.'

'I'm sure.' Nate brought her hand up to his mouth and kissed her fingers. 'I want you, Greer. I want to share my life with you. I want to be a part of yours. I want to travel with you and laugh with you and hold you and be there for you. You are all I'll ever need.'

Greer nodded, a relieved smile on her lips. 'Me too.'

'About Callum,' he said, his voice thick with emotion. 'I hope he'll always be a part of my life.'

'Of course he will. I understand your bond. It's one of the reasons I love you. And I know you're scared to forget Dylan, but how could you when you have Callum as a reminder? When Dylan is a part of you too?' She pressed her hand to his chest over the thump of his heart.

'I love you,' he said roughly, pressing his lips back to hers. Before he could become distracted by her kisses, Nate added, 'I know one day Maggie will be ready to move on. She's still desperately in love with my brother— she cried for him, for their love, when I told her I'd almost lost you. I think she could see I was in love with you before it finally struck me. But one day, there'll likely be another man in Callum's life and that's fine with me.'

'You'll always be his Uncle Nate.'

'I will,' he said, hoping that Dylan could rest knowing that Nate would always be there for his son.

Greer smiled lovingly, sliding her fingers through his hair. 'Maybe we could get Maggie and Callum over for a barbecue before Lily goes to Manchester. It would be good for us all to meet properly.'

'It would,' he agreed, his heart pounding with another wave of love for this incredible woman. 'If we're all going to be a funny little family of sorts.'

She nodded, her fingertip tracing his cheekbone and the line of his jaw. 'That we are. How would you feel if I resigned from Kensington Hospital?'

He froze, his heart lurching. 'Is that really necessary? I want to work with you.'

'I want to work with you too,' she said. 'But it would solve the tricky issue of me being your boss. Either way, I'm going to inform HR that we're an item.'

Nate's arms tightened around her, his lips grazing hers as if he'd forgotten their taste. 'I love you being my boss. But the other option is that I apply for the next consultant post that arises in our hospital. Then we'd be equals.'

'We're already equals. But if you want that then I'd support you. You're definitely ready.'

'I'd rather we worked at the same hospital if possible. I don't want to miss you.'

'I'd miss you, too.' She smiled and pressed herself against him, bringing their lips back together. 'You just want to lure me back into that on-call room for another quickie, don't you?'

Nate grinned, kissing her once more. 'I mean, you're not wrong. I do. That was seriously hot.' He pushed her hair back from her face and stared deep into her eyes. 'But I'll support whatever decision you make, Greer.'

'Whatever decision *we* make,' she whispered, her breath mingling with his.

Nate nodded. 'As long as you're happy. I want you to be happy and fulfilled and secure.'

'And with you, I am all of those things.'

Nate held her closer, kissed her deeply. His love for her finally free. And because he loved her, because she was naked in his arms, her legs entwined with his, his body responded, becoming aroused again.

Greer pulled back from the heated kiss and gasped in mock delight. 'Again so soon?' she asked teasingly, parting her thighs when her rolled on top of her, her smiling stare, sexy and eager, locked to his. 'Oh, the marvellous benefits of dating a younger man.'

She laughed joyously and Nate kissed her again and again, their playfulness turning into the serious business of loving each other once more.

EPILOGUE

One year later...

GREER HAD DONE her research, discovering that the best time to visit Provence, but also to avoid the crowds, was early July, just before the school year ended. Not that term dates were a concern for Greer any longer. Lily had passed her A levels and breezed through the first year of her degree, making friends, learning new things, even falling in love with a second-year fellow astrophysics student.

'It's utterly breathtaking here,' she said, squeezing Nate's hand as they walked the path between the rows of lavender plants, the warm air sweet with their fragrance and the gentle hum of visiting honeybees.

They'd spent the day exploring Roussillon village, Provence's ochre jewel perched high on a ridge, walking the charming cobbled streets, pausing to enjoy galleries and cafés and take endless photos together, ending the day with a trip to one of the many lavender farms in the valley below.

'There's a table under the trees,' Nate said, plucking a lavender bloom, crushing the flower between his fingers to release the aroma, inhaling the scent before passing it to Greer. 'Let's sit for a while and enjoy the sunset.'

Greer sighed contentedly as they headed for the small copse of trees under which a single table sat with an on-brand purple shade umbrella.

'There's champagne,' she said as they stepped closer, spinning to face a smug-looking Nate. 'Did you organise this?'

'Yes,' he said. 'It seemed like the perfect end to a wonderful day.'

Greer sighed as Nate removed the bottle from a sweating ice bucket and popped the cork, pouring two glasses. He passed her one and took his own, their free hands clasped between them as they stood smiling at each other.

'A toast,' he said, holding up his glass. 'To the best year of my life. Waking up next to you, being in a relationship with you, getting to hold your hand as we shared the highs and lows of our work and daily life is a luxury I won't ever take for granted.'

'Me neither,' Greer whispered, her heart pulsing with the love she felt for this incredible man. Every day she felt lucky that they'd given each other a second chance. Every day, she praised herself for being brave enough to realise that what she wanted and needed was Nate.

'I know you said you never wanted to get married again,' he said as he placed his glass down, 'but I want to spend the rest of my life loving you, Greer.'

As Greer watched with surging excitement, he pulled a box from his pocket. 'If it's as your husband, your common-law partner or even your boy toy with benefits, I want you to have this as a sign of my commitment to us. To you.'

Greer placed her flute down before she dropped it as Nate opened the box and pulled out the stunning ring.

'Nate…' she said on a breathless gasp, her stare searching his to see his feelings for her swimming there.

'I asked Lily for her blessing first,' he said, removing the ring from the box and holding it up.

'You did? What did she say?' Greer shouldn't be surprised. Lily and Nate had become good friends this past year. Lily could go to him for sound, mature advice and Nate never missed an opportunity to know Greer's daughter a little better.

Nate smiled his sexy smile, the one she saw every day. The one she would never take for granted or tire of. 'She said she wanted you to be happy. So it's all over to you.' He held the ring a little higher so the diamond glinted in the sun.

'Yes,' Greer said without hesitation, throwing her arms around his neck. 'I will marry you. I want you to be my husband, as long as we can also keep the boy toy with benefits on the table.' She smiled against his lips as they kissed, his joy igniting her own as he held her in his strong arms, their hearts racing side by side.

'Yeah, we can.' His arms tightened around her waist, his smile the sexy one she adored.

Greer pulled back, cupping his face between her palms. 'I love you, Nate. You're the only man for whom I would make an exception. But know that if you put that ring on my finger, then that's it for ever. Just you and me.'

Nate's smile stretched, his eyes sparkling. 'In that case…' He took her left hand and she spread her fingers as Nate slid the ring onto her finger. 'Now you're mine for ever,' he said, picking her up and twirling her around as the scent of sun-baked lavender filled the warm air. 'And I'm yours.'

He loosened his grip and her body slid down his until

her feet touched the ground once more and he kissed her passionately.

'Wait,' Greer said, when she came up for air. 'We didn't drink to the toast. Doesn't that mean we might have seven years' bad sex?' She reached for their glasses of champagne and handed one to him, clinking the flutes together for good luck.

One arm around her waist, Nate held her close and stared deep into her eyes, his wickedly playful. 'With you? Impossible,' he said, brushing her lips with his and groaning sexily.

'In that case,' she said, because she knew there would never be any worries on that score, 'cheers to years of incredible sex. And to us.'

Holding her stare as if he might suggest a quickie under the trees, a divine possibility for which Greer could muster no reluctance, Nate touched his glass to hers once more, sighed as they each took a sip and then kissed her again.

* * * * *

If you enjoyed this story, check out these other great reads from JC Harroway

The Paramedic Roommate Pact
Mistletoe Baby Mix-Up
One Night to Royal Baby
One Night to Sydney Wedding

All available now!

MILLS & BOON®

Coming next month

GREEK HOSPITAL, RED-HOT REUNION
Tina Beckett

Ana shrugged, but curled her fingers around his, not quite ready to break the contact. 'When we first saw each other at the hospital, and I sensed how uncomfortable we both were, I did think it. That I would try to avoid you as much as I could. When Natalia told me I'd have to rotate through surgery, I was horrified. Wasn't sure if I could even do it.'

'And now that you've done it. Are you still horrified?'

'No. I'm actually looking forward to our next time.'

'Our next time.' Dimitry unhooked his hip from the car and took a step closer. 'Are you, Ana?'

God, he evidently felt it too. She swallowed as her senses went on high alert.

'Yes. Very much so.' The words came out as a whisper. Why had she never noticed him like this in school? Hadn't she? She could remember at least one time when she had.

Dangerous. This was moving into territory she had no business exploring. What about working on herself? Wasn't that what she was supposed to be doing?

He took another step and that muscle in his cheek bunched again. This time, though, she knew he wasn't irritated.

She had a feeling it meant something else entirely. That—like her—he was fighting his inner impulses, while being dragged slowly and methodically closer.

'What else are you looking forward to, Ana?'

'Can't you guess?'

His left hand slid behind her nape and he leaned forward until his lips were at her ear. 'Is guessing really what you want me to do?'

'No.' She turned her head so their lips were mere inches apart. 'I want you to kiss me.'

Continue reading

GREEK HOSPITAL, RED-HOT REUNION
Tina Beckett

Available next month
millsandboon.co.uk

Copyright © 2026 Tina Beckett

COMING SOON!

We really hope you enjoyed reading this book. If you're looking for more romance be sure to head to the shops when new books are available on

Thursday 21st May

To see which titles are coming soon, please visit
millsandboon.co.uk/nextmonth

MILLS & BOON

FOUR BRAND NEW BOOKS FROM
MILLS & BOON MODERN

Indulge in desire, drama, and breathtaking romance – where passion knows no bounds!

OUT NOW

Eight Modern stories published every month, find them all at:
millsandboon.co.uk

TWO BRAND NEW BOOKS FROM
Love Always

Be prepared to be swept away to incredible worldwide destinations along with our strong, relatable heroines and intensely desirable heroes.

OUT NOW

Four Love Always stories published every month, find them all at:

millsandboon.co.uk

OUT NOW!

Available at
millsandboon.co.uk

MILLS & BOON

LET'S TALK
Romance

For exclusive extracts, competitions and special offers, find us online:

- **f** MillsandBoon
- **X** @MillsandBoon
- **◉** @MillsandBoonUK
- **♪** @MillsandBoonUK

Get in touch on 01413 063 232

For all the latest titles coming soon, visit
millsandboon.co.uk/nextmonth